Praise for F

"A delightful novel that weaves tog ry
mystery involving Jane Austen." le

"Part mystery, part love story, *First Impressions* is a 100 percent thumping good read and a loving homage to one of literature's most beloved authors. Lovett takes readers on a rollicking adventure that cleverly weaves in the best elements of Austen's novels, while also giving life to Austen's own personal history in a satisfying and captivating way. It's a giddy novel that celebrates books and the people who love them as much as it entertains, making it the perfect read for bookworms and Janeites alike."

—*BookPage*

"[Lovett's] story weaves together both past and present, fact and fiction, in pursuit of a secret that threatens to turn the literary world upside down. . . . This novel is, at its heart, a love letter to fiction—not just for its writers, but also for its readers." —*The Washington Post*

"Delightful . . . An inventive tale with elements of romance and suspense, wrapped around a bookish mystery."

—Deborah Harkness, #1 *New York Times* bestselling author of *The Book of Life*

"A charming, entertaining story . . . Lovett's storytelling and humor keep you captivated from the first page to the last." —*The Burlington Times News*

"Fans of Austen will devour the backstory . . . Lovers of intrigue and romance will relish the present-day journey . . . Bibliophiles will savor the interconnectedness of both stories . . . *First Impressions* is an Austen appetizer—leaving the reader eager to explore or revisit works that have touched us for more than two centuries." —*The Mountain Times* (Boone, NC)

"Beautiful and exciting . . . A must-read." —*Historical Novels Review*

"A completely captivating and charming book . . . The reader gets a nice adventure story, a little bit of romance and mystery, and a real feel for book collecting and for the author's love of Jane Austen. If it's a love you share, you may well find this book irresistible." —*Mystery Scene*

"An intriguing story [about] an author whose stories have not lost their romantic appeal in two hundred years." —*Suspense Magazine*

"[An] ingenious novel." —*Publishers Weekly*

"Lovely and entertaining." —*Shelf Awareness*

"[An] appealing combination of mystery, romance, and bibliophilism . . . An absolute must for Austen fans, a pleasure for others." —*Booklist*

"A delightful read that Janeites will love . . . [Lovett] adds bookish intrigue to the life of another luminary of English literature." —*Library Journal*

"Lovett's love of books and libraries once again energizes his storytelling." —*Kirkus Reviews*

"A thoroughly engaging story that keeps us enthralled to the very last page. Austen herself would adore the counterpoint heroine, the bright and delightful Sophie Collingwood. A pure gem."
—Katherine Reay, author of *Dear Mr. Knightley*

"Brimming with charm and intrigue, Charlie Lovett's new novel will leave a lasting impression on lovers of books, literary enigmas, and the eternally fascinating Jane Austen. *First Impressions* spans centuries, but time ceases to exist as Lovett's riveting story begins to unfold."
—Erika Robuck, author of *Hemingway's Girl*

"It is a truth universally acknowledged that a reader in want of a marvelous mystery and lovely literary fiction must be in want of *First Impressions*. With a deep understanding of Jane Austen and a deft hand at mystery, Lovett strikes the perfect chord between literature and a first rate thriller."
—Craig Johnson, *New York Times* bestselling author of the Walt Longmire mysteries, the basis of the hit series *Longmire*

PENGUIN BOOKS

# FIRST IMPRESSIONS

Charlie Lovett, author of *The Bookman's Tale*, is a former antiquarian bookseller, an avid book collector, and a member of the Grolier Club, the oldest and largest club for bibliophiles in North America. A playwright and former teacher, he has written plays for children that have been seen in more than three thousand productions. He and his wife split their time between Winston-Salem, North Carolina, and Kingham, Oxfordshire, in England.

# FIRST IMPRESSIONS

## A Novel of Old Books, Unexpected Love, and Jane Austen

CHARLIE LOVETT

PENGUIN BOOKS

PENGUIN BOOKS
An imprint of Penguin Random House LLC
375 Hudson Street
New York, New York 10014
penguin.com

First published in the United States of America by Viking Penguin,
a member of Penguin Group (USA) LLC, 2014
Published in Penguin Books 2015



THE LIBRARY OF CONGRESS HAS CATALOGED THE HARDCOVER EDITION AS FOLLOWS:
Lovett, Charles C.
First impressions : a novel / Charlie Lovett.
pages cm
ISBN 978-0-525-42724-7 (hc.)
ISBN 978-0-14-312772-7 (pbk.)
1. Women college students—Fiction. 2. Austen, Jane, 1775–1817—Authorship—Fiction. 3. Austen, Jane, 1775–1817. Pride and prejudice—Fiction. 4. Women novelists, English—Fiction. I. Title.
PS3612.O86F58 2014
813'.6—dc23
2014004514

Printed in the United States of America
3 5 7 9 10 8 6 4 2

Set in Electra
Designed by Sabrina Bowers

FOR JANICE

*Who will always be to me*
*what Elizabeth is to Darcy.*

# FIRST
# IMPRESSIONS

## *Steventon, Hampshire, 1796*

**FOND AS SHE WAS** of solitary walks, Jane had been wandering rather longer than she had intended, her mind occupied not so much with the story she had lately been reading as with one she hoped soon to be writing. She was shaken from this reverie by the sight of an unfamiliar figure, sitting on a stile, hunched over a book. Her first impression was that he was the picture of gloom—dressed in shabby clerical garb, a dark look on his crinkled face, doubtless a volume of dusty sermons clutched in his ancient hand. Even the weather seemed to agree with this assessment, for while the sun shone all around him, he sat in the shadow of the single cloud that hung in the Hampshire sky. Realizing how far she had come from home, Jane thought it best to retrace her steps without interrupting the cleric's thoughts as he had unknowingly interrupted hers. During the long walk home, across fields shimmering with the haze of summer heat, she amused herself by sketching out a character of this old man, storing him away, like so many others, for possible inclusion in some novel yet to be conceived. He was, she decided, a natural history enthusiast, but his passion lay not with anything beautiful like butterflies or wildflowers. No, his particular expertise was in the way of garden slugs, of which he could identify twenty-six varieties.

By week's end, Jane had filled in the pathetic details of his life. Disappointed in love, he had turned to natural history, where the objects of his pursuit were less likely to spurn his advances. As his passion for his study grew, and as he shared it more enthusiastically with those around him, his invitations to dine gradually declined until he was left alone on most evenings with his books and his slugs. He was a melancholy figure, which made it all the more shocking to find him, on Sunday morning, not only seated in the Austen family pew, but smiling broadly and greeting her by name.

Jane had led the family procession from the rectory to the small stone church of St. Nicholas, where her father was rector. The church stood on the far outskirts of the village, flanked by flat, green meadows. After passing through the rectory gates into the narrow lane that led to the church, the Austens had fallen in with several villagers. When she had concluded her pleasantries with these acquaintances, Jane had not a moment to respond to the stranger's greeting before the service began and she found herself separated from him by her mother and her sister Cassandra; of her six brothers, none were currently in residence in Steventon.

The man's robust baritone voice, evident in his hymn singing, exuded a spirit that was anything but melancholy. Jane endured a sharp elbow from Cassandra for not attending to the gospel reading; instead, she was trying to watch the man out of the corner of her eye. She failed to follow the thread of her father's sermon, lost as she was in a reevaluation of the stranger's history. By the time the service ended she was thoroughly intrigued and determined to secure a proper introduction to satisfy her curiosity about the true nature of his character.

"Go along home and I shall wait for Father," she told her mother and Cassandra as they stood beside the ancient yew tree that clung to the west end of the church. Jane felt certain that a visiting clergyman with leave to occupy the Austen pew must be known to her father, and she expected Mr. Austen to make the necessary introduction, so it came as a surprise when she felt a tap on her shoulder and turned to face the stranger, who addressed her in a cheerful voice.

"Miss Jane Austen, if I am not mistaken."

"You are at an advantage, sir," said Jane. "You know my name, but I do not know yours."

"Mansfield. Reverend Richard Mansfield at your service," he said with a slight bow. "But we have nearly met already."

"What can you mean, sir?"

"Only that two days ago you emerged from the waving grain of Lord Wintringham's field and stopped in your tracks when you spotted me reading on a stile just outside Busbury Park. At the time I conceived the idea that you were a rather dull and impetuous young lady, but I already begin to suspect that I may have been mistaken." His eyes twinkled in the morning sun as he said this, and his smile transformed from one meant for the general public to one that seemed to be reserved solely for Jane.

"I hope you will come to believe so, Mr. Mansfield. I have been accused of having many faults by those who know me well, but neither dullness nor impetuousness has been among them."

"And of what faults do they accuse you?"

"My worst, or so I am told, are a too highly developed interest in fictionalizing my acquaintances and a tendency to form opinions of others hastily."

"Opinions such as the one you formed of me when you saw me alone with my book?"

"You do me wrong, sir. You assume first that I saw you, second that I gave your appearance sufficient thought to form an opinion, and third that my opinion was ill considered."

"In the first case," said Mr. Mansfield, "I observed you myself, for though your mind may have been elsewhere, your eyes were certainly on me; in the second case, your father tells me, somewhat to my surprise, that you aspire to write novels, so I can only assume that anyone you meet may become a victim of your imagination; and in the third case it seems impossible that you would have guessed the extent to which our interests overlap."

"I confess that shared interests did not occur to me. I imagined you a student of natural history, reading . . . but you will laugh when I tell you."

"I enjoy a good laugh," said Mr. Mansfield.

"I imagined you reading a book on garden slugs."

Mr. Mansfield did laugh, long and heartily, before confessing the true nature of his reading. "It may shock you, Miss Austen, but in fact I was reading a novel."

"A novel! You *do* shock me, sir. Do you not find novels full of nonsense? I myself find them the stupidest things in creation."

"Then you read novels?"

"Novels! I'm surprised at you, Mr. Mansfield, suggesting that a young lady such as myself, the daughter of a clergyman, no less, could occupy her time with such horrid things as novels."

"You tease me, Miss Austen."

"Indeed I do not, Mr. Mansfield, for though you know that I aspire to *write* novels, you cannot expect that I would take my interest in the form so far as to actually *read* them." Because Mr. Mansfield was old enough to be her grandfather, Jane took the bold step of adding a wink to this statement and turned toward the rectory. The congregation had dispersed and only the sounds of birdsong and the breeze in the yew tree disturbed the silence of the morning. Jane was pleased when Mr. Mansfield fell into step beside her as she made her way up the tree-lined lane. With the summer sun now high in the sky, she was grateful for the cooling shade.

"Surely, Mr. Mansfield, your shortest route to Busbury Park lies in the opposite direction," said Jane.

"Indeed it does, but you are assuming again, Miss Austen. First that I am staying at the park, and second that I am taking my luncheon there."

"And my novelist's imagination has deceived me again?"

"Not entirely," said Mr. Mansfield. "For I am a guest at Busbury Park, but though he can offer me only cold mutton, your father has asked me to take my luncheon at the rectory."

"I confess, Mr. Mansfield, I am sorry to hear it."

"And why is that? Are you so embarrassed to be seen in the company of a novel reader?"

"On the contrary, it is *because* you are a novel reader that I had rather hoped to keep you to myself. Once you enter the doors of the rectory, you will become a friend to my mother and my sister Cassandra, and you will no doubt retire after lunch to the study with my father and abandon the rest of us."

"Surely, Miss Austen," said Mr. Mansfield, "I can be both a visitor at the rectory and a special friend of the rector's younger daughter."

"I believe, Mr. Mansfield," said Jane as she took the clergyman's arm, "that I should like that very much indeed."

## *Oxfordshire, Present Day*

**AFTER FIVE YEARS** at Oxford, Sophie Collingwood had mastered the art of reading while walking. She knew every curve of the Thames Path from Oxford to Godstow, and had the ability to sense and avoid oncoming pedestrians. This was a useful skill for someone so absorbed by the books she read that she often pictured herself at the center of whatever romance or mystery or adventure played out on their pages. On a sunny day in July, she was walking opposite the wide expanse of Port Meadow, where horses and cattle stood grazing as they had for centuries. On the river a quartet of picnickers were making their way back downstream in a punt, and the smooth sound of the flat-bottomed boat gliding across the water seemed the perfect accompaniment to the day. In the midst of this idyll, Sophie spotted, over the top of her well-worn copy of *Mansfield Park*, a young man lying under a tree, reading. His artfully relaxed sprawl and his intentionally disheveled clothes radiated a combination of arrogance and apathy. *Slovenly* would be the best word to describe him, she decided—the unwashed hair, the shredded jeans, the faded T-shirt. It was a style that both puzzled and annoyed her. Sure, Sophie didn't always go out of her way to look good, but to go out of one's way to look *bad* just seemed rude. As she drew level with him he greeted her in a lazy American voice.

"How's it goin'?" he asked, but Sophie only raised her book higher and walked on, pretending his question had been lost in the breeze. As she rounded the next bend in the river and was lost to his sight, she had a sudden recollection. She had heard that voice before. It had been two nights ago, at the Bear. She had been standing at the bar waiting to order drinks for a group of friends who were discussing the relative merits of *Mansfield Park* and *Persuasion*, when that brash American accent had cut through the clamor of the crowd.

"What really gets me is these Austen fangirls. Running around pretending the sun rises and sets with some chick who wrote soap operas two hundred years ago." And then, in a mocking imitation of an English girl, he had added, "I think *Mansfield Park* isn't properly appreciated by the establishment." Sophie had crossed back to the table with her drinks, and the sound of his voice had been blessedly swallowed up by the noise of the crowd, but the damage had been done, for it had been Sophie who had made the remark about *Mansfield Park*, not five minutes earlier. When she told her friends what she had heard, they had all had a good laugh about the whole thing and had quickly come to the conclusion that this conceited American was a prat.

After a half-pint of bitter in the garden of the Trout, Sophie headed back toward Oxford. It would take her just over an hour to walk the four miles to Christ Church, and that should be enough time, she thought, to see Fanny and Edmund married. But, just as things were beginning to look inevitable for the two young lovers, Sophie heard once again that insufferable voice.

"Whatcha reading?" it asked, as Sophie approached. He spoke louder this time, and she couldn't pretend she hadn't heard.

"Not that it's any of your business," said Sophie, "but I happen to be reading Jane Austen."

"The person, be it gentleman or lady, who has not pleasure in a good novel, must be intolerably stupid."

Sophie was so taken aback that she almost smiled in spite of herself. After his comments in the Bear the last thing she expected from him was a Jane Austen quote.

"Surprised to hear me say that?"

"It's just that that's a rather obscure Austen quote for a . . . a . . ."

"A what?" asked the man. "An unsophisticated, uncultured, unenlightened dilettante?"

"That's not what I meant," said Sophie. "It's just that most people haven't read . . ."

"*Northanger Abbey*?"

"Exactly."

"And you're surprised since I'm not wearing tweed and sitting in a dusty study, that I have the first idea about Austen."

"On the contrary," she said politely. "I think lounging on the banks of the Thames on a sunny summer day is the perfect way to read Austen."

"Well, to be fair, there are two reasons I can quote that passage so precisely. First, I saw it on a T-shirt in the Bodleian shop yesterday, so it's not as obscure as you think."

Sophie could barely conceal her irritation at this. "And the second reason?" she said icily.

He held up a battered paperback copy of *Northanger Abbey*. "I just read it about ten seconds before you walked up. I'm Eric. Eric Hall." He extended his hand without raising himself off the ground, simultaneously tossing his hair out of his eyes. Sophie fought to keep her face from betraying that she already knew he was a jerk. And yet she sensed that behind his studied appearance and almost scripted insolence there was something softer. It wasn't just that he read Jane Austen. It was the way he waited for her response with almost painful anticipation—like a little boy seeking approval.

"Sophie," she said, offering her hand but not her surname.

"Pleasure to meet you."

"Is it really?" said Sophie. "I thought you didn't care for Austen fangirls."

"Whatever gave you that idea?"

"You said so yourself, in the Bear. And don't you think that Jane Austen is just a chick who wrote soap operas?"

"You heard that?" said Eric. "Well, I only meant that I don't care for people who worship what they don't understand. You have to admit, there are an awful lot of girls bouncing around Oxford whose main impression of Jane Austen is Colin Firth in a wet shirt."

Sophie smiled in spite of herself—much as she hated to admit it, Eric had a point. She recalled one doe-eyed girl lurking at the edge of her circle of literary friends in the Bear. From her few intrusions into the conversation it seemed that she thought Mr. Darcy's principal character trait was the "adorable" way his wet hair hung across his forehead.

"Now," said Eric, "if you're walking back into Oxford, I think I'll join you. We can keep talking about Jane Austen if you like." He stood up without brushing the dirt and grass from his pants and slipped his book into his pocket.

"Do you promise not to imitate my voice?" said Sophie.

"What do you mean?"

"I think *Mansfield Park* isn't properly appreciated by the establishment," said Sophie, doing her best impersonation of his impersonation.

"That was you?"

She only scowled in response.

"Well, come on," said Eric, "it's such a clichéd line—all that stuff about *Mansfield Park* not being appreciated. It may not make as good a movie as some of the others, but of course it's appreciated."

"Even if you were right, that's entirely beside the point."

"And what is the point?"

"That you're an ass," said Sophie.

"Yes, but wouldn't talking to me be more interesting than walking alone?"

She stared at him, detecting an intensity in his eyes that belied his relaxed attitude. Finally she sighed and said, "Marginally."

"Great," said Eric, starting toward Oxford. She wasn't sure how it happened, but by the time they reached the edge of Port Meadow, they were deep in conversation about the youthful style of *Northanger Abbey*.

"Listen, tomorrow's Saturday—I thought I might drive down to Steventon," said Eric at a lull in the conversation. "You want to come?" Sophie had, in fact, never been to Steventon, the village in Hampshire where Jane Austen had spent the first twenty-five years of her life and had written the first drafts of three of her novels. She would have loved to go, but not with him, and in any case she couldn't help laughing at his transparency.

"Does that work?" she asked.

"Does what work?"

"That ploy. You find out a girl's favorite author and then offer to drive her to Jane Austen's birthplace, or George Orwell's gravesite, or Charles Dickens's favorite pub."

"I don't like Dickens."

"How can you not like Dickens?"

"All that poverty. It depresses me. At least Austen's heroines end up in nice big houses."

"Setting aside the fact that I find you disagreeable," said Sophie, "the truth is I have plans tomorrow."

"Oh, I don't think you find me disagreeable," said Eric.

"Then how do you think I find you?"

"I think you're intrigued by me—and even though I'm rude and generally unpolished, you think you might have finally met someone who appreciates Jane Austen as much as you do."

"When I heard you the other night, my first impression was that you were a prat," said Sophie, annoyed that he had so accurately guessed what she was thinking. She had dated Clifton for two years and he *never* knew what she was thinking. This guy had known her for twenty minutes and he could read her like a book. It was unnerving.

"First impressions can be misleading," said Eric. "Just ask Eliza Bennet. Come to Steventon with me."

"I have plans."

"What plans?"

"I have to go home for the weekend. My mother's having a . . . thing."

"A thing?"

"A garden thing," said Sophie. "It's a sculpture show. My mother is a bit obsessive about her garden. She thinks it's the finest in Oxfordshire."

"What sort of things does she grow?"

"Latin things," she said. "English names aren't good enough for my mother. Everything is Latin." She hadn't meant to sound quite so harsh.

Sophie actually liked her mother's use of Latin—it reminded her of her Uncle Bertram reading Horace to help her fall asleep when she was a girl.

"I take it you're not a gardener," said Eric.

"I like to *read* in the garden," said Sophie, "and I can tell a flower from a shrubbery and a shrubbery from a tree, but my thumb has always been distinctly black."

"And your father?"

"What about my father?"

"What sort of chap is he?" asked Eric.

"Oh, really, don't use the word 'chap.' You're American; don't try to pretend otherwise."

"Sorry, what sort of bloke is he?"

Sophie rolled her eyes. "He likes to shoot things. They're quite the pair, my parents. Mother only wants to grow things and Father only wants to kill them."

"Sounds like you don't like them very much."

"Mother and I get on well enough," she said. "She's not much of a reader, but we like to sit in the kitchen and talk all morning over coffee. I don't get to do that as often as I used to." It suddenly struck Sophie that, in spite of her apathy about her mother's garden, she was really looking forward to the morning *after* the sculpture show, when she and her mother could have one of their long relaxing talks.

"So it's your father you don't like. Is he just annoying or is it something worse?"

Eric's question cut a little too close to the bone, so she turned the conversation on him.

"What about you? Are you on one of those American university study abroad programs?" she asked.

"Hardly," he said. "I'm a little old for that." He explained that after getting his M.A. he had taught at Berkeley for two years but was now between jobs, so he was taking a year off, hitchhiking across Europe, and reading great books in beautiful places. "You know, Proust in Paris, Dante in Florence, and Jane Austen in the English countryside. I suppose you think that sounds a bit pompous."

"I think it sounds wonderful," said Sophie, who could think of no better way to spend a year. "But, if you're hitchhiking, how were you going to drive me to Steventon?"

"Good question," said Eric. They had reached Osney Lock. He leaned against the white metal railing that separated the nineteenth-century lock, with its hand-cranked wooden gates, from the narrow width of the path. They stood watching as the water pouring into the lock slowly raised up a long, narrow canal boat. Sophie loved the locks and almost always stopped to watch the traffic whenever she passed one.

"I would have found someone to loan me a car," Eric said as the boatman cranked open the upstream gates and the boat began to move slowly away. "I'm very persuasive."

She wasn't quite sure how he had done it, since she had thought they were both watching the canal boat, but suddenly she found him looking directly into her eyes and she felt her knees go weak. The desperation and need for approval were gone, replaced by a confidence that both frightened her and drew her in. She turned away and continued down the path toward Oxford, convinced now that he could, indeed, be very persuasive. She resolved not to look into those eyes again.

"I don't get along with my father, either," he said, falling back into step with her.

"I'm shocked," said Sophie. "I mean, unkempt and unemployed—he should be so proud."

"Sarcasm!" said Eric. "Bully for you."

Perhaps she was being too harsh—after all, they had been having a pleasant conversation—but the way he'd gazed into her eyes had really thrown her. "I'm sorry," she said, more gently. "Tell me about your father."

"I'd rather talk about yours," he said. "I look forward to meeting him."

"Oh, I hardly think that's going to happen."

"You never know."

"Actually, I do know. You don't have a job, you don't cut your hair, and you love books. You represent everything my father abhors."

"You've got to introduce us. I could learn to shoot things."

"I don't think arming you is a very good idea," said Sophie.

"Well, even unarmed, I'm sure he'd find me delightful."

"You have an awfully high opinion of yourself, don't you?"

"Not really," said Eric. "I mean, not like you do. I'm just American. Maybe we're better at joking around and having fun."

"What makes you think I have a high opinion of myself?"

"Well, you think you're better than me, right?"

Sophie felt chastened. They had arrived at the gentle stone arches of Folly Bridge, and the Oxford traffic was now just ahead of them, at the top of a long flight of stone steps.

"Look," said Eric, gently laying a hand on her arm and pulling her to a stop. "I'm not very good at first impressions. But think about it—we both like Jane Austen, we both like walks in the countryside, and I'm an uncouth American who would drive your parents crazy. I'm kind of a catch."

She stared at the stones beneath her feet and felt her cheeks turn hot.

"We don't have to get married or anything," said Eric. "I just thought we had a nice walk and it might be fun to hang out or get a coffee or something. I'm only in Oxford for a few more days anyway."

Sophie was dying to look at him, to give him her number, even to kiss him on the cheek and walk away with a toss of her hair, but she had never been good at this. And at the moment his insensitive impersonation of her was still pounding in her ears, doing its best to drive away that feeling she had had when he looked into her eyes.

Still looking down, she pulled away and said, "It was nice to meet you, Eric." She was halfway up the steep stone steps that led from the riverside to the street when she impulsively turned back and called to him, "It's Collingwood, by the way. I'm Sophie Collingwood. You can reach me at Christ Church. Just leave a message with the porter."

Ten minutes later, Sophie stood in the Upper Library of Christ Church, surrounded by neoclassical bookcases of highly polished oak filled with bindings of leather and vellum and cloth that contained the library's greatest treasures. Although she worked in a modern office downstairs, this was her favorite room in the college—second among Oxford spaces, in her opinion, only to Duke Humfrey's Library in the Bodleian. For the past five years, through two degrees, she had come here whenever she needed a place for quiet reflection, a place to center herself before diving back into the raucous world of Oxford. Sophie had finished her master's degree three weeks ago and was taking the Long Vacation to explore her career options. The college librarian had said she could keep her part-time job until the new term started. So, for a few more weeks, Sophie could stay connected to the world of education—a world she had been immersed in her entire life and where answers always came, if only you looked in the right place. Now she stood alone in the center of this glorious room and wondered if any of her questions—what to do about a man like Eric, how to soften her own sharp edges, and above all what to do with her life—could be answered by the priceless books that surrounded her.

## *Hampshire, 1796*

"I FELT THAT, as a young lady whose love of books is equaled only by my own, you would enjoy such a spot," said Mr. Mansfield.

"You were, as usual, correct, Mr. Mansfield," said Jane, running her finger along a row of gleaming leather spines and sighing audibly.

They stood, by invitation of his lordship, the Earl of Wintringham, in the library of Busbury House. Jane was overwhelmed. The trove of books in her father's study at Steventon paled in comparison with this treasure house. Shelves seemed to stretch for miles, nearly disappearing overhead.

"I generally prefer to keep to my own sitting room," said Mr. Mansfield, "but as you mentioned that you had just finished reading *Camilla*, I thought you might enjoy looking for new material in his lordship's collection."

"Indeed, Mr. Mansfield," said Jane, "I feel as if I could spend my life searching for things to read in a library as grand as his lordship's. I see it was not just the possibility of friendship with young ladies who love novels that drew you to Hampshire. I am surprised you do not *live* in this room."

Though their acquaintance had extended for only two weeks, Jane already felt that she and Mr. Mansfield were old friends. As she had learned at luncheon in the rectory that day when they had first spoken, Rev. Richard Mansfield was the rector of Croft-on-Tees, Yorkshire.

When he had entered his ninth decade a few months earlier, his physician had encouraged him to seek warmer climes, so he had hired a curate and decamped to Hampshire, where he was now a guest of Edward Newcombe, the Earl of Wintringham, at Busbury Park. Earlier in his career, Mr. Mansfield had been a schoolteacher, and Robert and Samuel, the two sons of the earl, had come under his tutelage. He had since remained a friend of the family, and was now ensconced in a disused gatehouse at the end of the long east drive.

"I am asked to dine with his lordship regularly," said Mr. Mansfield as Jane pulled a lusciously bound copy of *Amelia* off the shelf, "but I prefer not to stay here. A drafty gatehouse is much more to my liking."

"And, I suspect, gives you an independence you might not otherwise enjoy," said Jane. Mr. Mansfield smiled.

"Let us say that the conversation at his lordship's dinner table is not what I have come to expect from you, Miss Austen. It is far too much composed of gossip, especially when his lordship's sister and her daughters are visiting from London as they are at present."

"And you would rather have your intrigue in the form of novels," said Jane, holding up *Amelia* and waving it at him, "than in the form of idle speculation by his lordship's sister concerning her neighbors."

"Though you jest, Miss Austen, you are correct. Why, just three nights ago, Lady Mary informed us all with breathless delight that she had heard, while staying with his lordship's cousin in Kent, that a nearby house had been let to a bachelor with four thousand pounds a year. She told us this as if it were news as momentous as the French Revolution."

"But you have said that Lady Mary has daughters," said Jane, "so to her the news was certainly much *more* momentous than the beheading of a few thousand French nobles."

"I am afraid you have lost me with your youthful logic."

"Surely you know, Mr. Mansfield, as any good mother of daughters does, that a bachelor of such means wants nothing more than a wife. No doubt Lady Mary has a high enough opinion of her daughters to believe that he will choose one or the other of them. Marrying one's daughter to a wealthy man is certainly more important than anything that could happen in France."

"I did not think such a thing could happen, Miss Austen," said Mr. Mansfield with a wink, "but I think it is altogether possible that you have read too many novels."

"Well then," said Jane, "I shall return *Amelia* to the shelf and borrow this volume of *The Spectator* to see if, in fact, it 'tempers my wit with morality.'"

Summer was in full bloom on the grounds of Busbury Park, and Jane took to making almost daily visits to Mr. Mansfield. They walked in the park, through gardens, along carriage paths, and across fields, occasionally catching a glimpse of the impressive edifice of the main house, but more often enjoying the views across the gently rolling park. Jane loved the way the sheep gathered under the isolated trees in the meadows at the hottest time of day. She relished the view of the stone bridge at the far end of the lake and the broader vistas that one particular hilltop provided beyond the boundaries of the estate and across the fields of Hampshire. They talked of nothing but books—what they had read, what they hoped to read, and, in Jane's case, what she hoped to write. When they returned to the gatehouse after their walks, Jane would invariably read aloud the latest chapter of her current project, a novel in letters called *Elinor and Marianne*. Mr. Mansfield would sit with his eyes closed listening to the gentle sound of her voice, then ponder the reading silently when she had finished. These were tense moments for Jane, for she valued his opinion, and knew that he would give it eventually. Often he approved of every word; other times he grimaced as he made suggestions.

"You needn't make such a face, Mr. Mansfield," said Jane on one such occasion. "I take no offense at your criticism. Quite the contrary, I am honored that you grace me with your honest opinion. An opinion, I might add, which I believe strengthens my work."

"I only felt that if Sir John Middleton were a more affable sort—the type to throw parties or host picnics—your younger characters might be thrown together with more frequency."

"I confess I had not yet given much thought to the character of Sir John," said Jane. "But I think you are right. And it should not take much rewriting to set him on a course to host picnics and balls aplenty."

"It is, I think," said Mr. Mansfield, "the sign of a well-crafted novel when the minor characters are as fully realized as the hero and heroine."

"Wisely spoken, Mr. Mansfield. And I am certainly guilty of giving less life to those whose time upon the stage of my novel is but brief. It is a fault I shall endeavor to correct."

"Tell me, Miss Austen—you have said that you read these same pages at the rectory. Do you receive advice from your listeners there as well? Does your sister Cassandra offer you suggestions?"

"Alas no, sir—though I often entreat her. I fear she believes her honest reaction would harm my feelings or somehow damage our intimacy, and so she says only that she thinks each chapter 'marvelous,' or, what is worse, 'the best yet,' without giving any indication how the inferior previous chapters might be brought up to the level of quality of the most recent. Your honesty, sir, is one of many reasons I so value our friendship."

Another reason was that, at his age, Mr. Mansfield posed no threat as a suitor. Though Jane took delight in writing of the courtship and wedded bliss of her characters, she was quite uncertain how she would react should the opportunity for such courtship fall into her own path. The chance to spend so much time with a mind so in sympathy with her own without the slightest thought for romance made Mr. Mansfield, to her, the perfect companion.

## *Oxfordshire, Present Day*

"OF COURSE YOU CAN come for a visit," said Uncle Bertram. "You know you're always welcome."

"More than a visit this time," said Sophie. "I need some advice."

Her encounter with Eric Hall yesterday had driven home the fact that she was at a crossroads in her life. So, as the green fields of Oxfordshire slipped past the window of the train bearing her toward Kingham, she had called the person who had always helped her find direction—her Uncle Bertram.

"Nothing you want to discuss on the phone?" said Uncle Bertram.

"It's more of what we've been talking about this past year," said Sophie. "What I'm going to do now that I've finished my master's. But it's more complicated than that." She paused for a moment and heard the patient, steady breathing of her uncle. "I met a man yesterday who's taking a year off and traveling around Europe reading books."

"Sounds delightful," said Bertram.

"Well, *he* wasn't delightful," said Sophie, "not exactly. But he did make me think."

"An essential quality in a man," said Bertram. "Now, I'm off to a lecture at the V and A, but you come down any day this week and we'll have a long chat."

**SOPHIE'S SISTER WAS WAITING** for her on the platform at Kingham station. After hugging her, Victoria tossed Sophie's bag in the back of the Land Rover and pulled out of the car park for the ten-minute drive home.

Bayfield House, the country home where Sophie had grown up, stood at the top of a hill looking out across a wide valley in which sheep grazed. On the far side of the valley was the dark green of Bayfield Wood. Unlike most of the buildings in the towns and villages nearby, built with the local stone in a warm honey color, Bayfield was a gray stone edifice three stories high, built around a central courtyard, into which Victoria now steered her car. To some visitors it seemed a cold and imposing country house, but to Victoria and Sophie, who had delighted in exploring its mysteries as children, Bayfield was home.

Although Bayfield boasted an impressive library, her father had always treated books as decor, not repositories of knowledge or stories or inspiration. He kept the library locked, opening it only for monthly tours conducted for the sightseers who stalked the country homes of England and for the annual parties that coincided with what he considered the triumvirate of high holidays—Christmas, Ascot, and Henley. Even on those occasions, the wire mesh doors that covered the bookcases remained locked. When Sophie, at the age of six, had the audacity to ask if she could look in the library for something to read, her father replied, "Those books aren't for reading."

Sophie's love of books and her father's apparent resentment of their very presence in his home was just one root of the distance that had grown between them over the years—a distance Eric Hall had sensed and Sophie had refused to discuss. She knew that her own birth had caused complications that meant her mother couldn't bear any more children; she knew, too, that while her father doted on Victoria, he resented Sophie for not being a boy. More than anything he had wanted a son, and, in ways subtle and not so subtle, he had reminded Sophie of this fact for as long as she could remember. Maybe that, as much as anything, was why she had turned to his younger brother, her Uncle Bertram.

The only time she had ever seen the bookcase doors of the Bayfield library unlocked was on Christmas, when Bertram visited. Every year, he threw open the doors of the library and withdrew from the pocket of the silk waistcoat he insisted on wearing to Christmas dinner a tiny golden key, with which he unlocked one of the bookcase doors. He never perused the shelves or took his time deciding which door to open. He always seemed to know exactly where to go, and within seconds of entering the room he had pulled a single volume off the shelf, relocked the cabinet door, pocketed the key, and proclaimed, "Merry Christmas to me!" Sophie was the only member of the family who seemed to find this ceremony worthy of attention. Victoria, older by three and a half years, had explained its origins to her one year when they were children:

"It's an agreement he has with Father," whispered Victoria. "Uncle Bertram gave Father some sort of money or inheritance or something to help keep the house, and he gets to take one book out of the library every Christmas."

"Father says those books aren't for reading," said Sophie.

"I'll bet Uncle Bertram reads them," said Victoria, winking at her little sister.

**"IT'S ANOTHER OF MOTHER'S** classic events," said Victoria now, as they got out of the car. "Good intentions and dreadful sculpture."

Sophie laughed. "I've missed you, Tori," she said.

"Edinburgh is too far away," said her sister. For the past six months she had been working for an Internet advertising company in Scotland. "But we have all day to catch up. Trust me, you won't want to spend your time looking at the art."

The sculptures were indeed hideous. It looked as if the artist had made plaster casts of the most unattractive people he could find, and then broken off body parts and scattered them around the garden. Arms hung from trees, heads floated in the pond, legs grew up next to the rosebushes. It was supposed to be some sort of social statement. As far as Sophie and Victoria were concerned it was a statement that the artist should get into another line of work.

"We're not allowed to say how awful it is," said Mrs. Collingwood to her girls as they were setting up the refreshments table. "We just smile and pour tea and remember it's all for charity."

"But did you know?" said Sophie. "I mean, how bad it would be?"

"Oh, my dear, of course not. But we'll have a good laugh about it in the morning."

And so Sophie, in her favorite summer dress, spent the day walking through the garden telling people that cream teas were available in the summerhouse, bringing cups to old ladies too tired to move from the benches around the pond, and talking to her sister while the two of them washed dishes.

Late in the afternoon, as the crowd was waning, the two sisters were strolling up the garden looking for abandoned teacups when their mother called to Sophie from where she stood chatting with a young man.

"Sophie, come here. There's someone I want you to meet."

"Good thing I have a boyfriend at the moment," said Victoria with a giggle, giving Sophie a playful shove in the direction of their mother, whose matchmaking was notorious.

She didn't recognize him at first. He had cut his hair and shaved, and although he was wearing jeans, they were new and untattered, and he wore them with a checked button-down shirt that made him look almost civilized.

"You must be Sophie," he said, holding out his hand to her as she approached. She was just on the verge of revealing him, of saying, "Eric, I see you've met my mother," but he caught her eye again—how did he do it?—and something in his gaze made her play along.

"Yes, Sophie Collingwood," she said, gripping his hand as firmly as she could, wondering if she could cause physical pain.

"Eric Hall," he said. "I was just admiring your mother's viburnum."

"I'm sure you were," said Sophie. "It's so admirable."

Sophie's mother ignored her daughter's sarcasm and said, "Eric here is a book lover, like you, Sophie. Although it doesn't keep him from appreciating a fine garden."

"No indeed," said Eric. "Or fine sculptures. I especially like the pile of torsos next to the rhododendron." Sophie and her mother glanced at one another and each suppressed a laugh. "I would love to have an escort round the garden, Mrs. Collingwood, but I'm sure you must be much too busy."

"Sophie will be happy to show you round," said Mrs. Collingwood. "Won't you, Sophie?"

"Blissfully," said Sophie. Her parents were constantly trying to force her into an attachment—usually with a wealthy young man who might one day be counted on to preserve Bayfield House for the Collingwoods. That her mother was now thrusting the hitchhiking academe Eric Hall on her she found more than a little amusing.

"So, Mr. Hall, was it?" said Sophie. "What brings you to Bayfield House?"

"I've come to admire the sculpture," said Eric.

"Oh come on, you know as well as I do that this stuff is abominable," she said, turning and walking up the garden.

"Well, that's one more thing we have in common."

"How did you find us, anyway?" asked Sophie, genuinely curious. Though she found his showing up uninvited a bit annoying, walking with Eric was certainly more pleasant than fetching tea for old ladies.

"'Open Garden and Sculpture Show at Bayfield House'—the signs are in every tearoom in Oxford. And I told you I could borrow a car."

"But I never told you I lived in Bayfield House."

"No, you didn't. Lucky for me the only other open garden and sculpture show in Oxfordshire today was only forty miles from here. I should've known yours would be the house near Adlestrop."

"Why Adlestrop?" said Sophie.

"You must know why," said Eric. "Jane Austen's cousins lived there. She visited, what, two or three times?"

"Three," she said, smiling. "So how was the other sculpture show?"

"Well, the sculpture was much better, but the company wasn't nearly as nice."

"You need to work on your lines," said Sophie, almost instantly regretting her abrasiveness.

"You know, I'm not a horrible person. And I'm not trying to get you into bed or anything. I just fancied an afternoon in the country and I thought you would make good company."

"I know. I'm sorry," said Sophie. She had promised herself, standing in the Upper Library yesterday, to stop being so defensive, stop assuming—for she had finally admitted to herself that this was what she had been doing—that every man she met would break her heart the way Clifton had. "Maybe we could start over?" she said.

"Why not? Hi, I'm Eric Hall." When he held out his hand Sophie felt charmed and, she was surprised to find, a little disappointed (that he wasn't trying to get her into bed).

"Sophie Collingwood," she said, shaking his hand once more, but this time without trying to crush it. "You'll have to forgive me; university life has made me a bit of a cynic when it comes to men."

"Look," said Eric, "I'm sorry about the other night in the pub. I could claim that I was drunk or something, but the fact is I was an ass, and I apologize."

"Apology accepted," said Sophie.

"So, what was it like growing up in a grand country house?"

"The best part was lots of empty rooms to escape to with a good book and lots of woods and fields to tromp round in with my sister. The worst part was listening to Father complain constantly about how there isn't enough money to replace this roof or rebuild that wall. That, and having people constantly ask, 'What was it like to grow up in a country house?'" she teased.

"Another topic, then," said Eric. "Your mother tells me you're quite the bibliophile."

"My mother used the word 'bibliophile'?"

"Not exactly," he said with a laugh. "She said something about the miracle of pulling Sophie away from her books for an afternoon."

"A bibliophile raised in a family that doesn't know the word," said Sophie. "That's me."

"So how did you become a book lover?"

She leaned against the stone wall at the end of the garden and gazed out across the glowing Oxfordshire countryside toward the ridge five miles away, where she could just see the silhouette of the church tower in Stow-on-the-Wold.

"My Uncle Bertram," she said.

**SOPHIE HAD ALWAYS LIKED** Uncle Bertram. He told her stories and engaged her in conversation in a way that other adults at Bayfield House rarely did. She had been eight years old when her uncle brought her to London for a weekend to see a Christmas panto. "He took *me* when I was eight," said Victoria, by now a sage of eleven and a half. "You won't like it. His flat smells funny and there aren't any toys and there's no garden." Sophie was unimpressed with the panto—it all seemed rather silly to her. When Uncle Bertram asked her afterward what she wanted for dinner she couldn't think of anything, so he took her for pizza. She didn't particularly care for pizza.

She gritted her teeth as she stood on the doorstep of his flat in Maida Vale, prepared for the odor Victoria had warned her of, but as they walked in and Bertram busied himself turning on lights, Sophie found she quite liked the smell. It was something like dust and candle wax, and if she took a deep breath it burned her nose the tiniest bit. It seemed almost alive. Only when she had stepped into the sitting room did she begin to suspect its origin. The walls were lined with books from floor to ceiling. Stacks of books stood neatly arranged on every horizontal surface—tables, windowsills, even the top of an unplugged television. Since Sophie had been forbidden to explore the library at home, her only real experience with books had come at school and from the few children's picture books that lay on the bottom shelf of a cabinet in the nursery. She sensed immediately that this was something altogether different. It was a library, yes, but she knew these books had been *read*. They weren't arranged in long lines of matching bindings like the ones in Bayfield House, and almost every volume had slips of paper protruding from the top. She wondered if Uncle Bertram had marked all the best bits.

"Shall we have a story?" said her uncle, when he had hung up their coats.

"Yes, please," said Sophie.

"What would you like?" he asked.

"You pick."

And so he did. They settled onto the couch, Bertram with a cup of tea and Sophie with a mug of cocoa. He began to read and Sophie's world was transformed—this was not like the insubstantial children's stories her mother read to her at bedtime. This was ever so much more.

"*The Wind in the Willows*," read Uncle Bertram. "Chapter One, The

River Bank. The Mole had been working very hard all the morning, spring-cleaning his little home." Sophie closed her eyes and fell into the story.

After every chapter, Uncle Bertram said, "Perhaps that's enough for now," but chapter after chapter, Sophie pestered him for more, until finally he said, "I think it's time we switched to another book. I do believe it's past your bedtime." And only because he promised to keep reading once she was tucked up in bed, Sophie brushed her teeth and put on her pajamas at lightning speed. She discovered that not only the sitting room but every room of the flat had book-lined walls. Even the narrow corridor was made narrower by tall shelves of books.

"What's this one called?" she asked when Uncle Bertram drew a small fragile-looking volume from the shelf next to her bed.

"*The Odes of Horace*," he said. But this time when he began to read, the words made no sense to Sophie.

"I don't understand," she said.

"It's Latin," replied Uncle Bertram. "Think of it as music, and just listen."

And so she fell asleep to the musical sound of Uncle Bertram intoning Horace, with visions of Rat and Mole and Toad dancing around her. She didn't wonder until much later whether it had been the kind attentions of Uncle Bertram and his gentle voice or the story itself that had so delighted her. She only knew, then, that she had never been happier.

They did not leave the flat for the rest of the weekend. The next morning Uncle Bertram finished reading *The Wind in the Willows* while Sophie had tea and toast for breakfast. After that, she explored every room and every shelf, climbing on a stepladder to reach the rows of books that towered over her eight-year-old head. Uncle Bertram's books were not arranged by author or title or, more perplexing to little Sophie, by size or color. "You have to read a book to understand its place on the shelf," said Uncle Bertram. And he showed her how *The Wind in the Willows* ("a book about life on the river") sat next to *Three Men in a Boat* ("a book about a journey on the River Thames"), which sat next to *Alice's Adventures in Wonderland* ("a story that was first told on the banks of the Thames"), which sat next to Freud's *The*

*Interpretation of Dreams* ("because *Alice* is a dream story"), and so on. Sophie longed to read every book, to understand every relationship. If other books were as exciting as *The Wind in the Willows,* she could not imagine a better way to spend her life than unlocking the puzzles of her uncle's bookshelves. She found it mystifying that this library was so alive, while the library back at Bayfield House seemed so dead.

"Why does Father never look at the books in his library?" asked Sophie as she and Uncle Bertram sat at the kitchen table eating tomato soup for dinner.

"Your father has always resented that library," said Uncle Bertram. "I think he feels like he's its prisoner at times."

"Why?"

"Well, you see, Sophie, our father died when we were young, and since your father was the older brother he inherited the estate—that's the house you live in and all the gardens and fields around it. And that also included the books in the library."

"You didn't get any books?"

"Not exactly," said Uncle Bertram. "You see, our father made a sort of rule before he died that none of the books or the furniture in the house could be sold or given away unless your father and I both agreed."

"And you wouldn't agree to sell all those books!" said Sophie gleefully.

"Exactly. Your father thought he needed money and the easiest way to get it would be to sell the books. And since he didn't care for books, especially old dusty books, that didn't make him very pleased with me."

"But old dusty books are the best kind."

"I think so, and you think so, but your father doesn't think so."

"So you bought all these books yourself?" said Sophie, waving her soup spoon to indicate the entire flat.

"Almost all," said Bertram. "Your father and I made a deal. I agreed to let him sell some paintings and things to raise the money he needed to fix up the house, and he agreed to let me have one book from the family library to take home each year."

"The Christmas book!" said Sophie.

"Exactly, the Christmas book. So every year at Christmas I pick one book to keep for my own." He took her by the hand and led her into a small bedroom at the end of the corridor. "Do you see this shelf right here next to my bed? Those are all the books I've picked over the years. It is my very special shelf."

"It must be exciting to go into a big library and get to pick any book you want."

"I'm glad you think so, Sophie. Because I want you to do the same thing. I want you to pick any book in my flat to take home with you and keep."

"Really?" she said, her face lighting up.

"Really," said Bertram. "After all, it's almost Christmas."

"Any book?"

"Any book. But choose carefully," said Uncle Bertram. "A good book is like a good friend. It will stay with you for the rest of your life. When you first get to know it, it will give you excitement and adventure, and years later it will provide you with comfort and familiarity. And best of all, you can share it with your children or your grandchildren or anyone you love enough to let into its secrets."

"**AND WHAT BOOK DID** you pick?" asked Eric as Sophie fell silent.

"I can't tell you that," she said, turning to look at him for the first time since she had begun her story. "It's personal."

"Wait a minute, let me get this straight," he said. "You can tell me all the intimate details of your family and their finances and your relationship with your uncle, but what book you chose is personal?"

"That's right," said Sophie. "What could be more personal than a book?"

"It just seems like a strange place to draw the line when you're talking to a perfect stranger."

"You're not *quite* perfect," she said, turning to walk back up the garden. Most of the "art enthusiasts" had moved on, leaving behind the occasional teacup on a low stone wall or a garden bench.

"It was *Pride and Prejudice,* wasn't it?" said Eric, running to catch up with her.

"I was eight years old."

"Yeah, but I'll bet you were a pretty brainy eight-year-old. If Jane Austen was reading Samuel Richardson when she was seven, I'm sure you were reading Jane Austen when you were eight."

"What makes you think Jane Austen was reading Richardson when she was seven?"

"I don't know. Didn't I read that somewhere?"

"I really don't think so."

"Well, I still think you picked *Pride and Prejudice*."

Sophie, in fact, had not picked *Pride and Prejudice*. She had chosen an oversize copy of *Grimm's Fairy Tales* with dark, ghoulish illustrations by Arthur Rackham. She discovered years later that it was a signed limited edition, worth hundreds of pounds, but Uncle Bertram had placed it into the hands of his eight-year-old niece without hesitation. It still occupied a place of pride in her collection—the first in a row of sixteen volumes, each of which she had chosen as her annual Christmas gift from Uncle Bertram.

After that first visit, Uncle Bertram had become Sophie's special friend. He loved all his family, he told her, but Sophie knew their relationship was different. Her mother could see how much genuine joy Sophie derived from her visits to Uncle Bertram and would not let Mr. Collingwood's resentment of his younger brother interfere with the relationship. As she spent more time with her uncle, Sophie felt less and less connected to her father—but she didn't care. Uncle Bertram understood her in a way her father never could. It wasn't just that they both loved books. It was that Sophie, as a little girl, had yearned for mystery and adventure—something beyond her ordinary life at Bayfield House. At home she had to settle for getting her mystery from books, but her visits with Bertram were filled with adventure.

By the time she was ten, Uncle Bertram was fetching Sophie every other weekend for a London visit, a pattern that would continue until she entered university. During the long holidays at Easter and in the summer, she would often spend a week or two in town. She and Uncle Bertram walked the streets of London together, exploring any neighborhood or building with a literary connection. They visited museums and libraries that displayed rare books and attended plays and musicals based on books, but most of all they shopped—Sophie delighting in spending her carefully saved allowance on "dusty old books." Uncle Bertram knew every bookshop in the city, every antique stall with a shelf of books tucked into the back, every street vendor in the markets of Portobello Road or Camden Passage who might have a book or two laid out on a blanket. And without fail, after a day of stalking the books of London, they would return to the flat in Maida Vale, curl up by the fire, and read. At first Uncle Bertram always read to Sophie, but soon enough she shared the task, and they would pass *The Ingoldsby Legends* or *The Secret Garden* or *Robinson Crusoe* back and forth at the end of each chapter.

Sophie had a particular fondness for first lines—they were so laden with potential. Simple first lines were the best, she thought—"Alice was beginning to get very tired of sitting by her sister on the bank, and of having nothing to do"; "Whether I shall turn out to be the hero of my own life, or whether that station shall be held by anybody else, these pages must show"; "In a hole in the ground lived a hobbit." And she had never forgotten that frozen winter's day when she and her uncle had returned to the flat in the dark of early evening after an afternoon of book hunting and he had pulled down a volume from an upper shelf, settled in his chair with a cup of tea, and read a line that, even though she was only ten, seemed to Sophie so intriguing and mysterious that she could not wait to see where it would lead: "It is a truth universally acknowledged, that a single man in possession of a good fortune, must be in want of a wife."

## *Hampshire, 1796*

"I **AM AFRAID** I am to leave Hampshire in a few days' time, Mr. Mansfield," said Jane as they stood beside the lake, which glistened in the August heat. "My brother and his wife have written from Kent and I am to go for a visit of some weeks."

"I confess, Miss Austen, that it will grieve me to be parted from you for such a time, but it may grieve me even more to be parted from the Dashwoods. Are you to leave me at such a delicate point in their story?"

"It cannot be helped, sir. But perhaps you will write a letter of support to their creator so that you might see their story ended."

"Do I understand, Miss Austen, that you are holding the misses Dashwood hostage with a ransom of my correspondence?"

"Indeed I am, sir," said Jane with a laugh. "For how can I hope to write a word in such a place as Kent without your encouragement?"

"I believe, Miss Austen, that you could write anywhere with no more encouragement than paper and ink, but you may depend upon me as a correspondent nonetheless."

As they climbed out of the valley and toward the gatehouse, Mr. Mansfield fell unusually silent. Jane thought at first it was due to the steepness of the hill and she worried that perhaps he was unwell, for just a few days earlier they had climbed the same path and he had interviewed her the entire way about her progress with *The Spectator.*

"Do you feel well, Mr. Mansfield?" she asked at last. "For I have not known you to eschew conversation with me for so long unless you have a book in your hand."

"You must forgive me, Miss Austen. I am only silent because I feel I must chose my words carefully so as not to give offense."

"Surely, Mr. Mansfield, you need never concern yourself with giving offense to me. Are you angry with me?"

"Certainly not," he said. "Nothing could be further from the truth; it is only that your imminent departure forces me to express an opinion which I hope you will take in the kind spirit with which it is intended."

"I could do nothing less with you, Mr. Mansfield. But you frighten me. Tell me what you have to say."

"I am concerned," he began, but then he broke off.

"Concerned?" said Jane. "What gives you concern? Certainly no improper words or actions on my part?"

"On your part, no," said Mr. Mansfield. "I am concerned about Mr. Willoughby."

Jane gave a little laugh. "Mr. Willoughby? Please, Mr. Mansfield, say what you will against him, for I confess I am relieved that it is he and not I who has earned your disapprobation, especially as he is fictional and therefore it is much easier to reform his ways than my own."

"I only feel that when Mr. Willoughby first comes into the lives of the Dashwoods, one already has the sense that he is a scoundrel. The shock of Miss Marianne's rejection would be so much more powerful if we had no reason to suspect Willoughby of duplicity until his true character is revealed."

"So Willoughby should come onto the stage as more of a hero?"

"Exactly. That is precisely how I should put it. I do hope you do not think me impertinent to say so."

"Mr. Mansfield, I have always expressed my sincere appreciation for your criticism, and I do not except this attack on Mr. Willoughby." Lost in their conversation, Jane tripped on a root that lay across the path and stumbled forward. Mr. Mansfield caught her arm and steadied her, and the two walked on. "Perhaps it is that simple," said Jane.

"You have an idea, I can see," said Mr. Mansfield, "but I confess I cannot detect its nature."

"Perhaps Marianne, walking alone and without a kind octogenarian to keep her upright, falls and twists her ankle and Willoughby rescues her. He could thus be a hero from the moment we meet him."

"I am relieved that you not only welcome my criticism," said Mr. Mansfield, "but that you are so quickly able to solve the problem. I did not feel I could send you into Kent to write of a Willoughby who was less than he might be."

"And for that I am most grateful," said Jane. They had reached the gatehouse, and Jane, who was to depart early the following morning, took her leave. "Do not forget that you have promised to write. Know that I will always be grateful for words from you—even when, or I may say especially when, they are critical of my creations." Mr. Mansfield accompanied her through the gate of the estate and watched as she turned down the lane in the direction of Steventon. She turned back just before the opening in the hedgerow, where she would leave the road and set off across the fields, for a final glimpse of Mr. Mansfield, who stood by the gatehouse, waving.

**AS IT HAPPENED, JANE'S** stay in Kent was so filled with visits and balls and long conversations with her brother Edward and his charming wife, Elizabeth, that she had little time for writing beyond the mandatory letters to Cassandra. She had not the heart to write to Mr. Mansfield of the scant progress she had made in the adventures of the Dashwood family, and so to his letters of literary encouragement she replied only with brief notes of family news and an account of a ball. To this last, Mr. Mansfield replied:

**Dear Miss Austen,**

**Busbury Park is a lonely spot without you. I find neither Mrs. Harris, the housekeeper, nor the swans on the lake are able to converse on literary topics, and as for the residents of the main house, their interests lie much more in the way of shooting than reading. While I do not begrudge your brother a visit with his sister, you must return soon if my mind is not**

**to atrophy. And please bring the Dashwoods with you. They are missed, though not as much as their creator.**

**Yours Most Affectionately,**

**Rev. Richard Mansfield**

Laying this letter on her dressing table, Jane was surprised to find that a well of emptiness seemed to open in her heart. She had felt slightly odd during her visit, almost as if she were watching herself from a distance, and she had given that feeling no serious thought until this moment. Now she realized that she not only missed Mr. Mansfield, but she missed him terribly—in a way that she did not miss Cassandra or her parents. To be true, she felt their absence and looked forward to returning to the bosom of family, but this ache for Mr. Mansfield was something altogether different. It was not, she knew, the ache of a lover, for though she had not yet felt that ache herself, she knew enough of it from novels to know that the symptoms were entirely different. But she found that she could no longer think of him merely as a friend or companion.

That night she lay awake considering her feelings toward Mr. Mansfield. Certainly she was grateful to him for his kindness and encouragement, his honest criticism and his insightful suggestions—but one might feel the same way toward a schoolmaster, she thought. No, there could be no doubt about the matter: Jane loved Mr. Mansfield—not with the love of a heroine for a hero, but with a love that was slower and gentler, more intellectual than passionate, more . . . the word *avuncular* occurred to her but, though she certainly loved her uncles, her relationship with them was nothing like that with Mr. Mansfield. With him there was a meeting of the minds that she supposed was rare, even between husbands and wives. It was as if a part of her mind dwelt in him and a part of his mind dwelt in her, and when she was separated from him a part of herself was missing. She wondered if it was this, more than her busy schedule, that had kept her from returning to *Elinor and Marianne*.

That his letter arrived a few days before Jane's departure for Hampshire only increased her desire to be home again, and the pain of parting from her brother and his family was eased, if not completely allayed, by the thought of returning not just to Cassandra and her parents, but especially to her frequent intercourse with Mr. Mansfield.

## *Oxfordshire, Present Day*

"THE GARDEN CLOSES in a few minutes," said Sophie to Eric, glancing at her watch. "It was nice of you to come."

"I love the way the English tell people to go away," said Eric with a laugh. " 'It was nice of you to come' sounds so much more civilized than 'Get out.' Anyhow, your mother's invited me to stay for a late supper."

"I might have known."

"It's remarkable what a young man can catch around here with no more bait than a clean-shaven face and an admiration of viburnum."

"I hate to tell you, but all it takes to wrangle an invitation from my mother is a Y chromosome and a pulse."

"If you want me to leave, I'll leave," said Eric, grabbing Sophie by the hand and pulling her to a stop before they approached the spot where Mrs. Collingwood was chatting with the last of the visitors.

Sophie looked down at her hand held in his. It felt electric, and that both excited and frightened her.

"No," she said. "Don't leave. If you've charmed my mother, then you should stay."

"I was hoping I might charm other members of the family."

"Well my sister has a boyfriend at the moment and I don't think you're going to like my father," said Sophie with a laugh.

"I gather *you* don't like your father," said Eric. "All conversational roads seem to lead back to that point."

"It's not that I don't like him," she said, dropping his hand and starting toward the house. "I've nothing against hunting and Barbour jackets; that's just not my cup of tea. My cup is served in a cracked mug decorated like an old Penguin paperback."

"Somehow I think there's more to it than that," said Eric, "but you don't have to tell me if you don't want to."

They walked back toward the house in companionable silence until Eric said, "What is a late supper anyway? Is it different from dinner?"

"Supper is in the kitchen instead of the dining room and it means Mother doesn't fix her hair and nobody changes clothes."

"It's a good thing I met you, Sophie Collingwood," said Eric, following in her wake.

"I'm reserving judgment," she said.

Sophie, Eric, Victoria, Mrs. Collingwood, and a few other guests had been sipping cocktails in the parlor for more than an hour when Sophie's father finally appeared. He seemed determined that it be a very late supper indeed. By that time, Eric had charmed everyone, mostly with his American accent and his story of the "amazing coincidence" of having met Sophie on the Thames Path and then stopping by to view the sculpture only to discover the same "delightful young lady."

"You didn't tell me you already knew Eric," said Sophie's mother, pulling her to the side of the room where her father stood.

"You didn't ask me," said Sophie. "Besides, I wouldn't say I know him."

"He seems a nice enough chap," said Mr. Collingwood. "What does he *do* in America?" Sophie knew her father meant how did he earn a living. Mr. Collingwood was a great admirer of those landed gentry who had married off their eldest sons to American heiresses.

"He's a pig farmer, Father," said Sophie. "He comes from a long line of pig farmers."

"And is there money in that?" asked her father, oblivious to her sarcasm.

"I'm going to fix another drink," she said.

At first she thought the meal might not be so bad. Her mother seemed to have tempered her opinion of Eric, on the advice of her husband, who was suspicious of the swine in Eric's past, and was not thrusting him upon her quite so shamelessly. Mr. Collingwood was deep in conversation with another guest about the foxhunting ban. Eric ate his salad quietly across the wide table from Sophie, separated from her by a massive centerpiece of flowers from the garden; but on the rare occasions when he caught her eye, she detected a mischievous twinkle. The main course passed peacefully enough, as Eric chatted with Victoria, who sat to his left, about games the Collingwood girls had played when growing up at Bayfield. Not until Sophie's father was serving the trifle did things begin to deteriorate.

"So, Mr. Collingwood. I hear you have quite a book collection here at Bayfield House," said Eric, winking at Sophie. She did her best to silence him with a glance, but she had never perfected the necessary subtlety of expression, nor did she think Eric would have stopped if she had. "Do you use the library often?"

"Not often," said her father with what Sophie knew was false politeness. "We have receptions there on occasion."

"No," said Eric, "I meant do you use the *books* often. It must be a pleasure to have such a fine collection at your fingertips."

"'Pleasure' is not the word I would use," said Mr. Collingwood in a low voice that was clearly intended to discourage Eric from further pursuit of the subject.

"And do you frequently add to the collection?" said Eric.

"Do I . . . ?" Mr. Collingwood could hardly have looked more shocked if Eric had asked him if he often performed human sacrifices in the parlor. "Do I *add* to the collection?"

"Yes. I'm sure you must frequent the auction houses and the antiquarian book fairs."

"Tell me, young man, if you were swimming in the sea and there was a millstone tied round your neck, would you add another one?"

"I don't swim," said Eric. "Never learned."

"That is entirely beside the point. The Bayfield House library is not something which I wish to add to; quite the contrary." Sophie could see in her father's expression that he was desperately trying to think of some new topic of conversation to introduce to avoid discussing family finances, and she was about to rescue him by mentioning the upcoming music festival at Chadlington, but Eric forged loudly on.

"Then I suppose your brother must add to the family collection. Sophie tells me he's quite the bibliomaniac."

"My brother?" spat Mr. Collingwood, now red in the face and clenching the spoon with which he had been dishing out the trifle as if it were a dagger he was about to wield on Eric. "Not that it's any of your business, but my brother would have been a disappointment to his father and he is a disappointment to me. He has frittered away his inheritance on a flat full of worthless old books and has never contributed twopence to the upkeep of his family estate. Not that any of that gives you the right to call him a maniac. Now—trifle?"

He held a spoonful of trifle over Eric's bowl and Sophie feared that if Eric said yes her father would hurl the pudding downward with such force that it would spatter everyone at that end of the table.

"Actually," said Sophie, "Eric has to be going. Remember, Eric? You said you needed to be back in Oxford by eleven."

"Why, look at the time," said Eric, standing up. "I really am most grateful, Mrs. Collingwood. Mr. Collingwood, I hope we have a chance to continue our conversation sometime."

Sophie's father did not seem to have any idea how to respond to this comment, and Sophie grabbed Eric by the wrist and led him gently toward the door.

"Good night," he said, waving to the table with his free hand.

A moment later, standing in the garden, Eric tried to pull her toward him. "Thanks for getting me out of there," he said.

Sophie pushed him away and dropped his hand. "Why did you goad him on like that?" she said. "I told you what a sore subject the library is for my father."

"I just showed your father for the buffoon he is. I thought you'd like it."

"My father is not a buffoon."

"He is a little. You practically said so yourself."

"Right—*I* said so, not you. I'm allowed to call him that; you're not." Sophie was trying very hard to stay angry with Eric—it was unforgivable that he had made such a scene—but every time she pictured her father brandishing a spoon full of trifle like a weapon, she could feel laughter bubbling up inside.

"I just wanted to make you laugh. I mean, if you read Jane Austen you have to think that was funny. Your father is Thomas Palmer, right out of *Sense and Sensibility*."

"My father is not Mr. Palmer," insisted Sophie, but she giggled when she realized how apt the comparison was.

"You know who I'd really like to meet is your Uncle Bertram. I'm a bit of a book collector myself."

"I suppose Uncle Bertram would know what to do with you," said Sophie with a smile. She could just imagine her uncle's laughter when she told him about Eric, her father, and the trifle.

"But I don't suppose I ever will meet him," he said, suddenly serious.

"I don't suppose so," she said with a sigh. "Listen, Eric, it was very nice of you to come out and pretend to like that awful sculpture and talk with me about books and everything, but it's late and I'm exhausted, and now I have to go back inside and placate my father by telling him that Americans don't understand manners or something like that. So maybe you'd better just go."

"Kiss me."

"I beg your pardon?"

"We're two lovers of old novels in a garden in the moonlight. Kiss me."

Sophie suddenly felt that she should like to do nothing more. So what if he was an ass now and then? He loved Jane Austen and he had driven all over Oxfordshire to find her and he made her laugh—and she had to admit he looked rather handsome with his hair cut.

"I thought you weren't interested in getting me into bed."

"I'm not. I'm interested in kissing you."

"I'm not sure that's a good idea."

"Look, I'm leaving for France in the morning and then Italy and then back home to America. When I walk out of this garden we'll never see each other again, but we'll always remember that kiss on a warm summer night."

"You're incorrigible," said Sophie, weakening.

"Kiss me." He did not move toward her or try to take her hand. He just stood there in the moonlight that filtered through the leaves of the willow tree and said it one more time, so softly that the words themselves were like shadows. "Kiss me." And Sophie raised herself up on her toes and gently pressed her lips to his. He did not embrace her or even touch her except with his lips. He only kissed her and she kissed him and her knees went weak and her heart raced and she thought for a moment that she saw fireworks. Then he pulled away and ran a hand through her hair and whispered, "Good-bye, Sophie." When he was gone, she stood alone on the grass, shivering in spite of the warmth of the night, and wondering what the hell had just happened.

## *Hampshire, 1796*

**JANE WAS NOT RETURNED** to Hampshire above twenty-four hours before she ventured to Busbury Park and found Mr. Mansfield just setting out on his afternoon constitutional. "I confess, as pleased as I am to see you, that I am sorry to hear that the Dashwoods have been so neglected these past weeks," he said.

"I assure you, Mr. Mansfield, now that I am back in your company, they shall not be neglected until their story is complete." Jane had not confessed her epiphany about her feelings toward him. There would be time for that later. Now she wanted nothing more than to talk about literature and feel that connection of the intellect she had missed so in Kent.

"I hope, though you will not neglect the Dashwoods, as you say, that you will still have time to visit a poor old man with few friends and empty days."

"You paint a self-portrait of much pathos, Mr. Mansfield," said Jane with a smile, "but despite your exaggerations, I assure you I shall return to you as often as the Dashwoods allow me."

**AS AUTUMN CAME** to Hampshire and the weather turned cool, Jane and Mr. Mansfield often curtailed their walks, instead taking tea by the fire in the sitting room of the gatehouse. Jane was writing more quickly now, as her novel rushed toward its denouement, and her reading often took up nearly the whole of her visit. By the beginning of October she had almost finished, and, as she wished to prolong the pleasure of reading, she was delighted with a sudden turn in the weather—a last bit of summer warmth before the grip of autumn became unbreakable—that allowed them to take a lengthy walk around the grounds.

"I was shocked when you read yesterday of the marriage of Mr. Ferrars," said Mr. Mansfield as they turned in to a walk between two rows of oaks. "I had thought for certain that Elinor and Mr. Ferrars were destined for one another, but I see it is not to be."

"The story is not finished, Mr. Mansfield."

"Yes, but Mr. Ferrars has married a young and healthy woman in Lucy Steele, and even if you were to kill her off, Elinor Dashwood should be no man's second choice."

"Mr. Mansfield, I suspect that you are trying to get me to tell you the ending. I certainly would not do so, even if I knew it myself."

"While I believe, Miss Austen, that you are within your rights as a novelist to withhold the end until it is the end, I cannot believe that, so near the conclusion of your tale, you yourself do not know the fates of all involved."

"Am I a novelist, Mr. Mansfield?" Jane had never been called such, but found that she rather liked the appellation.

"Certainly one who writes novels is a novelist—I believe even that great lexicographer Mr. Johnson would define you as such."

"But I can claim no true novels to my credit. No words of mine have been set in type or printed on paper or bound in covers."

"Do you imagine, Miss Austen, that a novel is a novel only when it is set in type and bound in covers?"

"I imagine exactly that, Mr. Mansfield. Surely you would not call Christopher Wren an architect if he had merely dashed out some worthless sketches that were never turned into buildings."

"You cannot think that what you have written is nothing but worthless sketches."

"They are worthless if no one pays me for them," said Jane. "Is that not Mr. Johnson's definition?"

"Indeed it is not," said Mr. Mansfield. "Unless I am very much mistaken, Mr. Johnson's definition of worthless is 'having no value.'"

"And what value do my sketches have?"

"Anything that brings pleasure to others has inestimable value," said Mr. Mansfield. "And your novel has brought great pleasure not only to me, but to all at the rectory who have the joy of hearing you read. But we are straying far from your question. You asked if you are a novelist. Let me ask you this, Miss Austen. Are you able to prevent yourself from writing?"

"Indeed not. I find that my stories will not cease to crowd all other thoughts from my mind until I have committed them to paper."

"And do you have the utmost respect for both the truth of your characters and the emotions of your readers?"

"Though I cannot claim to have readers in the traditional sense, I believe that I do."

"Then, Miss Austen, let there be no doubt about it—you are a novelist."

They walked a little farther in silence as Jane digested this proclamation. "Do you know, Mr. Mansfield," she said, "how Mr. Johnson defines the word 'novel'?"

"Indeed I do," he said. "'A small tale, generally of love.'"

"'A small tale,'" said Jane. "Novel writing seems an altogether less intimidating occupation when one considers that one only need produce a small tale."

"And that brings us back to my grave concern about the fate of Elinor and Mr. Ferrars. For I can see no way that their tale can be of love. You must tell me what you contemplate for them."

But Jane merely tossed her head, smiled, and remarked, "How lovely it is here in the walk with the leaves turning."

## *Oxfordshire, Present Day*

**SOPHIE LAY AWAKE** that night, longing for a good novel to take her mind off that kiss. Just before she'd turned in, Victoria had popped her head into Sophie's room with a wicked grin on her face.

"So," she said, "this Eric Hall. Marry, kill, or shag?"

"Kill," said Sophie, almost certain she was lying. "Definitely kill."

"I doubt that," said Victoria, and smiled at her sister before going to bed with assurances they'd talk about it in the morning.

Now Sophie was left alone pondering that damn kiss. God, it wasn't like she hadn't stumbled home from parties in Oxford and had a snog in the shadows with some guy whose name she would forget the next day. She had done that several times since Clifton, actually. But this had been sober and deliberate and done with the full knowledge that it could lead nowhere. And she wasn't even sure she liked him. When she remembered the way he made her laugh and how comfortable she was walking with him along the river or up the garden, she was sure she did. But when she thought of how he had acted at the pub and at dinner with her father, she wanted to hit him. But she couldn't hit him because he was gone. Her mind shuffled through every page of Jane Austen, looking for a kiss like the one in the garden. What would Eliza Bennet think? Or Marianne Dashwood? *I do not like him*, she tried repeating to herself as she stared up at the cracked ceiling. *I do not like him*. But if that was true, then why did she feel so miserable that he would never return?

At three, she finally gave up on sleep and crept downstairs. On a hook in the kitchen she found the key to the library. Even though she had no idea where her father kept the key to the bookcases, just sitting in the dark room surrounded by the smell of all those books calmed her. Tomorrow, she decided, she would go to London and join Uncle Bertram at an antiquarian book fair and Eric Hall would be forgotten. She could just imagine what her uncle would say when she told him about all this: "Dive into life, Sophie; have the adventure!" As she finally fell into sleep, she heard his voice telling her, "Sometimes you think too much."

**BAYFIELD HOUSE WAS USUALLY** quiet on Sunday mornings. Sophie's father would don his tweeds and head out into the countryside; her mother would pull on her gloves and slip out into the garden. Church was rarely on the docket. When she awoke late the next morning, however, Sophie heard loud voices and ringing telephones. Doors banged and feet pounded up and down stairs and a car started up in the courtyard and sped away, spewing gravel against the side of the house. In spite of all the commotion, no one seemed to notice that the library was unlocked and that Sophie was lying on the couch. When she finally made her way bleary-eyed into the kitchen in search of tea, her mother was sitting at the table staring at an uneaten slice of toast. Victoria stood looking out the window, her face impassive.

"Good morning," said Sophie tentatively.

"He's gone to London," said Mrs. Collingwood, almost as if she hadn't heard her daughter.

"I beg your pardon?"

Before Sophie realized what had happened, her sister had wrapped her in an embrace and was sobbing on her shoulder. Sophie's pulse quickened with fear.

"Your father's gone to London to attend to business," said Mrs. Collingwood.

"What's wrong?" said Sophie, as Victoria dropped her embrace and slipped into a chair. "What business could Father have on a Sunday?"

"Pour yourself a cup of tea and sit down, Sophie," said her mother, turning at last to face her daughter. Sophie could see that she had been crying—her eternally stoic mother had been crying. Her eyes were red and puffy and she gripped a wad of tissue in one hand. Sophie felt a rock in the pit of her stomach.

"Mother, Tori, what's happened?" she asked.

"Sit down," said her mother hollowly.

Sophie sat and reached for her mother's hand.

"Oh, you poor, poor child," said Mrs. Collingwood.

"Me?" said Sophie. "What about me?"

Mrs. Collingwood stared at her daughter blankly for several seconds before she continued. "It's your Uncle Bertram," she said at last, her voice barely above a whisper.

"Uncle Bertram?" said Sophie, dropping her mother's hand.

"There's been an accident," said Victoria.

"What do you mean there's been an accident? Is he all right? Where is he?"

"He's . . . Sophie, your Uncle Bertram is dead," said her mother.

"No," said Sophie, unable to even process the words. "No he's not. Tell me what happened really."

"He slipped and fell down the stairs outside his flat," said Victoria, reaching for her sister's free hand.

"No," said Sophie, pulling away and standing up. "No, I want to talk to him. I need to talk to him. Where is he?"

"He broke his neck, they think," said Victoria in a dull monotone. "They found him this morning."

"That's not right," said Sophie, whose eyes had begun to glaze over. "I just talked to him." The air seemed to have left the room. Something was wrong, very wrong. Perhaps she was still asleep and this was only a nightmare.

"Your father's gone to London to tend to . . . things. He wants to have the funeral here, though, so we'll have to put on a brave face and . . . Sophie? Sophie, are you all right?"

Sophie thought perhaps there were more words, but they came from the end of a long black tunnel, and then she was falling and falling and then everything was fine. She was twelve years old and she and Uncle Bertram were walking home from a book fair laden with purchases.

"Am I a book collector, Uncle Bertram?" she asked as they reached the quiet streets of Maida Vale.

"What do you do with a book when you get it?" Uncle Bertram asked.

"I read it," said Sophie. "Or else I ask you to read it to me."

"And then what?"

"And then I put it on my shelf so I can look at it again whenever I want to."

"And do you ever want to throw it away or sell it?"

"Of course not," said Sophie. "What a silly question."

"I have one more silly question, and then I can tell you if you're a book collector."

"What is it?" she asked earnestly.

"After you get a new book and you read it and you put it on your shelf, do you love it?"

"Oh yes!" said Sophie.

"Then you are a book collector," said Uncle Bertram. "Just like me."

She laughed with glee. "I'm happy that I'm like you, Uncle Bertram."

"I'm happy, too."

"**SOPHIE! SOPHIE, ARE YOU** all right?" Somehow Uncle Bertram was gone and faces swam above her. She lay on something cold and hard, yet her whole body felt sweaty. Everything above her—faces, cracks in whiteness, bits of color—was spinning slower and slower and then she was lying on the kitchen floor looking up at her mother and her sister and Uncle Bertram was dead and her world had been turned upside down.

## *Hampshire, 1796*

JANE HAD LITTLE TIME to relish the thought that the word *novelist* could rightly be applied to her. What happened the following day put all thoughts of novel writing out of her head, and instead convinced her that, while she had previously thought herself to be, though sinful from birth, essentially a good person, she was in fact one in whom virtue and vice mixed unequally. And the evil in her own soul, of which the events of the day were such a brutal reminder, meant that in her case the mixture was unequal in favor of vice. When she next met Mr. Mansfield, she sought him out not as a friend or fellow lover of literature, but as a clergyman—perhaps, she thought, even as a confessor.

"A lovely day for a walk, Miss Austen," said Mr. Mansfield when he opened the door to the gatehouse to find Jane on the doorstep. "I had rather hoped you would come by. I've just finished reading a new novel and I wanted to discuss it with you. Let me fetch my coat and we shall stroll through the grounds while I tell you all about it."

"I would rather we speak inside, Mr. Mansfield," said Jane, her eyes on the ground.

"If you prefer," he said, stepping aside to admit her into the house. "I'll just put the kettle on for some tea."

"I care not for tea, Mr. Mansfield. Please let us sit, so I may unburden myself."

"You are troubled?"

"Deeply, sir. And I find I cannot share this trouble at the rectory. There my niece Anna plays and my brother Henry visits and all is stories and songs and delight and there is no room for the darkness in my heart. I would not wish it even on my dearest Cassandra—especially not on Cassandra."

"You may share your load with me," said Mr. Mansfield. "After all, I am not only your friend; I am a priest."

"You are my tower of strength, Mr. Mansfield."

"God is your tower of strength, my child."

"And to him I have already spoken, and at length."

"Then speak to me."

"Yesterday," began Jane, "as I have done many times before, I accompanied my father on a visit to a certain house in Whitchurch where a widow of some means has founded a home for fallen women desiring to repent and reform their lives. Father has been clergyman to these women, who are frequently too ill to be removed, for the past several months, the local rector, so he says, being too busy with his other duties. Too often, Father's visits come at the time of death for one of these poor women, and he knows well that the presence of a young woman such as myself is sometimes a comfort to those facing judgment.

"Yesterday was one such time, and after Father had performed the order for the visitation of the sick, I was left alone at the bedside of a woman whose years were not many beyond my own but who was so disfigured from illness that I should not have recognized her if she had been my own sister.

"With death's embrace near, she felt a need to tell me her story, and I was happy to listen, knowing it was the only thing I could do to bring her comfort. She had come ten years ago, she said, to London, penniless and without prospects. Begging, she found, did not feed her and she soon turned to the only profession that offered her a chance of survival—that sinful and insidious practice that infects our capital. Once the fatal step had been taken, try as she might she could not rise above this evil way of life. Two children she bore, and two children died in her arms, for the price of her virtue was still not enough to feed a family. When illness deformed her face, robbing her of what little beauty she still possessed, the price she could ask for her services declined to the point that she was living in the street when she was found by a clergyman and taken to the home in Whitchurch. There she could do little more than wait for death to come. It was a tale I had heard all too often in that place, though it did not fail to move me. She gripped my hands in hers with what little strength remained in her broken body, so I could not wipe away the tears her words brought to me.

"And then she did the most extraordinary thing. She sat up in her bed, looked me in the eye, and said, 'I forgive you, Jane.'"

"That seems not so very remarkable," said Mr. Mansfield. "I have often known those on their deathbeds to have a desire to bestow forgiveness, and as you were the only soul present, she naturally bestowed it upon you."

"But, Mr. Mansfield, she called me Jane."

"It is true that 'Miss Austen' would have been more proper."

"And yet equally surprising, for we had not been introduced. I did not know her name, and she could not have known mine."

"And yet she did."

"And to understand how, Mr. Mansfield, you must first know what happened at Reading."

## *Oxfordshire, Present Day*

"IT'S NEVER LOOKED so nice," said Victoria, squeezing her sister's hand. "He would have liked it."

"He loved the books," said Sophie. "He never worried about dust."

"Are you OK?" said Victoria.

"No," said Sophie, "but keep asking."

The two stood in the library of Bayfield House, which would be crowded with visitors later that day. Their father had decreed that the library be opened for the reception following Bertram's funeral. The housekeeper had dusted furniture and washed windows and polished doorknobs in preparation.

"Tori, do you really believe Uncle Bertram's death was an accident?" said Sophie.

"What else would it be?"

"I don't know. It's just that Father said he slipped on the stairs because he was reading while he walked."

"Well, he did read all the time. You know that better than anyone."

"Yes, but not while he walked. I remember once we were walking down Elgin Avenue and I was reading and he said I shouldn't read while I was walking because one day I would walk out in front of a taxi. And I laughed and put my book away and told him that would never happen because it was impossible to get a taxi in his neighborhood."

"But don't you think maybe he read while walking when you weren't around?"

"I guess it's possible," said Sophie, "but something just doesn't seem right."

"You've read one too many mysteries," said Victoria. "You're always trying to turn everything into Agatha Christie."

"You're right, it's silly," said Sophie. "Maybe I just want someone to blame."

"But there's no one."

"Would you mind if I sat here alone for a few minutes?"

"Of course not," said Victoria, giving Sophie a light kiss on the cheek. "I love you, you know."

"I know," said Sophie. "I know."

Alone in the library, Sophie settled into the sofa in front of the fireplace—the same sofa that had so recently offered her refuge. That conversation with Bertram about walking and reading replayed again and again in her head. Tori was right—Sophie did let her imagination run wild sometimes, especially as a girl when she'd seen herself as a kind of Hercule Poirot or Miss Marple, but something about Uncle Bertram's death wasn't right. She could think of only one way to banish these thoughts. From the pocket of her black suit jacket she withdrew a note that had arrived in the post that morning. She had lost track of how many times she had read it since then, but she unfolded it once more and whispered the words to the empty library.

**Dear Sophie,**

**I was so sorry to hear about your uncle. I heard the news from a bookseller here in Paris. I know how much he meant to you. I know I may come across as a bit insensitive, but believe me when I tell you that I genuinely feel for your loss. If your uncle was anything like you, and I suspect he was, then he was a special person indeed. I can only imagine how much you will miss him, and, though it may be little comfort, I hope you know that you are in my thoughts at this difficult time. I'm sorry about my behavior at dinner—I guess**

**I acted rather selfishly that entire day, but as our friend Jane would say, "Selfishness must always be forgiven you know, because there is no hope of a cure." I feel like I should apologize for that kiss, too, but I won't because I'm not sorry. I'll be at this address for a few weeks, though I don't expect you will feel like writing.**

**Yours,**

**Eric Hall**

Even though she had little hope of ever seeing Eric again, his note brought her comfort. Outside of the constant solicitous attention of her sister, it had been one of only two sources of solace in the past few days. The other had come when she and Victoria took the train into Oxford to retrieve some books from Sophie's room. She had returned home with a box containing the sixteen books she had selected from Uncle Bertram's library at Christmastime over the years. They sat on a shelf by her bed in chronological order of acquisition—although she had somehow managed to switch *Pride and Prejudice* with Boswell's *Life of Johnson*. At Bayfield House she had carefully emptied the contents of the box onto her dressing table, stroking the spine of each book as she fitted it into place.

Only when she had reconstructed her shelf of Christmas books and sat there remembering her selection of each volume did the full import of a conversation she had had with Uncle Bertram last December suddenly strike her.

She was sitting by the fire in Uncle Bertram's flat and they each had a book—he was reading Thomas Carlyle and she was reading *Far from the Madding Crowd*. She had reached that delicious point in the narrative where the hero seems to have all the forces of the universe arrayed against him, yet she knew that he would triumph, that Gabriel and Bathsheba would, before the pages had been exhausted, make that short walk to the church and happiness.

She laid the book in her lap to rest her eyes for a moment and Uncle Bertram did the same.

"Do you like it here?" he asked, as they both gazed into the dying fire.

"Uncle Bertram," said Sophie with a laugh. "What a silly question. I'm never happier than when I am here."

"You are never happier than when you are there," said Bertram, pointing to the open pages of her book. "But I was speaking more generally. Do you like being in London?"

"Of course. You're the only Collingwood who really understands me."

"I did think I had taught you to listen better," said Bertram. "You still haven't answered my question. Take me out of the equation, even take Thomas Hardy and Jane Austen and Charles Dickens out of the equation and tell me, do you think you would like living in London?"

Sophie was silent for a long moment. She had never considered the experience of London independent of the experience of being with Uncle Bertram. She had rarely been in the city without at least seeing him, and it took a great effort of imagination to consider how she should like the one without the other.

"I think I would," she said at last. "When I think of all we have seen and done here, I'm inclined to believe Dr. Johnson was right."

"That the man who is tired of London is tired of life?" said Bertram.

"Exactly. But I still consider *you* London's chief attraction."

"So after Oxford you might think of moving here?"

"I don't know what I'm going to do after Oxford," said Sophie. "You know that. But I do know I'd like living in the same city as you."

"But I won't always be here, you know. I'm not a young man."

"You *are* a young man," she said. "At least too young to be having this conversation."

"And you, my dear, are perhaps too young to understand the need for such a conversation. There's something I'd like to tell you."

Sophie leaned forward in her chair and placed a hand gently on her uncle's arm. "You're not sick?"

"No, no," said Bertram, standing. "This is news for the distant future, I hope. But someday, when my time comes, I would like for you to have all this." He waved his hand to indicate the room.

"The books?" said Sophie, for an instant breathless with delight, until she considered that the gift was contingent on her uncle's death.

"Not just the books, but the flat as well. No one I know would be happier here."

"Oh, uncle!" cried Sophie, wrapping her arms around him. "But I hope to be a very old woman before I sit by this fire without you."

"I hope that as well," said Uncle Bertram. "But I thought you should know. Now, since you will have to wait to get your hands on all these musty old volumes, and since Advent is nearly done, I think it's time you picked out this year's Christmas book."

**NOW SOPHIE'S CHRISTMAS** volumes could soon be returned to Uncle Bertram's flat and reunited with the rest of his books. Only it wasn't Uncle Bertram's flat and they weren't his books. It was all hers now. But while the books she had chosen over the years comforted her; the promise of owning *all* of her uncle's library did not. To be in that cozy flat among those glorious books but without her uncle meant that something was deeply wrong with the world.

"Sophie, it's time." Victoria stood in the library doorway, a silhouette in her black dress, holding out Sophie's handbag for her. Five minutes later they were in the back of a black car, crunching down the drive.

The funeral was a simple service in the local parish church. Uncle Bertram had been cremated, and his ashes were buried in the churchyard. It ought to have been a cold winter day, with clouds hanging low in the sky and a sharp wind whistling through the unmown grass of the graveyard; but it was lovely—a warm blue sky, immaculately trimmed green grass, and a gentle breeze to keep the heat from bearing down on the black-clad mourners.

Back at Bayfield House, Sophie, feeling like the unacknowledged chief mourner, drifted through the visitors—distant cousins she had never met, business associates of her father, friends of her mother—without making any meaningful contact. Victoria and her mother were both in full hostess mode, and in the crowd Sophie felt more alone than she had all week. She was in the library peering through the metal grid at a shelf of travel narratives when she heard a voice beside her.

"I was so sorry about your uncle, Miss Collingwood. He was such a wonderful man." Sophie turned to see the short, round, and balding figure of Augustus Boxhill, one of London's leading antiquarian booksellers. She had met Mr. Boxhill many times at his shop in Cecil Court when on the prowl for books with Uncle Bertram.

"It was kind of you to come, Mr. Boxhill."

"I suspect," said the bookseller, looking around the room, "that you and I may be the only people here who really knew your uncle."

"That looks like the first edition of *Voyage of the Beagle*," she said, nodding at a row of four volumes at the end of a shelf. "I'm sure Father will be happy when he finds out what that will fetch at auction."

"Thanks to your uncle, you know more about books than most collectors twice your age," said Mr. Boxhill.

"And without my uncle," said Sophie, "I'll have no one to share all that with."

"Bertram was a good customer," said Mr. Boxhill, "but more important, he was a good friend. I think he'd want me to tell you that there are a lot of us out there who share your passion. You're not alone, Sophie."

"I know," she said, softening. "That's very kind of you, Mr. Boxhill."

"If there is ever anything I can do for you," he said, pulling a card from his pocket and pressing it into her hand, "I hope you won't hesitate to call on me."

But what could he do for her, thought Sophie. More important, what should *she* do? Uncle Bertram's death and her inheritance of his books and flat seemed to have forced the issue that she was expecting to spend the next several weeks wrestling with—what to do with her life now that her formal education was finally over. Once again, she could hear her uncle's voice telling her to embrace life and have adventures—but she could also hear his books calling to her and she could imagine sitting in his flat reading, communing with him through all those volumes and all their connections to him and each other. She pondered the relative merits of a quiet life alone in a flat full of books and a bold plunge into a world outside her comfort zone. She hadn't even noticed as the din of the reception slowly faded, but she was alone in the library, looking out the window over the garden, when she said aloud, "Why not both?"

"Sophie, are you all right?" said Victoria, stepping into the room.

"I might be," said Sophie. "I've made a decision."

"About what?"

"I'm going to London."

"For a visit?" said Victoria.

"To live," said Sophie.

"What will you do?"

"I don't know," said Sophie, turning toward her sister. "But it will be exciting."

**THE NEXT SUNDAY,** Sophie stood waiting for the London train, holding a small suitcase and a box containing her Christmas books. Eric's letter still rested in her pocket—somehow it had helped her find the courage to follow through with her plan. Victoria had returned to her job in Edinburgh, and, after a brief infestation of lawyers and a flurry of paperwork, calm had returned to Bayfield House. Sophie had resigned from her job at Christ Church and planned to return to Oxford before her lease was up at the end of the Long Vacation to pack the rest of her belongings.

"You sure you'll be all right, dear?" said her mother as the train approached the platform.

"No," said Sophie, "I'm not at all sure. But I've been in Oxford long enough. Uncle Bertram thought I'd like living in London, so that's what I'll do."

"You'll call us," said her mother hopefully.

"Of course, Mother," said Sophie, and she embraced her mother tightly.

**SOPHIE HAD PROMISED** her sister that she wouldn't obsess over the circumstances of their uncle's death, but she couldn't help replaying two versions of the event in her mind as she and Mr. Faussett, the solicitor handling Bertram's estate, mounted the stairs to her uncle's flat. In one scenario, Uncle Bertram emerged from his flat engrossed in a novel, stepped on a circular advertising Chinese food, and tumbled headfirst down the long flight of stairs. This was the official version of the story. But in the other version, Sophie saw a shadowy figure struggling with her uncle and hurling him down the stairs to his death. She shivered as she stepped over the very spot where, she imagined, her uncle's body had lain.

"There is still a lot of paperwork to go through, Miss Collingwood," said Mr. Faussett in what seemed to Sophie a falsely cheerful voice, "but there's no reason you can't stay here. We got everything cleaned up for you." He leaned a shoulder into the door.

Sophie knew something was wrong as soon as the door opened. The flat didn't smell right. Instead of must and dust and paper and leather, it smelled of lemon and lavender and bleach. Sophie clung to her box of books like a life preserver as she stepped through the door. Yes, the flat was cleaner than she had ever seen it—no dust hung in the air—but there was something else. Only when she walked through the entryway and into the sitting room did she see them: empty shelves. Miles and miles, it seemed, of empty shelves. There was not a single book in the room. Sophie dropped her box and screamed. Without a thought for the mystified solicitor in her wake she dashed through the flat, only to discover the same thing in every room: sickening tidiness and empty shelves. Aside from the box she had dropped on the floor of the sitting room, there was not a single book in the entire flat.

"What have you done!" she shrieked, nearly hysterical.

"I'm afraid I don't understand, Miss Collingwood. Is there a problem?"

"A problem? A problem! Of course there's a problem. Look around you. Where are they?"

"Where are what?"

"The books! Where are his . . . that is, where are *my* books?"

"Aren't those your books there on the floor?" said Mr. Faussett.

"Not those, the others. All the books. This flat was filled with books. Where are they?"

"Ah yes, we took care of all that according to your uncle's will."

"What do you mean according to my uncle's will? Uncle Bertram left those books to me. He told me so himself."

"That may have been his intention," said Mr. Faussett. "I gather he drew up his own will, which is never a good idea. He left you his flat and its furniture, but the residue of the estate he directed to be liquidated with the proceeds going to your father."

"Residue! You're calling his books residue?"

"Now if he had put 'furnishings' instead of 'furniture' that might have included the books. But as it is—"

"You *liquidated* my uncle's books?" Sophie collapsed into her favorite chair—the chair where she had sat for hundreds of hours reading with or to Uncle Bertram.

"We sold them, yes. Your uncle had debts, you see, and the only way to pay them and the death duties and still leave you with the flat was to—"

"Then you should have sold the flat and kept the books," said Sophie weakly.

"I'm afraid that wasn't an option. Legally, I mean. We had quite a few dealers come through. Things went very quickly."

Sophie no longer had the strength to shout. She felt as if what was left of her heart had been ripped out of her chest. The library Uncle Bertram had spent his life building had been scattered to the winds, and instead of spending the rest of her life connecting to him through his collection, she was left with sixteen books to remember him by.

"Do you know who bought them?" said Sophie softly. "I mean which dealers." Of course she couldn't afford to buy back even the smallest percentage of the collection, but still.

"I could send you a list," said Mr. Faussett.

"Thank you," she said.

"If there's nothing else, Miss Collingwood, I have an appointment. I'll leave you my card in case you need anything."

"No, that's all," said Sophie. "Thank you." The solicitor laid a business card on Uncle Bertram's desk and showed himself out.

She sat in silence for nearly an hour after he left, her mind as empty as the shelves around her. Finally she got up to retrieve the books that had spilled out of the box she had dropped on the floor. They were more precious now than ever, and she checked each one for damage before starting to place them in a neat row next to the fireplace. It flashed across her mind to line her Christmas books up on the shelf where Uncle Bertram had kept *his* Christmas books, but as soon as she thought it, she realized that would be sacrilege. If she lived in this flat for the rest of her life, if she bought enough books to fill every shelf, *that* shelf would remain empty. Nothing could replace those volumes.

**UNCLE BERTRAM HAD NEVER** kept a catalog of his library, but he knew the names and locations of every book—especially the Christmas books.

"How do you remember them all?" Sophie asked one day when she was ten years old.

"Do you remember where all your fingers are?" asked Uncle Bertram.

"Well yes, silly, but that's because they're a part of me, and I use them all the time."

"Well, it's just the same with me and my books," said her uncle with a smile.

"I don't think I could remember this many fingers," said Sophie, waving toward the bookshelves.

"But that's because you came upon them all at once. I met these books one at a time. Now this book," he said, drawing a thick leather-bound volume out of a plastic bag, "I shall remember because I bought it today with you. We took a walk in Hyde Park, and then we took the tube to Tottenham Court Road and walked down Charing Cross and you sat on the floor looking at illustrated books while I convinced Mr. Boxhill to sell me this for fifty pounds. And it was raining when we left, so I had him wrap it up in a plastic bag for me."

"And then we went for ice cream," said Sophie.

"Exactly. We went for ice cream. Now how could I forget all that?"

"But that's just one book," said Sophie. "You can't have gone for ice cream every time."

"No," said Uncle Bertram with a laugh, "not every time. Now before I put this book on the shelf, I need to make sure everyone knows it belongs to me."

"How do you do that?" asked Sophie.

"Watch," he told her. He took the book to his desk by the window and picked up his fountain pen. Opening to the first blank page, where the dealer's original price of seventy-five pounds was still visible in pencil, he wrote, in a neat script, "*Ex Libris* B.A.C."

"What does that mean?" said Sophie.

"*Ex Libris* means 'from the library of,'" said Uncle Bertram. "It's Latin. And B.A.C. are my initials—Bertram Arthur Collingwood."

"Do you write that in all your books?"

"Not all," said Uncle Bertram. "Come with me." He led her into his bedroom, to the shelf where his Christmas books from Bayfield House stood. "Look into one of those."

Sophie pulled a tall thick volume out of the bookcase. She barely managed to maneuver it onto the bed, where she opened the cover. In the center of the blank first page was the inscription "*Natalis Christi* B.A.C. 1984."

"*Natalis Christi* means 'Christmas,'" said Uncle Bertram, "and 1984 was the year I chose that book from Bayfield House."

And now, out there on the shelves of London booksellers, or perhaps already in the homes of collectors, were the books that Bertram had labeled "*Natalis Christi* B.A.C. 1985" and "*Natalis Christi* B.A.C. 1992" and dozens more. Sophie had followed her uncle's habits, and so the books that she now carefully shelved in the sitting room each bore their own "*Natalis Christi*" inscription—some in the scrawl of her childhood, others in the more decorative script she eventually taught herself. She had shelved about half the books when her mother rang.

"Oh, dear, I'm so sorry. I've just heard about the books."

"I can't believe Father didn't tell me," said Sophie, too tired to be really angry anymore. "I suppose it was his idea."

"You mustn't blame your father, Sophie," said her mother. "It broke his heart; it really did. He told the solicitor to find some other way, but in the end it was the only way to settle the debts of your uncle's estate, and you know what pressure your father is under about money."

"I know," said Sophie. She wanted to blame her father for selling the books, just as she wanted to blame someone for Uncle Bertram's death, but she knew her mother was right. She knew, also, that her father had lived his entire adult life under the edict placed on him by his own father on his deathbed—preserve Bayfield. At all costs preserve Bayfield. He had promised to do it, and, Sophie thought, that promise had ruined his life.

"Your father has promised to let you take a few books from the library next time you're here. Something to start filling the shelves. He feels awful; he really does."

"So do I," said Sophie. "I just wish he had told me instead of letting me find out like that."

"You know how your father is," said Mrs. Collingwood.

"Not so good with bad news," said Sophie grimly.

"Exactly," said her mother. "You get some rest, dear, and things will look brighter in the morning. We'll chat again soon. I just wanted to . . ."

"I know," said Sophie. "Thanks."

She sat quietly for a minute, then returned to the task of shelving her Christmas books. When she took the last book from the box, she saw Eric's note in the bottom, where she had left it. She sat again in her chair, slipped the paper out of its envelope, and read.

After she had read the letter twice over, she closed her eyes and did her best to do what she knew Victoria would tell her to do—mentally take stock of her situation. She had a flat in London, sixteen books, and a sweet letter from a man who had promised never to see her again. The question was: What should she do next?

## *Hampshire, 1796*

"**EVEN AS A CHILD,** I had an unquenchable thirst for novels," said Jane, ready now to confess to Mr. Mansfield what she had told no living soul. "It began in Oxford, when I discovered, on the bookshelves of Mrs. Crawley, to whom Cassandra and I had been dispatched for schooling, a copy of *The History of Sir Charles Grandison* by Samuel Richardson. I was seven years old, if you can believe it, yet I consumed it in a matter of days, and after that I never lost a chance to read any novel that came my way."

"I confess," said Mr. Mansfield, "that my history is not dissimilar, though you had a rather earlier start than I."

"At ten," said Jane, "I went with Cassandra to the Ladies Boarding School at the old abbey in Reading, and I suppose you could say that I was at the center of a somewhat illicit trade in novels that took place amongst several of the girls. You would have loved the abbey, Mr. Mansfield. It was an ancient building with winding staircases, dusty turret rooms, and a plethora of hiding places for those of us youngsters whose reading material was unlikely to meet with the approval of Mrs. Latournelle, who ran the school. And as long as I spent an hour or two with my tutor in his study each morning, no one seemed to take the slightest interest in where or how I filled my days. So they were filled with *Pamela* and *Joseph Andrews*, and the abbey was a paradise.

"There was another adult who lived at the abbey—a narrow, rangy young woman known to us only as Nurse. I suppose she earned that sobriquet because among her many duties was the care of children who had been taken ill. She moved slowly through the halls—tending fires, doing laundry, helping serve meals, and doing a thousand other tasks necessary to our daily life and comfort. She shut up the dormitory at night and woke those girls who slept through the bell in the morning. She saw to it that the younger girls were properly dressed. On nights when thunder crashed outside the abbey, Nurse would stay with us in the dormitory, and tell us stories. It didn't take me long to realize that her stories came from *Robinson Crusoe* or *Moll Flanders* or *Tristram Shandy*, and that therefore Nurse must be a fellow reader of novels. I never saw her with a book in her hands, but I knew. Nurse was a reader like me, and therefore I felt that Nurse, in some small way, belonged uniquely to me. I never would have said such a thing out loud, least of all to Nurse herself, but it comforted me that she and I were linked by the worlds of *Evelina*, and *Tom Jones*, and *Amelia*.

"There was only one rule at the abbey that was enforced with threats of punishment: Once the girls were secure in their beds for the night we were to remain there until the bell rang the following morning. Oh, Mr. Mansfield, I cannot tell you the fear placed upon me on those two occasions when we were forced to watch as Mrs. Latournelle took a birch twig to the back of the legs of a girl who had snuck out at night. The screams of those girls and the blood running down their legs gave me nightmares for weeks."

Jane shivered with the recollection and fell silent for a moment. Mr. Mansfield did not urge her on or offer her false comfort; he merely sat quietly and waited. Jane liked that—liked that he knew her well enough to know that the rest of the story would come, like all stories, in its own time.

"It was on a night in early December that I faced what seemed to me the greatest dilemma of my young life. In the long days of August I had been able to read in bed, but as I lay awake this night, darkness had fallen hours ago. A full moon had risen over the wall of the garden, but the shadow of the building opposite did not admit its beams into the dormitory. On most nights I would have returned my book to its hiding place in the mattress, but I was deeply engrossed in Miss Burney's *Cecilia*."

"And who can blame you?" said Mr. Mansfield. "It is one of my favorites."

"Well, try though I did, I could not fall asleep. While the other girls slept around me, my sister Cassandra breathing heavily in the next bed, I finally crept to the window and gazed longingly at a corner of the garden, brightly illuminated by moonlight. I could not imagine that, at this deep hour of the night, Mrs. Latournelle would be anywhere other than sound asleep in her room, so, tucking the third volume of *Cecilia* under my nightshirt, I eased open the window and caught hold of the ivy that grew on the abbey's stone wall. With little effort I was soon safe on the ground.

"Oh, the enchantment of midnight in that garden, Mr. Mansfield—no breeze stirred the trees, no nightingale sang; it was the perfect place to read. I made my way to that corner of moonlight, pulled out my book, and perched on a small stone ledge that protruded from the garden wall. To my delight, the moonlight was bright enough for me to read the words, in which I instantly lost myself. But hardly had I read a page when I heard the snap of a twig, a small enough sound in itself, but to me it seemed to rend the silence of the garden like a thunderclap.

"Only a few yards away, I saw the familiar figure of Nurse making her way swiftly toward a corner of the garden wall. I slipped into the nearby shadows, trembling with fear lest I be detected. I thought perhaps she was merely out for a late-night walk, suffering from the insomnia that a particularly exciting passage of a novel can produce. But as soon as I conceived this explanation, I was forced to discard it, for a cloaked figure suddenly appeared, climbing over the garden wall from the streets of town. I was just close enough to hear, as the two figures conversed, that the stranger was male, but their whispered voices were too low to understand. As you can well imagine, Mr. Mansfield, being only ten and having learned from a careful reading of literature that no other relationship is possible between two people who meet in a garden by moonlight than that of lovers, I immediately began filling in with my imagination the gaps that their unintelligible whispers left in the evidential record.

"Nurse had a secret lover, no doubt the son of a wealthy landowner whose father had forbidden him from consorting with a housemaid. That maid had been banished and had come to Reading, but her lover had followed, and on nights when the moon was full they met in the garden where he made love to her with poetry and pledges of undying fidelity. It was a doomed romance, but all the more beautiful for its hopelessness. So firmly had this story taken root in my imagination, that I continued to embellish it even after the man had slipped back over the wall and Nurse had returned inside. I was just on the verge of infecting the lover with some deadly disease or perhaps having him join the navy at the insistence of his father when the weighty hand of Mrs. Latournelle fell upon my shoulder.

"'And what can you be doing in the garden at this time of night, Jane?' she growled. I needn't tell you that my blood ran cold with fear.

"Back in Mrs. Latournelle's study I could think of only two things—protecting the backs of my legs and preventing Mrs. Latournelle from discovering my secret consumption of novels. The story my imagination had created was so real to me that I had no difficulty repeating it. I had heard a noise in the garden and feared for the safety of the children. When I went to fetch Nurse, I found her already headed for the garden, and so I followed to render assistance. There I saw the two lovers consorting.

"Secure in my bed a few minutes later, with the promise that I would suffer no punishment, I breathed a sigh of relief. I only hoped that Mrs. Latournelle would discover neither the book I had left in the garden nor the unlatched window of the dormitory.

"Having lost much of the night's sleep, I was shaken awake after the bell had rung by my dear Cassandra. The dormitory was abuzz with the news that Nurse had not made her usual morning appearance. I thought only that she, too, had overslept after the excitement of the previous night. Not until we assembled for breakfast and morning prayers did Mrs. Latournelle reveal the sobering truth. Nurse had been sent away. Only I knew the reason, for the schoolmistress did not dwell on details. 'Nurse's behavior has forced me to dismiss her,' was all she would say.

"That night, I sat on my bed surrounded by a frenzy of speculation. I had retrieved my book from the garden, where I had dropped it into a shrubbery, and had closed the latch on the window without detection. I was safe. But I did not participate in the conversation that consumed the dormitory. Even when Cassandra asked me, 'What do you think Nurse did?' I only rolled over and pulled my pillow close. Only I knew the depth of my betrayal of the only adult at the school with whom I felt true empathy. A week later Cassandra and I went home for Christmas and never returned to the abbey.

"And I didn't see Nurse again," said Jane, sinking back into her chair, "until yesterday, when she died in my arms."

## *London, Present Day*

**SOPHIE COULD NOT SLEEP.** She lay awake filled with grief, anger, and confusion. Finally she called Victoria. In the sprawling Bayfield House, the sisters had occupied adjacent rooms, and on many nights during their childhood one of them, unable to sleep, had crept into the other's room and slipped under the covers. Sometimes the visitor simply fell asleep; other times they talked until morning. Sophie missed that. She hated that Victoria lived so far away and that they could only talk on the phone, which could never convey the same warmth as Victoria's presence.

"Can't sleep?" said her sister.

"You don't know the half of it," said Sophie. She told Victoria everything—the injustice of Uncle Bertram's books being sold, her confusion about her feelings toward Eric, and how directionless she still felt.

"I wish I could be there with you," said Victoria.

"I just don't know what to do," said Sophie.

"About what?"

"About any of it."

"Well, let's take things one at a time," said Victoria. "First of all, why didn't you tell me about that letter from Eric? The last time I saw him you were escorting him out of the dining room after he was so rude to Father."

"He was so arrogant."

"He was hilarious," said Victoria, laughing at the memory.

"OK," admitted Sophie, "he was hilarious, but he wasn't polite. You know, he kissed me in the garden. Or maybe I kissed him. I'm not sure."

"Why, Sophie Collingwood, I'm shocked. Tell me more."

"There's nothing more to tell. He's left the country, I'll never see him again, I don't have his number, and I'm not even sure if I like him or not."

"So do the only thing you can do, outside of forgetting all about him," said Victoria. "Write him back."

"Write him a letter?"

"Sure," said Victoria. "He wrote you, didn't he? It's charming when you think about it."

"I suppose I could," said Sophie. "But what would I say?"

"You'll figure that part out," said Victoria. "Now, the next problem is Uncle Bertram's books. It's too late to stop them being sold, so what can you do?"

"I suppose I could make the rounds of the bookshops and see if I can find some of them," said Sophie.

"So you'll do that."

"I can't afford to buy very many of them."

"But you can afford to buy some, and some is more than you have now."

"True."

"That just leaves the problem of what to do with the rest of your life."

"Honestly, right now that one worries me less than the others," said Sophie.

"But there's something else, isn't there?"

"It's annoying how well you know me," said Sophie.

"Like a sister," said Victoria. "What is it?"

"Those stairs. I walked up them today and I just can't imagine someone in Uncle Bertram's state of health falling down them unless . . ."

"There goes your imagination again," said Victoria. "Don't you think if there were anything suspicious about Uncle Bertram's death the police would be investigating?"

"I suppose," said Sophie reluctantly.

"So forget about foul play and do what you can do. Get some sleep, write Eric, and try to get some of those books back."

"You're very much about making plans of action, aren't you?" said Sophie.

"I think I get that from Father," said Victoria.

"I love you, Tori."

"I love you, too, Soph. Call me tomorrow."

"OK," said Sophie. Five minutes later she was asleep.

**THE NEXT MORNING SOPHIE** put Victoria's plan into motion. After a quick walk to the corner shop for breakfast things, she sat down at Uncle Bertram's desk and pulled out a piece of his thick letter paper. Paper, pens, and envelopes, it seems, had not attracted the interest of the vultures that had descended on Maida Vale to pick clean her uncle's library. As she took up his favorite fountain pen, she shivered to think that he had probably held it himself just before he died. He always penned correspondence first thing in the morning. She had composed her letter in her head as she walked back from the shop, so it took her only a couple of minutes to write.

**Dear Eric,**

**Thank you for your note. This may surprise you, but it's been a comfort to me to know that someone outside the family seems to understand a small part of my loss. My mother and sister do their best, but I think it's possible only a fellow bibliophile can truly understand how I feel. Maybe that bibliophile is you. If so, you'll be shocked to hear that all my uncle's books have been sold, and I am now living in his flat in London surrounded by empty shelves. I hate empty shelves. So, you see, it is nice to have a friend, even one who is far away. Don't feel that you have to answer this. I only wanted you to know that your note was very much**

**appreciated. If you ever have news to share of a bookish nature, you can reach me at the address above.**

**Fondly,**

**Sophie**

Her first task accomplished, Sophie couldn't resist doing a little bit of detective work, despite Victoria's discouragement. But the only way she could think of to investigate Uncle Bertram's death was to ring Mr. Faussett's office and ask for the report of the inquest. They promised to send her a copy. With nothing more she could do on that front, she turned to book buying. Rebuilding her uncle's library might be the work of a lifetime, but, as Victoria had pointed out, that was no reason not to start today.

**"UNCLE BERTRAM," SOPHIE HAD** asked one December after she had selected her Christmas book, an edition of *Pride and Prejudice* illustrated by Hugh Thomson, "how is it that you always know in advance exactly which book you want for Christmas? I took all afternoon to pick mine out."

"My father had a different attitude about the library than your father does," said Bertram. "He let us use it whenever we wanted. I say 'us' but the truth is your father rarely set foot in there. He just never cared for books, and I think he resented the time I spent in the library when I should have been, so he thought, outside doing things with him. I suppose we both grew up rather alone. Anyway, over the years I got to know every book in that library. After our father died and your father and I made our little arrangement, I never had to search for the book I wanted."

"You always knew what it was going to be?"

"Not in January, perhaps. I pick books that interest me at the time, and my interests are always changing. But I've never walked into that library at Christmas without knowing exactly which book I would be taking home."

"Even the very first time?"

"Especially the very first time," said Uncle Bertram. "Remember that. Let me show you one of my favorites." Bertram led Sophie into his bedroom, where he pulled a tall thick book in a cracked leather binding off the end of his *Natalis Christi* shelf.

"It's not very pretty," said Sophie. At twelve, she still had a tendency to judge books by their covers.

"On the contrary," said her uncle. "I think it's one of the most beautiful books I own, but not because of how it looks; because of what it says." He opened the cover to reveal a title page printed in red and black.

"Latin again," said Sophie with an exasperated sigh. She had learned a little Latin from her uncle, but that ancient language, which appeared so often in his books, was still largely a mystery to her.

"When my father became ill, I was still at school, and one of the things I studied was physics. We learned all about Isaac Newton and his great work the *Principia Mathematica*. When I found out we had a copy at home, I was fascinated. I learned Latin so I could read this book. My father died during my first year at university and when my brother and I made our arrangement, I knew that I wanted this book."

"Is it a first edition?" asked Sophie, who had already learned a great deal about rare books at her uncle's side.

"No," said Bertram, "I'm afraid the library at Bayfield House isn't quite *that* grand. It's a third edition, the last to be printed in Newton's lifetime."

"So it must not be worth much."

"Sophie, you know I have never chosen books for what they are worth to others; only for what they are worth to me. I hope you do the same."

"Yes, Uncle," said Sophie, feeling scolded.

"I chose this book because in these pages mankind first understood why everything in the universe is attracted to everything else."

"Does it explain why you are attracted to books?" asked Sophie.

"No," said her uncle with a laugh. "I don't think anyone could explain that. But, Sophie."

"Yes, Uncle?"

"Even though this is a third edition, you must be quite careful with it. I did not choose it for its value, but it is nonetheless one of the most valuable books in my collection."

"But you would never sell it."

"Of course not," said Uncle Bertram. "But I must take especially good care of it so that people may enjoy its treasures for hundreds of years to come."

**SOPHIE NOW HELD THOSE** treasures in her hand in a bookshop in Bloomsbury. It was her third stop of the day. She had already found six books from her uncle's library at the other two shops—ordinary editions of ordinary books that cost her a total of fifty pounds. Now she sat on the floor in the upper room of Tompkins Antiquarian Books, one of the more posh bookshops in London, holding her uncle's beloved copy of Newton's *Principia*.

Uncle Bertram had not, as a rule, patronized bookshops with glass-fronted cases and deep-pile carpeting. Though his collection had been filled with valuable books, he had never been able to afford to pay much for any one volume. He had bought wisely, and often recognized a significance in a volume that a dealer had missed, but his haunts were more likely to be the poorly lit basement rooms of used bookstores than the antiseptic environment of the high-end antiquarian bookseller. He had only ventured into Tompkins Antiquarian Books on rare occasions when there was something in the window that caught his eye; he had never bought anything there. "Obscenely overpriced," he would always say. He would be furious to know that Gerard Tompkins now owned his *Principia*.

On the same page where her uncle had made his very first *Natalis Christi* inscription was penciled the current asking price: fifteen thousand pounds. Sophie could no more afford this book than she could bring back her uncle, and rage welled up within her as she held what she knew ought to be hers and yet could never be hers. The world owed her a library, she thought. And if the world couldn't afford that, then it owed her the shelf of her uncle's Christmas books. And if that wasn't forthcoming, then, at the very least, the world owed her *this* book.

Gerard Tompkins, who sat downstairs deeply engrossed in pricing a pile of new stock, had not recognized Sophie, though she had been introduced to him several times at the London Antiquarian Book Fair. She got the distinct impression he was one of those rare dealers who cared only for money—not for books or people. Sophie had never stolen anything before, but this wouldn't be stealing, exactly, she told herself. It would be restoring a book to its rightful owner. A single book in exchange for an entire library—if that was a criminal arrangement between her and the world, surely she was the victim, not the perpetrator. Her hand shook and she felt sweat break out on her forehead as she slipped the book into a carrier bag that held two other volumes. Surely Tompkins would search the bag. Surely the book had been tagged and would set off an alarm. Surely anyone who took even a casual glance at her would be able to tell that something was wrong, would stop her, and discover the *Principia*. But in the end it was easy. She just walked out the door. Tompkins didn't even look up from his work—no doubt having pegged her as a curious browser rather than a serious collector. Sophie was now a book thief, and she was surprised to find that, rather than guilty or afraid, she felt exhilarated.

## *Hampshire, 1796*

"So," **SAID MR. MANSFIELD** as Jane finished her story, "the woman who offered you forgiveness was the very Nurse whose dismissal was caused by your dishonesty."

"A fact I did not realize until she called me by name. Even then I questioned her as to how she knew me, and then she told me the rest of her tale. While at the abbey, she had received a letter from her brother that her mother was ill. He would arrive two days hence by the midnight coach and wished to meet her as soon as he arrived. She replied, suggesting that he come to the abbey garden, where she would wait for him. She kept the appointment and warmly embraced the brother she had not seen for over three years. His news was distressing. Their mother, it seemed, was near death. Yet pressing business meant that her brother must leave Reading before dawn and could not return for her for three days. Then, he promised, he would take her to their mother's bedside. But a young child lurking in the darkness accused her of consorting with a lover and she was sent away before the brother could return. She never saw either brother or mother again." Jane fell silent, as tears coursed down her youthful cheeks.

"A heavy burden for you indeed," said Mr. Mansfield. "But you say she offered forgiveness, as does God to all who repent their sins."

"She died before I could discover her name," said Jane. "Before I could even offer any apology for my dreadful sin."

"You were a child, Jane. And though your intellect and the quality of your writing belie it, you are little more than a child even now."

"I did not come to you to help me make excuses, Mr. Mansfield," said Jane, wiping away her tears and drawing herself upright. "Or even for comfort. I came because I thought you might help me to discover an act of atonement. Not that any act can give life back to Nurse or to her two children, but I must do something or I shall die as well."

"Only God can assign punishment, and only he, through Christ, can offer forgiveness. He offers it to Nurse and he offers it to you," said Mr. Mansfield. "But perhaps there is something you can do that would both honor Nurse and do good to both yourself and others."

"Anything you suggest that would accomplish all that, I would gladly do."

"Tell me, Miss Austen, what is your sin?"

"That I judge others," said Jane. "Not outwardly, but in my mind. I embellish the truth of their lives with the lies of my imagination. And I allow first impressions thus formed to guide too much my opinions."

Mr. Mansfield sat in silence for a moment, his fingertips pressed against each other. "I believe I begin to see a way in which you might make reasonable amends for your sins and at the same time do great service to one who, though he has known you but a short time, is blessed to call you more than a friend."

Jane blushed deeply at the compliment, recalling her epiphany about her own feelings toward Mr. Mansfield. To be so clearly loved at a time of such great personal shame touched her deeply.

"It is I who am blessed by your affection and concern, Mr. Mansfield, and I am open to whatever you might suggest."

"First, Miss Austen, I know enough of the way you work to tell you this. Before you embark on any act of contrition, you must clear your mind of *Elinor and Marianne*, and the only way to do this is to finish writing their story. I tell you this not merely as a passionate listener who cannot bear the thought that learning the fate of the Dashwoods should be delayed by what I have in mind, but as one who knows that whether you want them to or not the Dashwoods will inhabit your thoughts until you have recorded the end of their story."

"You do not speak falsely, Mr. Mansfield. For though my heart aches for the sin which I have committed against God and my dear Nurse, my mind is nonetheless racing with the happenings at Barton Cottage."

"It is no sin to begin your atonement with a mind emptied of such encumbrances," said Mr. Mansfield, "even if it means delaying that act by a few days or even weeks."

"Truly, I think you are closer to the mark when you say days, for though you may not believe it, if our conversation in the park before my departure to Kent is truthful evidence, the story of the Dashwoods is nearly at an end."

"Then you must bring the novel to its conclusion, read it to your family and to myself, and then with uncluttered minds and open hearts we can begin the project which I have in mind."

"You have not yet said what form this project takes, Mr. Mansfield, or in what way it could possibly provide me with atonement for the sins I have committed."

"Finish with the Dashwoods, Miss Austen. Then I shall tell you of my plan."

## *London, Present Day*

**ALMOST WITHOUT THINKING,** after she had stolen the *Principia*, Sophie had walked to Cecil Court, a short pedestrian lane between Charing Cross Road and St. Martin's Lane that was lined on both sides with bookshops. Cecil Court, with its rows of tall glass windows framed by green painted woodwork and filled with displays of every type of book imaginable, was the heart of London's secondhand book trade. The world seemed to move more slowly here, just around the corner from the traffic of the West End. Dealers perched behind counters reading catalogs and sipping tea while customers strolled from one shop to the next, their carrier bags growing ever heavier. Above the window in front of which she now stood, painted in gold letters, were the words AUGUSTUS BOXHILL, SECONDHAND AND ANTIQUARIAN BOOKS. Sophie thought a friendly bookseller might be just the thing to help her banish the thought of Gerard Tompkins pawing through her uncle's books. She pushed open the door and stepped inside as a tinkling bell announced her entrance.

Unlike Tompkins Antiquarian Books, Boxhill's smelled the way a bookstore ought to smell. It was a deeper and more intense version of the smell that had permeated Uncle Bertram's flat before the removal of his books, and Sophie stood for a moment breathing in the rich aroma of dust and knowledge.

"Miss Collingwood, what a delight to see you." Mr. Boxhill sat behind a tall counter at the back of the tiny shop, barely visible through the stacks of books arrayed in front of him.

"Good morning, Mr. Boxhill."

"Please, call me Gusty. It's a silly name, but it's what everyone calls me."

"Then you should call me Sophie."

"I must say, Sophie, I was appalled by what happened to your uncle's library. Vultures, they were, swooping in like that without anyone even calling you. I was out of town, I'm afraid, or I should have let you know and tried to save a few things for you. I know how much your uncle meant to you."

"That's very kind of you, Mr. . . . I mean, Gusty. It was a shock to find his books gone. I'm living in the flat now, you know."

"Oh, dear, I didn't. Well, we must get you some books. I can't bear the thought of those empty shelves. Your uncle had me to tea a few times and we had some delightful hours perusing his library."

Sophie stood for a moment, not sure what to say. Her search for books from Uncle Bertram's library could not be furthered here at Boxhill's, and she was on the verge of saying good-bye and moving on, but something about the store called out to her. It wasn't just the smell and the clutter—both of which transported her to days spent with Uncle Bertram. Perhaps it was the way the sunlight caught the dust motes in the air and the careful lettering on boxes of old postcards and playbills stacked in front of the counter. Or the way the books on the highest shelves—out of reach of all but the tallest customers—were perfectly aligned, while those at eye level showed every sign of having been pulled off the shelves and examined again and again. Or the chipped paint on the molding and the worn floorboards under her feet. Above all, it was a feeling that all of this pressed into her bones, that while there might be valuable and collectible books hiding on the shelves of Boxhill's, the books in this store were not meant for displaying behind locked glass doors—they were meant to be read. Standing in Boxhill's Sophie felt, for the first time since her uncle's death, at home. And as soon as she realized this, she knew what to say to Gusty.

"At Bayfield you said that if there was ever anything you could do for me . . ."

"Name it," said Gusty matter-of-factly.

"I need a job," said Sophie.

"You saw the sign in the window?" he said.

"No . . . I just thought . . ."

"Your timing is impeccable. My shop assistant left last week and I'm desperate for help. When would you be able to start?"

"I could start . . . now," said Sophie.

"Well, you have been coming to the shop for most of your life. You're certainly qualified. Overqualified, even. Now we'll have to sort out details like salary and hours, but in the meantime I suppose there's nothing for it but to say welcome to Boxhill's."

"You mean I'm hired?"

"Who else am I going to find who knows half as much about books as you do?"

"That's . . . well, that's just marvelous," said Sophie. "I'd very much like to give you a hug, if you weren't behind that counter."

"Well, suppose I come out from the counter and we pop round the corner for a spot of lunch and then I'll show you the ropes?"

**SITTING AT A TABLE** by the window of the Salisbury, on St. Martin's Lane, Sophie settled into a comfortable conversation with Gusty about books, bookselling, and her Uncle Bertram.

"He always spoke so fondly of you," said Gusty. "I think since he didn't have any children of his own, he really thought of you as a daughter."

"Can I ask you something, Gusty?" said Sophie.

"Why, certainly."

"Do you think there is anyone who would have wanted to hurt my uncle?"

"I thought he died . . . that is, I thought it was an accident."

"It was," said Sophie, "officially. But to me it just doesn't add up."

"Well, I certainly never heard anyone speak a harsh word against your uncle," said Gusty. "You know as well as I do how much he was loved in the book community."

"True."

"Bertram always said you had an active imagination," said Gusty. "Are you sure you haven't just read too many Sherlock Holmes stories?"

"Maybe so," said Sophie, forcing a smile. She had read all of them.

"I wouldn't give it another thought. Besides," said Gusty, pushing his chair back and standing, "we've got work to do."

By midafternoon Gusty had shown Sophie most of the inner workings of the shop. At four o'clock he left her in charge while he went off to an auction.

She could hardly believe her good fortune to be left alone in such a place. There was no doubt that working at Boxhill's could ease the pain of having lost Uncle Bertram's library. Gusty, she reflected, was the closest thing to Uncle Bertram she could hope to find. The two men had to be about the same age, and they shared not just a love of books, but a great joy in sharing that love with others. Gusty seemed equally happy with a customer who stopped by to chat about books for a half hour and bought nothing as with the man who walked out with an armload of purchases. More happy, Sophie thought. She wanted to take care of him and was soon discovering scores of things she could do to improve the shop, to get on with the business of selling books, so that Gusty could enjoy his full-time occupation of loving them.

**A WEEK LATER,** Sophie was just turning the handle of the flat's front door when the morning post came cascading through the letter box. It looked like the usual assortment of bookseller catalogs addressed to her uncle. She would look through them this evening, she thought, and was just setting the post on the table by the door when a postcard of the Eiffel Tower fluttered to the floor. She picked it up and read:

> **Dear Sophie,**
>
> **The Bibliothèque Nationale de France has some very nice old books on display, but when you look at them closely they're written in some sort of gibberish. It's like they use a**

**whole different language or something. Missing Jane Austen; I think she's better for me than Proust, don't you?**

**Eric**

Sophie chuckled at Eric's joke. She was resigned, she told herself, to the fact that she had no romantic future with him, but perhaps they would become transoceanic correspondents. She liked that idea. After all, Jane Austen had had correspondents. Writing letters to Eric and reading what he had written to her seemed deliciously civilized. She smiled, slipped the postcard into her handbag, and headed off to work.

She arrived at Boxhill's just before opening time and found a note from Gusty on the door: *Off to Surrey to see about buying some books at an estate sale. Close up whenever you need to go. Sorry for the short notice. Gusty.* She was delighted to again be ruling this tiny kingdom of books.

Sophie wasn't in the habit of undressing men with her eyes, but when the first customer strode through the door, she felt she owed it to herself to at least admire his muscular shoulders. He was tall and broad and wearing a tight designer T-shirt that concealed little of his toned physique. A pair of sunglasses was propped on his perfectly disheveled shock of blond hair. He was tanned, and smiling broadly, and wearing expensive leather shoes with his khakis, and Sophie thought he must be Italian or Spanish or at least Southern Californian until he greeted her in an accent right out of Mayfair.

"Good morning. Miss Collingwood, I presume."

"You presume correctly," said Sophie. "But how do you know my name?"

"It seems everyone in Cecil Court knows your name," said the man. "Gusty's been bragging about his new employee up and down the street. I'm Winston. Winston Godfrey. A pleasure to meet you." He held out his hand and Sophie timidly took it. It was warm and dry and strong and she found herself imagining how it would feel on the small of her back.

"I understand you're the person to talk to about eighteenth-century imprints."

"I can't imagine what gave you that idea," said Sophie. "I've only been working here a week."

"You may have been working for Gusty for a week, but from what every other bookseller on Cecil Court says, you've more or less grown up here."

"That's true," she said, "but I don't have a particular expertise in the eighteenth century. If anything I'm more of a Victorian."

"Look, Miss Collingwood."

"You can call me Sophie."

"Sophie. The fact is I'm looking for a rather ordinary book, and I could explain all about what I need to any of a number of tweed-wearing middle-aged men up and down the lane, or I can come and have a nice chat with the beautiful young lady at number seven. Put yourself in my shoes. Which would you do?"

Sophie felt herself blushing. She'd never imagined bookselling as a way to meet men. Most of the male customers she had seen in bookshops over the years had been much as Winston had described the proprietors—tweedy and middle-aged. Winston didn't look much older than she was.

"Well, Mr. Godfrey—"

"Winston."

"Yes, Winston. I'd be happy to help you in any way that I can." She was trying very hard to concentrate on books, but she could think of any number of ways she would like to help Winston Godfrey—none of them appropriate within the confines of the shop.

"I'm looking for this book." He pulled a slip of paper out of his shirt pocket and slid it across the counter. Sophie unfolded it and read:

"'*A Little Book of Allegorical Stories* by Rev. Richard Mansfield. Published in Leeds, 1796.' Don't you just want to wait for the film to come out?"

"Surely it's not the strangest thing a customer has asked for," said Winston.

"Like I said, I've only been here a week, so actually it is."

"Well, it gets worse. I need the second edition."

"The second edition?" said Sophie.

"That's right."

"You're a collector of fine second editions?" said Sophie, now meeting his blue eyes boldly with her own.

"I have the first already," said Winston, returning her gaze.

"It must have been a fascinating read," she said, trying to decide if this conversation had a subtext, or if this Adonis really just wanted a boring book by an eighteenth-century clergyman.

"So do you think you can help me?" asked Winston.

"Well, second editions of obscure books don't turn up in catalogs very often, but I can ask around. Why this book in particular?"

"Do you ask all your customers such personal questions?"

"I haven't really established any habits with regard to customers."

"Well, I have a personal question for you, Sophie Collingwood. What time do you get off work?"

"And why do you ask that question?"

"Sophie," he said, leaning against the counter and once again staring into her eyes. "I think you know and I know that the chances of a young man meeting a beautiful woman in a rare book shop are minuscule. It must be fate. So the least we can do is go out for a drink."

"Are you asking me out?" said Sophie, willing calm into her voice.

"That's exactly what I'm doing," said Winston.

"In that case, I'll be closing the shop at five."

"The sign on the door says six."

"Do you really want to wait an extra hour?" said Sophie, shocked at her own audacity.

"I'll see you at four thirty," said Winston.

**SOPHIE FOUND A DUSTY FILE BOX** under the counter labeled "Customer Wants" and filled out a blank card with the title and author of the book Winston Godfrey was looking for, along with his contact information. It was an odd request, to be sure, but she knew from hundreds of hours spent in bookshops that it was not unusual for a customer to come in looking for an old and obscure book. Not everyone had both the bank account and the inclination to collect first editions of Jane

Austen or Charles Dickens. Perhaps some ancestor of Winston's had written *A Little Book of Allegorical Stories*, or perhaps it contained a tale that Winston remembered from his childhood, or maybe he just collected allegories written by eighteenth-century clerics.

Sophie spent the next few hours working the Customer Wants file. Obviously no one had looked at it for some time—by early afternoon she had found several items in the shop that matched cards in the file and had reached three very happy collectors by phone with the news that she had found the books they were looking for. The delight in their voices was a pleasure to hear, and she hoped she could provide a similar delight for Winston by finding his book of allegories. Most wants, she knew, fell into one of two categories: those that could be found fairly quickly with a little digging, and those that would probably never show up. If *A Little Book of Allegorical Stories* was in the former, perhaps she could surprise Winston over drinks with good news.

After two hours of checking online, flipping through catalogs, and phoning most of her uncle's favorite dealers, she could find no one who had listed any books by Richard Mansfield for sale, nor, for that matter, anyone who had even heard of either Mansfield or his book of allegories. Even the British Library catalog listed only the first edition of the book. She had just concluded that she would have to tell Winston that the chances of his book turning up anytime soon were slim to none, when a customer came through the door. Sophie spent the next hour in a conversation with a middle-aged man about the bibliographical intricacies of various books of nineteenth-century poetry. It was nearly five when the gentleman left, with a carrier bag full of books, a smile on his face, and a considerably lightened wallet. Winston had been loitering outside the shop, pretending to browse through the bargain books, since exactly four thirty. As soon as the poetry lover was out the door, Winston came in.

"If you're not planning to take anything home, you really shouldn't loaf around scaring off the customers," Sophie teased.

"Actually, I do see something I'd like to take home," said Winston, staring right at Sophie.

"Oh, really?"

"Yes," he said, pulling a book off a shelf without even looking. "This copy of . . . *Lectures and Essays* by the Earl of Iddesleigh."

"Really," said Sophie. "That's what you want to take home with you?"

"Oh, yes, I'm a big fan of the Earl of Iddesleigh."

"I'm sure you are, but I'd stick to the lectures if I were you. They're much better than the essays." Winston laughed and put the book back on its shelf. "Come on," said Sophie. "Help me bring in the bargain books." For the next few minutes they worked together in silence, toting the books from the outside display back into the shop. Once everything was inside, Sophie retrieved her handbag, turned out the lights, and locked up.

"Well," she said as they both stood in the middle of Cecil Court, "I was expecting a nice young man to come take me out for drinks."

"Guess you'll just have to settle for me," said Winston, holding out his arm. Sophie took hold of it, and they set off toward Covent Garden.

## *Hampshire, 1796*

**JANE'S WIDOWED BROTHER,** James, had recently been offered by their father the curacy of Deane, and so he now resided in that village just a mile and a half distant from the family home. His daughter, Anna, a beautiful and clever child of four and a half, had come to stay at the rectory in Steventon under the care of her two maiden aunts. Cassandra especially enjoyed indulging the child, and to Jane's stories Anna would listen in raptures. In early October, Jane had, as Mr. Mansfield suggested, completed her draft of *Elinor and Marianne* and read the ending to various groups at the rectory, including, one gloomy afternoon, Anna and Cassandra. Her niece's delight in the story brought a lightness to her heart that she had not felt since attending the death of Nurse, and she began to feel that, especially now that the completion of her novel would allow her to turn her undivided attention to whatever project Mr. Mansfield proposed, she might regain that joy in life she had lost when confronted with her childhood sin.

Such thoughts, as any, were short-lived with little Anna in the house, for barely had Jane laid down the manuscript of *Elinor and Marianne* than Anna was expressing her eagerness for another tale. When Jane informed her little niece that her store of fiction was exhausted, Anna disappeared and returned a few minutes later, holding out a slim clothbound volume.

"If you have no more stories, Aunt Jane," said the little girl, "would you please read one of these?"

"What book have you here, Anna?" said Jane.

"I don't know," said Anna.

Jane smiled at the expectant face of her niece. "Where did you get this book?" she asked gently.

"From Grandpapa," said Anna.

"He gave it to you?"

Anna looked down at the floor and did not answer.

"Answer me honestly, now, Anna. I will not scold. Where did you get this book?"

"From his study. It was on his desk."

Jane laughed and swept the child up in her arms. "I doubt that any book you find on Grandpapa's desk will make for very good reading," she said. "Let me see it. It's most likely theology or science, which I am afraid you would find quite dull."

"But it says 'stories' on it," said Anna. Cassandra had been teaching the child to read and she was a remarkably quick study.

"Does it, now?" said Jane. She set Anna down and took the book from her. The words "Allegorical Stories" were embossed on the cover.

"There's another word, too," said Anna. "But it's a rather long one."

"Yes it is," said Jane, "and a rather difficult one as well." She opened the volume to the title page and her eyes widened. In another moment she burst into a fit of laughter.

"What is it, Aunt?" said Anna, smiling with delight at Jane's amusement. "Why do you laugh so?"

Jane quickly composed herself and again picked up the child. "Come, Anna, I shall read you one of these stories and we shall discover if they are clever and exciting or dull and tedious."

"I hope for exciting!" cried Anna.

"So do I," said Jane. "So do I."

**THE FOLLOWING DAY,** Jane wore her usual smile when Mr. Mansfield opened the door to the gatehouse, eager, he said, to hear the conclusion of *Elinor and Marianne,* which he had been promised. She breezed by him into the sitting room without offering a greeting or receiving an invitation to enter. When her host followed her she turned on him and spoke in a tone of measured censure.

"Mr. Mansfield. I am shocked, sir, shocked to discover after all these weeks of intimacy that you have been withholding from me the one secret from your past which you well know would most influence my opinion of you."

"Miss Austen, I cannot think what you mean by this. Surely I have kept no great secrets from you."

"You, sir, are not what you seem."

"I assure you, Miss Austen, I am no more or less than an aging clergyman with a passion for literature."

"No less, that is certain, but you are more."

"Of what do you accuse me, Miss Austen?"

"Quite simply of a crime which I only wish I had known about when first we met. You, sir, are an author." Jane threw down on the table the volume Anna had brought to her the previous afternoon, and though Mr. Mansfield blushed deeply, he also smiled with relief.

"It is, I am afraid, not worthy of your notice."

"You do yourself wrong, Mr. Mansfield," said Jane. "I assure you that Anna, at least, thoroughly enjoyed it. It is not the quality of your writing but the content of the inscription that offends me." She picked up the book, opened the front cover, and read, " 'To Rev. George Austen from the Author.' Where, sir, is the copy inscribed to your student Miss Jane Austen?"

Mr. Mansfield laughed and took the volume from Jane. "I only gave a copy to your father because, as a fellow clergyman, I thought he might find it useful. It is certainly not literature. It is only a collection of allegorical stories, intended to teach moral lessons, and perhaps a helpful aid for preaching. However, when next I return to Croft, I will bring you a copy."

"I must say," said Jane, taking the book back from Mr. Mansfield, "from one who criticizes the title of my novel *Elinor and Marianne* as being too plain, I am a bit disappointed in the title of your little book of allegorical stories." She held up the title page to his face. It read: *A Little Book of Allegorical Stories*.

Mr. Mansfield laughed. "Perhaps I can do better in the second edition," he said. "But tell me, did your father show you my book? For I expressly asked him not to do so."

"You needn't think ill of him," said Jane. "It was the curiosity of my little niece that brought your efforts to my attention. Having heard the ending of *Elinor and Marianne,* she entered his study in search of stories and discovered this lying on his desk."

"And you read it?"

"Only the first story, and that only because Anna insisted. I thought it best, since I have read my work to you, to allow you to read yours to me."

"Tomorrow, perhaps, after you have read me the end of your novel."

"Indeed not, Mr. Mansfield. You must suffer some punishment for hiding your light under a bushel. Today you shall read me your allegories and tomorrow I shall conclude the adventures of the Dashwood sisters."

"Very well," said Mr. Mansfield, and he settled himself in a chair by the fire, opened the book, and began to read.

## *London, Present Day*

"So, ANY LUCK FINDING my book?" said Winston as they settled into a table in the back of the Lamb and Flag. Sophie loved dark-paneled pubs—they felt almost like libraries—and was happy to discover this cozy example just a short walk from her new job.

"Did you really expect me to find it on the first day?"

"Not really," said Winston. "But I thought maybe you'd try to impress me."

"The fact is," said Sophie, blushing, "I did try to impress you, but I can't find any sign of Mr. Mansfield or his little book of allegories anywhere. Even the British Library only has a first edition."

"But you'll keep looking," said Winston.

"It's in the 'want' file," said Sophie, "so there's always a chance. But I wouldn't get your hopes up."

"You seem awfully young to know so much about the antiquarian book world," said Winston.

"I'm not that young," she said—hoping, at least, that she was not too young for him to consider . . . well, she wasn't quite sure what just yet; she just hoped she wasn't too young.

"Let me guess," said Winston. "Fresh out of Cambridge, you read history and worked in the library and so you thought you'd work in a bookshop for a while."

"It's nothing like that," said Sophie. "I'm fresh out of Oxford; I read English literature and worked in the library."

"Can't believe I was so far off the mark."

"But that's not why I came to Boxhill's," said Sophie. "That was because of my uncle."

"Boxhill is your uncle?"

"No, my uncle was named Bertram Collingwood," she said, and by the time she had told Winston the whole story of how Bertram had helped her fall in love with books, she had finished her pint and it was time for Winston to order another round.

"And his books are just gone?" asked Winston, when he had settled back in his chair.

"Gone," said Sophie. "I've found a few of them, but even if I could find them all, I certainly couldn't afford to buy them back." She did not mention her acquisition of the *Principia*.

"So you'll build your own library. What do you collect?"

Uncle Bertram had asked her the same question earlier that summer when they were sitting together in Hyde Park reading. She was deep into *Jude the Obscure*—one of the few Hardy novels she had not yet read, and he was reading a new translation of Pindar's *Odes*, making pencil notes in the margin whenever he disagreed with the translator. Their peace had been disturbed by a sudden outburst from the ducks on the Serpentine, and Bertram had laid down his book and turned to Sophie.

"What sort of books would you like to collect?"

"You always told me to buy whatever appeals to me at the time," said Sophie. "That's what I've always done. That's how you did it, isn't it?"

"True, but as much as I love my library, sometimes I wish I had started with a little more focus. What do you like to read?"

"You know that," said Sophie. "I like stories. I like characters and plots and intrigue and romance and not knowing what's going to happen next. I seem to be less interested in nonfiction these days. If I want that, I can just go outside. And I like corsets and Empire waistlines and poorhouses and debtors' prisons and the countryside. I could never get excited about novels written after the Great War. Except mysteries, of course."

"So you'll collect novels," said Uncle Bertram. "Victorian novels. Or perhaps I should say nineteenth-century, so you don't miss out on Jane Austen."

"I suppose I already do collect novels," said Sophie, thinking of her room in Oxford. "If you read English literature, you can't really help it."

"But be honest, my dear," said Uncle Bertram. "Are your books anything like the books of any other student of English literature?"

"No," said Sophie, who never settled for the cheap paperback editions at Blackwell's. Whether it was Dickens, or Austen, or Hardy, she always managed to find a secondhand hardcover copy—the older the better, as far as she was concerned. One girl in her tutorial had complained of the moldy smell wafting off Sophie's copy of *Little Dorrit*, and Sophie had retorted, "This is the first book edition. Without the mold it would have cost me twice as much."

"You've always been a collector," said Uncle Bertram. "But now, beware, Mr. Dickens and Mr. Trollope and Miss Brontë and especially Miss Austen, for Sophie Collingwood is on your trail and she will not rest until she has caught you." And Sophie had laughed and Uncle Bertram had joined her, and the ducks had flown up off the water, the sound had startled them so.

It was the last day she had spent with her uncle.

**"I COLLECT NOVELS,"** said Sophie to Winston. "Nineteenth-century, mostly, but some later. Mysteries are my guilty pleasure. I always rather fancied myself a sleuth. But mostly English lit. You know, 'The person, be it gentleman or lady, who has not pleasure in a good novel, must be intolerably stupid.' "

"Oh, I don't know about that," said Winston. "I prefer nonfiction myself, and I don't think I'm *intolerably* stupid."

"It's a quote," said Sophie. "It's from *Northanger Abbey*. You know—Jane Austen."

"Never read her," said Winston.

"You've never read Jane Austen?"

"We didn't do her at school. We did Dickens, though."

"I'd love to own a Dickens novel in the original monthly parts," said Sophie, trying to ignore the fact he had never read any Jane Austen. "Can you imagine what that must have been like, to be reading *David Copperfield* and to have to wait a month for the next installment?"

Winston nodded, taking a sip of beer. "Hey, I just found out this was Charles Dickens's favorite pub," he said. "There's a sign behind the bar."

Sophie almost choked on her beer as she suddenly remembered accusing Eric of whisking women off to Charles Dickens's favorite pub. She thought for a split second that Winston was using the same ploy—but something about his nonchalance told her that not only had he not known this was Dickens's favorite pub; he didn't care.

"Dickens's parts are a bit out of my price range," said Sophie, regaining her composure, "but if I ever had a set I would read them. I never could understand collectors who lock up their books in glass cases and don't read them."

"Me neither," said Winston.

"But listen to me, going on and on about my uncle and his books and my books and books I don't even own yet and will probably never own. What about you? What do you collect? Why do you collect?"

"Maybe that's a question for the second date."

"So is this the first date, or is this just drinks?"

"I was hoping this was the first date. I would ask you to dinner, but my father is up from the country house and he expects me to take him out."

"Oh, your father is up from the country house, is he?" said Sophie, affecting a posh accent.

"Sorry, that sounded pompous. My father's a solicitor in Gloucestershire, but he comes to London so often for business that he finally bought a little flat in St. John's Wood. So now, I'm living in the flat and when Father's in town I get to sleep on the sofa and take him out to dinner."

"And when Father's not in town?"

"I suppose it becomes my bachelor pad, though so far that's mostly meant me home alone watching the footy." Sophie doubted this very much. It couldn't possibly be that difficult for a drop-dead gorgeous, charming, intelligent man like Winston to find women willing to visit his flat.

"And since Father's in town I have to take myself home?" she said.

"I'm sorry about that," said Winston. "I promise the next time we'll have a proper date. Dinner and everything." Sophie was afraid to ask what "everything" included.

"And when do you propose we have this proper second date?" she said.

"Well, today is Tuesday and if I call you tomorrow it will look like I'm overeager and desperate, so how about Thursday?"

"I'll have to check my engagement calendar," said Sophie teasingly. "And if it's a proper date, I'll need to change out of work clothes and fix my hair and put on proper nighttime makeup."

"I think you look lovely," said Winston, and Sophie blushed for the second time that day. She did not mind a bit.

She reached into her handbag for a pen and wrote Uncle Bertram's address on a napkin. She slid it across the table to Winston. "Pick me up at seven?"

"I thought you had to check your engagement calendar."

"I'm sure I can squeeze you in," she said. And she was just getting up and hoping this was the perfect exit line when Winston leaned over and picked something up off of the floor.

"You dropped something," he said, holding up the postcard of the Eiffel Tower. Sophie snatched it out of his hand before he could look at it.

"A postcard from my sister," she said quickly. "See you on Thursday." It wasn't quite the flirtatious exit she had hoped for, but she had at least avoided any awkward questions about Eric Hall.

## *Hampshire, 1796*

**HAVING READ FOUR** of his allegorical stories, Mr. Mansfield expressed a wish to be allowed to hear the ending of *Elinor and Marianne.* Jane would not allow it.

"Had you not kept your book a secret from me," said Jane, "I would consider four stories an adequate compensation for the final four chapters of the adventures of the misses Dashwood, but because you hid your talents from the very friend who is best able to appreciate them, you shall not earn your reward until the book is finished."

"I count myself lucky that it is but a slim volume," said Mr. Mansfield. "Were you to strike a similar bargain with the author of, say, *Robinson Crusoe,* that would be inhumane. But surely you understand, Miss Austen, it is because you are best able of all my acquaintances to judge my work that I have been hesitant to share it with you."

"Yet I allow you to judge my work every day, and I profit from the judgment. Might you not wish to do the same?"

"It is an infuriating thing, Miss Austen," said Mr. Mansfield with a smile, "to be taught wisdom by one a quarter of one's age."

"You shall find a way to bear it, Mr. Mansfield. Now please continue."

Mr. Mansfield settled back in his chair and read on.

## GREGORY THE HERMIT

### A MORAL TALE

*Happiness is the wish of every individual. It is pursued by the wise and the foolish, the wealthy and the indigent; and, though the attempt is generally unsuccessful, it is continued with avidity till death closes the scene, and puts a period at once to our hopes and our labors. We should indeed be oftener successful did we search for Happiness where she may be found, in a mediocrity of the gifts of fortune, and in the smiling valley of Content. But, dazzled with the fascinating glare of riches, and the ostentatious parade of power, we seek her in places where she was ever a stranger, and at last, when it is too late to correct our error, we are convinced that we have been deluded by a phantom, and pursued a fleeting insubstantial shadow.*

The story went on to tell of the simple-living Gregory and the wealthy and ostentatious Alphonso. Gregory counseled Alphonso away from his worldly ways, saying, "The calm blessings of uninterrupted health, and the placid comforts of a mind at ease are not to be bartered for the noisy joys of riot and excess." But Alphonso did not listen, and only accepted that "the paths of virtue only are the paths of peace" after his palace was destroyed by a volcanic eruption.

"Do you truly believe," said Jane, "that the primary motivation of humankind is, as I believe the Americans call it, the pursuit of happiness?"

"I do," said Mr. Mansfield, "though that in itself is not an evil thing. It is only when we attach happiness to those things which are worldly and unimportant that our lives become corrupted."

"And what of me?" said Jane. "Am I wrong to pursue the happiness I believe would come to me with the publication of my writing?"

"To answer that question, one must first know why you yearn for publication. Do you envision riches and the opportunity for the 'noisy joys of riot and excess'?"

"You jest with me, Mr. Mansfield, for you know that I do not. You know that, although I enjoy the occasional ball, I am happiest when I am here with you, sharing our thoughts, reading to one another, living simply in the world of the mind. It is not riches that I seek but rather the possibility that my published words might allow me to have a similar communion of thought with those unseen."

"Then I think we can safely say that you have not fallen into the trap that claimed Alphonso. By your labors at the writing table, Miss Austen, you do anything but, as Gregory says, 'sacrifice your prospect of distant happiness to the delusive pleasure of an hour.' I should say you do quite the opposite."

"It comforts me to hear you say that, Mr. Mansfield."

"I am pleased to give you comfort," said Mr. Mansfield. "However, while I am happy that my stories stimulate self-reflection, as was their intent, if we are to discuss the place of each in our own lives, it may be weeks before I discover the fate of the dear Dashwoods."

"You are right, Mr. Mansfield. In my self-concern I am too cruel. Pray continue."

And for the next hour, he read, until four more of his stories were finished.

"I wonder," said Mr. Mansfield, laying the book aside, "if by listening to my meager attempts as a writer you have perhaps come to understand how accomplished you are at that same endeavor?"

"I do not admit to a difference in quality between your work and my own," said Jane, "only in style and perhaps intent."

"Nonetheless, were my intent wedded to your abilities, it might produce something rather new," said Mr. Mansfield.

"You'd best continue reading, Mr. Mansfield," said Jane, "or we shall never return to *Elinor and Marianne.*"

*London, Present Day*

**THE NEXT MORNING** Sophie rang her sister, still feeling delightfully light-headed from her time with Winston.

"I met someone," she said.

"Marry, kill, or shag?" said Victoria.

"Shag," said Sophie. "Definitely shag."

"So you've forgotten all about your American?"

"I wouldn't say that," said Sophie. "But Winston has the distinct advantage of being located in this country."

"Winston? Sounds yummy," said her sister. "Here I thought I was the woman of action in this family, and in a week you've gotten a job, a stack of Uncle Bertram's books, and a boyfriend."

"He isn't my boyfriend."

"Well, I'm glad you had a good day."

"It was a good day," said Sophie, "but that doesn't mean I've forgotten about Uncle Bertram."

"I know. Oh, God, my boss is coming into the office. I have to go. Love you, Soph," said Victoria, and she was gone.

**SOPHIE SPENT THE MORNING** in the basement of the shop, sorting through new acquisitions. The most promising volumes she set aside for cataloguing, ordinary but desirable stock she brought up to Gusty to be priced and shelved in the shop; the dregs she relegated to the bargain display outside. When she had carried the third armload of bargain books outside and stood in the doorway brushing the dust from her clothes, Gusty commented, "You look happy."

"I am happy," said Sophie.

"Oh, by the way, I had an old customer in here this morning. He's on the trail of something and since you seem so talented at mining the want file, I'll let you take care of him." He handed Sophie a card on which was written the name George Smedley and a phone number. Below that were the words "Richard Mansfield. *A Little Book of Allegorical Stories*. 2nd edition. 1796."

"Is this some sort of joke?" said Sophie with a laugh.

"Not at all," said Gusty. "I know it's an odd request, but bibliophiles are an odd bunch."

"I don't suppose this Smedley is tall and blond and broad-shouldered and good-looking?"

"No," said Gusty. "I'd say he was my height. Hair is dark and curly and he's certainly built solidly but he's hardly classically handsome. Has a face like . . . well, like a bull terrier. Looks rather frightening, but he's harmless. Used to come in here quite often a year or two back but I haven't seen him in a while."

Sophie was on the verge of telling Gusty that another customer had come in yesterday looking for the same book, when it suddenly occurred to her that here, at last, was a real mystery to solve.

"I'll see what I can do for Mr. Smedley," she said.

Once back in the basement, Sophie picked up the shop phone and dialed the number on the card Gusty had given her. She heard a click on the line, but no answer.

"Hello?" she said. "Is this Mr. George Smedley?"

"It is," said a brusque voice. Sophie guessed the accent was from somewhere up north. To her ear he sounded more like an aggravated plumber than a book collector.

"I'm calling from Boxhill's Bookshop."

"Why, what rapid service," said the voice, a bit more cheerfully. "I knew old Gusty would pass my request on to his new shop assistant. Have you found my little book of allegories already?"

"No, sir. I just thought I would give you a call to see if I could get a little more information."

"And what other information could you possibly need," said the voice, turning cold again. "You have the title and the author. You know, I presume, that I require the second edition of 1796. You clearly have my name and number. I suggest you get to work."

"Well, I just wondered—"

"Young lady, I want you to understand that I am willing to pay a lot of money for this book. A lot of money. More than others will be willing to pay. Do you understand?"

"I believe so," said Sophie, though all she really understood was that this phone call was getting stranger by the second.

"And I can offer you certain, shall we say, *protections* that others will not."

"Protections?" she said, for the first time feeling genuinely frightened by this strange man.

"Let us say simply that if you find this book for me there will be rewards; if you find it for someone else . . ."

"Are you threatening me, Mr. Smedley?" said Sophie, doing her best to sound confident.

"That's exactly what I'm doing," said the voice. "And another thing. You are to keep this conversation—you are to keep *all* our conversations—confidential, even from your employer. It would be a shame to drag poor Augustus into all this."

Sophie shivered at the implications of this statement, and the line was silent for a moment. "Now," said Smedley, "are you looking for my book?"

"Actively," said Sophie, trying to keep her voice from trembling. "I've done some research and I think I may have one or two leads." This was stretching the truth considerably.

"You'd better not be lying."

Sophie swallowed hard and decided not to be intimidated. If she was going to get to the bottom of this, she thought, she needed to find out everything she could about Smedley. She pretended to ignore his comment and put on her cheeriest voice.

"Do you live in London?" The line was silent. "I only ask because I thought perhaps we might get together sometime, to discuss your interest in . . . book collecting."

"Don't try to outsmart me."

"I just thought it would be nice to meet," said Sophie, who could think of nothing less nice than meeting this particular customer. "When I worked at the library at Christ Church it was so much more interesting to meet researchers face-to-face than to talk on the phone or e-mail."

"You were at Oxford, then," said Mr. Smedley, softening. "I was at St. John's, but I'm sure before your time."

"You don't sound that much older than me."

"Suppose we dispense with the detective game."

"Fine," said Sophie. "Then I'll just ask you a question, plain and simple. Why this book? What possible interest could it have?"

"Young lady," said Mr. Smedley, ignoring her question, "my patience is not infinite, and I don't think you would like me when I lose my patience." And with these ominous words he rang off.

"I don't like you when you *are* patient," said Sophie aloud to the phone. Her attempts to ferret out information had been all but fruitless. If she was going to discover what was so special about Richard Mansfield's book, she would have to find another way.

She sat on a stool in the basement, her mind cluttered with questions. Why had two such different customers come to the same shop looking for the same obscure book? None of the other dealers she had talked to the day before had ever heard of Richard Mansfield, much less had requests for his book of allegories. And why was one of these customers issuing not-so-veiled threats? Obviously there was more to this book—or to this particular edition—than met the eye. She wondered if she ought to tell Winston that a mysterious man was after what she had already begun to think of as *his* book, but Mr. Smedley's threats and demands for secrecy still rang in her ears. She would honor his wishes, until she found out more. But she couldn't imagine finding two copies of *A Little Book of Allegorical Stories*, and, she reasoned, Winston had asked first. So if she did find a copy, by all rights she should sell it to him, regardless of the price Mr. Smedley was willing to pay. But what if his threats of punishment were serious?

Her first thought, as she pondered this puzzle, was that Uncle Bertram must have owned a copy of the book, and that was why both men had come to her. But if he had, how would two different collectors have known? Besides, whether or not Bertram had owned such a book was immaterial now. His books were scattered; finding any specific one was virtually impossible. As she thought over the situation, she could hear the voice of her sister in her head: "What can you do? Figure out what you can do and do it and don't worry about the rest." What she could do was find out everything she could about Richard Mansfield and his book of allegories.

In a case in the basement, Gusty had a substantial reference library—bibliographies, biographical dictionaries, and biographies of well-known authors. Maybe one of them would include an entry on Richard Mansfield.

She had plowed through most of the biographical dictionaries without success when she finally came across an entry in *Alumni Oxonienses,* a four-volume work that listed every person to attend Oxford University from 1715 to 1886.

> **MANSFIELD, RICHARD NORMAN, 1s. Tobias Charles, of Bloxham, Oxfordshire, cler. Balliol Coll., matric. 1734, aged 18; B.A. 1737, M.A. 1740. Curate of Bloxham 1743, Master of Cowley Grammar School 1758–1780, Rector of Croft, Yorkshire, 1780. Died 4 Dec. 1796.**

So, his father was a clergyman, Richard had attended Oxford, he had worked in his father's church, taught school for more than twenty years in what was now the Oxford suburb of Cowley, and then gotten a parish of his own in the north. Nothing in his biography sounded remotely interesting. Mansfield, like his book, was completely ordinary. So why all this fuss about his allegories?

"Gusty," said Sophie, emerging from the basement, "do you mind if

I do some work over at the British Library this afternoon? There are some bibliographical questions on some of these want cards that I'd like to work out." She had already phoned her friend Nigel Cook at the British Library and arranged to have their copy of the first edition of Mansfield's book waiting for her.

"Of course, of course," said Gusty. "Wednesdays are always slow once the matinees start." Thirty minutes later, Sophie was settling into a chair in a light and airy reading room holding a copy of Richard Mansfield's book.

She copied down the bibliographical details—size, number of pages, and the publication information: "Printed in Leeds by Gilbert Monkhouse, 1795"—and then turned to the text.

Sophie had not previously read any allegorical tales from the late eighteenth century, and it didn't take her more than a page of *A Little Book of Allegorical Stories* to realize why. Mansfield's stories had the triple distinction of being heavy-handed, poorly written, and dull. When she read Jane Austen, Sophie felt transported back two hundred years and found herself in a place and time she loved to inhabit—attending balls, taking walks in the countryside, paying visits, all in the company of witty and charming heroines. Reading Richard Mansfield, she found herself in the same era yet in the company of people so dull they would pay actual money to own and read these dreadful stories. It made her want to run screaming back to the present. How could two such different authors, united by a desire to write fiction, represent the same world? In a way, slogging through Richard Mansfield was a revelation to Sophie. We judge the past, if we are readers of novels, only by the output of the best writers, she thought. How differently might we feel if instead of viewing the turn of the nineteenth century through the lens of Jane Austen, we viewed it through the lens of Richard Mansfield?

The best Sophie could say about Mansfield's allegories was that they were blessedly short. A typical example was titled "Sickness and Health," and began:

> *When the original chaos was first reduced to form, and primeval darkness and confusion were superseded by light and harmony,*

> *the Gods joined together Exercise and Temperance, and sent them down among mortals to facilitate and hasten the population of the new world. These two had not lived long on earth, before they were blessed with a daughter called Health.*

It continued on in this vein, talking of all the good things this daughter HEALTH brought to the world until after many generations the men of earth became insolent and "rebelled against the Gods," who then sent INDOLENCE and LUXURY to "sojourn upon earth," and wouldn't you know it, they had a daughter named SICKNESS, and you know what trouble she's made for everybody ever since. What on earth could Winston Godfrey want with this rubbish?

Sophie scanned the rest of the book, checking for any marginal markings and making a few notes on stories with such scintillating titles as "The Pleasures of Benevolence," "Youth and Vanity," and her favorite: "General Depravity of Mankind." What a wonderful Christmas gift *this* book would make!

By five o'clock she could take no more, and she returned the book to the desk, pushed her way through the glass doors into the brick piazza, and headed toward the tube at King's Cross. She had looked at every page of the book, racking her brain for any reason why not just one, but two people would want to buy the *second* edition of something so utterly ordinary. This was something worth making veiled threats and offering large sums of money? It simply didn't seem credible. Sophie wondered if it was all some elaborate hoax perpetrated by Winston. Perhaps *he* was the second customer, disguising his voice on the phone. But then she remembered that Gusty had met Smedley and he looked nothing like Winston. Besides, she couldn't imagine why Winston would play such a trick. Then again, she also couldn't imagine why he wanted the second edition of a book that preserved for future generations stories like "General Depravity of Mankind."

## *Hampshire, 1796*

**THE DAY AFTER** she had forced Mr. Mansfield to read her his book of allegories, Jane read to him the final pages of *Elinor and Marianne.* She was pleased to find that he in no way anticipated the possibility that Lucy Steele had married not Mr. Edward Ferrars but Mr. Robert Ferrars. Her friend even uttered a little squeal of delight when she revealed this twist in the plot.

"It is a triumph," said Mr. Mansfield. "A truly magnificent first draft."

"What can you mean by that, Mr. Mansfield?" said Jane. "Do you imply that it needs improvement?"

"Certainly not in story or character," said Mr. Mansfield. "But I do believe, and I know that you are understanding enough to take my suggestions as encouragement, not as criticism, that it might benefit from being written as a conventional narrative."

"You feel a novel of letters is inferior to a narrative?"

"Not in your capable hands," said Mr. Mansfield, "but I do fear this practice of writing novels in letters may be no more than a passing fashion. I should think it a waste if, in the decades to come, your novels were given no more attention than other passing fashions."

"Tell me, Mr. Mansfield, do you truly believe that my novels will ever be read by anyone outside my circle of friends and family?" said Jane.

"I am certain of it," said Mr. Mansfield. "Trust me, Miss Austen, your name will be known when all around you are long forgotten." Jane blushed at this prediction, touched by his confidence in her success.

"I must say, Mr. Mansfield," she replied, laying her manuscript aside, "I continue to be amazed at your unconventionality."

"And in what ways am I unconventional?"

"First, that you are a clergyman of the older generation who delights in novels rather than scorning them from the pulpit as evil influences on the weak minded."

"Only because I have passed four score years will I allow you to refer to me as of the 'older generation' without censure."

"And second, that you treat a woman—that is, myself—as an intellectual equal."

"I am afraid you are wrong on that count," said Mr. Mansfield. "I never meant for you to think that I viewed you as my equal. I am afraid you exceed me by a wide margin in matters of intellect."

"You are kind to say so, though it be said in jest."

"It is not said in jest, I assure you," said Mr. Mansfield. "But why do you call my opinion unconventional?"

"Surely you know, sir, that a more commonly held position among the men of your generation and even of my own is that a woman unfortunate enough to be in possession of knowledge should do her best to conceal that fact."

"It is a sentiment I have met with, though I cannot say I condone it. But let us turn from the question of my unconventionality to more pressing matters. I have news from the north." He picked up a letter from the table by his chair and waved it in the air.

"What news, Mr. Mansfield?" said Jane.

"It has to do with us," he said. "For it bears on our little project of atonement. It is a letter from Mr. Monkhouse."

"And who, pray tell, is Mr. Monkhouse?"

"Only the finest printer in Leeds and the man responsible for creating the book I have just read to you."

"I would remind you, Mr. Mansfield, that you yourself have said that the author and not the printer is the true creator of a book, were I not eager to proceed to the neglected topic of your assignment to me. An assignment that you promised to reveal as soon as I had completed the saga of the Dashwoods."

"The fact is, Miss Austen," said Mr. Mansfield, "that, dry as my little book of allegories may be, I have heard from many quarters—most recently from the headmaster of the school where I was privileged to spend so many years shaping the character of young men—that my allegories have proved useful both in the pulpit and in the schoolroom. And so I begin to contemplate a second edition—and your recent confession has suggested a way in which I might be able to expand my little collection. But, for one of my years, it is an onerous task, and to achieve what I envision I shall need your help."

"Whatever they may be," said Jane, "my talents are at your disposal."

"And they are talents which I believe could bring much improvement to my little book, and thus help many who may benefit from its lessons."

"To use my talents of imagination—the very talents that condemned Nurse—to help you help others seems a fitting act of atonement, Mr. Mansfield."

"I am pleased that you think so."

"I do hope," said Jane, after they discussed the details of Mr. Mansfield's proposal for a new and expanded edition of his book, "that this work will not make you so busy as to prevent your sparing some of your time for reading and pleasant conversation with your student."

"I shall never be too busy to spare time for you—I am not like Alphonso, who does not recognize the true chances for happiness, but I cannot but think that I am your student as much as you are mine."

"You are kind to say so, Mr. Mansfield, and again I would debate the question were I not too respectful of the wisdom which must come from your highly advanced years."

He gave a deep laugh at this jibe, stood from his chair, and crossed to the table by the window, where stood a small selection of books from the library of Busbury House.

"Now, the question that rests in the heart of this ancient sage is—what are we to read next? While we embark on my little project, we must have some story to occupy those moments when our minds need rest. Having exhausted all your own writings, I fear we must turn to some inferior author. Mrs. Radcliffe, perhaps?"

"There are some of her books I have read with pleasure," said Jane.

"I had thought *Udolpho*," said Mr. Mansfield. "When I first read it I could not lay it down; I remember finishing it in two days—my hair standing on end the whole time."

"You didn't find *Udolpho* a bit . . . horrid?"

"Perhaps," said Mr. Mansfield. "And perhaps that explains the hair."

"There is a class of novels," said Jane, "into which I am afraid I must place *Udolpho*, of which I am not particularly fond. They all have titles such as *Mysterious Warnings* or *Horrid Mysteries*. I can say only that of these gothic novels, *Udolpho* is perhaps the most intriguing."

"And yet still not a favorite of yours."

"Charming as Mrs. Radcliffe's works are, Mr. Mansfield, I do not find human nature, of the English variety, reflected in them. They may perhaps give a faithful representation of the Alps and the Pyrenees, with their dark forests and their mysterious vices. There I can imagine that those who are not as spotless as an angel might be as dark as a fiend. But among the English," said Jane, thinking of the recent revelations she had had about the weaknesses in her own character, "I find a general, though unequal, mixture of good *and* bad."

"Then there is only one thing to be done," said Mr. Mansfield.

"And what is that?"

"We must read *Udolpho*; we must revel in the mystery of the black veil; and then, when our current project is finished, you must write a satire on the whole genre. Bring the gothic novel to England and see how it behaves in a more civilized environment."

"I confess, Mr. Mansfield, your suggestion is not wholly without merit. I could give it some suitably gothic title such as *The Mystery at Midnight* or *The Abbey Ruins*."

"I suddenly remember—or perhaps misremember," said Mr. Mansfield, "the name of a village my brother Henry mentioned to me years ago. What do you think of *Northanger Abbey*?"

## *London, Present Day*

**SOPHIE AND WINSTON** sat at an outdoor table at a Chinese restaurant in Little Venice, just a short walk from her flat. Every few minutes a canal boat chugged by, and the cool summer breeze wafted the diesel smoke away from them, leaving only the smell of the flowers in huge pots that dotted the terrace. Winston had picked her up at precisely seven—she had met him at the street door—and, after properly admiring her dress, he had taken her by the hand and led her to the canal. She had ordered wine as soon as they sat down, and Winston had told the waiter to bring a bottle. The starters had been cleared and the mains had not yet arrived when they began a second bottle.

"I went to the British Library this afternoon and had a peek at the first edition of that book you're looking for," said Sophie when the waiter had refilled their glasses. "It made for fascinating reading."

"You read it?" said Winston, leaning forward in his chair.

"OK, I admit," said Sophie, "I'm a little embarrassed to be seen in public with a man whose idea of a good read is a book with a story in it called 'General Depravity of Mankind.'"

"I never said it was my idea of a good read."

"You're trying to find the second edition when you already have the first. There must be something you like about it."

"You're trying to get me to tell you why I want that book."

"Well, it's the second date, so you must find me a little charming—

I thought maybe I could use my wiles to get you to tell me your little secret."

"I find you more than a little charming," said Winston, reaching for her hand.

"That's very kind of you," said Sophie, pulling her hand away, "but holding my hand isn't going to make me forget my question."

"Then why did you pull away?"

Sophie stared into his eyes for a moment and sighed. "Because holding your hand would make me forget my question."

"I never heard you ask a question," said Winston.

"Why do you want that damn book?"

"If you really want to know, I'll tell you."

"I really want to know," said Sophie.

"The fact is I'm fascinated by printing—preindustrial printing. In the nineteenth century, with the industrial revolution, everything changed, but even in the late eighteenth century, printing wasn't that different from what it had been for Gutenberg three hundred years earlier. So I collect obscure books of the second half of the eighteenth century."

"By obscure you mean cheap."

"Exactly," said Winston with a chuckle. "You see, unlike books of a century later, you can really feel the craftsmanship of the individual printers. Before the machines took over, type was set by hand and every typesetter had his own style. I like that feeling of connecting with a particular workman over the centuries."

Sophie wondered if it was anything like the feeling she had of connecting with an author.

"Anyway," said Winston, "I discovered that if I could put together a run of different editions of the same book, I could get an even greater sense of the men who printed it. Most eighteenth-century press runs were pretty small. They would set the type and print off five hundred or a thousand copies of a book, and then put the type back in its cases for the next project. Then a few months later they would get an order for another five hundred copies and they'd set the whole thing up again and print a new edition. And I found all these differences in the editions—differences in design and spelling and even in the way the lines were justified. With books from some of the smaller printing offices, I can practically identify the individual typesetters—not by name, of course, because nobody kept records of these men, but I can tell that the same person set the first edition of this book and the third edition of that book; that sort of thing."

Sophie had nearly forgotten her original question. Winston's fascination both intrigued and puzzled her. Although she loved the feel of an old volume, and the experience of reading a book that had been read by others throughout the generations, she had never stopped to think about who had made it. To Winston those men, for in the eighteenth century they certainly would all have been men, defined his experience of a book more than the author did. She couldn't quite decide if Winston was opening up a new vista or completely missing the point of books.

"One of my favorite printers," he continued, "was a man named Gilbert Monkhouse in Leeds. Ever heard of him?"

"Not until today when I wrote his name down," said Sophie.

"I'm not surprised. He only seems to have been in the business for a couple of years—all his books are dated 1795 or 1796, but I've found several of them, and some of them in multiple editions. He did beautiful work."

"He was the printer of *A Little Book of Allegorical Stories.*"

"Exactly," said Winston.

"So the reason you want the second edition has nothing to do with the text."

"I don't give a toss about the text," said Winston. "Richard Mansfield or Henry Fielding—it's all the same to me. I collect Gilbert Monkhouse."

"Well," said Sophie, "*A Little Book of Allegorical Stories* might be the one book that I can agree is more interesting for its typesetting than for its text."

They stayed at the restaurant talking long enough to consider a third bottle of wine, a suggestion Sophie rejected, not wanting Winston to get the wrong idea. As it was she felt unsteady when they stood up and was happy to take his arm as they walked back toward Maida Vale. The tree-lined street outside her flat was quiet at eleven o'clock and Winston pulled her to a stop in the shadows just outside the light of a streetlamp.

"It's a delicate moment, isn't it?" he said.

"I can't imagine what you mean," said Sophie. She told herself she was trembling because of the cool night air, but she didn't quite believe it.

"Well, I like you, Sophie," he said. "I'd like to see you again, and seeing you again means a third date, which probably means seeing a good deal more of you, if you know what I mean."

"You come straight to the point," said Sophie, at the same time gripping his arm a little tighter.

"And this is the first good-night kiss. I don't want to cock it up."

"Well, good night, then."

Winston leaned down and Sophie closed her eyes and she felt his lips press into hers with just the right pressure for just the right length of time. Everything about the kiss was just right—as if it had been rehearsed a thousand times. Ten out of ten for technical merit, thought Sophie. So who cared if there were no weak knees, no rapid heartbeat? A perfectly executed kiss from a gentleman who had asked her on a second date was a lot better, she told herself, than one with a guy she would never see again, even if it had been in the garden in the moonlight. Still, as she mounted the steps to the street door and Winston turned toward the tube station, she wished he had not been *quite* so much of a gentleman.

Sleep eluded Sophie for the next few hours, and as she lay in bed she did her best to steer her thoughts toward the mystery of Mr. Smedley and away from Winston Godfrey. Winston had given her a perfectly reasonable explanation why *he* was looking for Richard Mansfield's book; and Winston, after all, was not threatening her and offering huge sums of money for a worthless volume. It was a shame, thought Sophie, that she had never considered the craftsmanship that went into printing books, especially considering the origin of her own family library.

"**WHERE DID ALL OF** the books at Bayfield come from?" she had asked Uncle Bertram one day. "I know Father didn't buy any of them."

"They're the family library," said Uncle Bertram. "Our father bought a few of them, but most of them go back at least to our grandfather, and many further back than that."

"But not every family has a library," said Sophie.

"That's true. Not every family has a great big house, either," said Uncle Bertram. "But the beginnings of our library are rather special. Usually families like ours have lots of money and then decide to build a house and then decide to buy lots of books—mostly to impress people. We were a little different."

"How?"

"In our family, to a small extent at least, the books came first. Some of the books at Bayfield House date back to before the family had any money at all. You see, originally we weren't dukes or earls; we were printers."

"We made books?" asked Sophie.

"We did," said Uncle Bertram. "A very long time ago. Over the years the family got into different businesses and made a lot of money and bought land and built Bayfield House. But it all started with books. And there are a few books in the library that go all the way back to that printing-office."

Sophie sat bolt upright in bed. Was it possible that the printer who started the Bayfield library was Gilbert Monkhouse? And might some of Monkhouse's books still sit in the family library? And did Winston know all this and think he could somehow extort these books from Sophie with his charm and good looks and promises of sex? Her train of thought nearly jumped the rails when she allowed the thought of sex with Winston, which had been buzzing around the edge of her consciousness ever since their conversation in the street, to articulate itself, but she pushed that from her mind as best she could and, without regard for the time, reached for her phone and rang Bayfield House.

"Sophie is that you?" said her father's groggy voice. "What's wrong? What's happened?"

"Nothing's happened," said Sophie.

"Then why are you ringing at three o'clock in the morning?"

"We're descended from printers, right?" said Sophie, ignoring her father's question.

"Sophie, this really isn't the time for this conversation. Can't you ring back in the morning?"

"It's just a quick question, Father. You're already awake."

"Yes, yes, I suppose there are some printers dangling in the branches of the family tree."

"Are any of them named Monkhouse?"

"What sort of a name is that?"

"It's just a name, Father. Are any of my ancestors named Monkhouse?"

"I'm not a genealogist, Sophie."

"Yes, but the printer, the one who started the library. Is there any chance he was named Gilbert Monkhouse?"

"Is that what this is about? The library?"

"The name, Father. What was the name of the printer who started the family library?"

"He started the family fortune, more important," said her father. "Don't recall his Christian name, but his surname was Wright."

Sophie fell back on her pillow in relief. Winston was a gentleman after all. How could she ever have doubted him? She forgot all about Richard Mansfield and Gilbert Monkhouse and Mr. Smedley and let the thoughts she had been avoiding since she got home, thoughts of her third date with Winston Godfrey, wash over her. In ten minutes she was fast asleep, and what dreams did come.

## *Hampshire, 1796*

**OVER THE NEXT** two weeks, Jane was rarely seen at the rectory. Cassandra indulged her desire to be with Mr. Mansfield, for Jane had whispered a hint that they were involved in a literary project, and Cassandra was never one to interfere with her sister's endeavors in this direction.

"Still, I feel almost as if you are away in Kent," said Cassandra one evening as they sat together reading. "Perhaps you could send me a letter from Mr. Mansfield's residence to inform me of all the goings-on there."

"I assure you, sister, nothing goes on but reading and writing, and the occasional consumption of a bit of beef or bread to keep up our strength."

It was nearly November, and the wind whistled through the barren branches of the trees when Jane presented herself at Mr. Mansfield's door to find her friend looking unusually cheerful.

"Should you be out alone in such weather, Miss Austen?" he said as he ushered her into the warm sitting room.

"It is only my characters," said Jane, thinking of Marianne Dashwood, "who are careless when walking in less than perfect weather, Mr. Mansfield. Now you must tell me what inspires this smile that does not leave your face."

Mr. Mansfield presented Jane with a sheaf of papers. "It is finished," he said.

*"Allegorical Stories and a Cautionary Tale,"* she read. "Not A *Little Book?"*

"With the addition, it won't be so little."

"You must have been up all night finishing this," said Jane.

"I wanted you to be able to read it through without stumbling across my marks and corrections, our deletions and emendations."

"I wonder if you would mind, Mr. Mansfield, if I did more than read it through. It occurs to me that, with this project of atonement completed and your new edition ready for the press, the new cautionary tale, as you call it, might serve as the germ of an altogether larger project—perhaps even a new novel."

"What a capital idea," said Mr. Mansfield. "I do not doubt that in your talented hands the story could be much more than what it is now. You must keep the manuscript for as long as you need."

"You are indeed generous, Mr. Mansfield, and I confess that, with the work I envision, such a carefully written and unmarked copy will be of great benefit. But you must keep this for yourself a little longer, for I am eager to hear you read."

"I had hoped, perhaps, that you would read to me, as I have, as you surmise, been awake much of the night."

"Then I am afraid my dulcet voice would lull you straight to sleep," said Jane. "No, on this occasion I should like to sit in comfort by your fire, close my eyes, and hear *you* read to *me*."

"I would argue your point, if I did not already know the futility of doing battle with you," said Mr. Mansfield with a chuckle. "If you will allow me to pour a mug of tea to bolster my aging voice, I shall indulge your wishes."

Jane fell into a chair as Mr. Mansfield lifted the kettle from the fire, filled the teapot, and poured two mugs of tea. "Now," he said, "I shall dispense with the revised versions of stories you have already heard and skip directly to the new material, which I know is of most interest to us both." He shuffled through the manuscript until he had found the place he wished to begin, picked up a page, and read: *"First Impressions."*

The shadows had deepened in the sitting room by the time Mr. Mansfield turned to the final page. He had been forced to light a lamp, but neither he nor Jane seemed willing to break off mid-story, and so he read on until he reached the final letter:

*Pemberley, Thursday*

*My Dear Lydia,*

*It has always been evident to me that such an income as yours and Wickham's, under the direction of two persons so extravagant in their wants, and heedless of the future, as yourselves, must be very insufficient to your support; however, you will not be surprised to learn that I had much 'rather not' speak to Mr. Darcy of securing any place at court for your husband. Such relief, however, as it is in my power to afford, by the practice of what might be called economy in my own private expenses, I shall happily send you. Though Darcy can, of course, never receive Wickham at Pemberley, I hope that you may be an occasional visitor. I have found in Georgiana a true sister, and I believe you may grow to love her as I do. Lady Catherine remains extremely indignant on the marriage of her nephew, and Darcy proclaims all intercourse with her at an end, yet I hope to persuade him to seek a reconciliation. As I consider my happiness with Darcy and how nearly it was lost, and as I ponder your life with Wickham, I cannot help but be reminded of the dangers that befall those who succumb to their first impressions.*

*Your Loving Sister,*

*Elizabeth Darcy*

**MR. MANSFIELD LAID THE** final page in his lap and stared into the dying fire. "I admit to being rather proud," he murmured.

"But would you call it an allegorical story?" said Jane.

"As you have pointed out yourself, I chose to present it as a cautionary tale," said Mr. Mansfield. "And it certainly is that. Especially in the differing fates of the two sisters—one who has the wisdom and courage to discard her faulty first impression of a gentleman and the other who does not. It is a message that may do much good."

"That must be our earnest hope, Mr. Mansfield. Now, for turning this cautionary tale into something more rich and substantial, I think of telling Eliza's story as a narrative novel, much as you wish me to do with *Elinor and Marianne*."

"You must do so," said Mr. Mansfield. "And with all expediency, as I hope to live to see the results of your efforts."

"While I expect you to be with me for many years to come, Mr. Mansfield, it is nonetheless my intention to begin the work as soon as possible, so as not to retain your manuscript any longer than necessary."

"Now, Miss Austen, it has grown too dark for me to allow your return to Steventon alone. Allow me to send the gardener up to the house to fetch a gig for your transport. I do not think Lord Wintringham would begrudge his guest such a favor."

Jane accepted this offer, as the shortening days and cloudy sky meant she would certainly have walked much of the way home in darkness. Her arrival at the rectory in a gig belonging to Lord Wintringham was cause for much speculation that evening, but once she had assured everyone from her father to little Anna that it was an indication only that she and an elderly clergyman had lost track of the time while discussing literature and not that she was courted by one of the sons of the estate, the matter was dropped in favor of a discussion of plans for the upcoming Christmas theatricals.

## *London, Present Day*

**IN THE MORNING POST,** which Sophie sifted through as she ate her breakfast, was a large brown envelope from Mr. Faussett containing the promised copy of the report of the inquest into Uncle Bertram's death, along with the list of booksellers who had bought items from Bertram's library. The latter she reluctantly put aside for now while she examined the inquest report.

The inquest had taken just a few minutes, the finding of accidental death, Sophie thought, being almost predetermined by everyone involved. Uncle Bertram had left for a walk and, reading a book, had slipped on a circular and fallen down a flight of stairs. His neck had been broken and he had died almost instantly. As much as she tried to read the report as a disinterested investigator, Sophie could not help feeling heartbroken as she imagined poor Uncle Bertram lying lifeless at the bottom of those stairs.

In addition to the inquest report, the envelope contained several other pages—the report of the police who had been called to the scene, an autopsy report—and Sophie read through them all, looking for anything that might suggest foul play. The last page was a list of personal items that had been retrieved from the body:

**1 gentleman's shirt, plaid**

**1 gentleman's jacket, tweed**

**1 pair trousers, brown**

**1 gentleman's undergarment**

**1 belt, brown**

**1 pair shoes, brown**

**1 pair socks, brown**

**1 gentleman's leather wallet containing identification, two credit cards, one photograph of a young woman, thirty-seven pounds, and an Oyster card**

**1 copy of *Collected Poems of Robert Burns***

**UNCLE BERTRAM HAD LOVED** to read Burns in the summertime. And of course the photograph in the wallet was of Sophie. In the end, at least he had been with her and with a favorite book. Sophie had to admit that the case seemed cut-and-dried. Even though she knew that Bertram never read while walking near traffic, she could imagine him reading Burns as he descended the familiar stairs from his flat.

Sophie herself almost tripped as she walked out the door of the flat, her foot catching on a package that lay on her doorstep. It had been sent from Paris, the address written in Eric's now familiar scrawl. What on earth was Eric sending her from France? She was running late, so she tucked the parcel under her arm and headed for Cecil Court.

"Somebody sent you some books, I see," said Gusty when she set the package down on the counter.

"How do you know it's books?" asked Sophie.

"What else would somebody send you?"

"He does know I love books," she said.

"A boyfriend, then?"

"More of an acquaintance. He was just visiting England when we met."

"A mysterious foreigner," said Gusty, handing her a pair of scissors, with which she began to cut the tape.

"I wouldn't say mysterious," said Sophie, "but he is an American."

She pulled the paper apart and four slim clothbound volumes fell onto the counter.

"This looks intriguing," said Gusty. "Early nineteenth century, I'd guess from the bindings."

Sophie picked up one of the volumes and opened to the title page. "My French is a little rusty, I'm afraid," she said. She handed the volume to Gusty.

"Oh my goodness," he said. "This is quite a find."

"What is it?" asked Sophie.

"*Orgueil et Préjugés,*" said Gusty. "My pronunciation is probably a bit off, but this is the second French translation of *Pride and Prejudice*. It's quite a rarity."

"You're kidding," said Sophie, taking the book back from Gusty. "Eighteen twenty-two? I had no idea Jane Austen was getting translated that early."

"There was a completely different French translation a year earlier," said Gusty. "Of course, Austen's name didn't appear on either one of them. No copyright laws in those days."

Sophie looked at each volume and found number one. She opened the cover and a folded sheet of paper fluttered out. She opened it and read:

**Sophie,**

**Found this for a song at one of those bookstalls along the Seine. I have a feeling it might actually be worth something—I don't think the dealer knew what he had. Anyway, I knew no one would appreciate this as much as you. Do you read French? I can barely order food here. Paris is hot and empty of Parisians. I'm starting to think I should have made you give me your phone number, but I have a feeling you prefer ink and paper. If you have some of each perhaps you'll write.**

**Yours,**

**Eric**

"In this kind of condition," said Gusty, picking up another volume and admiring it, "this was an expensive present."

"He says he bought it for a song at a stall along the Seine."

"I doubt that," said Gusty. "Even if there were a bookseller in Paris who didn't recognize the importance of this book, some other dealer would have snatched it up before any American tourist got his hands on it."

"Are you saying my friend is lying?"

"I thought he was an acquaintance. Gives you a nice book and he gets upgraded to friend, huh? Anyway, a man who buys a woman a book this nice is looking to be more than just an acquaintance."

Sophie worked the counter that day, but business was slow. Between shelving new acquisitions and ringing up the few sales, she read over Eric's letter several times. Was he really lying about how much he had paid for the books? And did he really want to be more than friends? Maybe he was as unable to shake the memory of that kiss in the moonlight as she was. Eric remained an enigma, so she turned her attention to the volumes he had sent her. She knew a little French and knew *Pride and Prejudice* well enough that she could pick out a familiar scene or bit of dialogue here and there, but unlike every book she had ever bought for herself, she couldn't sit down and read these through. Uncle Bertram's library had had plenty of valuable rarities in it, but they had always been books that he at least intended to read, and most of them he had read many times over.

"That's the beauty of rare books," he had said one evening when he was reading a first edition of *Cecilia*. "If you mail a rare stamp it becomes worthless. If you drink a rare bottle of wine, you're left with some recycling. But if you read a rare book it's still there, it's still valuable, and it's achieved the full measure of its being. A book is to read, whether it's worth five pounds or five thousand pounds." Of course, Uncle Bertram could read not only French, but German, Latin, and Greek.

But Sophie couldn't read these books; she could only admire them. She tried to imagine, as Winston did, the people who had set the type and printed the pages. French people, she supposed, in the days of the Bourbon Restoration. She could almost smell the print shop wafting off the pages. She imagined, too, some young upper-class French woman, who had the privilege of literacy, opening the first of these volumes and reading Sophie's favorite first line in literature, but reading it in French. She turned to the first page and read: *S'il est une idée généralement reçue, c'est qu'un homme fort riche doit penser à se marier.*

Sophie's French wasn't good enough to understand every nuance, but it was good enough to see that that perfect opening lost a great deal in translation. As near as she could make out, the French read something like: "It is an idea generally received that a rich man must be thinking of marriage." If Jane Austen had started out *Pride and Prejudice* with those words, she might occupy the same place in literary history as Richard Mansfield.

Still, Sophie yearned for more. She wondered if she could brush up on her schoolgirl French enough to read these books. She shivered every time she picked up one of the volumes. Whether because they had come from Eric or because they represented the earliest days of Jane Austen spreading across the globe, she could not be sure. Certainly no one except Uncle Bertram had ever given her such a nice set of books. She had just decided that she had better write Eric and thank him, when her phone rang and she found herself on the line with Winston.

"I thought you weren't supposed to call the day after a date," said Sophie. "You said it would make you look too eager."

"I am eager," said Winston.

"Eager for another date?" asked Sophie. "Or just eager to get your hands on Richard Mansfield?"

"Well, I am eager to acquire a certain second edition," he said, "but that's not exactly what I'm imagining getting my hands on at the moment."

"Whatever can you mean?"

"I believe that's a question I'd prefer to answer in person," said Winston. "My father has gone back to Gloucestershire. How would you like for me to cook dinner for you tonight?"

"Seriously? You're good-looking *and* you cook?"

"You think I'm good-looking?"

"Oh, come on," said Sophie. "I'm sure you must have seen a little thing called a mirror before. It's really a remarkable invention."

"I'll stop by the shop at closing time and we'll walk up to Selfridges and see what looks good in the food hall and then head back to my place for dinner."

"This sounds like a rather transparent plan to get a single girl into your flat."

"Are you single?" said Winston. "I had no idea."

"Do you think a respectable young lady should dine in a gentleman's flat on the third date?"

"You said you were single; you didn't say you were respectable," he said. "Besides, you have to eat. I'll see you at six." Before Sophie could respond, he rang off. She thought she had protested enough to maintain an air of propriety. On her lunch break, she popped round the corner and bought a toothbrush.

## *Hampshire, 1796*

**UPSTAIRS AT STEVENTON RECTORY** was a small sitting room, which the Austen family was pleased to call the "dressing room." It contained Jane's piano, several shelves full of books, and a large oval looking glass. The walls were cheaply painted and the furniture scanty. In one corner stood a small round table and a simple slat-back chair. In this room and in this chair and at this table, as November passed, Jane ensconced herself for several hours a day. The other residents of the rectory would at times hear her playing the piano, but never for more than a few minutes. Then silence would return, and only Cassandra, who sometimes passed through the room, would hear the sound of a quill scratching on paper that was nearly continuous during those days. While everyone at the house was inured to Jane's writing and knew to give her privacy in which to create her stories, no one had ever seen her this driven.

One morning, when the strains of a minuet could be heard drifting down from the dressing room, Cassandra dared to enter and address her sister.

"Is it a new story? Or are you giving us more of *Elinor and Marianne*?"

"I believe we've had enough of *Elinor and Marianne*," said Jane, dropping her hands from the keyboard. "This is a new one."

Cassandra waited for Jane to elaborate, but no elaboration was forthcoming. "You seem less . . . less cheerful than you usually are when you start a new story. Is it giving you difficulties?"

"On the contrary," said Jane. "It flows from my pen almost fully formed. At times I feel I cannot write fast enough to keep up with the tumble of words."

"And yet I still sense that something troubles you, sister. You have always told me your troubles in the past. Will you not do so now?"

"Perhaps it is only that I am tired," said Jane. Although the work she now undertook moved far beyond any act of atonement as the cautionary tale Mr. Mansfield had so carefully written out blossomed into a novel more complex and nuanced every day, as she wrote Jane still felt sobered by the events that had first set her on this journey. But she had resolved not to share the burden of Nurse's fate with her sister. Cassandra, after all, had been in Reading, too. She had known Nurse and loved her—if not as deeply as Jane had, certainly as much as any of the other girls. "This story haunts my dreams as well as fills my days," said Jane to Cassandra. "I feel I cannot escape its grip until it is written down."

"Can you yet share it with us?" asked Cassandra. "Little Anna runs wild with curiosity when I forbid her to enter the dressing room."

Jane considered this for a moment. She was not ready to share any part of her new novel, but perhaps Cassandra and Anna would like to hear a bit of the source material. On its surface, the story was not so very different from others she had read to them. Out of the context of Mr. Mansfield's book, it might seem merely a romance inhabited by characters with simple human weaknesses. Sharing it with others, setting it free from the pages, might loosen its grip on her and ease somewhat the strain of her recent, almost frenzied efforts.

"With you I shall share it, and with Anna. But not with the others, not yet. And for now, I shall give you only a taste."

Cassandra smiled and clapped her hands in delight. "For those who are hungry, a taste is ever so much better than nothing at all. Mother has taken Anna to Deane for a visit with her father, but she returns this afternoon."

"This afternoon, then," said Jane, and she rose from the piano and returned to her writing table. As Jane dipped her quill in the inkwell, Cassandra knew the interview was ended and quietly left the room.

Later that day, Jane finally set aside her quill and turned to the four eager eyes looking up at her from the floor. Cassandra leaned against the wall and Anna sat expectantly in her lap. Jane picked up a sheet of paper.

"It began as a story in letters," she said, "but I am working to expand it and make it a narrative piece. Still, for now I shall read to you from the letters. That should be sufficient to give you a taste." And she began.

## *First Impressions*

*My Dear Sister,*

*What do you think? Netherfield Park is let at last! And not only let, but taken by a young man of large fortune from the north of England by the name of Bingley. I am told he is to take possession before Michaelmas, and some of his servants are to be in the house by the end of next week. It is, of course, a fine thing for our girls—it is very likely that he may fall in love with one of them. Mr. Bennet has expressed his opinion that Lizzy is the most likely, though Lizzy is not a bit better than the others; and I am sure she is not half so handsome as Jane, nor half so good-humoured as Lydia. And yet Mr. Bennet insists on calling Lydia "silly and ignorant." I do believe he takes delight in vexing me. He has no compassion for my poor nerves. Nonetheless I have made him promise he will pay Mr. Bingley a visit as soon as he is settled. He does not understand that the business of my life is to get my daughters married. Do give my regards to Mr. Philips.*

*Your Affectionate Sister*

Jane had read only three letters to Anna and Cassandra when word came that dinner was served and the three made their way downstairs, Anna taking her aunt by the hand and Jane impressing upon her niece as they went that she was not to breathe a word of *First Impressions*. As they left the room, a small draft wafted one of the pages of the manuscript from which Jane had read to the floor. Cassandra picked it up to return to the pile and was perplexed to see that the hand was not her sister's. When Anna called to her impatiently from halfway down the stairs, she quickly returned the page to its place and hurried after them, thinking no more about the matter.

## *London, Present Day*

**THE SHOP WAS EMPTY** when Victoria rang Sophie a few minutes before six.

"Sorry I haven't called," said Victoria. "I've been so busy this week, but I have to know how it's going with your two boyfriends."

"I wouldn't call them boyfriends, exactly," said Sophie, "but I think maybe it's going really well."

"Details, please," said Victoria.

"Well, it's possible that Eric has moved from the 'kill' column to the 'marry' column."

"Do tell."

"He sent me this amazing book from Paris," said Sophie. "An early French translation of *Pride and Prejudice*."

"The quickest way to Sophie Collingwood's heart."

"On the other hand," said Sophie, "there's a strong possibility that after tonight Winston's presence in the 'shag' category will no longer be theoretical."

"You have been a busy girl. I was going to ask if you wanted me to come down next weekend, but it sounds like you have things well under control."

"Oh, do come down," said Sophie. "That would be lovely. If things go well with Winston I can introduce you and if they don't you can help me drown my sorrows."

"We're closed on Friday," said Victoria, "and I might be able to take Thursday off, too. Make a long weekend of it."

"Perfect," said Sophie. "Oh my God, here he comes." Winston had just appeared in front of the shop window and was smiling and waving at Sophie.

"Have fun, little sister. Don't do anything I wouldn't do."

"Does that narrow it down at all?" teased Sophie.

"Very funny," said Victoria. "I expect a full report."

**THE DINNER WINSTON PREPARED** for Sophie was simple but delicious: roast chicken, potatoes, and veg with a bottle of red wine. "You don't have to be a great cook," he said when she complimented him on the meal. "You just have to have access to fresh rosemary. And I know you're supposed to have white wine with chicken, but I prefer red."

"So do I," said Sophie, draining her glass and holding it out for a refill. Winston emptied the bottle into her glass.

"Shall I open another?" he said.

"Better not," said Sophie. "I wouldn't want to . . ."

"Lose your inhibitions?"

"Something like that."

"Well, if we're through with dinner, then I have a little something for you." He disappeared and returned a moment later with a small brown bag, which he presented to her. From it, she withdrew a plastic package holding some sort of doll about six inches high.

"I don't understand," said Sophie. "What is it?"

"It's a Jane Austen action figure," said Winston, flashing a grin like a pleased schoolboy.

"But I don't understand," she said, turning the blister-packed figurine in her hand. "What does it do?"

"Nothing, I suppose," he said. "It's a joke. Just a bit of fun. I figured you had all the books, but you probably didn't have the action figure."

"You were right about that," said Sophie, still not sure what to make of this gift. She saw now that it did bear a certain resemblance to the one known portrait of Austen—a colored sketch by her sister, Cassandra.

"Anyway, they didn't have a Richard Mansfield action figure," said Winston, pushing back his chair.

"No," said Sophie, laying the figurine on the table. "I imagine they didn't."

"Now, would you like to see my little collection?"

"Sure," said Sophie. "I'd love to. Where do you keep it?"

"In the bedroom."

"I might have known," she said. She had been thinking about this moment all afternoon, reveling in the delicious anticipation of it, but she hesitated for just a beat. There he was, smiling at her with those straight white teeth, holding a muscular arm out to her. A man like Winston had never asked Sophie Collingwood to his bedroom. Her hesitation melted and she stood up and took his hand. "Well, lead on," she said.

**WINSTON ACTUALLY DID SHOW** Sophie his collection—about fifty books, including a dozen or so printed by Gilbert Monkhouse. They were mostly in poor condition—tattered covers or no covers at all, missing pages, torn pages. "The worse the condition is," he said, "the cheaper they are, which fits my current budget just fine. Besides, I'm only interested in the printing." Sophie was beginning to think that in spite of all the flirtation and innuendo, all Winston really wanted to do was show off his book collection, but as she was turning the pages of his first edition of Richard Mansfield's *Little Book of Allegorical Stories*, he reached down, gently took the book from her hands, and wrapped her in his arms. For the next two hours she forgot all about books and printing and mysterious customers. She even forgot about that damn moonlight kiss with Eric.

They made love with the lights off, and Sophie was glad about that. She wasn't exactly comfortable being naked in front of Winston. Not yet, anyway. But if embarrassment and awkwardness and inexperience kept Sophie from feeling any deep emotional connection, they certainly did not preclude physical enjoyment. Winston did things she hadn't even read about and did them in a way that betrayed a degree of experience she did not care to contemplate. The world was reduced, at times, to a few molecules of her body—and not always the molecules she expected. She had disdained girls at university who talked of relationships as being "purely physical," but perhaps that was because she had not yet experienced the ministrations of Winston Godfrey. Purely physical, as it turned out, was bliss.

Even though they had been together for almost two years, Sophie had always found sex with Clifton, her first real boyfriend, awkward and forgettable. He got it over with quickly, was about all she could say for him. She knew from old American movies watched late at night with her sister that bookish girls always ended up bespectacled and chaste. Nights of sexual nirvana were not meant for the likes of Sophie Collingwood. However, no one seemed to have informed Winston of this.

She was certain, she thought, as she lay in bed the next morning listening to Winston banging about in the kitchen, that she did not love him. But it was early days. Perhaps that would come. Sophie thought she could learn to love anybody who could curl her toes the way Winston had. And he loved books, too. In a different way than she did, perhaps, but still. Sparks, she thought, trying not to think of Eric, were overrated.

"Good morning, my little Pekingese," said Winston, peeping into the bedroom.

"Really?" said Sophie. "That's my pet name? The name of an actual pet?"

"Well, it's just that you made noises last night I've only ever heard from my neighbor's puppy."

"Very funny," said Sophie, glad that the dimness of the room hid the deepness of her blush. "If you'll excuse me, I need to get dressed."

"I've got coffee and croissants when you're ready," said Winston, not moving from the doorway.

"Well, go drink your coffee," said Sophie, eying her clothes scattered across the floor.

"I was hoping to catch a glimpse."

"You caught your glimpse last night."

"It was dark last night."

"Go drink your coffee," said Sophie. If he didn't leave pretty soon, she was afraid she might try to drag him back to bed.

"**YOU'RE ALL DRESSED UP** for a Saturday morning," said Sophie as she sat at the kitchen table in her rumpled clothes from the night before. Winston was wearing a suit and tie and a perfectly pressed shirt.

"Big meeting for work," he said.

Sophie took a deep drink of coffee. She had already had one mug and polished off a croissant smothered in butter and jam. She was trying to decide if it would be unladylike to take another. Sex seemed to have given her quite an appetite. "So what is work?" she asked. "You know all about my job, but I don't know anything about yours."

"It's appropriate, I suppose," said Winston. "You work at one end of the book food chain and I work at the other. I'm a publisher."

"You're a publisher?" said Sophie. "Aren't you a little young to be a publisher?"

"It's not quite as impressive as it sounds," he said. "I worked with a big publishing company when I finished at university. Started out as an intern reading dreadful manuscripts and eventually worked my way up to editor, working with actual authors on actual books. It was OK, but I really wanted to get into the business side of publishing. So I saved some money, found a partner who knew as much about books as I did about pounds and pence, convinced my father to be an investor, and opened a tiny little house of my own a couple of years ago. We have three employees and we published nine books last year. My father says it's kind of like a hobby that doesn't lose too much money, but we're growing. Slowly."

"That's fantastic," said Sophie, reaching out for the last croissant. "I mean, the only thing I can imagine that might be as great as spending your days discovering old books is spending them creating new ones."

"It's very rewarding," said Winston. "At least in an 'I'm doing something interesting' sort of way. Not in a 'putting pounds into my bank account' sort of way."

"What sort of things do you publish?"

"So far, things only a few people buy. First novels of unknown writers, a couple of literary biographies. My partner picks everything; I just deal with printers and distributors, that sort of thing. We did publish one book you might have heard of. It was sort of a sequel to *Mansfield Park*. Everyone else is publishing *Pride and Prejudice* spin-offs, but Godfrey House has cornered the market on *Mansfield Park* spin-offs. It was called *Mansfield*."

"I've read that," said Sophie with delight. "I have a copy in my room at Oxford."

"Well, that was us," said Winston. "I guess I ought to read it."

"It was really good," she said. "Something to be proud of."

"I am, I suppose. But it all won't last much longer without either a best seller or an infusion of cash. That's why I'm all kitted out. I've got a lunch meeting with some potential investors. Now," he said, clearing away Sophie's empty plate and mug, "how would it be if I rang for a taxi to take you home?"

"That would be very gentlemanly," said Sophie.

"Oh please, don't accuse me of being a gentleman," said Winston. "Would a gentleman do this?" And he pulled her out of her chair and wrapped her in his arms and kissed her long and hard.

## *Hampshire, 1796*

**FOR TWO DAYS** rain fell steadily outside the windows of the rectory. Unable to play in the garden or run in the fields, Anna kept her aunts busy with constant demands for games and stories. Jane did not write, and she did not read any more of *First Impressions* to her niece and sister, but she thought about the Bennets and the other inhabitants of the story nearly constantly. When Anna was finally asleep on the second night of rain, Jane and Cassandra stole a few minutes in the dressing room to talk.

"Father believes the weather will clear tomorrow," said Cassandra. "I shall take Anna for a long walk so that you can work."

"I should like to pay a visit to Mr. Mansfield, if it does clear," said Jane. "After that I shall write."

"Is your friend quite well?" said Cassandra. "You have seemed distracted these two days since you saw him last."

"He is, I believe, as well as anyone of his age can rightfully expect to be. But it is not Busbury Park or Steventon or Deane that distracts me. My mind, I fear, has been dwelling at Longbourn, and Pemberley, and Meryton."

"Jane, are you courted by some gentleman unknown to me? I have never heard of any of those places."

"Courted?" said Jane with a laugh. "Indeed you might say I am courted, but not by a gentleman; rather by a story."

"The book you have been working on? The one you refuse to give us more than a page of?"

"I read you three full pages," said Jane. "And it is not a book yet. But it is well on its way."

"And will you read us more soon?" asked Cassandra in an eager voice.

"Indeed I shall, sister. But for now I shall retire. Little Anna has quite exhausted me."

"And will you not give me even a hint of how those few letters you read to us are to become a novel?" entreated Cassandra.

"There is one thing," said Jane, pausing in the doorway. "I have spent the better part of the afternoon trying to form a single sentence that would encapsulate the essence of the story."

"The opening line?"

"Precisely."

"Oh, Jane, you must tell me. I shall not sleep if you don't."

Jane had tried a number of different openings before it occurred to her that her words to Mr. Mansfield when he had first confessed to being mystified by the importance Lady Mary placed on the appearance of a wealthy single man in her cousin's neighborhood needed only slight alteration to provide the perfect beginning to her novel. "What do you think of this?" said Jane, assuming the air of a little girl giving a recitation. "It is a truth universally acknowledged, that a single man in possession of a good fortune, must be in want of a wife."

## *London, Present Day*

**SOPHIE WAS WORKING** the front of the shop Monday morning when the phone rang and she found herself again talking to Mr. Smedley.

"Still haven't solved the mystery?" he said. "I'm afraid you're making me angry."

"You asked me to find a book for you," said Sophie. "Sometimes that takes months or even years. Sometimes they never get found." The weekend's events had emboldened her. Why should she feel threatened by a strange man on the phone who wanted a worthless old book? She was going to find that elusive second edition, but not for this creep.

"But I am not your only customer for this particular book," said Mr. Smedley.

"What makes you say that?"

"Don't play games with me, Miss Collingwood," he spat, and suddenly lowering his voice, he added, "I assure you, you won't win."

Sophie's confidence suddenly evaporated. "How do you know my name?" she said, feeling cold.

"I know all about you . . . Sophie." He said her name with a hiss. "Why do you think I came to Boxhill's? Why do you think Winston Godfrey came there?"

Sophie began to shiver. "Mr. Smedley," she said, "if you have something you want to tell me, why don't you just tell me?"

"What I have to tell you is there's a reason I told Gusty to get his new girl to ferret out this particular book. If you don't find it soon, others will come to you, and they won't be as friendly as your little boyfriend."

"What do you know about my boyfriend?" said Sophie, finding the word distasteful. It seemed both too much and too little to describe what Winston was to her, but worse, the way Mr. Smedley used it, it sounded tawdry. And how the hell did he know about Winston anyway?

"The Chinese restaurant, Selfridges, these are public places. Did you really think you could keep your little dalliance a secret from me?" Sophie leaned against the counter, feeling dizzy. Her stomach jolted and she felt sweat begin to dampen her forehead. Had Smedley been tailing her? She had written him off as an eccentric collector, maybe a little aggressive, but basically harmless. But now it seemed he might pose a real threat to her safety, and perhaps to Winston's, too.

"You've been following me?" said Sophie, almost unable to breathe.

"Find that book, Miss Collingwood. You're the only one who can do it, now that your uncle is gone. And I'd hate to see you take your own tumble down the stairs." He rang off, but Sophie didn't know it. She had fallen to the floor in a faint.

**FOR A MOMENT,** Sophie thought it was Uncle Bertram's voice calling to her. All she could see were books and the silhouette of a man leaning over her. She had fallen asleep in the corner of a bookshop, a copy of *Alice's Adventures in Wonderland* propped on her knee. Uncle Bertram had been talking and talking to the bookseller about things Sophie did not understand, and, just like when she was at his flat and he read to her in Latin at bedtime, their words had lulled her to sleep.

"Come, my little Sophie," he said, slipping his arms around her and picking her up. "I've made you do too much walking round London for a nine-year-old. Let's get you some tea."

"I don't mind walking," she said when Uncle Bertram had set her down on the pavement outside the shop. "It was just that I was reading about a dream and your voices were like Alice's sister in the book."

"Well, it's true," said her uncle with a chuckle, "that we were talking about a book with no pictures or conversations in it."

"Did you buy it?" asked Sophie.

"Not today," he said. "I'm afraid it was too expensive for my budget."

"What makes a book valuable, Uncle Bertram?"

"An excellent question," he said, taking her hand and guiding her down the street toward the nearest café. "There are two kinds of valuable. A book might have special value to me that it wouldn't have to anyone else. For instance, the old family prayer book at your father's house. It's not a rare edition and it's got a loose cover and a lot of torn pages. Nobody would pay much for that at a bookshop. But to our family, it's irreplaceable. It has our history in it—not just in the baptisms and marriages and burials listed in the front, but in every tear and every smudge. So that book is valuable."

"But what about the book you wanted to buy today?"

"Ah, that's a very different matter. That's a book that is *expensive*, which is not quite the same as valuable."

"What was it?"

"It was an early edition of a very important English translation of a book called *Plutarch's Lives*. In other words, it's a very old book about history."

"That doesn't sound very interesting," said Sophie.

"Ah, but interesting and valuable and expensive are all different," said Uncle Bertram. "A book can be interesting or valuable to one person and not to another, but an expensive book is expensive for all of us."

"And why was the Pluto book so expensive?"

"Plutarch," said her uncle, ushering her into the café and settling in at a table. "Well, it's expensive for several reasons. First, it's an important book. Plutarch was one of the great historians of the ancient world. And this particular translation is important, because it's the one Shakespeare used to research some of his plays."

"Shakespeare, like A *Midsummer Night's Dream* in the park last summer?" said Sophie.

"That's right."

"He's funny," she said.

Uncle Bertram dosed a cup of tea generously with milk and sugar and handed it to Sophie, who took a long drink.

"So, the book I was looking at today was historically important and it had an important literary connection to a famous author. Those things made it valuable. What made it expensive was that it was in very good condition, added to a simple equation."

"Equations like math?" said Sophie. "I hate math."

"This is simple math," said her uncle. "It's called supply and demand. If there are not very many copies of a book but there are lots of people who would like to have one, then the book will be expensive. A book can be valuable without being expensive, but it's not likely to be expensive without being valuable."

"So if there was a book that only had one copy," said Sophie, "and everybody in the world wanted it, that book would be expensive!"

"It certainly would," said Bertram.

"**SOPHIE! SOPHIE, ARE YOU** all right?" She realized that this voice was not Uncle Bertram's, that she was not nine years old, and that she had not fallen asleep.

"Is that you, Gusty?" she managed to say softly.

"What happened?" said Gusty, his voice tinged with panic. "I heard a bump and I found you passed out on the floor."

Sophie hoisted herself up on an elbow, feeling dizzy and a little queasy. "I guess I didn't get enough breakfast," she said.

Gusty helped her into a sitting position and pulled a box of books behind her so she could lean against it. "You stay there, while I get you some water." He disappeared downstairs and Sophie concentrated on breathing for a minute. She tried not to think about Smedley or anything he had said. There would be time for that later. For now she breathed in the aroma of old books and worn floorboards and it worked better than any smelling salts. By the time Gusty was back from the basement, Sophie had pulled herself up from the floor and was sitting in a chair behind the counter.

"I told you not to move," he said, handing her a glass of water.

"I'm OK, really," said Sophie. "It was just low blood sugar." Smedley's warning about not talking to Gusty had suddenly returned to her mind.

"Have one of these," said Gusty, holding out a packet of digestive biscuits. The last thing she wanted to do was eat, but he insisted, and she did feel a little steadier after a glass of water and a biscuit. "You need to go home and get some rest," he said. "Take the rest of the day off."

"That might be a good idea," said Sophie. "I think I'll go home and try to sleep, if that's OK."

He wouldn't hear of her taking the tube home, so he closed the shop, walked her out to St. Martin's Lane, hailed a taxi, and gave the cabbie a twenty-pound note and instructions to see Sophie safely to her door. Thirty minutes later, locked in her flat, sitting in a room of empty bookshelves, she finally allowed herself to relive Mr. Smedley's phone call.

It seemed the suspicions about Uncle Bertram's death that she'd fought so hard to shake may have been right after all, and that somehow that crime—if it was a crime—was tangled up in the mystery of *A Little Book of Allegorical Stories*. Smedley had used that word: *mystery*. Sophie had always wanted to find herself in the midst of a mystery and now she was—but this wasn't like curling up in Uncle Bertram's sitting room with a volume of Wilkie Collins or Agatha Christie on a cold winter night. This was real.

"There are two things you need to know about mysteries," Uncle Bertram had said one night as they settled in for *Murder on the Orient Express*. "If there is a sword on the wall in the first chapter, someone is going to take it down and use it in the last chapter."

"I don't think there's going to be a sword on a train," said Sophie, who, at eleven, was starting to discover the joys of challenging adult authority.

"There isn't always one," said Uncle Bertram gently. "And it isn't always a sword. It could be a hunting rifle or a cricket bat."

"What's the other thing?" asked Sophie.

"Beware of red herrings."

"I don't like herring."

"Red herrings aren't fish," said her uncle. "They are false clues. A red herring will lead you down the wrong path every time."

But now Sophie had no idea what were the swords on the wall and what were the red herrings. Did it matter that Winston was looking for the same book as Smedley, or was that just a coincidence? Winston had a perfectly good reason for wanting Mansfield's second edition, so she could set him aside for now. He was a red herring. What did she know about Smedley? Almost nothing. There were no swords hanging on that wall. Why had she been chosen to find this particular book? That certainly wasn't chance; Smedley had said as much. Was Sophie herself a sword on the wall?

She pulled out a sheet of paper and wrote down a series of questions:

**Why me?**

**Why now?**

**Why this book?**

**Why two different collectors?**

She paused for a moment, holding the pen over the paper, and finally allowed her mind to return to Mr. Smedley's final, chilling proclamation: "I'd hate to see you take your own tumble down the stairs." At the top of the list, in capital letters, she wrote:

***WHAT HAPPENED TO UNCLE BERTRAM?***

In the excitement of being courted by Winston, she had almost forgotten about the inquest report that still lay in her uncle's desk drawer. Now she returned to those stark pages knowing that her suspicions about her uncle's death were based on something more than paranoia and shock. On top of the neat stack of pages, where she had left it, was the inventory of personal items recovered from her uncle's body.

Were there any clues in this generic list? The only thing that set Uncle Bertram apart from any other dead male body was the presence of a book—and for him it would have been more unusual if he hadn't been carrying one. And that thought made Sophie pause to consider—what *didn't* he have with him?

It was easy to think of things that weren't on the list. Everything else he owned was not on the list. But she did her best to channel Hercule Poirot. How would he approach the problem? She had left Uncle Bertram's apartment with him a thousand times. What did he take along?

**"ARE YOU READY?"** called Sophie down the hall, eager to be on their way. Uncle Bertram had decided that, at thirteen, Sophie was old enough to go to a book auction, and she was worried they would be late.

"You realize the book I'm bidding on is lot 375," said Bertram. "It won't come up for at least three hours."

"But I want to see it all," said Sophie.

"You want to see it all," he repeated. "Why am I not surprised? Well, just let me see that I have everything. Has it stopped raining?"

"The sun is out," she said, bouncing with impatience.

"No umbrella, then. Do you have a book to read?"

"Don't ask silly questions," said Sophie. "Of course I do."

"And of course I do, too. I have my hat, I have my auction catalog, I have my wallet, and I have my niece."

"Let's go, let's go."

"Right," said Uncle Bertram. "Off we go." He picked up his keys from the bowl by the front door, and they were on their way.

Sophie looked back at the list. His keys. If Uncle Bertram had been going out, why didn't he have his keys?

## *Hampshire, 1796*

**AFTER HER TWO DAYS'** confinement at the rectory, the weather did clear, and despite the mud through which she was forced to walk, Jane, having taken an early luncheon, arrived at the gatehouse of Busbury Park just after midday. To her surprise, she found the house a hive of activity. The front door stood open, a large trunk stood on the floor of the sitting room, and into this the housekeeper was just placing a small parcel of books. Mr. Mansfield came tottering down the stairs with a heavy coat over his arms.

"I shall wear this, Mrs. Harris, so you needn't worry about fitting it in the trunk. Now if I can only find my . . . ah, Miss Austen," he said, noticing Jane in the doorway. "I had hoped you might come today so I could say good-bye."

"Good-bye, Mr. Mansfield? What gives you need to say good-bye?"

"It's my curate, I'm afraid. He has written to say he has been presented with a living and will be leaving me within the fortnight. I must return to Croft until I can secure a replacement."

"But surely such matters could be handled by post," said Jane.

"I am afraid, Miss Austen, that the hiring of a curate to serve my parish is not something I take lightly. One must meet the candidates face-to-face. Do not worry. I shall not be gone for more than a month. Oh dear, I'm afraid I have forgotten my boots."

Mr. Mansfield was just turning to go back upstairs when Mrs. Harris called out. "I've packed them for you, sir, not to fear."

"I do believe," he said, turning to Jane again, "that I should quite forget to take my head with me if it were not for Mrs. Harris. Sudden departures do not befit eighty-year-olds."

Jane felt a chill as her friend turned to inspect the contents of the trunk. Sudden departures, she thought, await us all, especially those of such an advanced age as Mr. Mansfield.

"I have heard again from Mr. Monkhouse, Miss Austen," he said. "He proposes to print my second edition before Christmas. Once I have unpacked I shall go over to Leeds and deliver my manuscript in person."

"And how," said Jane with a smile, "do you propose to do that?"

"I'm afraid I do not follow you, Miss Austen. Though no doubt there has been some rain in the north, the road to Leeds is generally quite passable at this time of year."

"I only meant, Mr. Mansfield, that you might find it difficult to deliver to a printer in Leeds a manuscript, part of which lies on the writing table of your friend in Hampshire."

"The manuscript!" cried Mr. Mansfield. "I knew I had forgotten something. Is there time for me to stop by the rectory and still make the coach?"

"Mr. Mansfield, you needn't—" began Jane, but her friend was too flustered to listen.

"Here is the revised portion," he said, pulling a sheaf of papers out of his trunk and then plunging them back again. "But how foolish of me—the new material is—"

"Is right here," said Jane calmly, holding out the pages of *First Impressions*. "I had come to tell you that my vision of how to turn this cautionary tale into a full-length novel is now fully formed, and I no longer require your pages."

"Oh, Miss Austen, bless you," said Mr. Mansfield. "What should I do without you?"

"You should perhaps get more sleep and be less flustered and always know the locations of your manuscripts."

"Foolish, foolish girl," he said, turning to look at her. He seemed in an instant to age a decade, and the sparkle in his eyes dulled as he took her by the hand. "I shall miss you terribly," he said.

Jane trembled at the touch of his hand, and wanted desperately to find a way to tell him what she had discovered in Kent the last time they had been separated—that she loved him. But though that love was engraved on her heart, she did not have the words to explain its nature. For Jane to lack for words was only evidence of the depths of her emotion. Squeezing his hand in hers and hoping that small gesture might somehow do what words could not, she said softly, "When do you leave?"

"The gig arrives any moment to take me to the London coach. But come—sit with me while I wait and keep me company."

"Nothing would give me greater pleasure," said Jane. "I shall write to you, while you are gone," she added as they settled into their usual chairs.

"I would rather you spend your ink on the Bennet family," said Mr. Mansfield. "So that I may learn more of them on my return. I must admit, though, it is your companionship, more than anything, that will lure me back to Hampshire."

"I shall count the days," said Jane, "though I do not know how many they will be. Can it be only four months since we met? It seems I have always known you."

"And how strange," said Mr. Mansfield, "to remember what our thoughts were that first day . . ."

"When we formed such false impressions of one another," she said, finishing his thought.

"And on that Sunday when we first spoke," he said, "you said you wished to have me as your special friend. I certainly did not guess what a gift that would be." They sat for a moment without speaking. Jane was struck with how very old Mr. Mansfield's eyes looked. She was so used to thinking of him as an equal that she felt she had never truly comprehended the reality of his age.

"I am afraid this journey will be wearying to me," he said.

"Do take care of yourself," said Jane. "And come back to me."

"I shall," he said, and he reached for her hand and kissed it gently with his dry lips. They continued to talk until the gig arrived a few minutes later and Mr. Mansfield was forced to make his departure. Jane watched as the gig disappeared down the lane.

"Cup of tea before you go?" said Mrs. Harris, who stood in the doorway wiping her hands on her apron.

"No, thank you," said Jane firmly, brushing a tear from her eye. "I have work to do."

## *London, Present Day*

"WHAT ARE YOU SAYING?" asked Victoria.

"I'm saying that I was right," said Sophie. "It wasn't an accident. Uncle Bertram was killed." She had rung her sister as soon as she realized about the missing keys. "The police couldn't get into the flat until they came back with Father and his keys *six hours* after they found the body. The only way to lock the door to the flat is with the keys, but Uncle Bertram's keys were *inside* the flat. That must mean someone came to the flat, Uncle Bertram opened the door, the killer grabbed him and threw him down the stairs, and then went into the flat and locked the door from the inside."

"So you're saying whoever pushed him down those stairs was *in* the flat when the police came," said Victoria.

"It's the only explanation," said Sophie.

"I'm sure it's not the *only* explanation."

"Gives me chills just thinking about it."

"So how did your mysterious murderer get out and still leave the door locked and the keys inside?" asked Victoria.

"I'm not sure," said Sophie, "but I think I know who it was."

"Seriously?"

"Have you got a few minutes?"

"Boss is out to lunch," said Victoria. "I've got at least an hour." So

Sophie told her everything about Richard Mansfield and his *Little Book of Allegorical Stories*, and the threatening phone calls from Smedley.

"I don't know why this book is so special," she said, "but Smedley wants it badly."

"Badly enough to kill?"

"He basically said as much," said Sophie. "I think he thought Uncle Bertram had a copy, he showed up, pushed Uncle Bertram down the stairs, hid in the flat until the police left, and still had three or four hours to search for the book."

"But he must not have found it," said Victoria, "or he wouldn't be hounding you."

"Exactly," said Sophie, pausing for a moment as the sobering truth sank in. "He killed Uncle Bertram for nothing."

"What the hell is so special about that book that somebody would kill for it?" said her sister, her voice wavering.

"No idea," said Sophie, gritting her teeth. "But I'll tell you one thing—I'm going to find that goddamn book, I'm going to use it to lure this Smedley out into the open, and I'm going to find a way to prove that he killed Uncle Bertram." Sophie did not share the thought that, much to her terror, leapt into her head at that moment—if she couldn't prove Smedley's guilt, she would do the next best thing: She would kill him.

She told her sister good-bye, walked to the window, looked out on the quiet street, and said aloud, "Now, time to get the son of a bitch."

**SHE WONDERED,** for a moment, if she should warn Winston. Smedley clearly knew that Winston was also looking for the Mansfield book, and even if Winston's reasons were indeed innocent, he might not be entirely safe. But was Winston innocent? If one person was willing to kill for Mansfield's book, why not two? Sophie shook that thought away and decided if she had to pick one of these men to trust, it would obviously be Winston. Maybe she could even use him as—what did the American crime dramas call it?—backup.

She looked at the list of questions she had drawn up. She thought she knew the answer to the first one, "What happened to Uncle Bertram." That left four more:

**Why me?**

**Why now?**

**Why this book?**

**Why two different collectors?**

The question that mattered most, she thought, was the third one: Why this book? Answer that and she might be able to answer the others. She had to find the second edition of *A Little Book of Allegorical Stories*.

She knew that her uncle had not shared his literary life with anyone else in the family; it was unlikely that Sophie's parents would have the first idea about the location of what they would see as some worthless old book. The only person she knew who might have some insight into the mystery was Gusty, and she needed to ring him anyway, to let him know she was OK.

"I'm feeling much better, really," Sophie said in answer to Gusty's queries about her health. "I had a little something to eat and took a nap," she lied, "and I'm right as rain."

"You need to take better care of yourself," scolded Gusty. "What would your Uncle Bertram think if he knew I was letting you faint dead away on the floor of my bookshop?"

"Gusty," she said, "could I ask you a question about Uncle Bertram?"

"Of course, my dear."

"Do you know if he had any secret hiding places? You know, for special books?"

"Secret hiding places?" said Gusty. "Well, if he did he never told me about them. Your uncle believed that books belonged on shelves, where he could see them and read them and love them. He would have something worth a thousand pounds sitting next to a tattered paperback. No, I'm sorry to say the only place your uncle hid books, so far as I know, was in plain sight."

"Do you mind if I take a few days off, Gusty?" said Sophie, already planning her next step. "I have to clear a few things out of my room in Oxford before the end of the month." This, at least, was true.

"And by a few things I suppose you mean your books."

"Naturally," she said, smiling for the first time since Smedley's call.

"Take as long as you need."

Sophie thought it was unlikely she would uncover any hiding places in Uncle Bertram's flat. Smedley had had hours to look for Mansfield's book and he hadn't found it. Nonetheless, a thorough search of the flat was the first order of business. She turned over the mattresses and pulled cushions out of chairs and sofas. She knocked on the back panels of kitchen cabinets to check for hidden compartments. In her uncle's bedroom she discovered an unlocked window that opened right next to a large drainpipe. Doubtless Smedley had climbed down this to make his escape. She locked the window and continued her search.

An hour later she had found nothing. She sat on Uncle Bertram's bed staring at the shelf where his *Natalis Christi* books had stood. Now, only one book occupied the shelf—the *Principia* she had stolen. Smedley's threats and Winston's attentions had pushed the loss of those precious Christmas books from her mind, but now, as she sat defeated in Uncle Bertram's bedroom, she thought that shelf looked emptier than any other in the flat.

Her search of her uncle's desk had revealed only writing paper and pens and a few empty file folders. She had pulled the drawers completely out of the desk to check for anything hidden behind them, but had felt nothing but bare wood as she ran her hands inside those dark openings. Now she dragged herself back to the sitting room and started returning the drawers to their proper places. She was just about to insert the lower left drawer when she felt something on its underside. She turned the drawer over and expelled a sharp breath. Taped to the bottom was a copy of Uncle Bertram's business card, and taped to the card was a small key.

Sophie knew at once that this was the key to the cabinets in the Bayfield House library. She had seen her uncle withdraw it from his silk waistcoat pocket when he strode into the library to select his Christmas book. She slipped the key into her pocket—glad to have it, but still not sure what it meant for her search.

She took another look at the business card. Her uncle had rarely discussed his career with Sophie, but she knew he had worked for an accounting firm in the West End. "It means I can prowl the bookshops on my lunch hour," he had said. She wondered if it would be any help to ring the firm where he had worked. She absentmindedly flipped the card over and her eyes widened. On the other side, in Uncle Bertram's handwriting, was a cryptic message:

*NC 1971 Bulwer-Lytton*

NC must *certainly* mean *Natalis Christi*. But Sophie was almost positive Uncle Bertram had chosen the first of his Christmas books in 1972. She ran to his bedroom and pulled the *Principia* off the shelf. The inscription read "*Natalis Christi* B.A.C. 1972." There was no *Natalis Christi* 1971. Uncle Bertram had told her that the *Principia* had been the first book he had chosen. Or had he?

"My father died during my first year at university," he had said, "and when your father and I made our deal, I knew that I wanted this book." He had been speaking of the *Principia*; but she now realized he hadn't said it had been his first pick, only that he knew he wanted it. Something else he said that day suddenly bubbled up in her mind. When Sophie had asked if he had known what book he wanted the first time he got to choose, Uncle Bertram had said, "Especially the very first time. Remember that." Why did he want her to remember? Did he know that one day she would be searching for *Natalis Christi* 1971?

Sophie knew the contents of the *Natalis Christi* shelf like old friends. *Principia* had always been the first book. Not only that, but Uncle Bertram had loathed Bulwer-Lytton.

"Even *The Last Days of Pompeii*?" asked Sophie as they sat at breakfast one morning. At fifteen, she was going through a stage of being fascinated with salacious literature, and *The Last Days of Pompeii* had seemed deliciously sexy.

"Especially *The Last Days of Pompeii*," said Uncle Bertram.

"But why?" asked Sophie.

"We all have our personal tastes, my dear." She had noticed that, while Uncle Bertram would tell her if he didn't like a book she was reading, he would never tell her exactly why. She supposed he wanted to let her form her own opinions, but she wanted to understand his, so she pressed him.

"You can't expect me to learn about great literature if you won't tell me why you think something *isn't* great," she said.

"Very well," said her uncle, laying his *Essays of Elia* on the table. "You are a lover of great first lines, correct?"

"Yes," said Sophie.

"And what is your favorite?"

"*Pride and Prejudice*—you know that," she said.

"As perfect an opening line as you will find in English literature. Now, at the other end of the spectrum, we have Mr. Bulwer-Lytton."

"What do you mean?"

"Your friend," said Uncle Bertram, nodding at Sophie's copy of *The Last Days of Pompeii* on the table, "is responsible for the most criminally horrendous opening line in all of English literature."

"What is it?" asked Sophie, leaning forward eagerly.

Uncle Bertram affected a spooky voice and intoned, "It was a dark and stormy night." He scowled at his niece and then burst out laughing.

"It's not so very horrible," said Sophie, who, honestly, did think it was a pretty wretched first line when compared to Austen or Dickens.

"As I said, my dear," he said, picking up his Charles Lamb, "you are entitled to your opinion and I am entitled to mine."

And knowing Uncle Bertram's opinion, Sophie could not comprehend why he would have chosen Bulwer-Lytton as a *Natalis Christi* book. And even if he had, why had it never been on the shelf with the others? And what could it possibly have to do with Richard Mansfield?

Sophie was finally forced to admit that the search of Uncle Bertram's flat had been fruitless. If he had possessed the Richard Mansfield book, it was long gone now. But if Smedley had murdered Uncle Bertram and stayed behind in the flat, then he had certainly searched through Uncle Bertram's books without finding *A Little Book of Allegorical Stories*. Yet he had still approached Sophie thinking that she was the one person who could find the book. What could that mean?

She sat down at her uncle's desk, and her eye fell on the little golden key that had been taped to his business card. Was it possible that Richard Mansfield was hiding in the library of Bayfield House? It seemed unlikely, but Sophie could think of no other place to search. A moment later she had her father on the phone.

"I thought I might come up for dinner and maybe spend the night," she said.

"Your mother would like that, I'm sure," said Mr. Collingwood.

"Father, when did Grandfather die?" asked Sophie, still puzzled by the mystery of the first *Natalis Christi* book.

"Why this sudden interest in family history?" he asked.

"Well, Uncle Bertram's books are all gone, so stories are all I have left," said Sophie, unable to resist twisting the knife just a bit. But her father seemed not to notice.

"It was in February the year after I married your mother," said Mr. Collingwood. "So it must have been 1971."

So perhaps there had been a *Natalis Christi* 1971. Uncle Bertram had been nineteen. Was it possible that he was still as fascinated by Bulwer-Lytton then as Sophie had been at fifteen? Did he later hate Bulwer-Lytton because he had wasted a precious Christmas choice on something like *The Last Days of Pompeii*? It didn't really matter, Sophie decided. What mattered was finding the Mansfield book and somehow using it to prove that Smedley was a killer. Five minutes later Sophie had packed an overnight bag and was stepping out the door on the way to Paddington Station. She met the postman in the stairwell and he handed her the post. Something to read on the train, she thought as she strode toward the station. In her rush she had forgotten to bring a book.

**THE POST CONTAINED FOUR** book catalogs, two advertising circulars, and yet another letter from Eric. She did not open it until she was comfortably seated on the five-fifteen for Kingham.

**Dear Sophie,**

**I suppose you are growing tired of getting letters from Paris from that rude American who accosted you by the river. I promise this will be the last, because I don't think I can take much more of Paris. It's not that the French are rude (although the few French I have encountered aren't exactly polite). It's something that makes this letter difficult for me to write. I finally figured out last night, sitting alone by the Seine and looking up at Notre Dame, why I hate Paris. You aren't here. I miss you Sophie. I know that's probably not what you want to hear, but I had to say it. The fact is, I'm giving up on Florence and coming back to England. I need to see you, and I need to see if there was more to that kiss than I thought at the time. You probably think I'm an ass, but anyway, this ass is coming to find you and hoping you'll give him a second (or is it third by now) chance.**

**Affectionately (that's how Jane Austen signed her letters),**

**Eric**

Sophie read the letter over three times, feeling more and more guilty about the thrill it gave her. Just reading it felt like cheating on Winston; *enjoying* reading it was even worse. But she couldn't help herself. She still wasn't sure how she felt about Eric, but the thought that he was coming back to England to see her left her a little breathless. She had just stowed the letter in her handbag and was turning to the catalogs when her phone rang.

"Where are you?" asked Winston. "I stopped by the shop and Gusty said you were sick and when I rang the flat there was no answer."

"I'm fine," said Sophie. "I'm on the train. I'm going up to Oxford to get my things."

"I could meet you there," said Winston. "We could spend the night. Take a room at the Randolph; I could show you all my old haunts."

"Can you afford a room at the Randolph?" asked Sophie, who slumped a little deeper into her seat as she imagined a night with Winston in the freshly laundered sheets of Oxford's finest hotel.

"Not exactly," he said, "but don't you have a room?"

"I have a room with a very narrow single bed."

"I'm sure we could come to some sort of arrangement."

"You never told me you were at Oxford," said Sophie, changing the subject before she weakened further and agreed to let him come meet her.

"I read economics at St. John's," he said. "Longer ago than I care to think."

"Yes, you're *so* old," she teased. "Much too old for me, I imagine."

"So shall I meet you at the Eagle and Child around eight?"

"I'm actually going home for the night," said Sophie. "To my parents', that is."

"I could come up tomorrow," said Winston. "We could take a punt out, maybe have a picnic in the meadow."

It was a glorious vision, but Sophie would not be distracted from her quest. "Not this time," she said. "I have too much work to do cleaning out my room. I'll call you, though. And maybe when I get back to town we could . . ." She left her sentence unfinished, but they both knew what she meant.

"We certainly could," said Winston.

## *Hampshire, 1796*

**NOVEMBER HAD FADED** into December and Christmas was on the horizon. Jane had worked several hours a day on the new and much expanded version of *First Impressions*. In the afternoons she read from her newly completed pages to Cassandra and Anna—a habit which further motivated her to write more pages each day. She did not breathe a word about the impending publication of the story from which her novel had been taken, nor did her sister ask about why that story had been written in someone else's hand.

Two weeks after his departure, she had written hastily to Mr. Mansfield:

**_Steventon, November 23, 1796_**

**My Dear Mr. Mansfield,**

**I have shared _First Impressions_ only with Cassandra and my niece Anna, to whom I read each afternoon. Anna, I'm afraid, is so excited about the story that she keeps mentioning the names of Eliza Bennet and Mr. Darcy downstairs in the sitting room, and I'm sure the other occupants of the rectory must be filled with curiosity, but so far your little project**

**remains, for the most part, a secret. I look forward to your return.**

**Yours very affectionately,**

**J. Austen**

**RICHARD MANSFIELD HAD NOT** slept well since his arrival in Yorkshire. The air was cold and the rectory drafty, and his body ached after being jangled for three days in coaches, but these were not the reasons for his insomnia. Even the search for a curate had occupied much less of his time and concern than he had feared. The son of one of the local landowners had lately completed his studies at Oxford and came recommended by both his tutors and the bishop. No, what occupied the mind of Richard Mansfield was Tobias Mansfield, known to his drinking companions, of whom he had many, as Toby. Tobias was Richard's only son and his greatest disappointment. The boy's mother had died when he was only three, in a failed attempt to bring a second child into the world, and since that day all of Richard's hopes had been invested in his son. He had sent him to Westminster School and Christ Church, Oxford, in hopes that Tobias would follow in his father's footsteps, but his son had let him down at every turn. At Oxford he drank with the toffs more often than he visited his tutors. After only a year he left that establishment in the company of those whom he called friends and had spent more than two decades bounding from one country house to another, living off his acquaintances, drinking, playing cards, and . . . Richard shuddered to think what else. On rare occasions Toby found himself between friends and only then did he return to his father, not for love or counsel, but only to ask for a "loan"—monies Richard always gave and Tobias never repaid.

Richard had returned to Croft to find Tobias had been an unwelcome guest at the rectory for several days. He knew that Tobias would leave as soon as his financial stability was secured, and so, because he feared these might be the last days he ever spent with his son, he had delayed making the loan for nearly two weeks. Tobias did not suffer this delay patiently, and, rather than cherishing these days spent with an aged father, he spent his hours in loud complaint—about the meanness of the meals, about the hardness of his bed, and most of all about his father's total lack of need for the nearly one thousand pounds a year brought to him by the Croft living. With such a troublesome guest, Richard found it difficult to conduct his business, and impossible to indulge in those recreations he so craved—reading a good novel and corresponding with Miss Austen. Though he realized full well that not all boys grow up to be like Tobias and not all girls grow up to be like Jane, he wished, when lying in bed on those sleepless nights, that he had had a daughter. And on the last night before he finally resolved to give Tobias a banker's draft and see him off, he went even further—he wished that Tobias were not his son and that Jane were his daughter. He regretted that he had not told her just how much he loved her.

"I take the midday coach to London, Father," said Toby, who sprawled in front of the drawing room fire, his muddy boots propped on the fender. "I cannot wait much longer." In his hand, Toby held a sheaf of papers that had been sitting on a table near the fire. Richard planned to deliver the manuscript of his revised and expanded little book to Gilbert Monkhouse as soon as he was rid of Tobias. In his sleeplessness the night before, he had stoked the fire in the drawing room and read *First Impressions* again.

"What is this nonsense?" said Toby, waving the papers in his hand. Richard felt a flash of anger toward his son.

"A story for the new edition of my book. Did you read it?"

"Enough of it to know that it's rubbish and a waste of your time," said Toby.

Richard could bear it no longer. He feared he would lash out at his son and speak words he would live to regret—and if those words were the last he ever spoke to his own flesh and blood, well, better that he pay the boy and be done with it. He reached into his coat pocket, pulled out the banker's draft he had written earlier that morning, and held it out to Tobias.

"Now that," said his son, snatching the draft away, "is a worthy use of pen and paper."

"Will you come to morning service with me?" said Richard, knowing the answer. Whenever in residence at the rectory he always read the daily offices at the church.

"Perhaps I shall see you afterwards," said Tobias. But Richard knew he would not see him afterwards. He knew that when he returned his son would be gone and he would likely never see him again.

**THAT AFTERNOON,** Mr. Mansfield traveled to Leeds and handed the manuscript of *Little Allegories and a Cautionary Tale* to Gilbert Monkhouse with instructions that a proof copy be sent to him at Busbury Park. On his return to Croft the following day, he searched the shelves in his study and found his only remaining copy of the first edition of *A Little Book of Allegorical Stories.* Opening it to the first blank page, he wrote: "To J.A. Judge not too harshly, but like me reserve First Impressions for second editions. Affectionately, R.M." Besides the book and a few personal items, there would be little else to pack. His new curate had arrived the previous week and seemed to have matters well in hand. It was time to return south.

## *Oxfordshire, Present Day*

**TRAIN TRAVEL MADE SOPHIE** feel romantic—she supposed it had begun with Agatha Christie's description of the Orient Express. As she rattled into the Cotswolds and gazed out at the green fields dotted with sheep, she felt torn in at least three directions: Her body ached for Winston; her heart fluttered when she thought of Eric; and her mind told her there was a very good chance they were both bad news. As the train pulled into Kingham, she shoved this quandary out of her mind. Finding that book, proving Smedley's guilt—these things were more important than her love life.

Her father had sent a taxi to meet her at the station and drive her to Bayfield House. Sophie arrived just as her mother was serving dinner.

"Sophie, do you know Mr. Tompkins?" said her father, when she had greeted her mother and dropped her bags in the corner of the kitchen.

A man in jeans and a white dress shirt stood and extended his hand to Sophie. "I don't believe I've had the pleasure," he said. "Gerard Tompkins."

Sophie suppressed a smile. He had, in fact, had the pleasure, she thought as she shook his hand, but she wasn't about to remind him that he was her uncle's least favorite bookseller or ask him if he had checked to be sure his copy of Newton's *Principia* was still on the shelf. She ought to be nervous facing a man she had stolen from; instead she felt powerful.

"Sophie Collingwood," she said. "What brings you to Bayfield House?" She slid into her seat, feeling sure she knew the answer.

"Your father is interested in thinning out the library a bit, now that—"

"Now that the opportunity presents itself," said Mr. Collingwood, interrupting Mr. Tompkins. "I've asked Mr. Tompkins to sift out some of the more valuable items so I can afford to fix the roof."

"What you mean," said Sophie, unable to stop herself, "is now that Uncle Bertram is reasonably cold, you're going to sell off our family history to the highest bidder, who no doubt is Mr. Tompkins here, judging from the ridiculous prices in his catalogs." She was feeling more justified every minute in having stolen the *Principia*.

"Sophie," said her father calmly, "if I don't raise some funds to repair this house, there won't be any library. It will become the victim of first the rainwater and then the bankruptcy court."

"You didn't get enough money from Uncle Bertram's library—which he'd intended to go to me, by the way?" Sophie was no longer making any attempt to keep her voice at a civilized level. "I'm sure Mr. Tompkins here got some gems from that sale. Are they selling well, Mr. Tompkins?" The bookseller did not answer, and Sophie took this as confirmation that he was both an ass and a fool—how could he not know that someone had stolen a fifteen-thousand-pound book?

"Sophie, I loved my brother," said Mr. Collingwood, "but he was not a responsible man. He left debts and the only way to pay those debts out of his estate was to sell his books. As it is I'll be several thousand pounds out of pocket by the time everything is settled."

"If you loved him, you never would have sold his books," said Sophie, rising from the table.

"Please, let's not argue," said Mrs. Collingwood. "Sophie, sit down and have some dinner."

"I'm not hungry," said Sophie, and she stomped out of the room.

Locked in her bedroom, she punched her pillow with anger and grief until she exhausted herself. Then she washed her face, brushed her teeth, and considered her next move. She would need the key to the library from the hook in the kitchen, and she would need privacy, so there was no point in stirring from her room until everyone was asleep.

But she had to strike as quickly as possible. The Bayfield House library, Uncle Bertram had once told her, contained nearly six thousand volumes, and tomorrow every one of them was a potential victim of the sword of Damocles that was the unscrupulous Mr. Tompkins. Sophie would have only a few hours to find the Mansfield book, if it was even there, and to make her escape. She sat in the chair by her window, looking into the garden, where the late-summer light was fading fast, and listened for the sound of her parents turning in. To pass the time, she started reading the catalogs that had come in that morning's post.

It was on the first page of a catalog from a dealer in Bath: "Austen, Jane. *Orgueil et Préjugés*, being the second French translation of *Pride and Prejudice*." The description fit Sophie's copy perfectly, right down to the nineteenth-century inscription: "Marie Bonnel, 1847." The price was fifteen hundred pounds. So, Eric had not found her gift for a song at a stall along the Seine. He hadn't even bought it in Paris. He must have gone to Bath after that scene in the garden—it would make sense for an Austen enthusiast. Jane Austen had lived in Bath for more than five years and had set important parts of her novels there. But it was one thing for a hitchhiking American to wander around Bath in the footsteps of Jane Austen; it was another for him to go into a bookshop and spend fifteen hundred pounds on a book for a girl he hardly knew. Was it a grand romantic gesture or something more sinister?

Before she could decide whether to be touched or disturbed by this new knowledge, she heard the door to her parents' room click shut. She cracked her own door and watched until the light under their door was extinguished. She waited another few minutes before creeping out of her room and down the stairs—stepping over the creaky fifth step as she and her sister had done so many times in childhood when sneaking downstairs for a late-night snack. Sophie went first to the kitchen, where the key to the library was hanging on the hook she had seen her father take it off of every Christmas. Finding a torch took a little longer, but she finally found one that worked on a high shelf in the laundry. She tiptoed down the long main corridor, past gloomy portraits of forgotten ancestors, until she reached the solid oak doors of the library. She unlocked a door, slipped inside, and locked the door behind her. Flipping on the torch, she shone it around the room. How could she have lived in a house with such a magnificent library and never been allowed access? How might her life have been different if she had spent her childhood and adolescence meeting the books on these shelves, curled up in front of the grand marble fireplace reading? What might she have become? She tried to comfort herself with the thought that if she had learned to love books here at Bayfield House, she might never have shared that part of her life with Uncle Bertram. He had been the one who introduced her to that world, and because of that he had been—well, she had never really named it before, but he had been, in a certain way, the love of her life.

It was quarter past midnight, and Sophie's father was an early riser. She figured she had about five hours to work—work made more difficult by the fact that she wasn't quite sure what she was looking for. Her uncle had left the key to the library cases with a cryptic note, and that might mean the Richard Mansfield book was here at Bayfield. Two different collectors had approached her and only her about the second edition, and *that* might mean the book was here at Bayfield. But a third and stronger possibility haunted her: There might be no second edition, here or anywhere else. There might be no way to prove Smedley was a killer, and furthermore, there might be no way to placate him and keep him from wanting to kill again. With this chilling thought, Sophie unlocked the case to the left of the fireplace and began her search.

She shone her torch across the spines and cursed the fact that she couldn't pull out every book to look at more closely. It was easy to skip over long sets of uniformly leather-bound volumes—*The Waverley Novels* or a long run of *Notes and Queries*—but as she moved to cases on the side of the room, away from the fireplace, the decorative sets disappeared, and every volume looked tantalizing. She knew the approximate size of the first edition of *A Little Book of Allegorical Stories*, but she also knew there was something different about the second edition, so she couldn't assume anything. She supposed she ought to be looking for books by Bulwer-Lytton, too, but thanks to Uncle Bertram's aversion, she had no idea what they looked like—her teenage infatuation had been limited to a paperback of *The Last Days of Pompeii*. Many of the older books had no titles on the spines, and Sophie's search was slowed by having to pull volumes off the shelves and flip to their title pages. She cringed to think that so many of these volumes—books she would love to use to populate Uncle Bertram's shelves—were soon to be lost, but she didn't dare steal more than what she needed to accomplish the job of entrapping Smedley. She wanted her father and Mr. Tompkins to be ignorant of the theft.

On a low shelf behind a sofa, Sophie found a battered copy of *The Book of Common Prayer* dated 1760. The front cover was barely attached and on the endpaper was a list of names headed "Baptisms." At the bottom of the list Sophie saw her grandfather's name: "Henry George Collingwood, December 3, 1928." She was just about to put the book back on the shelf when her eye caught a name, and a piece of the puzzle suddenly fell into place. Perhaps she *was* looking in the right place. Perhaps there was a very good reason why the Bayfield library should house a copy of *A Little Book of Allegorical Stories.*

An entry partway down the page read: "Sarah Monkhouse, daughter of Gilbert Monkhouse and Theresa Monkhouse née Wright. Baptized December 14, 1798." Sophie read through the entire list and confirmed her suspicion. She was descended from a printer named Thomas Wright, but she was also descended from Thomas's son-in-law, who was none other than Gilbert Monkhouse, the man who had printed the first edition of Mansfield's book. It was not surprising that both men were printers. What could be more natural than for an apprentice to fall in love with the master's daughter? Uncle Bertram had told Sophie that the family library began with a printer retaining copies of the books he had printed for others. It all made sense now. Smedley would only have had to do a little genealogical research to discover that Sophie was descended from the printer of Mansfield's book. A tour of Bayfield House would probably reveal the information that the library had begun as a collection of printer's samples. Smedley had assumed the book was either in Bertram's library or at Bayfield House. He had killed Uncle Bertram and searched his flat without success. His next logical step was to search Bayfield, but that was not so easy. So, why not threaten the young bibliophile in the family so she would do the job for him? But she still could not imagine why the second edition of a painfully dull book of allegories merited all this cloak-and-dagger intrigue.

That Smedley would stalk her, researching her family background, seemed not just creepy but nefarious. However, Winston might have done the same thing—yet in his case it seemed charming. Maybe the memory of sex with Winston was clouding her judgment, but his desire for *A Little Book of Allegorical Stories* seemed like nothing more than the bit of fate that had brought them together.

She returned *The Book of Common Prayer* to the shelf and continued her search. She felt much more sure, now, that the Mansfield book was in the library, and lacking any other clues, she began to focus on searching for Bulwer-Lytton. The light of dawn had been peeking through the cracks in the bolted shutters for some time when she found, on the top shelf of the west wall, a copy of *The Last Days of Pompeii*. Certain that it must contain the next clue from Uncle Bertram, she pulled it from the shelf. It was not even a first edition—just an ordinary copy that had clearly been read many times. It had no inscription, no marginalia, no bookmarks or notes slipped in between the pages.

She wanted more than anything to hurl that book across the room, but she didn't dare make a sound. She replaced it and sat on the floor. She had searched barely half of the library, and who knew what Mr. Tompkins would discover and cart away in the course of the day now dawning? If she did not find the second edition soon, she probably never would. Her mind was blurry from lack of sleep, but she pulled Uncle Bertram's card out of her jeans pocket and stared at it once again.

*NC 1971 Bulwer-Lytton*

What had her uncle told her about Bulwer-Lytton? All she could remember was that one conversation about the worst opening line in English literature: "It was a dark and stormy night." The answer struck Sophie with the force of a thunderclap at the exact moment that she heard footsteps upstairs. Knowing that she probably had no more than a few minutes, she scrambled back onto the library ladder and perused the shelf next to *The Last Days of Pompeii*. There were several other equally worn copies of Bulwer-Lytton novels. At the end of the shelf, she found what she was looking for: *Paul Clifford*.

The footsteps upstairs had become louder. Whoever was up was now wearing shoes and would probably be coming downstairs any second. She had to return the key to the kitchen before anyone discovered it was gone. Taking the book with her, and hoping that she was right, she left the library, carefully relocking the door. She slipped off her shoes and rushed to the kitchen in her stocking feet. Her handbag and overnight bag were still by the door, where she had left them. She returned the key to the hook, slipped *Paul Clifford* into her handbag, and had just put on her shoes when her father and Mr. Tompkins came into the room.

"Sophie, good morning," said her father. "I trust you're feeling better."

Sophie could not look at him but replied in as cheerful a voice as she could manage. "Much better, thank you. I'm sorry about last night. Still dealing with the shock of Uncle Bertram, I think."

"We all are, my dear," said her father. "We all are. Mr. Tompkins here is an early riser like myself."

"Hard to sleep when a treasure trove awaits," said Mr. Tompkins in a voice that was perfectly pleasant but that, to Sophie, sounded like a slobbering wolf's.

"I thought I might pop down to Oxford and clean out my room," said Sophie. "I have to vacate by the end of the month. Do you mind if a borrow a car?"

"Not at all," said her father. "Take the Vauxhall. They keys are hanging by the door. Have you had some breakfast?"

"Yes," Sophie lied. "I had some tea and toast." She was turning to leave when a thought occurred to her. "Father, Uncle Bertram once told me that there is an old family prayer book in the library with the baptism dates of all the family in it. Do you think perhaps you could save that for me?"

"Of course, dear," said Mr. Collingwood. "I'm not trying to sell off the family history; I'm not even trying to empty the library. I'm just trying to keep Bayfield solvent."

"I understand," said Sophie softly. And though it broke her heart, she did.

"I'll keep an eye out and set it aside for you," said Mr. Tompkins.

She tossed her bags in the Vauxhall and pulled away from the house. Halfway down the long gravel drive she stopped the car and fell against the steering wheel as she thought of Mr. Tompkins carting away treasures from Bayfield House.

She wanted more than anything to burst out sobbing—to cry the tears she hadn't been able to cry at Uncle Bertram's funeral, the tears that had seemed locked inside her ever since she had heard the awful news of his death. But try as she might, she could not unlock them. Her chest tightened and her throat constricted, but there was no release of grief or emotion or tension. After five minutes, she drew a breath and bit her lip and stared herself down in the rearview mirror. She would find time to cry later. She was on a mission. She reached into her handbag for *Paul Clifford* and instead drew out Eric's letter. She hadn't had much time to think about it, but Eric was coming for her. Eric who could be rude and insensitive, Eric who had deceived her about the Jane Austen volumes, but also Eric who knew nothing about Richard Mansfield, Eric who made her laugh, and most important, Eric who had kissed her in the garden. She knew that as long as she kept up the fabulous sex with Winston—which was something she very much wanted to do—there could be no more moonlight kisses. She knew she should feel guilty for even forming this thought—but knowing that Eric was coming somehow made her feel safe. Instinctively glancing around to be sure no one was watching, she gave Eric's letter a little kiss, and slipped it back in her bag.

I'm a proper book thief now, thought Sophie as she drew out the copy of *Paul Clifford*. I've stolen from a dealer and a private collector. I suppose a library is next. The book was bound in drab cloth, faded from years of sunlight in the days when the library wasn't shut tight all the time. The spine was chipped, and the corners were rubbed, but it was still a solid copy. Not exactly collector quality, but then who collected Bulwer-Lytton? She opened to the first page of text and read:

> *It was a dark and stormy night; the rain fell in torrents—except at occasional intervals, when it was checked by a violent gust of wind*

*which swept up the streets (for it is in London that our scene lies), rattling along the housetops, and fiercely agitating the scanty flame of the lamps that struggled against the darkness.*

In the margin next to this opening sentence was a penciled note in her uncle's hand: *You see, Sophie, I told you it was awful. Take better care of English literature than BL did.* She tried to fan out the pages of the book to see if it contained any other notes from Uncle Bertram. Only the first few pages would cooperate, however. The rest seemed to be stuck together. Sophie flipped ten pages and stopped, a smile spreading across her face. Not only had the rest of the pages been glued together; their interior had been cut away, leaving a neat rectangular container. The book that Uncle Bertram considered a travesty against English literature had been reduced to little more than a slipcase, and within it lay a small volume, bound in rough green cloth.

Sophie turned over *Paul Clifford* and the second book fell into her lap. She opened the cover and read the inscription: "*Natalis Christi* B.A.C. 1971." For whatever reason, Uncle Bertram had thought, at the age of nineteen, that this was the most desirable book in the family library. Sophie carefully turned to the title page and read:

**LITTLE ALLEGORIES AND A CAUTIONARY TALE**

**BEING THE SECOND EDITION OF**

***A Little Book of Allegorical Stories***

*BY* **REV. RICHARD MANSFIELD**

**PRINTED AT LEEDS BY GILBERT MONKHOUSE**

*1796.*

## *Hampshire, 1796*

"JANE, WHAT DO YOU THINK?" exclaimed Cassandra, entering the dressing room and waving a letter in her hand. "It is a letter from our aunt. We are to make a visit to Bath."

"Not for Christmas, I hope," said Jane, laying aside her quill.

"For a fortnight only, but what a delight for us. And how kind of Aunt Jane and Uncle James to have us both together. It is still the autumn season and there will be balls and concerts and visitors galore."

"And no time for writing, I fear," said Jane.

"The whole winter will stretch before you when you return," said Cassandra. "*First Impressions* will wait."

"Actually, I think of calling it something else, to distinguish it from . . . the original version," said Jane, standing up and taking her sister by the hand. "And you are right—Bath will be a delight and doubly so because we are there together."

While Jane would never have said so to either her aunt or her sister, she did not find Bath a delight. She found the whole city to be much like her first ball there—crowded, noisy, and, in spite of a plethora of persons, impersonal. On the first morning Jane accompanied her uncle on his walk to the pump room for his daily glass of the bitter local water, and unlike her walks in Busbury Park, this excursion involved navigating around the dresses of approaching women, the refuse in the gutters, and the puddles on the pavement—all the while being deafened by one passing wagon after another. Her aunt had laid before them a schedule of visits, concerts, and theatrical evenings which promised to leave Jane little time for correspondence, let alone any real writing. The social calendar began with a ball on their third night in Bath. The following afternoon, in a rare moment of quiet, Jane composed a letter to Mr. Mansfield.

***Bath, December 4, 1796***

**My Dear Mr. Mansfield,**

**It may surprise you to find that, in your absence, I have been forced to seek other companionship for my walks. Of course none of the residents at Steventon or Deane would do, nor anyone from Basingstoke or Andover or even Winchester. No, your abandonment has forced me to seek all the way to Bath, where I walk with my uncle on a morning circuit around the city. All work on *First Impressions* has ceased. But do not think my visit wasted. Every time I meet a young woman, whether in the street or in my aunt's parlour, I am reminded of your idea about writing a satire on the gothic novel. Where better to find a heroine than in Bath? I assure you I have no model in mind, having learned my lesson about using my imagination to embellish the lives of others, but consider our experiences at the ball last evening if you need any convincing that Bath is the proper starting point for a gothic heroine.**

**My aunt and uncle accompanied Cassandra and myself. The room was crowded, and we squeezed in as well as we could. As for my uncle, he repaired directly to the card-room, and left us to enjoy the mob by ourselves. My aunt made her way through the throng of men by the door; Cassandra and I kept close at her side, and linked our arms too firmly within one another's to be torn asunder by any common effort of a struggling assembly. Though by unwearied diligence we gained the top of the room, we saw nothing of the dancers but the high feathers of some of the ladies. By a continued**

**exertion of strength and ingenuity we found ourselves with a comprehensive view of all the company. It was a splendid sight, and I began, for the first time that evening, to feel myself at a ball. We were not long able, however, to enjoy the repose of the eminence we had so laboriously gained. Everybody was shortly in motion for tea, and we must squeeze out like the rest.**

**When it was all over, I was struck that such a struggle might well suit the introduction of a heroine who will later face the dark challenges of Northanger Abbey—whatever they may be. You will accuse me, I am sure, of living altogether too much in the world of my own thoughts and tell me that I ought to have danced, no matter the crowd, to which I respond, sir, that had you been here, I most certainly should have.**

**I trust this letter finds you well and that you will soon be returned to Hampshire as I shall be myself.**

**Yours very affectionately,**

**J. Austen**

Jane had intended to put the letter in the next morning's post, but found when she came downstairs to breakfast that she had left it in her bedchamber. She resolved to post it in the afternoon but the letter that awaited her at the breakfast table—not from Mr. Mansfield, but from her mother, at the rectory—rendered posting a letter to Yorkshire unnecessary.

***Steventon Rectory, Dec. 3***

**My Dear Jane,**

**We have had news from Busbury Park that your friend Mr. Mansfield has returned but was taken ill on the journey south. I do not like to ask you to cut short your visit,**

**but we are told that he asks for you and the illness seems quite serious. My love to your dear sister.**

**Your Loving Mother**

As much as she enjoyed the diversions of Bath, Cassandra was in agreement with Jane that they must return to Hampshire at once.

"But you've only just arrived," said their aunt. "And there are so many engagements. Surely if Jane must go there is no harm in Cassandra staying on until the end of the fortnight."

"I would not have my sister travel alone in distress," said Cassandra.

"But why should she be in distress?" asked Aunt Jane. "This man is not a family member. And from what Jane says I gather she has only known him for a few months."

"It is difficult for me to express, Aunt," said Jane patiently, "what he is to me. He is more than a dear friend, and hardly less than family. If he is ill, and it is in my power to offer him any succor, I shall do so with all expediency."

They departed Bath by the midday coach.

## *Oxfordshire, Present Day*

***LITTLE ALLEGORIES AND A CAUTIONARY TALE,*** thought Sophie as the car idled on the drive of Bayfield House, looked distinctly unpromising as far as literary treasures were concerned. Just as she was turning over the title page, she heard the sound of an approaching engine. Probably her father on some early morning errand, she thought. She had no desire to be subjected to questions about the book she was holding, so she shoved Richard Mansfield and Bulwer-Lytton back into her bag, put the car in gear, and headed toward Oxford.

She stopped off at the services on the way into town and bought two sausage rolls and the biggest cup of coffee they would sell her. Ten minutes later she was back in her old familiar room. She took Richard Mansfield's book out of her bag and began to flip through it, comparing it to her memory of the first edition she had examined at the British Museum.

"You have a superb textual memory," Uncle Bertram told her one day when she pointed out a difference between the first and second editions of *Sense and Sensibility* he had not noticed. They were standing at the booth of a high-end dealer from California at the international book fair in London. "It will make you a good book collector—that ability to spot variants that other people might miss."

The second edition of Richard Mansfield's book was filled with variants. Even without a careful reading, Sophie could see changes and additions on almost every page. The story formerly titled "General Depravity of Mankind," she was pleased to see, had been renamed "Lucy and the Hare," and even included the slightest hint of wit. But all the changes did not add up to more than a slightly less dull version of Mansfield's original text. After scanning two of his allegorical stories, she decided to skip to the big difference in the book, according to the title page, at least—the addition of something called "A Cautionary Tale." It must be a tale of some heft, thought Sophie, for this copy of the book was significantly thicker than the one at the British Library. She flipped through the pages until she saw the heading: "First Impressions, A Cautionary Tale." It couldn't be, she thought, and she began to read.

**AFTER THE FIRST SENTENCE,** Sophie found it hard to breathe. By the end of the first page she was forced to stand and open the window, hoping fresh air would help. A moment later she shut the window and pulled the drape, afraid that someone else might see what she was seeing. Even if her memory for text hadn't been almost photographic, she would have known these words—they were among her favorites in all of literature. But three things made reading them a breathless experience: Quite a few of them were missing; they were published in 1796, seventeen years before the version known to all the world; and they appeared to have been written by Richard Mansfield. *First Impressions* was an epistolary story, and the first letters had made it clear what story it was. Sophie sat nervously on the edge of her bed and read on.

*Dear Charlotte,*

*Jane has made quite an impression on Mr. Bingley, who danced twice with her last night at the Meryton Ball. It is decided by the Bennets, and I cannot dispute the conclusion, that Bingley is sensible, good-humoured, lively, and a gentleman of happy manners—much at ease, with perfect good breeding. I need hardly add that he is also handsome, which a young man ought likewise to be, if he possibly can. His character is thereby complete. What a contrast between him and his friend Mr. Darcy. He is the proudest man I have met—though I cannot be said to have actually met him. Mr. Darcy danced only once with Mrs. Hurst and once with Miss Bingley, declined being introduced to any other lady, and spent the rest of the evening in walking about the room, speaking occasionally to one of his own party. At one stage of the evening I was obliged, by the scarcity of gentlemen, to sit down for two dances and during this time I overheard Mr. Bingley encourage Mr. Darcy to allow him to make our introduction. Darcy replied, loud enough for me and many others to hear, "She is tolerable, but not handsome enough to tempt me; I am in no humour at present to give consequence to young ladies who are slighted by other men." I was amused and repeated the story with great spirit among my friends, but you can imagine the reaction of Mrs. Bennet who proclaimed Darcy a most disagreeable, horrid man, not at all worth pleasing. Bingley promises to throw a ball at Netherfield soon, for which I trust you will have returned from town.*

*Affectionately,*

*Elizabeth Bennet*

"**DID YOU KNOW,**" said Uncle Bertram, as he and Sophie were basking in the glow not just of the fire in the sitting room but also of having finished reading *Pride and Prejudice* to one another for the third time, "some scholars think the first draft was a novel of letters."

"Epistolary," said Sophie, rolling the word about on her tongue. She was sixteen and hungry for words of more than four syllables.

"We know the first draft of *Sense and Sensibility* was written in letters," he said.

"But it was called *Elinor and Marianne*."

"Exactly," said Uncle Bertram. "And not long after she finished that she wrote *Pride and Prejudice*. Between 1796 and 1797."

"And was it always called *Pride and Prejudice?*" said Sophie, who thought it a perfect title.

"That title actually came from a novel called *Cecilia* by Fanny Burney," said Uncle Bertram.

"We should read that," said Sophie.

"But the first version," said her uncle, "was called *First Impressions*."

**JANE AUSTEN HAD WRITTEN** *First Impressions* from 1796 to 1797. The book that Sophie now held—with its story in letters of the Bennet family and Fitzwilliam Darcy and George Wickham—was published in 1796, early enough for her to have . . . but it was unthinkable. Had Jane Austen plagiarized *Pride and Prejudice* from Richard Mansfield? The same Richard Mansfield who had written appallingly bad allegories with titles like "Sickness and Health" and "Youth and Vanity"? The text of *First Impressions* did not seem to fit at all with the rest of Mansfield's work. But she had noticed a marked improvement in his stories in this second edition. While they were in no way suggestive of Jane Austen, Sophie could easily imagine scholars making the case. Mansfield had been improving, and then, like many authors, he had had a breakthrough. Sophie could be holding in her hand the greatest literary scandal in history.

Did it matter, she wondered, that the most sublime novel of all time had, in a day before copyright laws, been pilfered from another source? Didn't Shakespeare take all his plots from other books? Well yes, he did, she told herself, but this was more than that. This was the wholesale lifting not just of an original plot and characters, but of sentences, even paragraphs of text. *First Impressions* wasn't just a source for *Pride and Prejudice*; it was the first draft.

When Sophie got to her favorite scene from the novel, she read Elizabeth Bennet's letter to her sister Jane over several times. She had never felt such a mix of emotions. On the one hand, everything she believed about her literary idol was crumbling. On the other hand, she was probably the only person alive who had ever read this original version of

Eliza and Darcy meeting at Pemberley. It was as if the meeting were happening for the first time and, instead of being witnessed by a hundred million lovers of literature, it was seen only by Sophie.

*My Dear Jane,*

*I write with news of a startling character. Of all places, the Gardiners were this day set on visiting Pemberley. I consented only because I believed Mr. Darcy to be away from home, but after the housekeeper had showed us round the house—which I shall describe to you on my return—we ventured into the park. As we walked across the lawn toward the river, the owner himself suddenly came from behind the stables. Our eyes instantly met, and both our cheeks were overspread with the deepest blush. He absolutely started, and for a moment seemed immovable from surprise; but shortly recovering himself, advanced toward us, and spoke to me, if not in terms of perfect composure, at least of perfect civility. He asked if I would do him the honour of introducing him to my friends—a stroke of civility for which I was quite unprepared. That he was surprised by our connection was evident; he sustained it, however, with fortitude, and even entered into conversation with Mr. Gardiner.*

*When he turned back to me, I, wishing him to know that I had been assured of his absence before coming to Pemberley, mentioned that his housekeeper had assured us he would not return until to-morrow. He acknowledged the truth of this, and said that business with his steward had occasioned his coming forward a few hours before the rest of the party with whom he had been traveling. "They will join me early to-morrow," he continued, "and among them are some who will claim an acquaintance with you—Mr. Bingley and his sisters." And then he said the most extraordinary thing. "There is also one other person in the party who more particularly wishes to be known to you. Will you allow me, or do I ask too much, to introduce my sister to your acquaintance during your stay at Lambton?"*

*He shortly took his leave of us, but what can this mean? That Mr. Darcy acts civilly not just to myself but to the Gardiners, that he wishes me to make the acquaintance of his sister? I must admit myself most astonished, and shall certainly write again if this unexpected introduction is made.*

*Affectionately,*

*Lizzie*

The text of *First Impressions* occupied the final fifty-two pages of *Little Allegories and a Cautionary Tale.* Certainly Jane Austen had expanded it significantly in her version, but the basics of the novel were here: the haughty behavior of Darcy, the charm and dishonesty of Wickham, the flighty matchmaking of Mrs. Bennet, and the poise of Elizabeth. Sophie wished she could channel some of that poise right now. What would Elizabeth Bennet do? Before she could give the matter much thought, her phone rang.

"I'm being a pest, I know," said Winston. "I'm not supposed to keep calling but I just felt like a chat."

"That's OK," said Sophie. "I could use a little cheering up."

"Rough night?"

"You could say that. My father brought in a book dealer to cherry-pick through the family library—so more of the Collingwood collection is to be lost forever."

"That's a shame," said Winston. "Didn't he even let you pick out a few items for yourself?"

"Oh, Father would never do that. What if I took a book that was valuable enough to repair the roof, or repaint the drawing room, or dig a moat?"

"Glad to see you haven't lost your sense of humor," said Winston. "I wouldn't want my favorite bibliophile to stop making me laugh."

Sophie sighed lightly at the thought that she was somebody's favorite something. She wished for a moment that Winston were there, that they were tangled up in the sheets on that hard narrow bed in her room, and that Smedley, and Mr. Tompkins, and Richard Mansfield would all just disappear. She was on the verge of asking him to come up to Oxford after all when she looked down at Mansfield's book, still open to the last page of *First Impressions*. Did Winston know? How could he not? And if he did, had this whole relationship just been his way of being sure that he, and not some other customer, would be the one to buy the book from Sophie? What was Winston's endgame? Did he want to discredit Jane Austen before the whole world? Or did he want to hide *First Impressions* away and protect her reputation? Sophie could think of a thousand reasons why she shouldn't trust him, but she also thought of the way his muscles had felt under her hands. Those muscles could be very useful in a confrontation with Smedley.

"Are you still there?" said Winston.

"Sorry," said Sophie, "my mind was wandering."

"And where was it wandering that could be more interesting than my scintillating conversation?"

"If you must know," said Sophie, "it was wandering back to your bedroom."

"I see," said Winston. "Jealous of my book collection, are you?"

"I wasn't thinking of your book collection," she said, deciding to take the plunge. "But now that you mention it, what would you say if I told you I think I have a lead on that book you're looking for?"

"I'd say great. But I'd rather have you tell me about it personally. Very personally."

"And what would you say," said Sophie, doing her best to suppress the thought of those arms wrapped around her, "if I told you that it's possible it might be a very valuable little volume?"

"I'd be surprised," said Winston. "I honestly can't see that it would have much worth. I suppose if it does, I won't be able to afford it."

"We'll see," she said. "Listen, do you still want to come up to Oxford and . . . get together?"

"I think I've made it abundantly clear that I would like to get together in every way possible."

"Give me some time to get things sorted," said Sophie, "and I'll give you a call."

"I'll be waiting by the phone," said Winston.

"You carry your phone in your pocket," she teased.

"Yes, well, that proves it, then."

**SOPHIE CLOSED** *Little Allegories and a Cautionary Tale* and returned it to her bag. Winston had seemed genuinely surprised when she had said it might be valuable. And he hadn't seemed too concerned about getting it from her right away. It was hard to believe it was a coincidence that he had come to her, but it was harder to believe that he was that good an actor. She would tell him the whole story when the time was right, but what was the whole story? Had Jane Austen really stolen her plot and much of her text from Richard Mansfield? Maybe she was naive to feel this way, but Sophie just couldn't believe it. The problem was, in the absence of other evidence, most people *would* believe it. She thought back over everything she knew about Mansfield (which wasn't much) and Jane Austen (which was quite a bit) but could imagine no connection between the two.

Unsure what to do next, she did know one thing: She couldn't keep her discovery entirely to herself. It was too fantastic a story not to share. She had to ring Victoria.

"Holy shit," said her sister when Sophie had explained about *First Impressions*. "Do you really think Jane Austen was a plagiarist?"

"No," said Sophie. "There has to be some sort of explanation and I have to figure out what it is. And I don't give a toss how much that book is worth or how many people want it—I'm not about to start showing it around until I can prove that Jane was innocent."

"So she's Jane to you now," said Victoria.

"I feel like I know her," said Sophie. "I feel like her fate is in my hands."

"Why don't you just burn the damn thing?"

"Don't think I haven't thought of that," said Sophie. "But I couldn't. It's just too . . . too . . . remarkable."

"The first draft of *Pride and Prejudice*," said Victoria wistfully.

"Yeah," replied Sophie with a sigh. She still couldn't quite wrap her mind around the momentousness of her find.

"There's something I've been wondering," said Victoria. "If this second edition is so damn rare, how did two different people know that it even existed?"

"Good question," said Sophie. "I never really thought about that."

"There must have been some other clue, something that made them believe there was a second edition."

"Tori, you're brilliant," said Sophie, jumping out of her chair.

"I am?"

"You're right. There has to be a clue and it has to be something they both saw. It's the sword on the wall."

"I beg your pardon?" said Victoria.

"Winston and Smedley must have crossed paths somewhere and wherever they crossed paths, that's where they found the clue. Where they crossed paths is the sword on the wall."

"I'm not sure I follow you."

"Oh God," said Sophie, her voice almost breathless. "I know what it is. There's one thing Smedley and Winston have in common."

"What's that?" said Victoria, still sounding confused.

"They both went to St. John's," said Sophie. "St. John's is the sword on the wall." And with these cryptic words, she rang off.

## *Leeds, 1796*

**GILBERT MONKHOUSE STOOD** in his printing-office in Leeds and inhaled the aroma of ink. It was a smell that had surrounded him since he was twelve years old and first went to work for Griffith Wright, printer of the *Leeds Intelligencer.* Griffith's son Thomas had taken over the business in 1784, and for eleven years Gilbert had worked in the shop, living in the embrace of that wonderful smell. Gilbert had learned how to read at an early age—it came naturally to him—and it was his ability to read that had led him to Wright's printing-office. From there, every night, he would take home the proofs of some book to read in his bed. Since he did not hold the position of reader in the printing-office, he never made marks on the pages, but he would remember any errors he noticed and point them out to the reader the next morning.

Gilbert had started out sweeping floors and carrying boxes of type and reams of paper. When he was fifteen Mr. Wright had set him to work casting off copy—calculating the number of words in a manuscript so that an estimate of printing costs could be made. From there he graduated to the job of distributing type into letter cases. Taking a handful of some ten or twenty lines of type from a previously printed book, Gilbert sorted the metal letters into the boxes within the letter cases. At first he was allowed to sort only a few pages of type each day, for his unskilled fingers slowed the pace of work in the shop, but soon he found he could read the lines of type (which meant reading in mirror image), memorize the words, and distribute the letters with his thumb and forefinger with lightening speed and perfect accuracy. Experienced compositors in the shop bragged of being able to distribute forty thousand letters in a day; by the time he was eighteen, Gilbert could match that; at twenty he could sort nearly fifty thousand.

What Gilbert, as a boy and as a young man, wanted more than anything else was to be a full-fledged compositor. He wanted to create books and newspapers by setting the type into words and lines and paragraphs and pages. True, authors might slave for months or years with quill and paper, but in the end all they created were texts. Compositors and printers created books, and that was what Gilbert wanted to do. When he turned twenty-one, Mr. Wright promoted him to the job of his dreams.

With fingers trained for years as a type sorter, Gilbert now set about the process of taking the tiny pieces of type from the letter cases and arranging them in composing sticks, each of which held several lines of type. The type from these sticks he then arranged into galleys, which, when each contained a full page, he placed in the proper arrangement on the imposing stone for printing. He had spent his entire youth watching compositors—never was a young man so well prepared for his vocation. From his first day, Gilbert could match the fastest compositor in the office, and the readers were always happy to get proofs that Gilbert had set—they were nearly error-free. He loved to visit the local bookshop and pull from the shelf some book for which he had set the type. He felt like much more than a workman; he felt like a creator.

In 1795, Gilbert's uncle, a solicitor in Manchester, had died, leaving Gilbert a modest inheritance. At the time, Thomas Wright's printing-office was having to turn away jobs—there simply wasn't enough space for another printing press, and Mr. Wright had no interest in expanding. Gilbert had gone to his employer with a proposal: If Wright would loan Gilbert the sum of two hundred pounds, he would take that money, together with his inheritance, and open his own printing-office. Leeds was growing rapidly, and Gilbert believed there was plenty of work for two printers. Thomas agreed. Though he was sorry to lose his best compositor, he felt the investment in Gilbert was a good one.

And so now, a year later, Gilbert stood in his own shop, blissfully happy. He had six employees, but he still worked as a compositor himself for several hours every day, and he still took proofs home every night. Tonight he had stayed at the shop late to finish printing the final pages of the proofs for a book unimaginatively titled *Little Allegories and a Cautionary Tale*. It was the second edition of a book he had printed the previous year—a rather dull collection of moral tales by a Yorkshire clergyman. What had surprised him about this job was the addition of the "Cautionary Tale." Though he would print anything he was paid to print, Gilbert was not above passing literary judgment on the works that came through his press. This long story was, he thought, one of the finest pieces he had ever set in type.

Gilbert was quite used to reading proofs in large, unfolded sheets, each containing, in this case, sixteen pages of the book. With a stack of these sheets draped over his arm, he locked up his office at half-past ten and walked the short distance to his lodgings—a small room above a milliner's shop in the high street. Lighting a lamp by his bedside, he settled in to read the proofs. Outside of his employees and those of Mr. Wright, Gilbert had few friends. His family lived far away, in Peterborough, and of female admirers he had none. One might be forgiven for thinking that the man reading the printer's sheets alone in his lodgings late at night was lonely or even unhappy, but nothing was further from the truth. Gilbert Monkhouse was the happiest man in Leeds—at least for a few more hours.

## *Oxford, Present Day*

**SOPHIE DRAINED HER** coffee, took a two-minute shower, and pulled on some fresh clothes. Out of term time, the library at St. John's would open at ten; it was quarter past by the time she walked out of the house onto the Woodstock Road and headed toward the center of town. It was a fifteen-minute walk to St. John's, and Sophie felt the cool morning air clearing her head. She had focus now, and a mission. Somewhere in the St. John's College Library was the precipitating clue—a book or a letter or a manuscript that had caused two very different men to go looking for the book that lay safely in her handbag. Whether that clue would exonerate Jane Austen, Sophie did not know, but finding it was her logical next step.

Having worked at the Christ Church Library for all of her five years at Oxford, Sophie knew librarians at just about every Oxford college. She was pleased to discover, on flashing her ID and gaining entry to St. John's, a familiar face at the circulation desk—a tall, lanky graduate student with a mop of black hair, a suit that looked as if he had slept in it, and dark-rimmed glasses.

"Sophie Collingwood, good to see you."

"Good morning, Jacob," she said, smiling. Seeing an old friend—even if in reality he was little more than an acquaintance—who was not a part of all this intrigue was refreshing. Here, at least, was someone she could trust.

"I thought I'd see you at the end-of-term do over at Worcester," said Jacob.

"Death in the family," said Sophie.

"Sorry to hear it. Well, it's good to see you anyway. Pretty quiet around here between terms, so always nice to see a friend."

"It's good to see you, too, Jacob," she said, smiling.

"Now, what can I do for you on a morning so fine that you really shouldn't be spending it in a library?"

"I'm doing some research on Jane Austen."

"You'd do better at the Bodleian," said Jacob. "Or even back at Christ Church. They both have better collections of Austen than we do."

"I've been there already," Sophie lied. "What I'm looking for could be anywhere. I'm trying to find a connection between Austen and an obscure northern clergyman."

"Sounds intriguing."

"It's really not," she said. "It's utterly boring and probably a waste of time, but I'm working for this rare book dealer now and one of his clients seems to think I'm his private researcher."

"As long as he's paying you," said Jacob.

"Would I be here if he weren't?" said Sophie with a smile. "Anyway, I'm looking through any early editions of Austen I can find for . . . well, I don't know what for—inscriptions, I guess, or marginalia. Anything that might show a connection."

"I'll go down to rare books and bring you anything we have with an Austen connection," said Jacob. "In the meantime you can have a look through the stacks and see if there's anything there. There won't be any early Austen, but who knows, you might find something."

Sophie spent the next hour paging through every book by or about Jane Austen in the stacks, beginning with the oldest ones, which were late-nineteenth-century editions of the novels. She didn't expect to find anything, but what if some other scholar had made a marginal note somewhere? When Jacob returned she was almost invisible behind stacks of books, none of which contained anything more than the occasional underlining by a thoughtless undergraduate who didn't understand the concept that library books were borrowed, not owned.

"Not a lot in rare books," said Jacob, holding up a small stack of volumes and a flat gray box. "A few early editions of some of the novels and a box of papers from the 1920s from a don who did some research on Austen. Doesn't look like he ever published anything, so it's just notes and a few odd chapters of typescript." He set the books and the box down on the table next to Sophie and returned to the circulation desk.

It took only a few minutes to discover that the books held no clues. There was an ownership inscription in the second edition of *Mansfield Park* and a date written on the endpaper of the first edition of *Persuasion,* which had been published posthumously in a set with *Northanger Abbey,* but no mention of Richard Mansfield. She was just about to turn to the box, which seemed much more promising, when it suddenly occurred to her what she had just held in her hand.

She laid the box down and picked up one of three nearly identical volumes. Turning past the title page, which identified the author only as THE AUTHOR OF SENSE AND SENSIBILITY, she reached the beginning of the text. At the top of the page, in large outlined capital letters, was the title, PRIDE & PREJUDICE; below that, a decorative line; then in small bold capitals the words CHAPTER I; and finally, that first glorious paragraph, with a large initial *I*:

> *It is a truth universally acknowledged, that a single man in possession of a good fortune must be in want of a wife.*

It took up four lines of text on the narrow paper, and seemed all the more important for taking up more than a third of the text space on the page. The words *acknowledged* and *possession* were both hyphenated. Those details—the narrowness of the book making the sentence cascade into nearly a third of a page, the initial capital, the hyphenated words—took that familiar sentence and made it look completely different.

Sophie had never held a first edition of *Pride and Prejudice.* She had never had the opportunity to run her fingers over those spectacular words as they had appeared in print for the first time. Somehow seeing them here in this volume from 1813 brought home to Sophie that Jane Austen had actually *written* these words. They had not simply appeared out of the ether. Sometimes, she thought, sentences like that become so famous that we cannot conceive a time when they did not exist. We can remember our own first encounters with those words, but that *mankind* should have had a first encounter with them seems almost impossible. But mankind did have a first encounter with Sophie's favorite sentence in all of literature, and she now held that first encounter in her hand.

On the lower corner of the first page of the first edition of *Pride and Prejudice* housed at St. John's College, Oxford, is a small circular water stain. It does not affect the text, nor is it significant enough to reduce the value of the book. But, like every mark in every book, it tells a story, and like so many marks in so many books, it is a story known to only one person and doomed to be lost forever when that person is no more. It is the mark of a single tear that dropped from the cheek of Sophie Collingwood as she stared at those words, and it is a testament to the power of literature.

Sophie wiped her cheek, but could not put the book down. Lost in the words, she read on, embracing both the familiar story and the unfamiliar way it appeared on the page. She felt herself somehow at one with the first men and women who read the novel; she felt especially connected to the person—she imagined her a lady of some wealth living in Bath—who first read this very copy.

Lunchtime came and went and she read on and not until she had reached the eleventh chapter did Miss Bingley startle her out of the world of Longbourn and Netherfield with the words: "*I declare after all there is no enjoyment like reading! How much sooner one tires of anything than of a book! When I have a house of my own, I shall be miserable if I have not an excellent library.*"

Sophie suddenly remembered that she was *in* an excellent library and with work to do. She was shocked to see from the clock on the wall that it was nearly two. Wistfully returning the first volume of *Pride and Prejudice* to its partners, Sophie removed the lid from the manuscript box and began looking through the contents.

She had some hope that these papers might provide the clue she was looking for, because they were unique to St. John's. First editions of

Austen's novels, as moving as they might be, were in many libraries around Britain, but nowhere else could one examine these particular papers. The don's name was Wilcox and his primary interest had been textual comparison. Sophie waded through two sheaves of notes on the variants between the first and second editions of *Pride and Prejudice* and *Sense and Sensibility*—page after page detailing changes in the locations of commas and in spelling. She was amazed that she could be both fascinated and bored at the same time. The typescript excerpts from a book apparently never published offered no more insight into Austen's connection to Richard Mansfield than the notes had. It was nearly closing time when Sophie finished examining the contents of the box.

Was it possible that she had been mistaken? Was there no sword on the wall of St. John's? Was it just another coincidence that both men had mentioned this was their college? Had Smedley even been telling the truth?

"Jacob," said Sophie, putting on her best smile as she approached the circulation desk. "Do you have a record of all the students at St. John's for, say . . . the past twenty years or so?"

"I've got a record of all the students here ever," said Jacob. "In a database, I mean. It's not much for browsing, but I can search specific names if you need."

"Just two names," she said. "The first is Smedley. George Smedley."

"Smedley," he said, typing away at his computer. "The last Smedley at St. John's took his B.A. in 1921."

"So that would make him . . ."

"About a hundred and twelve years old."

So Smedley had been lying. Maybe he had somehow listened in on the phone conversation when Winston had said he was at St. John's. But that couldn't be, because Smedley had told her he was at St. John's before Winston had mentioned it.

"What's the other name?" said Jacob.

"Godfrey," said Sophie. "Winston Godfrey."

"Let's see, Winston Godfrey. Nope. The closest I have is a Wallace Godfrey in 1946."

She did her best to hide her shock, leaning against the counter with one hand. Winston had been lying, too? But why? There was only one conceivable reason. He had been trying to lead her to St. John's. For some reason they both had. And since the one thing she knew they had in common was that they both wanted her copy of *Little Allegories and a Cautionary Tale*, there had to be something at St. John's that had led them to believe that book was important. But what?

"We close in about thirty minutes," said Jacob. "I need to take those Austen materials back to rare books."

"Right," said Sophie. "I'll put the rest of the things back in the stacks for you."

"Did you find what you were looking for?"

"Not exactly."

"Well, that's research for you. Nine times out of ten you don't find anything. That's what makes the tenth time so much fun."

Jacob gathered up the materials that had come from rare books and disappeared down a corridor. There had been a few other readers in the library during the afternoon, but they were all gone now and Sophie was left alone. She began to reshelve the books she had taken from the stacks, trying to think what she could have missed. What could be in this college that would make someone think that the second edition of a book by an unknown eighteenth-century clergyman was worth killing for? It had to be something that linked Mansfield and Austen, but it also had to be something that no one else, besides Winston and Smedley, had ever noticed.

She was putting the last of the books back into the stacks, accompanied only by the ticking of the clock, when the answer hit her with the force of a freight train. Of course, Jane Austen materials would have been ferreted out years ago, but what about Richard Mansfield materials? Who would go looking for those? No one. What if there was a Richard Mansfield item in the library that Winston and Smedley had somehow stumbled upon?

Jacob had still not returned and Sophie quickly scanned the theology section. It took her less than a minute to spot a slim unmarked volume, looking dusty and untouched, on the shelf between Herbert

Luckock's *After Death* and Frederick Maurice's *Theological Essays*. She carefully slipped the volume out of its place and turned to the title page—identical to the one she had seen at the British Library: *A Little Book of Allegorical Stories* by Rev. Richard Mansfield. She heard footsteps approaching down the corridor from the rare books room and acted almost without thinking. She rushed back to her table, grabbed her bag, dashed to the circulation desk, reached over and swiped Mansfield's book against the demagnetizer, and shoved it into her bag just before Jacob reappeared.

"Thanks again for your help, Jacob," she called.

"Sorry you didn't find what you were looking for," he said.

"Well, he's paying me by the hour, at least," said Sophie, feeling sweat breaking out on her forehead. She shouldn't be nervous, she thought. After all, she was becoming an experienced book thief.

"Maybe I'll see you in London sometime," said Jacob.

"I'm working in Cecil Court," she said, "at Boxhill's. Stop in and see me." And don't discover that I just used my skills as a librarian to steal a book from an Oxford college, she thought.

A moment later she was back out in the summer sun. The day had turned warm, and she was tempted to sit in the shadows of the cloisters and examine her purloined treasure, but she thought it best to get away from St. John's in case Jacob came upon her reading a library book that had not been checked out.

Of all her crimes, Sophie thought, this was the most appalling. It was one thing to steal a book that ought to have belonged to her from a dealer who had overpriced it, or even to steal a book from her own family library; but for a college librarian to steal from a college library—that was a violation of ethics that did not sit well with her. Not until she was safely back in her room and had a chance to examine the book more closely did she decide it had absolutely been worth it.

In most particulars, the book was identical to the one she had examined at the British Library. The binding was perhaps a bit less worn, the pages crisper—that probably meant the book hadn't been read much. Having read the text herself, Sophie couldn't really blame the readers of the past two centuries for neglecting this copy. She fanned the pages of the book and this cursory inspection showed a text unmarked in the margins, but when she turned to the front endpaper, she found an inscription in fading brown ink, in a slightly shaky hand: "To J.A. Judge not too harshly, but like me reserve First Impressions for second editions. Affectionately, R.M." To anyone who wasn't *looking* for a connection between Jane Austen and Richard Mansfield, it would have seemed innocent enough. It was easy to imagine how it might have been overlooked through all these years, especially in a book that people weren't likely to open very often. But here, surely, was evidence that Richard Mansfield had known Jane Austen. To Sophie, that was good news; but the further implications of the inscription left her more worried than ever that if her stolen books were made public, the world would believe that Jane Austen had plagiarized *Pride and Prejudice* from Richard Mansfield.

If only he hadn't included those two words: *like me*. As it was, the inscription certainly seemed to imply that Mansfield had written *First Impressions*. She closed the book gently and laid it on her dressing table. Staring at herself in the mirror, she wondered—is this the face of the woman who will destroy Jane Austen? What would those "fangirls" on whom Eric heaped so much disdain think of her? With the two books in her possession, Sophie had, perhaps, the ability to become the most reviled person in English literature fandom.

Of course, she had no intention of making the books public. She still wanted to do two things: find a way to prove Jane's innocence, and find a way to prove Smedley's guilt. Until she understood how both Smedley and Winston had come to discover Mansfield's book in the library of a college neither one of them attended, she didn't think she could make much progress with either goal. She certainly wasn't going to ask Smedley about the book, so that left her with only one option—she had to trust Winston, at least for now.

"I thought I was the one who couldn't stop thinking about you," said Winston when Sophie called.

"Can you come up to Oxford tomorrow?" she asked.

"Is that little bed of yours cold?"

She had a flash of spending the whole day in bed. Fireworks or no fireworks, sex with Winston would definitely take her mind off her troubles. But, as appealing as the notion was, it would have to wait.

"I was thinking lunch. There's a little café just outside the covered market."

"Puccino's. Sure, I know the place."

"Because you were at St. John's," Sophie prompted.

"Right," said Winston.

"So can you come? Say, noon?"

"I can come tonight if you like."

"I need to sleep tonight," said Sophie. "Come tomorrow and I'll meet you at Puccino's."

"Well, I suppose if we have to meet in a public place, I'll get by. At least I'll get to see you."

"It'll be fun," she said. "You can tell me all about your days at Oxford." And with this veiled warning she rang off.

It was only five o'clock, but, having missed an entire night of sleep, Sophie was exhausted. She bought two sandwiches from the shop on the corner, wolfed them down with the remains of a bottle of wine she found on her bookshelf, and was sound asleep as soon as her head hit the pillow.

## *Hampshire, 1796*

**THE COACH BEARING** Jane and Cassandra from Bath stopped at Devizes and did not reach Deane until nearly eight o'clock, by which time it had long gone dark. Jane was surprised to find a gig and driver waiting for them.

"Are you Miss Jane Austen?" asked the driver. When this was answered in the affirmative he continued. "Lord Wintringham says I am to bring you straight to Busbury Park."

"Oh, Jane, your friend must be quite unwell for them to send for you at this hour," said Cassandra, gripping her sister's arm. "We shall go at once."

But Jane did not move for a moment, though Cassandra pulled her toward the gig. Then, laying a hand on her sister's arm, she spoke. "I must go alone, dear sister."

"But surely you will want me with you at such a time."

Jane could not think how to explain to Cassandra the intimacy of her relationship with Mr. Mansfield, or the depth of her desire to be alone with him once more. It had nothing to do with romance but everything to do with love. She had found in him a mind so in sympathy with her own that when the two of them were together there seemed to be no one else in the world. If she could, she hoped to experience that feeling once more.

"You must deposit my sister at Steventon rectory on the way," said Jane, climbing into the gig as the driver hoisted up their trunks.

"Are you sure?" said Cassandra, taking her seat next to Jane.

"I am quite sure," said Jane calmly, and they rattled away into the darkness.

Jane did not alight from the gig at the rectory, though her family came out to greet the returning sisters. She leaned down to kiss her mother, then asked the driver to make all haste to Busbury Park. She could not bear the thought that she might not be in time, for now her mind was focused on a single aim—to make that confession to Mr. Mansfield that she had delayed making ever since her return from Kent. That she loved him—not with the love of a wife but with a love of the mind that, she imagined, was as deep as any other.

When they turned in to the east drive, the driver did not stop at the gatehouse. The windows were dark, and the gig continued up the drive until the main house came into view. Jane had not yet met the earl, but this impending introduction seemed not in the slightest momentous as the driver helped her down. She thought only of Mr. Mansfield.

In the light of the open door stood a middle-aged man, dressed for dinner, and wearing a look of fatigue on his face.

"Miss Austen, I presume," he said.

"Miss Jane Austen, at your service, my lord. I am most indebted to you for sending for me. I hope you will pardon my traveling clothes and take me to see Mr. Mansfield at once. I am desperate to speak with him."

"I shall take you to see him as you request, Miss Austen, but I am grieved to inform you that you will not be able to speak with him. Mr. Mansfield died not an hour ago."

Jane felt her knees buckle beneath her, and thought for a moment she would swoon, until the surprisingly strong arm of the earl steadied her.

"I am so sorry, my dear. I know it must come as a shock."

"Indeed it does, sir," said Jane, who had forgotten how to breathe for a moment. Now, as she forced herself to pull air into her lungs, it seemed to expel tears from her eyes. No gasps and sobs for her, just a steady trickle down her trembling cheeks. Her confession was not to be.

"But come in, Miss Austen. How cruel of me to keep you here on the doorstep. Will you sit for a moment?"

"No thank you, sir. I am quite well now. It was only the shock of the news. Will you take me to him?"

"If that is your wish, you may follow me, Miss Austen."

The walk up stairs and down corridors seemed to last forever. In other circumstances Jane might well have stored away the details of the house for use in some future story, but now she could think only of her friend. If only the letter had come the day before; if only the coach hadn't stopped at Devizes; if only Mr. Mansfield had lived a few more hours. That she should never again hear his gentle voice or walk with him to the lake or read to him by the fire seemed impossible, and yet it was so. She had heard the expression "an aching heart," yet never could she remember experiencing quite such a physical pain in her chest as this dreadful news had brought.

At long last they arrived at a closed door, outside of which the earl paused. "He is laid out here in the blue bedroom," he whispered, as if his voice could still disturb Mr. Mansfield. "I'm afraid I must go down to dinner, but you may ring for the upstairs maid to show you out. My man will drive you back to the rectory whenever you are ready."

"You are most kind, sir."

"It is the least I can do," said the earl. "Mr. Mansfield was among my oldest friends, though he preferred his books to social intercourse. When he did dine with us here, he spoke very highly of you. I believe your acquaintance was one of the great joys of his final months, and for being such a pleasure to an old friend, I shall always be indebted to you, Miss Austen."

"I assure you, my lord, he was a better friend to me that I could ever hope to be to him."

"He was a good man," said the earl with a quaver in his voice, and he turned and walked back down the corridor.

Jane turned the handle and pushed the door open. The room was dimly lit with candles and a lamp by the bedside. The elegant blue and gold drapes had been pulled shut. Mr. Mansfield, or the mortal husk of Mr. Mansfield, thought Jane, lay in the center of the wide bed. She sat on the edge of the bed for several minutes, looking at his serene face. He looked so well rested, she thought. She reached out and took his hand in hers. His skin was cool and dry. So often had she accompanied her father to funerals and burials that she knew most of the words of the service by heart. As she sat by the man she had loved so dearly, holding his hand in hers, she spoke aloud, once more reading to him, this time from memory:

> **I heard a voice from heaven saying unto me, Write, from henceforth blessed are the dead which die in the Lord: even so, saith the Spirit; for they rest from their labours.**

"So let it be with you, my love," she said, tears once again flowing freely down her face. "Rest. Rest in God's peace."

## *Oxford, Present Day*

**THE NEXT MORNING** Sophie awoke feeling hopeful. Somehow the decision to confide in Winston had already, in her mind, given her an ally. She was up early and at her computer, working on a plan of attack for the day. The first step was frighteningly easy. With nothing more than a fifty-pound membership fee in a genealogical research site, she was able, in less than an hour, to trace her ancestry back to Gilbert Monkhouse and Theresa Wright. Theresa's father, as the family prayer book had indicated, had also been a printer, which explained why Sophie's father didn't associate the name Monkhouse with the printing family from which he was descended. Of course, if Sophie could discover that connection, so could anyone else. Sophie imagined the old woman who conducted the monthly tours of Bayfield told the story of how the family library was begun when a printer kept one copy of every book he printed. Smedley suspected from the inscription in the St. John's copy of Mansfield's book that there was a connection between the second edition, Jane Austen, and *First Impressions*. It would have taken no great power of reasoning to deduce that if there were a surviving copy of that second edition, it might well be either in the inaccessible cases of Bayfield House or on the cluttered shelves of Uncle Bertram's flat. Smedley had searched Uncle Bertram's flat after he killed him; but he'd had to enlist Sophie to search Bayfield House. If threats and bribes weren't enough to rouse Sophie to action, he had dropped the hint about St. John's, hoping she would uncover the book that brought her beloved Jane Austen into the story.

Sophie's next task was to research Richard Mansfield. This proved more difficult. The genealogical site was no help this time. Beyond the brief biographical sketch she had found in *Alumni Oxonienses*, there was nothing. She pulled up *Alumni Oxonienses* online and looked at his biography again:

> **MANSFIELD, RICHARD NORMAN, 1s. Tobias Charles, of Bloxham, Oxfordshire, cler. Balliol Coll., matric. 1734, aged 18; B.A. 1737, M.A. 1740. Curate of Bloxham 1743, Master of Cowley Grammar School 1758–1780, Rector of Croft, Yorkshire, 1780. Died 4 Dec. 1796.**

He had been an undergraduate at Balliol, but they were not likely to have any records of his adult life. He'd served as a curate in the diocese of Oxford, so any records relating to that would be in the diocesan archives, but he had left there before Jane Austen was even born, so those records were not likely to be helpful. The records from his time as rector at Croft would be in the Yorkshire diocesan archives, a long day's drive away. That left the Cowley Grammar School. She had never heard of such a school, but a quick search of the online catalog for the Oxfordshire History Centre told her that it had existed from roughly 1750 to 1843. An entry in the catalog stated merely: "Records and papers related to Cowley Grammar School, masters, etc. Eight boxes."

It was a shot in the dark, but perhaps Rev. Mansfield had left his papers to the place he had spent the bulk of his career. Sophie had no idea if eighteenth-century clergymen had left their papers to institutions the way twentieth-century scholars had. It seemed unlikely, but since the Oxfordshire History Centre was just three miles away—in Cowley, coincidentally—there was no harm in looking.

Sophie stepped out of the house just before eleven. She would take a nice walk through the University Parks and along the river and still get back into the center of town in time to meet Winston at noon. She shivered to think that he was on the train right now heading to Oxford—

though she was not sure if it was a shiver of fear or of excitement. She was just passing the bus stop when she heard a voice call out, "Sophie!" She turned and her stomach fell. She had no idea what to say to Eric Hall, who now stood in front of her.

"Hi," said Eric.

"What . . . what . . . ?" She wanted to be angry that he had surprised her like this in the street, but she felt her cheeks flushing with an altogether different emotion and all she could think was: He found me. "What are you doing here?" she finally managed to say.

"Looking for you," he said. "Didn't you get my letter?"

"Yeah, but how did you know . . . ?"

"Well, your mom told me you were in Oxford and then this lady at the Christ Church Library told me you lived on Woodstock Road out near St. Antony's, so I figured I'd head out this way, and here you are."

"You said we were never going to see each other again," said Sophie.

"Yeah, well, the heart plays funny tricks, doesn't it?"

"Does it?" said Sophie. If he made some sort of crazy confession of love, she thought, she didn't know if she'd leap for joy or run away.

"I've been thinking about you and that night in the garden a lot and I decided to stop thinking and start doing something about it."

"You said you didn't want to get me into bed," said Sophie, remembering his words in the garden.

"What can I say? Paris is the city of lovers. It got me thinking. And I just couldn't get you out of my head."

At the mention of Paris, Sophie suddenly remembered the French books and Eric's deception. "Did you even go to Paris?" she said.

"What do you mean? Of course I went to Paris. Didn't you get my letters?"

"Then why did you lie about the books you sent me? You didn't buy them in Paris for a song; you bought them from a dealer in Bath for fifteen hundred pounds."

"I talked him down to twelve fifty," said Eric.

"That's beside the point. You don't spend over a thousand pounds on books for someone you hardly know."

"I know you well enough to know that you would love that set—

a piece of Jane Austen so close to the time she was alive. I lied because I didn't think you'd accept it if you knew how much it cost."

Sophie stared at the pavement for a long minute. "I did love it," she said at last. "But you can't just walk up to me on the street and expect me to drop everything and run off with you."

"I didn't ask you to run off with me," said Eric. "Besides, what are you doing that's so important that you can't take a half hour to have a cup of coffee with me and see if maybe there's something to this?"

"Actually," said Sophie, "I have a date."

"You have a date?"

"Surely if you are infatuated with me it must not be so hard to believe that someone else might have an interest as well."

"And who is this mystery man?"

It was none of his business, she knew, but somehow Sophie thought that naming the man she had romped around naked with just a few days earlier—and with whom she might very well do the same thing again tonight—would help her stop thinking about that kiss, and those sweet letters, and those amazing books.

"His name is Winston Godfrey."

"The publisher?" said Eric.

"Do you know him?" said Sophie, unable to hide her surprise.

"I'll say I know him," he said. "We were at Oxford together."

"You were at Oxford?"

"They do admit Americans once in a while."

"Let me guess," she said. "You were at St. John's."

"No, Balliol," said Eric. "But listen, Sophie, you've got to trust me on this. Winston Godfrey is bad news."

"You're hardly a disinterested party," she said. "And it just so happens that Winston is a perfect gentleman."

"Right, a total gentleman. Candlelit dinner on the first date, flowers on the second, dinner at his place followed by the best sex you've ever had on the third. Trust me, he'll push all those buttons about three more times and then he'll toss you aside like yesterday's paper. I saw it for two years. He went through girls like potato chips."

Sophie was disturbed by how accurately Eric had summarized her relationship with Winston. "Did it occur to you that Winston may have changed since university?"

"Guys like Winston don't change," said Eric. "Believe me, the guy may look good coming out of the lake in a wet shirt, but he's trouble."

"Listen, I appreciate the warning, I really do, but I can take care of myself. And I appreciate . . ." She wasn't sure how to word it. "Everything else. And I *would* like to have a coffee with you. Just not today, OK?"

"Can I give you my number?" he said.

"You give me your number and I'll give you my number and I'll be careful. And if Winston turns out to be what you say he is, I'll call you for coffee and you can say 'I told you so.'"

"And if he stays a perfect gentleman?" said Eric. "I don't want to walk down this street and never see you again."

"All right—no matter what happens, I'll call you for a coffee," said Sophie.

As she left Eric at Martyrs' Memorial, she realized she hadn't succeeded in simplifying her love life—anything but. But she didn't care. If Eric had come all the way from France to find her, maybe he did deserve another chance, particularly if Winston turned out to be as much of a scoundrel as Eric predicted.

On a whim she pulled out her phone and rang a friend who worked at the Balliol College Library. A quick query revealed that both Eric Hall and Winston Godfrey had been undergraduates there. Winston was a year ahead of Eric, but they had overlapped for two years. So Winston had lied about his undergraduate college and Eric had told the truth.

"Can you check one more name for me?" said Sophie to her friend. "George Smedley."

"Yep," he said. "George Smedley was here. Took his degree the same year as Winston Godfrey."

"Thanks," said Sophie. "That's very helpful."

So Winston and Smedley had not been at St. John's, but they had been at Balliol together. Sophie was beginning to think that her conversation with Winston might be very interesting.

## *Leeds, 1796*

**THE HEAT FROM** the flames brought a swelter to Gilbert Monkhouse's face, but his face would have burned if he were standing ten miles away. His beloved printing-office was in the last stages of destruction by fire, and grief and anger consumed him just as the flames consumed his paper and his press and melted his metal type. He had gone through in his mind again and again, since he had been shaken awake by his landlady in the predawn hours, the last moments he had spent in the shop, but he knew he had extinguished all the lamps; he knew this was not his fault. For the first time in his life he thought that his ability to recall almost any words set in type was a curse rather than a blessing, for now he could remember nothing but a small piece that had run in the *Leeds Intelligencer* a few weeks before. In a story about a fire that had been started by some idle boys playing with gunpowder, the penalties for that and related offenses had been stated:

> **Every person selling, or exposing to sale, any squibs, serpents, or fireworks, or permitting the same to be cast or fired from their house, or other place, into any public street or road, shall for every offence forfeit £5, half to the poor, and half to the informer.—And if any person through negligence, or carelessness, shall fire, or cause to be fired, any dwelling-house, out-house, or other**

**building, he shall forfeit £100 or be committed to the house of correction, to hard labour, for 18 months.**

Gilbert had little hope that anyone would be held accountable for the fire, and the catastrophe meant he had lost not just his personal savings and inheritance but also the two-hundred-pound loan from his former employer. For all intents and purposes, Thomas Wright now owned him.

Wright was not an unkind man. He was even among those who struggled to douse the flames that night. But he was also not foolish with regard to his investments. He gave Gilbert his old job back and allowed him to repay the loan little by little out of his wages. After only a week, Gilbert knew that he would work for Thomas for the rest of his life. He was not unhappy—he was, after all, still doing what he loved—but he would never forget that blissful year when he had made books on his own, sending them out into the world with his imprint, "Gilbert Monkhouse, Printer, Leeds," on the title pages.

In the commotion and emotion of the fire and the days that followed, Gilbert had forgotten all about the proof sheets that lay on the table in his room. It was almost a week later, working once again at his post as compositor for Thomas Wright, that he set a story in the *Intelligencer*:

**Rev. Richard Mansfield, 80, of Croft, died on December 4 in Hampshire. He was taken ill on a journey thence. Funeral services and burial were at the chapel at Busbury Park. Mr. Mansfield had been Rector of Croft for sixteen years and was much loved by his parishioners.**

Gilbert thought of Mansfield's book and realized that, like his own dreams, it would never come to fruition. He waited a few months, to see if any family members would contact him, but when no communication came, he took the pages to the bindery favored by Mr. Wright and had them bound up in a simple, unmarked cloth cover. He kept it always, as a reminder of what almost was.

Gilbert's dream of owning his own printing-office gradually faded and was replaced by other dreams—especially on the day that Thomas Wright's daughter, Theresa, stopped by the office on her way to the dressmaker. As a man in debt, Gilbert had given little thought to marriage, but after several weeks of walking with Theresa through the streets of Leeds on sunny days and taking tea with her in the parlor of the Wright home, Gilbert had the boldness to ask her father if he might have Theresa's hand.

Thomas Wright could see the joy that Gilbert brought to his daughter, and he not only gave his consent, but on the day they were married, he forgave the balance of Gilbert's loan and gave the couple a small cottage in which to start their lives together. Gilbert owed Thomas so much that he worked for him, and happily so, until the day some decades later when the old man sold the business and retired on the proceeds.

Theresa gave Gilbert a wonderful daughter; her father not only gave him employment, but allowed him to print an extra copy of any book that came through the press that interested Gilbert. By the time he died, Gilbert had built a collection of almost three hundred books, which he passed on to his son-in-law, Joseph Collingwood.

## *Oxford, Present Day*

"It's good to see you," said Winston, coming at Sophie for a kiss.

She turned her head and allowed his kiss to land on her cheek. "You too," she said. "Get me a coffee and a chicken baguette, will you?" She sat at an empty table in the small courtyard and pulled out her phone, pretending to check her messages. Anything to keep from looking at Winston until they had food as a buffer between them. When he returned with the sandwiches, Sophie took a big bite out of hers and chewed slowly while she continued to scroll through imaginary messages.

"Are we going to talk to each other, or is this literally just lunch?" said Winston, leaving his sandwich untouched.

Sophie took a gulp of coffee, laid down her phone, and finally looked at him. "Mostly you're going to talk," she said. "You're going to tell me why you lied about being at St. John's, and you're going to tell me why you lied about *First Impressions*, and then you're going to tell me who the hell George Smedley is."

"Did you find it?" he said eagerly, his eyes widening as he leaned toward her. Sophie could not decide whether he looked like an excited child or a ravenous dog. "Did you find the second edition?"

"I don't think you understand," said Sophie calmly. "I'm not here to tell my story; you're here to tell your story. From the beginning, with no more lies."

"From the beginning?" said Winston, leaning back into his chair.

"With no lies," said Sophie, picking up her sandwich and taking another bite. She thought she had done rather well. She hadn't raised her voice or made accusations that she couldn't support; she had just quietly asked for the truth.

"OK," he said, "from the beginning. I suppose it started with the family legend. My great-grandmother was a Mansfield, and her great-great-grandfather was the son of Richard Mansfield, who wrote *A Little Book of Allegorical Stories*. We didn't have a big library in my house—not like yours, certainly—but we did have a few books, and one of them was a copy of Mansfield's book that had been passed down through the generations. And there was a story that went with the book. My father thought it was bollocks, and my grandfather didn't seem to believe it either. But I heard it once from my great-grandmother. I was eight years old and her eyesight was failing, so she asked me to read her one of Mansfield's allegories. Then she told me.

"Her grandfather had heard the story from his grandfather, Tobias Mansfield. Tobias claimed that, right before his father died, he had paid the old man a visit and found a manuscript in his father's hand of an epistolary story called *First Impressions*. His father told him that it was a story he was adding to the second edition of his book of allegories, and Tobias read a few pages of it. Richard Mansfield died in 1796, so it was seventeen years later that Tobias picked up a review of a novel called *Pride and Prejudice* and saw a description of his father's story. Of course, Jane Austen's name didn't appear on the book anyplace . . ."

"It was published as 'by the author of *Sense and Sensibility*,'" said Sophie.

"And *Sense and Sensibility* was published as 'by a lady,'" said Winston. "Tobias read the book and figured it had been stolen from his father. Of course, there were no copyright laws then, and it's not like the book was selling millions of copies, so he told the story to his son and thought no more about it. And then his son told the story, and so on. The only things that changed as the story got passed down from generation to generation were that *Pride and Prejudice* gradually became a worldwide phenomenon and my family gradually stopped believing the legend.

"But it intrigued me. Anytime I had the chance, whether at a bookstore or a library, I always looked for copies of *A Little Book of Allegorical Stories*, but I never could find a second edition. And then I came up to Oxford."

"To Balliol."

"Right," said Winston sheepishly, "to Balliol. And one by one I searched every library in town. There are three copies of Mansfield's book in Oxford. One in the Bodleian, one at Worcester—"

"And one at St. John's."

"And one at St. John's. I never really believed the story until I saw the inscription in the copy at St. John's."

"'To J.A.,'" said Sophie, who had already memorized the inscription in the book that nestled in her handbag. "'Judge not too harshly, but like me reserve First Impressions for second editions. Affectionately, R.M.'"

"You've seen it, then. Sounds pretty incriminating, doesn't it?"

"Why didn't you just tell me all this to start with?"

"I didn't think you'd believe me," said Winston. "And I liked you—I do like you—so I didn't want you to think I was some sort of flake."

"And why lie about your college?"

"I had to be sure you found that book at St. John's. I thought about just telling you outright, but I thought if you found it on your own you'd be more . . . I don't know, committed to the cause."

"You knew I liked mysteries," said Sophie.

"True," said Winston.

"So you thought that where two centuries of Mansfields have failed to find the second edition of his book, little Sophie Collingwood, who's been a bookseller for about a week, would be able to succeed?"

"Oh, God, you don't know, do you? I thought you would have sussed that bit out by now."

"What bit?" said Sophie, who knew exactly what he meant, but needed to hear how he knew.

"Well, a lot of my friends know that I'm interested in eighteenth-century printing. One of those friends works at *The Book Collector* and not long ago he e-mailed me a piece that's going into the next issue—an obituary of your Uncle." Winston pulled out his wallet and removed a folded slip of paper, handing it to Sophie. "Read it."

She read:

> **Collingwood, Bertram Arthur—book collector, bibliophile, and expert on a wide variety of literary topics. He was descended from a printer of the late eighteenth century and often told the story of how his family library (Bayfield House, Oxfordshire) began as a collection of printer's samples. He is survived by his brother, Robert, and two nieces, Victoria and Sophie.**

"A collection that started as eighteenth-century printer's samples sounded fascinating to me, but of course I wanted to know which eighteenth-century printer. So I did a little genealogical research online and found out that Sophie Collingwood—"

"Is descended from Gilbert Monkhouse," said Sophie.

"So you *did* know," said Winston.

"Not until yesterday," she said.

"Well, when I called Gusty to check on an order and he told me Sophie Collingwood was working for him, I had to meet you."

"To add me to your collection, or just to gain access to the Bayfield library?"

"Neither," said Winston. "I mean, even with the inscription at St. John's I wasn't sure about that whole family legend. But it was too big a coincidence to ignore."

"So what's your goal here? Do you really think if I discovered the first draft of *Pride and Prejudice* in my family library I'd just sell it to you?"

"Of course not," said Winston. "I don't care what you do with it. I just think if there is an amazing literary artifact out there someplace, it should be found."

"So you stalked me."

"I didn't stalk you," he said. "I met you. And then everything changed."

"What do you mean?"

"I mean that now I don't care so much about Gilbert Monkhouse and Richard Mansfield and Jane Austen. I care a lot more about Sophie Collingwood." He leaned forward and took her hand in his. His sandwich lay untouched on his plate. "So let's forget all this nonsense about *First Impressions*, and . . . do something together. Take a walk in the countryside, or go to a gallery, or . . ."

"Or go back to my place?" said Sophie.

"Well, I admit, that would be my first choice; I just didn't want to seem forward."

It's a little late for that, Sophie thought, but in that moment, she decided. He had come clean, and he was more interested in her than in old books; otherwise he wouldn't be so nonchalant about what happened to *First Impressions*. She believed him.

"Do you want to see it?" she asked, leaning in toward him until their lips almost touched.

"See what?"

"See this," said Sophie. She opened her handbag and, careful not to let him see that there were two books inside, drew out the one that did not have a library sticker on the spine. Glancing around to be sure no one was looking, she held the unmarked volume up for him to see.

"Oh my God," said Winston, his eyes widening. "Is that it?"

Sophie looked right into those eyes for several seconds, trying to detect avarice, but she sensed only curiosity. "*Little Allegories and a Cautionary Tale*," she said, opening to the title page. "Being the second edition of *A Little Book of Allegorical Stories* by Rev. Richard Mansfield. And including the story *First Impressions*."

"It's really in there?"

"The last story," said Sophie. She turned to the beginning of *First Impressions* and read a few sentences. Winston's breathing stopped and his mouth fell open. "Sound familiar?" she asked.

"My God, I really didn't think it was true. Where did you find it? Does it belong to Bayfield House?"

"Actually," said Sophie, "it belonged to my uncle. It has his ownership signature on the flyleaf." She turned to the front of the book and showed Winston Uncle Bertram's inscription: "*Natalis Christi* B.A.C. 1971."

"Incredible," said Winston. "And the story? Is it really *Pride and Prejudice*?"

"Before we talk about that," said Sophie, "you need to answer my last question."

"Which question was that?"

"Who is George Smedley?"

"George Smedley? I have no idea who . . . wait, I think there was a chap named Smedley at Balliol with me. I don't remember much about him. Lived on the same staircase as me, but we didn't really go in the same circles. To be honest, he probably worked a lot harder than I did."

"And did you ever tell him this little family legend?"

"Sophie," said Winston with a sigh, "if you've been talking to people who knew me at Oxford, I'm sure you've heard all sorts of things. I was a womanizer, I didn't take my studies very seriously, I spent my nights at the pub drinking. I'm not going to deny any of that. I suppose we all make mistakes when we're young and I made more than my share. And I'm sure it's possible that on one of the hundreds of nights when I'd had too much to drink I bragged about my family legend within earshot of George Smedley. I did a lot of bragging in those days. It's funny how we brag the most when we have the least cause to."

"So it's possible that George Smedley knows all about *First Impressions*?" said Sophie, impressed that Winston had admitted to his past behavior. Apparently he *had* changed. What would Eric think of that?

"It's possible," said Winston. "Though I'd be surprised if he believed it. Why do you ask?"

"Because I believe that George Smedley murdered my uncle to try to get this book. And he's been offering me huge sums of money to find it for him and threatening me if I don't."

Winston expelled a laugh. "George Smedley? A murderer? He hardly seemed the type. Bit of a milquetoast, as I recall."

"People change," said Sophie.

"So what are you going to do with the book?"

"Here's the deal," she said. "I don't believe your great-grandmother's story. I believe *First Impressions* was written by Jane Austen, and I'm not going to sell or even show this book to anyone else until I prove it. And you're going to help me. Plus you're going to help me get George Smedley to admit that he murdered my uncle. Once we've done all that, I'll make the book public, your company will publish a facsimile of it, and we'll split the profits."

"That could save Godfrey Publishers," said Winston. "Can you imagine how many copies of that will sell?"

"Yes," said Sophie, who had been giving the matter considerable thought. "I can imagine it will sell enough copies that I can make some significant progress rebuilding my uncle's library."

"And what if we *can't* prove that Jane Austen was . . . was innocent? What if it looks like Mansfield really did write it?"

"I'd rather not think about that," she said. But she had thought about it. Once George Smedley was safely behind bars, Sophie would have to decide what to do: destroy a priceless literary artifact, keep the book a secret, or make it public anyway—whatever that meant for Jane Austen's reputation. It was a decision she had no desire to make. For now she would just have to be satisfied with believing that Jane was innocent, and that somewhere was evidence to prove it.

"So, are you with me?" she asked.

"Do you mean just as a . . . I don't know, a coconspirator, or as . . . as a partner in . . . in other ways?"

"Winston Godfrey, are you asking to be my boyfriend?"

"I'm just asking if we're going to have a relationship that extends beyond bibliographical intrigue."

"I don't know," said Sophie, feeling a twinge of guilt as she thought of Eric coming back from Paris. "We're not going back to my room right now, if that's what you're getting at."

"Where are we going?" said Winston.

"The Oxfordshire History Centre."

## *Hampshire, 1796*

**WINTER HAD GRIPPED** Hampshire early as Jane stood in the corner of the churchyard at the Busbury Park chapel. The wind bit into her cheeks and the dusting of snow that had fallen the previous evening swirled around among the gravestones, giving the whole scene an otherworldly appearance. Her family had accompanied her to Mr. Mansfield's funeral—her parents; her brothers, James and Henry, who had come home for Christmas; and of course Cassandra, who now held her hand tightly. Although even Cassandra did not know the depth of Jane's affection for or indebtedness to Mr. Mansfield, she, more than the others, comprehended that Jane had lost a dear friend, and she had been a great comfort and support to her sister in the past few days.

The Austens made up nearly half the congregation that had attended the funeral in the tiny chapel and now stood in the churchyard for the burial. Lord Wintringham was there with his two sons; his wife, Jane was saddened to learn, had passed away the previous spring. A large stone outside the door of the church marked her resting place, and here the two younger men had paused before the service to remember their mother. Jane had always found churchyards both heartbreaking and comforting, and today was no exception. Even on her most carefree childhood days, when some combination of Austen siblings would frolic among the gravestones in St. Nicholas churchyard at Steventon, she had never completely escaped the reality of what those stones represented.

Today that reality pierced her heart like a dagger, but at the same time the words of comfort spoken by the clergyman, and the knowledge that her friend rested in the bosom of Christ, served as greater comfort than any companionship of family—even of her dear Cassandra—could ever hope to.

When the Grace had been proclaimed, the tiny congregation began to disperse—some back toward the main house and some toward the village outside the park. The earl tipped his hat to Jane as she passed. The Austens were just passing through the churchyard gate when Jane felt a hand on her arm and turned to find Mrs. Harris, who had kept house for Mr. Mansfield.

"Mrs. Harris," said Jane. "How kind of you to come."

"I'm sorry for you, Miss Austen," said Mrs. Harris. "I know he was a good friend." She gave Jane a nod of her head and a look that seemed to say perhaps she knew more about the intimacy between Jane and Mr. Mansfield than she ought to have. Jane knew from novels that housekeepers often overheard private conversations, but she could easily forgive the gentle Mrs. Harris such eavesdropping.

"He was," said Jane. "And more than that."

"I thought you should know," said Mrs. Harris, "I unpacked his things when he returned, though they took him straight up to the big house. There was a book for you. I left it on the table there in the sitting room where you used to read to him. I thought you might still want it." Jane gave a tiny, inaudible gasp. Was it possible that this was the second edition of Mr. Mansfield's book?

"You are very kind. I shall stop by the gatehouse on the way home. And Mrs. Harris," said Jane, taking the older woman's hand in hers, "thank you so much for all that you did for him."

"'Tweren't nothing," said Mrs. Harris. "I cooked and cleaned same as I would for anyone else. You gave him nourishment I never could." Before Jane could respond to this kindness, Mrs. Harris slipped through the gate and hurried off toward the main house. Jane implored her family to start for home without her while she stopped off at the gatehouse, but Cassandra insisted on staying with her sister.

"So this is where you went off to all those days," she said to Jane as they stood before the gatehouse. It seemed lifeless now. No light shone from within, and a workman was busy closing up the shutters, sealing the house like a tomb.

"It was a pleasant spot for me," said Jane. "We spoke of literature and writing and . . . and other things. I shan't be a moment." Not wanting to prolong her stay in a room in which she had once felt so much joy but which now held no happiness, Jane dashed into the gatehouse, only to have her breath taken away. Not only was there no book on the table; the sitting room was nearly empty. Only a single heavy chair and the table by the window remained; the rest—furniture, books, rugs—was gone. Even the pictures had been removed from the walls, leaving rectangles of whitewash outlined in candleblack. Jane made a quick tour of the rest of the house and found the other rooms equally empty. Outside, she addressed the workman, now on a ladder closing out the sunlight from what had been Mr. Mansfield's bedroom.

"Excuse me, but can you tell me what happened to everything in the house?"

"Furniture went back up to the big house," said the man, not interrupting his efforts to look at Jane.

"But what about Mr. Mansfield's belongings? His books and his effects?"

"Sold by order of the heir."

"The heir?"

"Mr. Tobias Mansfield," said the man. "The son. Got wind that his father died and asked that all his things be sold."

"But there was a book there in which . . . that is, which Mr. Mansfield intended to present to me. As a gift."

"All I know, miss, is a fellow come up from Winchester yesterday and took away everything. Books included."

**IN THE MONTHS TO** come, Jane would search every bookshop in Winchester for the book that Mr. Mansfield had brought for her, but without success. She would carefully watch the advertisements in the literary journals, but she never saw an announcement for *Little*

*Allegories and a Cautionary Tale.* By the time she had finished expanding *First Impressions* into a full-length narrative novel, she had assumed that the original version had been lost forever.

The copy of the first edition of *A Little Book of Allegorical Stories* inscribed by Richard Mansfield to Jane Austen followed a path not so different from that of millions of other books. From the dealer in Winchester it was sold to a clergyman who kept it until his death. His books were bought by another bookseller and the volume was sold to another reader and on that reader's death the process was repeated. And so it went through the generations until the book was among a small collection left by a don to his Oxford college. There it was unpacked, cataloged, placed on a shelf, and ignored by readers for the better part of a century.

## *Oxford, Present Day*

**SOPHIE REMEMBERED** the first time Uncle Bertram had taken her to a library that was neither a place to check out books nor a public museum. He had just read a biography of Archibald Campbell Tait, the Victorian archbishop of Canterbury, and he wanted, he said, to know more.

"But you read the whole book," said Sophie, who was fourteen. "How can you know more?"

"The man who wrote this book couldn't read *all* the original source material," said Uncle Bertram.

"What's original source material?"

"Where do you think the author learned so much about his subject?" said her uncle. "He didn't know the archbishop. So he had to read his letters and his diaries and his sermons."

"Can't you just buy those things at a bookstore?" said Sophie, who had come to believe that all worldly knowledge could be found in any well-stocked secondhand bookshop.

"Not everything has been published in a book," said Uncle Bertram. "We're going to look at the originals—the actual handwritten letters and diaries and sermons."

He had taken her to the library at Lambeth Palace, the official home of the archbishop of Canterbury, on the south bank of the Thames in London. They had rung the bell next to a thick wooden door set into a high stone wall. When the door swung open, Sophie felt she was being admitted into a private castle. Traffic and tourists whizzed round them, but only she and her uncle passed into the quiet sanctuary. A librarian who seemed to be old friends with Uncle Bertram led them to a small reading room, where two or three other scholars sat at long wooden tables. Uncle Bertram enlisted Sophie's help in filling out small slips of paper requesting the materials he wanted, and a few minutes later she was carefully untying strips of cloth that held together dusty stacks of folded letters. She wondered if anyone had looked at them in the past century.

Sophie couldn't believe she was allowed to touch a notebook of sermons Tait had given in the 1840s or a series of letters to his wife. How could anyone who knew these things were right here in London not want to hold them, to experience the feeling of life and reality radiating off of them in ways that even a printed book could not provide?

Sophie came to love original source material. She loved the thrill that came with unfolding a piece of paper that had lain untouched for decades or even centuries and finding out something that other scholars had missed. At Oxford she spent as much time in archives working with unpublished materials as in libraries reading printed books.

The Oxfordshire History Centre was housed in a former church in Cowley. As Sophie and Winston entered, the high stained glass windows filtered colored light onto the researchers below. Winston gave a low whistle.

"You've never been here before?"

"Why would I?" he said.

"For a book collector, you have a lot to learn."

Sophie did not know any of the staff who were working that afternoon, and she decided that was just as well. Since she had come here hoping to engage in criminal activity, better that she not be recognized. She pulled out the paper on which she had written the catalog numbers of the Cowley Grammar School archives and began copying them onto request slips. "Each reader can only check out one box at a time," said Sophie, "so you sign requests for half of them and I'll sign requests for the other half."

"What are we looking for?" asked Winston.

"Anything to do with Richard Mansfield."

"I feel like a secret agent," he whispered in her ear. His hot breath almost made her wish they had gone to her room first, but when the archivist stepped up to the counter to take their request slips, all thoughts but research left her mind.

A few minutes later they sat side by side, sifting through the first two boxes of papers. Most were folded tightly and tied into packets with narrow strips of cloth. The cloth was almost black with dust on the outside and a clean white on the underside—a sure sign, thought Sophie, that no one had looked at these papers since they had first been bundled up. As the clock ticked slowly overhead, they carefully untied packet after packet, only to discover endless pages of accounts, correspondence with tradesmen, and lists of awards.

Sophie loved a story, and these papers told one. She found herself tracking the progress of certain students, following the troubles of tradesmen who did subpar work, and being drawn into the drama of hiring a new mathematics master. When Winston proclaimed he had finished his first box, Sophie was barely through the second bundle of at least a dozen.

"How did you get through so fast?" she asked.

"Same way I read all my assignments at Rugby—scanned everything and picked out the important words. There's nothing to do with Mansfield in here, trust me. Shall I go get the next one?"

"You can help me with mine," said Sophie. She didn't like the idea of his getting ahead of her. What if there *was* something related to Mansfield and Austen? And what if Winston, with his rapid scanning, found it before Sophie could? She realized that not only did she want Austen to be exonerated, but she wanted to be the one to do it. She handed him the most unpromising bundle in her box—a sooty pile of papers with a label tucked under the tie reading "accounts 1825–27."

"This is way too late for Mansfield," said Winston.

"Still, we'd better check," said Sophie. "You can't always trust labels."

She increased the pace of her own search, still not keeping up with Winston, but regretfully setting aside any number of dramas.

As soon as she opened her third box Sophie saw it. She turned her body slightly to shield Winston's view, but he was already rifling through the papers in his box, and besides, it was unlikely he would notice. Winston didn't catch subtle details. The cloth strip that tied one of the bundles in this box had several bits of white facing out. Unlike all the other bundles she had examined, this one had recently been untied and retied. She gently untied the cloth and turned over the slip of paper on the top of the bundle. It read: "Richard Mansfield 1758–80." Fingers trembling, she unfolded the first document. It was a list of students who had been at Cowley in 1758. She went on to the second item.

The documents appeared to be in chronological order, but Sophie resisted the urge to skip ahead to the end of the stack. A clue could be anywhere, she reasoned. Most of the documents had to do with mundane matters of school life. She was beginning to despair of finding anything, when she reached a small group of papers about an inch thick that had been tied together within the larger batch. Again, the fabric tie showed tell-tale bits of white. The label read: "R.M. papers after death 1796."

"Nothing here," said Winston, closing his box. "I'll go get my last one. They close in twenty minutes. You'd better get cracking. Anything good in yours?"

"Nothing yet," said Sophie, flipping the packet over to prevent him from seeing the label.

"Maybe Mansfield wrote the thing after all," he said.

She felt a surge of anger toward him that dissipated almost as quickly as it had come upon her. She needed him for protection against Smedley, she reminded herself; he was big and strong. And good in bed, she thought. He just wasn't a scholar or a particularly passionate defender of Jane Austen. Of course, if Mansfield really did write *First Impressions,* Winston would suddenly be descended from a famous author. Was it possible that he didn't *want* to exonerate Jane?

Sophie pushed these thoughts aside, realizing that she had only a few minutes to examine the final Mansfield bundle in private while Winston waited at the counter for his last box. She quickly untied the strip of cloth and began to scan the documents. The first several were letters from the headmaster who had followed Mansfield, asking for advice. These were arranged in chronological order, and the dates grew gradually further apart, until the correspondence became simple annual updates on the health of the school.

The last of these letters was dated January 1796. "I was delighted to receive your *Little Book of Allegorical Stories*," wrote the headmaster. "There are several of these that I will share with the boys from the pulpit on Sunday mornings, and they will appreciate them all the more knowing they come from a much loved former leader of their flock." At the bottom of the bundle were two unopened letters, both addressed to Mansfield at Croft Rectory, Yorkshire. Both were still sealed, with a wafer of gum and flour like those she had read about in Jane Austen, Sophie supposed. She glanced up and saw that Winston was still waiting for his box, casually chatting with a young woman behind the counter. She needed something with which to pry open the two letters—letters that neither Richard Mansfield nor anyone else had ever read. Her nails were too short to slip under the paper; her pencil was too thick. Desperate, she reached up and pulled out a hair clip. Thank goodness she had made some effort to look nice for Winston this morning.

Turning her back to the counter, she slipped the metal edge of the clip under the flap of the first letter and gently popped it open. She unfolded the single sheet of notepaper to discover a letter from a clergyman, asking if there were an open post for a curate at Croft parish. Sophie sighed in disappointment. She picked up the second letter and was just about to open it in the same way when she noticed a tiny cut just above the seal of the flap, as if someone had cut the paper with a razor blade. Whoever had untied this bundle had also cut into this letter. But why open the one and not the other? Willing herself to examine the clues one step at a time, rather than immediately unfolding the letter, Sophie turned the paper over and looked at the address. Eighteenth-century hands were hard to distinguish from one another, especially with a sample of only five words, but it certainly did look familiar.

Her whole body trembled now as she carefully unfolded the letter. She and Winston were the only researchers left in the room, and she could hear him still chatting with the girl behind the counter. She smoothed out the letter on the table and read:

*Steventon, November 23, 1796*

**My Dear Mr. Mansfield,**

**I have shared *First Impressions* only with Cassandra and my niece Anna, to whom I read in my room each afternoon. Anna, I'm afraid, is so excited about the story that she keeps mentioning the names of Eliza Bennet and Mr. Darcy downstairs in the sitting room, and I'm sure the other occupants of the rectory must be filled with curiosity, but so far your little project remains, for the most part, a secret. I look forward to your return.**

**Yours very affectionately,**

**J. Austen**

Sophie was thrilled and devastated all at once. Here was a previously unknown letter from Jane Austen that firmly established her connection to Richard Mansfield, but again it seemed to imply that Mansfield wrote *First Impressions.* It wasn't positive, she told herself, but at the same time she knew it didn't look good. The three pieces of evidence she now had—the inscribed first edition of *A Little Book of Allegorical Stories* from St. John's; the second edition, containing *First Impressions*; and this letter—together certainly pointed toward Mansfield as the author. But Sophie refused to believe it. She knew that Jane had written *First Impressions.* She just couldn't prove it. Not yet. Sophie looked up to see Winston taking delivery of the final box. Almost without thinking, she slipped the letter into the back pocket of her jeans. By the time Winston returned to the table she had retied the Mansfield bundle and was shutting up the box.

"She gave me the last two," said Winston. "And she says we can have an extra fifteen minutes."

"You work on those," said Sophie. "I need to pop to the ladies'."

"Nothing in that box, then?"

"Nothing," said Sophie. After returning the box, she went to the lobby, where she retrieved her handbag from a locker. A minute later she was secure in a stall of the ladies' loo and had slipped the Jane Austen letter into the St. John's copy of *Allegorical Stories*. Theft was getting easier and easier, she reflected.

Just as she was about to return to the lobby, she heard her phone vibrate from the depths of her bag. Pulling it out, she saw she had two texts from Victoria. The first read: "Managed to get off Thurs. so coming to see you," and the second, "Booked on the night train, will arrive London early." The thought that her sister would soon be on her way brought a surge of relief to Sophie. Here, at last, would be someone she could trust completely. She texted back, "In Oxford. Let me know what train and I'll meet you. Love you!"

She felt a lightness in her step as she returned to the lobby. Victoria would be able to help—she was always good at forming a plan of action. Jane Austen was not doomed yet. When she reentered the reading room, Winston was bent over one of the boxes, and only one librarian remained behind the counter. Sophie's mind returned from Victoria's text to those white flashes of cloth and that tiny cut in the Austen letter. Someone had been here before them. Someone without much experience dealing with eighteenth-century documents had slit the flap of the letter and been the first person to read it since Jane Austen had written it. And someone had been a little careless in retying that bundle. Either that or he didn't care about covering his tracks.

"Excuse me," said Sophie as she approached the counter. "I'm Sophie Collingwood. I work over at the Christ Church Library." She found that librarians were likely to do favors for one another they wouldn't necessarily do for other readers—favors that sometimes didn't strictly conform to the rules. "I'm researching the history of Cowley School and I'd love to share my work with anyone else who's interested. Can you tell me if anyone has looked at this box in the past few months?" She handed over her copy of the request slip for the box in which she had found the Austen letter.

The woman hesitated for a moment, glancing over at Winston. "Pretty nice for a research assistant, don't you think?" said Sophie. The woman blushed and looked down at the request slip.

"Let me take a look," she said. She busied herself at her computer and Sophie glanced back at Winston. He was writing something with his pencil on a page he had torn from the notebook that Sophie had not touched all afternoon. Might he have found something else useful? Something that would explain away the implications of the letter?

"Actually there was another reader who checked out that box," said the woman, looking up from her monitor. "That's strange."

"Well, it's a very interesting school," said Sophie earnestly, "so it's not too strange."

"No," said the woman, "what's strange is that the request was from today. It's got the same time on it as yours. Quarter past two."

Sophie felt the cold sweat breaking out on her forehead and her hands began to shake. Smedley had been here. He had been in the room with her. Maybe even across the table from her. Certainly close enough to see what she was checking out. He had been following her. And now he was one step ahead.

"It looks like he requested all the Cowley files, but this was the first box we delivered to him and then he canceled the request for the others at . . . three o'clock."

"What was his name?" asked Sophie, already knowing the answer.

"I'm not really supposed to tell you that," said the librarian.

"It's all right," said Sophie. "I won't tell anybody. I'll bet it was my old friend from Balliol. We used to talk about grammar school history all the time. What was his name? Smedley or something like that? He won't mind if you tell me." The woman stared down at her screen, apparently still uncertain. Sophie leaned over the counter and whispered, "It's OK, I'm a librarian. It was George Smedley, wasn't it?"

"I'm sorry," said the librarian, "I don't think I'm supposed to give out that information." Sophie jumped as Winston dropped the final two boxes on the counter. The moment of intimacy was broken.

"Thanks for letting us finish up, Fiona," he said. "Don't have too much fun tonight." Sophie watched as Winston ran his finger along the back of Fiona's hand. She could have hit him. Here she was, getting ready to grill Fiona about Smedley, and Winston walks up and starts flirting. And right in front her.

"Oops," said Winston, and Sophie thought she caught a hint of a wink as he looked right at Fiona. "Forgot my jacket."

He turned to retrieve his sports coat and Sophie grabbed Fiona by the wrist. "Tell me his name," she whispered. "It was Smedley, wasn't it? What did he look like?"

"I'm afraid we have to close now," said Fiona, her voice turning cold.

"Ready to go?" said Winston, slipping an arm around Sophie's waist. Half of Sophie wanted to lean into that arm, to lose herself in his touch. The other half wanted to push him away, to tell him never mind, she could do this on her own.

"I need to get my handbag," she said, shaking off his embrace. "Meet me outside." She took a minute to survey the contents of her bag in the empty lobby. Three stolen items: two books and a letter, all pointing to Jane Austen as a plagiarist. Maybe she should just quit now. Tell the police about Smedley and his threats and her suspicions, let Winston publish *First Impressions*, and let Winston . . . do other things. It was the path of least resistance, and Sophie had to admit it was attractive. She might be reviled among Austen fans, but she would still be famous in literary circles. She would have plenty of money for book buying, and she would have Winston in her bed on a regular basis. Unless, of course, he ran off with some flirt like Fiona.

And what about Eric? How did she really feel about him, and was there any truth to what he had said about Winston? After all, Winston had stood there chatting up that librarian right in front of her. Sophie had never felt more mixed up. All she was sure of was that she wasn't ready to give up on Eric, she certainly wasn't ready to give up on Jane Austen, she wasn't ready to *completely* trust Winston, and she couldn't wait for Victoria to show up so she'd have someone to talk to about all this. Until then, she would compromise. She would keep working with Winston to try to prove Jane's innocence, but she would keep a close eye on him. She certainly wouldn't show him the letter, just in case he was not what he claimed to be. After all, no one stood to profit more from the revelation of *First Impressions* than the publishing company that would present the story to the world.

## *Hampshire, 1797*

**A FEW WEEKS AFTER CHRISTMAS,** Jane sat at her usual spot in the dressing room, reading over a page of manuscript she had just completed. She had not spent a day writing since Mr. Mansfield's death, having been distracted first by the funeral and then by Christmas guests at the rectory—her brothers, sisters-in-law, nieces, and nephews. While the gathering demanded that she read to them frequently from her work—she had, in fact, given an encore performance of *Elinor and Marianne*—their enthusiasm for her incipient career as a novelist did not extend so far as to leave her in silence to write for any period of time. Now the rectory was experiencing a period of unusual calm and she had, that morning, taken back up her pen and returned to the project she had set aside at the time of Mr. Mansfield's death.

"Do you return to *First Impressions*?" said Cassandra, setting a cup of tea down on the table for her sister.

"Mr. Mansfield approved of my plan to expand it and tell it as a narrative rather than in letters. Though he is no longer with us, I believe he would want to see the work done." Jane, in fact, felt that she owed it to the memory of Mr. Mansfield to persevere with the work of expanding *First Impressions*, painful though it sometimes was to take up the thread of a story which reminded her of her absent friend at every turn.

"And will you share this new draft with us?" said Cassandra.

"Indeed," said Jane, "when I have made a bit more progress. I confess that, though I must read you the chapters in order, I have taken the rather rash step in my writing of skipping ahead to a particular scene which has been lurking, fully formed, in my head these many weeks. I find if I do not write it down, I cannot continue with the earlier episodes."

"Very well," said Cassandra, pausing in the doorway to smile at her sister. "We shall be patient while your mind flits ahead."

The scene was Eliza's first visit to Pemberley—a scene Jane had longed to write since a perfect day in autumn when, encouraged by the unusually warm weather, she had walked to Busbury in hopes of some intercourse with Mr. Mansfield only to find him not at home. Thinking he might have some business at the main house with Lord Wintringham, she resigned herself to passing the day without his company, yet she did not like to waste so excellent an opportunity for walking the grounds of Busbury Park, for which activity Lord Wintringham had issued to her, through Mr. Mansfield, an open invitation.

She set off on a familiar path down the hill and soon found herself sheltered from the sun by a descent through hanging woods to the edge of the water. Wishing nothing more than to circle the lake, which was at its best with a whisper of a breeze rippling its surface just enough to make it sparkle in the sun, Jane turned in to the path that set off in a circumnavigation of the water. As much as she loved to walk by the water, she had not previously taken this path, for it was her habit to walk with Mr. Mansfield, and she feared that a complete circuit of the lake might prove too taxing for a man of four score years, so they always turned back toward the gatehouse after admiring the water for a few minutes. Thus it came as a surprise when, after crossing the bridge that spanned the river feeding into the lake at the far end, she saw, at no great distance, Mr. Mansfield approaching—apparently taking the same path in the opposite direction. The walk being here less sheltered than on the other side allowed her to see him before they met, but soon enough they came face-to-face and Jane expressed her great delight in meeting her friend, though it meant her plans for a full circuit round the lake were dashed, as she turned back and continued in the direction Mr. Mansfield had been walking.

"Ah, Miss Austen," he said after they had traversed the bridge. "I thought perhaps you would be busy at home transforming *First Impressions* into a novel."

"Mr. Mansfield, you ought to be ashamed, speaking of novels in front of such an impressionable lady. But since you ask, I must tell you that yes, I have already begun to take the rash step of making *First Impressions* into something altogether . . . well, for the sake of propriety let me simply say—more substantial."

Mr. Mansfield laughed and offered his arm as they turned to follow the edge of the lake back toward the gatehouse path. "My reason for asking if you had yet begun the work, Miss Austen," he said, "is that I was struck just now by how our means of meeting one another, so unexpectedly while walking round the lake, might be just the way that Eliza ought to meet Mr. Darcy when she goes to Pemberley."

"Thus Eliza would have time to compose herself," said Jane, "as she might see his approach from a distance, yet she would also have no choice but to converse with him, as they would come together face-to-face far from the house or any other distractions. I like that, Mr. Mansfield. I like that very much indeed."

Now the sunshine and happiness of that day had given way to gloom and a dull ache in Jane's heart that throbbed into being whenever she thought of Mr. Mansfield. For him she would complete *First Impressions*, but with each stroke of the pen she would remember that perfect day, when she had taken his arm and they had strolled beside the lake, forgetting, for an hour, all the cares of the world.

## *Oxford, Present Day*

**SOPHIE PUSHED THROUGH** the outer glass doors of the history center to find Winston on the pavement, hands in his pockets, leaning against the stone wall at the edge of the car park. God, he looked smug, she thought, as her anger at his flirting suddenly resurfaced. "Jerk," she said as she stalked past him.

"Hey, what did I do?" said Winston, sounding genuinely surprised as he dashed to catch up to her.

"Don't have too much fun tonight," she said with a sneer.

"Sophie, what's wrong with you? Are you angry with me?"

"You were chatting her up right in front of me."

"Chatting who up? Fiona? I wasn't chatting her up," said Winston. "I turned on a little charm so she would let us stay past closing time, that's all."

"Did you get her number?"

"Of course I didn't get her number. Sophie, stop." He grabbed her by the wrist and she was forced to stop as he pulled her toward him and looked into her eyes. "That girl is nothing to me," he said. "I did it for you, because I knew you wanted to get through all those damn boxes. She was going to throw us out, so I flirted a little and it worked. You're good at research; I'm good at getting girls to bend the rules. I think that's called working as a team."

He was right. He *was* good at getting girls to bend the rules. She looked at his hand on her wrist and thought of all sorts of rules she would like to bend with him right there in the street. How could he do that with just a touch?

"Well, next time let me know about the plan first," she said, slipping her wrist out of his grip. "I wouldn't want to inadvertently interfere with your maneuvers." They walked for a few minutes in silence, and Sophie found herself reaching for his hand, silently apologizing for her anger as he slipped his strong fingers around hers.

"Is research always like that?" said Winston, as they walked up the busy Cowley Road toward central Oxford.

"Like what?"

"Hours of sifting through dusty old papers only to find nothing."

Sophie felt a twinge of guilt that Winston should be so convinced that their search had been fruitless, but only a tiny one. She still wasn't completely convinced he could be trusted. "Most days that's exactly what it's like," she said. "That's what makes the days when you find something so exciting."

"It was so quiet in there," he said. "I'm not good with quiet. I kept feeling like people were looking at me or talking about me behind my back."

"Oh, my god, I almost forgot," said Sophie. "Somebody *was* looking at us."

"What do you mean?"

"Somebody was there and looking at one of the same boxes we looked at," she said. "It must have been Smedley."

"What, this afternoon?" said Winston.

"*While* we were there," said Sophie. "God, that's creepy." She hadn't had much time to consider the fact that they may have been followed. She pressed herself into Winston, and he took the hint, encircling her waist with his arm.

"Don't worry," he said. "I may not be very good at research, but I make a passable bodyguard."

More than passable, thought Sophie. They had turned into High Street and were just passing the gates of Magdalen College when her phone rang.

"I haven't heard from you lately," said Smedley's voice. Sophie whirled around, certain he must be watching her, but she didn't see anyone else talking on a cell phone. She stepped away from Winston and spoke in a low voice.

"How did you get this number?" she hissed.

"Oh, your friend Gusty can be very helpful. Did you find anything exciting on your little excursion today?"

"You know exactly what I found because you found the same thing."

"I don't know what you mean."

"Anyway, it doesn't prove anything," said Sophie, "so if you came to me because I'm good at finding things out—"

"I'm sure by now you know why I came to you, Miss Collingwood. Now, I'm willing to let this little dalliance with your friend go on a little longer, but I warn you, my patience is wearing thin. If you've found what I'm looking for, it's time you handed it over."

"Or what?" said Sophie, emboldened by Winston's protection. "You'll push me down a flight of stairs?"

"There are others more dangerous than me, but if you bring the book to me, I can protect you."

"I'm not likely to trust you at this point, am I?" she said.

"It won't be long before you don't have a choice," said Smedley, and the line went dead.

"Who was it?" said Winston, when Sophie rejoined him.

"Take me home," she said softly. "Woodstock Road."

"Sophie, are you OK? You look pale."

"It was Smedley," she said. "Either he's following us or he's having us followed."

"I can't believe he would do that."

"Trust me," said Sophie, "he knew exactly what we'd been up to."

"If he's following us, we shouldn't go to your place," said Winston. He took her hand and swerved into Turl Street, pulling her quickly down the narrow passage. The next few minutes passed in a blur as Winston dragged Sophie down lanes, through the gates of colleges and out back entrances. Every porter in Oxford seemed to know him and none questioned his apparent need for speed and secrecy. He stopped frequently to look back, asking Sophie if she recognized anyone before they stepped into a street. Suddenly, after slinking through Balliol, they emerged in the sun at Martyrs' Memorial, where buses were taking on hordes of tourists after their day in Oxford. Winston took Sophie through the crowd that swarmed across the street from the Ashmolean. They turned in to a narrow alley and ducked through a gray metal door into a dimly lit passage. They waited in silence for a few minutes, Sophie's breath gradually returning to normal after the dash through Oxford. Winston certainly knew his way around, and he seemed to know how to shake a tail. Sophie wasn't sure if his actions were more suspicious or useful. Before she said a word to him, he pulled out a cell phone and placed a call.

"Derek? This is Winston Godfrey. . . . Yes, *that* Winston Godfrey. Listen, I need a favor. I need a room for the night under another name . . . you make one up. . . . The service elevator." Winston waited in silence for a minute, eyes still focused on the alley outside. "Four sixteen. Great."

"What are you . . . ?" Sophie began, but Winston held a hand up to her lips and led her down the industrial gray hallway. Once they were in the service elevator, he let go of her hand and fell against the wall.

"That was an adventure," he said. "Let's hope we lost him." A moment later the elevator opened onto an elegantly carpeted corridor. Winston turned left and Sophie followed. Four doors down the hallway was room 416. He pushed open the door and pulled her inside. It was the most luxurious hotel room she had ever seen—a four-poster bed draped in elegant covers, deep armchairs by the window, and a giant flat-screen television sitting on what looked like an antique chest of drawers.

"Where are we?" she said.

"The Randolph," said Winston. "The only hotel in Oxford good enough for you." Sophie had admired the elegance of the Randolph from the street a thousand times, but she had never been inside. She started across the room, but Winston dashed in front of her. "Stay away from the windows," he said, pulling the gold curtains shut.

"I thought you said you couldn't afford the Randolph," she said.

"Derek doesn't exactly charge me full price."

"Why am I not surprised that you have a secret contact who can provide you with a highly discounted, unlocked hotel room under an alias at a moment's notice?"

"I'll admit, you're not the first woman I've brought to this hotel."

"I'll bet your little undergraduate girls just loved beds like this," said Sophie, sitting on the edge of the four-poster.

"It made seduction easier," said Winston.

"I'm sure it was never hard for you," she said. Somehow the fact that he had been here with other girls only made her want him more. Now that they were alone in a hotel room, Smedley and the chase and the danger slipped from her mind as quickly as she knew Winston could slip her clothes from her body.

"Derek and I grew up together," said Winston. "He was a few years older and he always sort of looked out for me."

"If we're spending the night here, I have nothing to sleep in," said Sophie, trying to sound seductive.

"We can have something sent up." he said.

"That wasn't what I had in mind."

"What did you have in mind?"

"Come over here and I'll show you," she said, unbuttoning her blouse.

And he took her. He took her in a four-poster bed in a luxury hotel between the softest sheets she had ever felt and it was bliss. It was bliss because it reduced her consciousness to a few square feet of bed and eventually to a few square millimeters of flesh. It was bliss because she didn't care what it meant. It was bliss because, at that moment, with all the fears and confusion that lay in the world outside that hotel room, it erased everything else.

After the first time, they ordered room service. After the second time, Winston fell asleep and Sophie was just drifting off to the muffled sounds of the Oxford traffic when she remembered something and nudged him with her elbow.

"What were you writing this afternoon?" she said.

"What?"

"This afternoon, right before we left the history center. You were writing something. What was it?"

"Can we talk about this in the morning?"

"I can't sleep until I know. What was it?" Sophie sat up and turned on the lamp by her bedside. Winston blinked and grimaced.

"Do you have one of those brains that never stops?" he asked.

"Something like that," said Sophie. She could feel herself gearing up for battle. He was going to deny writing anything and her trust in him was going to slip a little further. "What did you write?"

"It's in my pants pocket, I think," said Winston, sitting up. "I forgot to tell you before because you got your knickers in a twist over that Fiona girl. In the last box I looked through there were some newspaper clippings and one of them was an obituary of Richard Mansfield. I'd never seen it before and you were in the loo, so I copied it down."

Sophie by now had reached Winston's discarded jeans, and pulled a folded piece of notepaper from his pocket. She jumped back in bed next to him, unfolded the paper, and read.

> **Rev. Richard Mansfield, 80, of Croft, died on December 4 in Hampshire. He was taken ill on a journey thence. Funeral services and burial were at the chapel in Busbury Park. Mr. Mansfield had been Rector of Croft for sixteen years and was much loved by his parishioners.**

"Where the hell is Busbury Park?" said Sophie.

"Must be in Hampshire," said Winston.

"Jane Austen lived in Hampshire," she said. "If some man hadn't lured me to a hotel to take advantage of me, I could look it up on my laptop."

"First of all," he said, "I think the question of who took advantage of whom is open to debate. And secondly, I have a smartphone." A minute later he had found a brief description. "Listen to this—it's for sale. Busbury Park, near East Hendred, Hampshire. Former estate of the Earl of Wintringham. Six hundred acres of parkland; large manor house needs significant repair. Outbuildings include stables, gatehouse, chapel. Serious enquiries only."

"Where's East Hendred?" said Sophie.

"Hang on," said Winston. "It looks like it's only about three miles from Steventon."

She leaned over his shoulder and looked at the map displayed on his phone. "Even closer if you happened to be walking across the fields in 1796. We should go."

"What, go to Busbury Park?"

"Yes," said Sophie, leaning into his back and trying to ignore the way his muscles felt against her naked breasts.

"Why would we go there?"

"Richard Mansfield is buried there."

"What are you going to do, dig him up?"

"Probably not."

"*Probably* not?" said Winston.

"OK, definitely not. But it's the only clue we have, the only other thing about Mansfield we know. We should at least find his grave and see if we can learn anything. Besides, I've never been to Steventon." She remembered that she had declined an invitation to Steventon from Eric less than three weeks ago.

"So you want to do what—drive to Hampshire in the morning?"

"Not in the morning," said Sophie. "Now."

"It's midnight," said Winston.

"The perfect time to slip out of town without Smedley seeing us."

"Listen," he said, "I don't think *you* should go anywhere. If this Smedley character is as dangerous as he sounds, I don't like the idea of your leaving this hotel room until we've taken care of him."

"Why do I think that's not the only reason you want me to stay in this hotel room?" said Sophie, once again pressing her breasts into his bare back.

"Let's at least wait until morning."

"I can't sleep," she said, bouncing up off the bed.

"I can."

"What's the matter, did somebody tire you out?"

"You could say that," said Winston.

"Fine," said Sophie. "You sleep. I'm going to curl up in this chair and read some Jane Austen." After all, Victoria would be there in the morning. Maybe she would join the expedition to Hampshire. She pulled the second edition of Mansfield's book out of her bag on the bedside table and, surprised by her own brazenness, sashayed across the room, sure that Winston's eyes were glued to her nakedness.

"Jane Austen or Richard Mansfield?" said Winston, teasingly.

Sophie slipped on a bathrobe she had tossed aside earlier and plopped down in one of the overstuffed armchairs. "Jane Austen," she said emphatically.

## *Hampshire, 1797*

THOUGH LORD WINTRINGHAM had made clear to Jane that his invitation to walk in Busbury Park whenever she wished had not expired with the death of Mr. Mansfield, Jane did not often avail herself of this privilege. Now, nearly a year after the death of her friend, she had come to Busbury on a painful errand. The November wind whipped across the fields as she approached Busbury House and turned down a short path to the chapel. Cassandra had urged her to wait for better weather, but Jane had protested that better weather was not likely to arrive for several months, and she felt her excursion to be of the most urgent nature. She refused, too, her sister's offer of accompaniment, saying that this was a visit she needed to pay alone.

Mr. Mansfield's grave in the corner of the churchyard, though now covered with grass, still seemed fresh to Jane. The small white marker gleamed even in the absence of sunshine. She stood by him for several minutes, before pulling a letter out of her pocket. It was a letter which, only a few days ago, had been invested with such high hopes that it hardly seemed possible that it had brought Jane here under these circumstances. She had spent much of the spring and summer of 1797 writing the narrative version of *First Impressions*. As she read each chapter to her family they became more and more convinced that here, at last, lay Jane's chance of publication. If people outside her family circle embraced her novel about Mr. Darcy and Eliza Bennet the way the

Austens had, she had reflected that it was perhaps a stroke of luck that the original version of the story had never seen the light of day.

She had finished the book—for even though it comprised nothing more than a sheaf of manuscript without printing or binding, she already thought of it as a book—in August, and since then had made such minor revisions to the story as had been suggested by her listeners. Her father, on rereading the entire manuscript in October, had proclaimed it as good as any novel in print and had undertaken to explore the possibility of its publication, which had given rise to the letter of which Jane now held a copy. Believing it to be the epistle that would launch her career as a published writer, she had insisted on copying it out before her father consigned the original to the post. She now unfolded the copy and read it to Mr. Mansfield.

**To Thomas Cadell, Publisher**

**Sir—I have in my possession a manuscript novel, comprising three volumes, about the length of Miss Burney's *Evelina*. As I am well aware of what consequence it is that a work of this sort should make its first appearance under a respectable name, I apply to you. I shall be much obliged, therefore, if you will inform me whether you choose to be concerned in it, what will be the expense of publishing it at the author's risk, and what you will venture to advance for the property of it, if on perusal it is approved of. Should you give any encouragement, I will send you the work.**

**I am, Sir, your humble servant,**

**George Austen**

"Should you give any encouragement," repeated Jane in a melancholy tone. Mr. Cadell certainly cannot be said to have given encouragement. He had declined the offer by return of post, bringing Jane's dreams of publication to an abrupt conclusion. Mr. Austen had not allowed her to see Mr. Cadell's reply to his letter, claiming that he had tossed it into the fire as soon as he had read the terse response declining to consider Jane's work.

"But declined it was," she said to Mr. Mansfield. "And now I know not what to do. Am I to write stories only for the enjoyment of my own family? And if that is the case, ought not my time be better spent in some more fruitful endeavor? Serving the poor in some way, perhaps? I am, sir, in desperate need of your advice and yet you lie there cold and unresponsive." Jane felt a tear course down her icy cheek. This was the moment, she thought, when she must decide once and for all whether to go on with her writing, to pursue it in the face of all rejection; or to lay aside her pen for some pursuit that might provide her with the opportunity to give lasting service to society rather than merely entertainment to her own family circle. She was inclining very much toward this latter option and expecting no interference in that decision from the corpse of Mr. Mansfield, when, as she knelt and laid a hand on his grave, she was suddenly struck by a recollection of the last time she had seen him.

It had been just a year ago, and she and Mr. Mansfield had sat for a few minutes in front of the dying fire in the gatehouse sitting room, waiting for the gig that would arrive to bear her friend away toward Croft and out of her life forever. Mr. Mansfield had confessed to feeling a weariness when anticipating the journey.

"How I wish," he had said, "that some enterprising young man would invent a form of transportation that would allow me to read while on a journey. The bumps of a carriage will not allow a book to stay in the same place long enough to accomplish the reading of a sentence, let alone a novel."

"You are a dreamer, Mr. Mansfield," said Jane, smiling. "What do you imagine? A room that will glide smoothly across the landscape, bearing you to your destination?"

"It is a consummation devoutly to be wished," said Mr. Mansfield with a laugh. "Instead I'm afraid I shall be bounced and jostled for the next three days, and am likely to arrive in Croft not only dull in mind but bruised in body."

"I'm sure you will recover from your journey and be pleased to sit in your own study once more, surrounded by your own books."

"I fear, Miss Austen," said Mr. Mansfield, "that recovery is not something that comes quickly at my age, and though the prospect of my own books is pleasing, the prospect of returning in a few weeks' time to your company is more so. I do hope I shall be back soon. But until then, you must make me a promise."

"Anything, my friend."

"Promise me that, until we meet again, whenever that may be, you will not cease to write. You will not cease to strive to better yourself in that work for which I am sure the Lord meant you."

"Though we shall meet again before the year is over, I promise," said Jane. "I shall do my best to make you proud in the tutelage and encouragement you have bestowed upon me, and I shall look upon what meager gifts I have as sent from God."

"Thank you," said Mr. Mansfield, rising from his seat as they heard the gig approaching. "And Miss Austen."

"Yes, Mr. Mansfield?" But she never heard what he wanted to say, for at that moment the driver of the gig had come through the door and insisted that if they did not leave immediately, Mr. Mansfield would miss his coach.

She wondered now, at his grave, what he had wanted to tell her. For her part, she wished once more that she had found the opportunity to confess her love for him. It was a confession she bitterly regretted never having made. But that was no matter. She had promised him, she thought as the cold earth turned her hand numb. She had promised him to keep writing until they met again. Had he known, when he extracted that promise, that they would not meet again on this side of the great divide? It did not matter, she thought. She had made him a promise and she intended to keep it.

When she returned to the rectory she tossed the crumpled copy of her father's letter into the fire and went upstairs to write.

## *Oxford, Present Day*

**THE MORNING SUN** had started shining through the gaps in the curtain when Sophie finished reading *First Impressions* for the second time. Winston was sleeping and she laid her three stolen artifacts next to each other on the coffee table. She sat in the armchair staring at them and wondering what to do next.

What would Uncle Bertram do? Give everything to Winston and let him deal with it? Hold a press conference and become the thief who destroyed Jane Austen? Burn everything and tell Smedley that there was no longer a reason to stalk her? Sophie had it in her to steal books, but she didn't think she had it in her to destroy them—especially these books. She knew they told a story, a remarkable story; she just wasn't convinced she had every chapter lying on that table in front of her. She knew what Uncle Bertram would do. He wouldn't rest until he knew the ending.

**"IT'S VERY HARD** to read a book with all of your rubbish in it," said Sophie one spring afternoon as she sat with her uncle on the narrow balcony of his flat. It was Easter holidays and she had decided to read something thick. Uncle Bertram had suggested *David Copperfield*, but his copy seemed to have a credit card receipt or a theater ticket marking a page at least once a chapter. And there were a lot of chapters.

"You know, I think I liked you better before you turned fourteen," said her uncle in a voice that betrayed his insincerity. "That's not rubbish."

"It may not be rubbish," said Sophie, "but every time I turn the page I end up in a fight with some old piece of paper that wants to blow off the balcony and into the street."

"It's a battle worth waging," said Uncle Bertram. "You know that every book tells a story, but every one of those bits of paper tells a story, too. I never kept a diary, you see. My books and my bookmarks are my diary. What have you got there?" he asked, indicating the slip of paper in Sophie's hand.

"It's a ticket to *The Winter's Tale* at the Royal Shakespeare Theatre," said Sophie.

"A matinee, right?"

"Two o'clock."

"It was a perfect summer's day in Stratford," said Uncle Bertram. "When the play was over I sat down by the river and watched the swans and read the chapter where David walks to Dover. It's always hard for me, that chapter, so it helped to be in such a beautiful place on such a lovely day. Whenever things started looking bleak for David, I could look up at the sun glimmering on the river and the white of the swans and the green of the grass and remember that he would be all right in the end. So you see, that bookmark reminds me of a special day. When I look at that bit of paper I'm back on that bench by the river feeling the warm breeze, and I'm also back with David on that cold road to Dover. So it's a special bit of rubbish because it reminds me of a special day."

"But they can't all be special," protested Sophie.

"Ah, that's where you're wrong, my dear. They each tell a story—it's just not always easy to know what the story is."

After that, Sophie often made it a game to guess the story of a particular bookmark. "This receipt for towels from John Lewis is to remind you that you walked over the Embankment into the Thames because you were so enthralled with chapter twenty-seven," she said the next day.

Uncle Bertram threw his head back and laughed. "Now I've learned something from you," he said. "My little bookmarks can tell a different story to every person who finds them."

"Yes, but my story isn't true," said Sophie.

"But truth and a good story are not always the same thing, now, are they?"

**SOPHIE WISHED VERY MUCH** that the objects in front of her would tell both the truth and a good story—and to her a good story was one in which Jane Austen was the heroine, not the villain. She finally put the letter and the St. John's copy of *Allegorical Stories* into her handbag, settled back into the armchair, and began reading *First Impressions* yet again. As she turned the first few pages, she felt overwhelmed with sadness that although this book had belonged to her uncle, there were no bookmarks. Every one of those thousands of stories stuck between the pages of his books was gone now, tossed into the rubbish bins of dozens of booksellers like so much worthless refuse. To Sophie, those receipts and tickets and takeaway menus were worth more than the books themselves, and even if she repurchased every book Uncle Bertram had ever owned, she would never have those stories.

In this melancholy mood, she flipped the pages of *First Impressions* to her favorite letter.

*My Dear Miss Bennet,*

*I am recently parted from my aunt who gives me such an account of her visit to Longbourn as to encourage me to believe that a similar journey of my own might not be wholly unwelcome by yourself. I entreat you not to trifle with me, but declare to you in all sincerity that my affections and wishes are unchanged from what they were last April. If your feelings are equally unaltered, I beg you to tell me so at once by return of post, and you shall never hear a word from me again. If, on the contrary, I have correctly understood the implications of my aunt's narrative, I should very much like to pay a visit to Longbourn to discuss with you, and with your father, a matter of great importance.*

*Yours,*

*Fitzwilliam Darcy*

Sophie loved this letter, even more than the corresponding scene in *Pride and Prejudice.* There was something about imagining Darcy being forced to wait for a reply that touched her deeply. She could imagine him standing at the door of Pemberley every day when the post arrived, his heart racing with hope—the great and noble Fitzwilliam Darcy turned into an anxious child by love.

She wondered if Jane Austen, or Richard Mansfield, or perhaps both of them were trying to tell her something about love. Winston was fun, but she couldn't imagine waiting by the door for a letter from him. She couldn't imagine him *writing* a letter, for that matter, not like Eric did. She knew she did not love Winston—not yet anyway—but what was wrong with a little casual sex? She read the letter again and tried to imagine what it would feel like to be so desperate for a response that you would drop all sense of dignity and propriety and dash from the house at the first sight of the postman. She remembered the leap in her chest she would feel whenever she received a letter from Uncle Bertram as a little girl—that was certainly love, but it was different. Poor Mr. Darcy, standing on the steps of Pemberley in the rain, waiting and hoping—how she envied him that perfect conviction that he had found the one. She saw him turning back toward the house, the letters in his hand lacking any communication from Eliza. He trudged through the rain without thought for his health or his appearance, already counting the hours until the next post.

**SOPHIE AWOKE FEELING STIFF** and confused. Mr. Darcy had disappeared and had been replaced by a ringing cell phone on the coffee table. She had not meant to fall asleep.

"Hello," Sophie mumbled.

"Soph, it's Tori. I'm on the train. Should be in Oxford in about twenty minutes."

"I'm at the Randolph," said Sophie. "Room four sixteen. You can walk from the station."

"The Randolph?"

"I'll explain when you get here," said Sophie.

Winston was neither in the four-poster bed nor in the shower. On the counter in the bathroom he had left her a toothbrush and toothpaste, no doubt obtained from the front desk, and a note written on a sheet of crisp ivory Randolph Hotel stationery.

**Darling Sophie,**

**I told you I wanted you to stay out of danger and I meant it. I think I know how I can lure this Smedley fellow into the open and wheedle a confession out of him. It shouldn't take more than a few hours. I'll call you this afternoon. In the meantime, stay put and order room service. It's on me. I'm afraid I had to borrow your car and of course I had to take the book with me, but all should be back safely by dinnertime.**

**Yours,**

**Winston**

She dashed back to the coffee table, where she had left the copy of *Little Allegories and a Cautionary Tale*. It was gone. Damn him! It was one thing to take her car without asking, but to take her book—even if it wasn't really hers—that Sophie couldn't forgive. Had Winston been playing her all along to get his hands on the book? Was he really stupid enough to think she would sit in a hotel room eating room service while he confronted the bastard who killed her uncle? He's either a shit or a moron, she thought. She crossed to the bedside table and opened her handbag. Even though Winston had taken her car keys, he had left both the St. John's copy of Mansfield's book and the Jane Austen letter it contained. If he was a crook, he wasn't a very smart one, thought Sophie. Luckily Victoria was on the way. Victoria, the woman of action—and action was what was required.

"Change of plans," said Sophie when she got Victoria back on the phone. "I need a car. That is, *we* need a car. Can you take the train up to Kingham and come back with the Land Rover?"

"Where are we going?" said Victoria.

"Hampshire," said Sophie. "A place called Busbury Park."

**SOPHIE WAS WAITING FOR** Victoria outside the hotel when she got a text from Eric. "I came round to your place last night," it said, "but you weren't there. Hoping you are OK. If you need anything, or even if you just want to talk, call me. I'll be waiting." He was sweet, she thought. She didn't know if Winston's disappearance that morning was proof that Eric was right about him or that he was dead wrong.

"OK, let's review the situation," said Victoria after Sophie had brought her up to date. "What do we think of Winston at this point? Marry, kill, or shag?"

"Well last night it was definitely shag," said Sophie, blushing. "Shag times two."

"Go, Sophie!" said Victoria.

"But after that stunt he pulled this morning I am seriously thinking about moving him into the kill column."

"So Winston is a question mark. What about Eric?"

"I certainly don't want to kill him," said Sophie. "He's a nice guy, I think. He's a friend. But I'm not sure he's in the shagging column yet."

"So you'll marry him."

"I doubt that."

They drove in silence for a time. Finally Sophie said, "I think there are more important things today than my love life."

"I know," said Victoria. "I was just trying to lighten the mood. If you'd rather, we can talk about the fact that Winston is a thief, Eric is a liar, and some guy named Smedley may have killed Uncle Bertram and be after you."

"Us, now," said Sophie.

"Right, he may be after us."

"You forgot the worst part."

"What's that?"

"That if we don't come up with some evidence to the contrary and fast, Winston might reveal Jane Austen as a plagiarist."

"That's the worst part?" said Victoria. "Not the whole 'somebody is trying to murder us' bit?"

"To me, it is."

"Well," said Victoria, "either way, we'd better get a move on."

**FINDING BUSBURY PARK WAS** not difficult, but finding a way in was another thing altogether. Driving along tiny lanes, they had nearly circumnavigated the tall stone wall that surrounded the estate when they could go no farther. In front of them was a hedgerow; to their left, the wall of the estate; and to their right, past a row of ancient shade trees, the open fields of Hampshire.

"What about that gatehouse a little way back?" said Sophie. "Maybe we can climb the gate." There was nothing else to do, so Victoria backed the car nearly a quarter of a mile down the lane and parked in front of the tall iron gate. There had been a matching gate on the other side of the estate that looked even more imposing. Sophie got the idea that this was the back entrance. It was not the sort of gate, in the end, that either of them could climb over, but Sophie managed to slide underneath and into the grounds of Busbury Park.

"You always were the skinny one," said Victoria. "There's no way I'll get under there."

"Wait there," said Sophie. "I have an idea." Next to the gate was a small two-story gatehouse, its outer wall forming part of the wall that surrounded the estate. Sophie was not surprised to find the door locked, but the board that covered one of the front windows was loose, and with one good tug, she pulled it off. The window behind had been broken and Sophie used the board to knock loose the glass hanging from the frame. In another minute she had climbed through and stood in a gloomy room, covered in what must have been several decades of dust. There was a simple stone fireplace against the far wall, and to her right was a solid carved chair and a heavy oak table. Rectangles of light on the sooty walls indicated where pictures had once hung, but other than the two pieces of furniture, the room was empty. She crossed the room, heading for a door to her left, when she suddenly felt a chill through her whole body.

"Somebody tread on your grave," Uncle Bertram used to say when the same thing would happen to her as a child. Sophie did not believe in ghosts or the supernatural, and had said so to Uncle Bertram many times when he guided her toward books like *Dracula* or *The Turn of the Screw.*

"A man with so many books should know what's real and what isn't," she told him one Christmas Eve when her father had let the two of them into the library at Bayfield House to read *A Christmas Carol.*

But Uncle Bertram had only smiled and shaken his head and said, "There are more things in heaven and earth, Miss Sophie Collingwood, than are dreamt of in your philosophy."

Well, she supposed Uncle Bertram had his answers now. After she had stood on the spot for a minute or two, the feeling, which was at once eerie and comforting, passed and she heard Victoria calling her name.

She opened the door to her left and found herself in a smaller but brighter room. There was no furniture, but the window, which looked out onto the lane, was intact. It was a simple matter to unlock the window, throw up the sash, and call out to Victoria. Sophie pulled her sister up through the window, and in another minute they had thrown the bolt of the front door and were standing outside in the grounds of Busbury Park.

"You might want this," said Victoria, handing Sophie her bag. "Didn't think you wanted to leave your stolen goodies on the side of the road where any passing bibliophile could just walk away with them."

"Thanks," said Sophie, horrified that she had left it behind.

"And I brought a torch," said Victoria. "Just in case. So what now?"

"Now," said Sophie, "we go find Richard Mansfield."

## *Hampshire, 1797*

"**YOU HAVE RISEN EARLY,** sister," said Cassandra as she stepped into the dressing room to find Jane at her writing table, working away by candlelight in the predawn of a December day.

"I find it peaceful to write while others sleep," said Jane.

She had hardly been away from her writing table for the past few weeks. Since her visit to Mr. Mansfield's grave, his voice had been driving her. All thoughts of Mr. Cadell's rejection were now forgotten, and Jane focused only on those words she had recalled so clearly in the churchyard at Busbury: "Promise me that, until we meet again, you will not cease to write." As she worked, she heard, too, Mr. Mansfield's voice from an earlier occasion—the day she had finished reading him *Elinor and Marianne*. "It might," he had said, "benefit from being written as a conventional narrative." It was, in fact, this task upon which Jane had focused all her efforts in the weeks since her visit to Busbury. She found that with Mr. Mansfield's encouragement the work seemed easy. Elinor and Marianne and the rest of the Dashwoods now occupied almost her every waking thought. With the Christmas theatricals, balls, and visits from family all on the horizon, she knew she would need to set aside her work soon, but that thought only drove her to rise earlier and stay up later than anyone else in the household.

"Is it still the revision of *Elinor and Marianne* that occupies you so?" said her sister. "I do hope you will share the new version with the family."

Jane laid down her quill and looked up at the smiling face of her sister in the candlelight. "I fear I have neglected you these past few weeks, my dear Cassandra," she said. "I am not a good sister when a story has hold of me like this."

"Nothing could keep you from being the most wonderful of sisters," said Cassandra, "least of all your commitment to a talent given to you by God."

"Your patience is a gift to me," said Jane, rising from her chair and crossing to embrace her sister. "Now I must tell you that, while I shall certainly fulfill your wishes and read from my novel when our family is gathered together, I shall not read from the pages of *Elinor and Marianne*."

"Indeed," said Cassandra with a little yelp of excitement. "Is there a new story on your table?"

"Not a new story," said Jane, "for the Dashwoods still fill my time. But a friend has suggested that a change of title would not be unwise and I have finally hit on one that I find satisfactory."

"And who is this friend with whom you discuss your work away from your own sister?" teased Cassandra.

"I should have said a late friend," said Jane quietly.

"Oh, Jane, I am sorry. It was Mr. Mansfield, was it not?"

"Indeed," said Jane, "and though he is no longer with us, it was Mr. Mansfield who gave me the idea for the new title. I was thinking of him this morning as I prepared to write about Willoughby's carrying Marianne in from the storm. The two of us made quite a pair—Mr. Mansfield and myself. I with the impetuous eagerness of youth and he with the level head of life experience."

"I cannot think you impetuous, good sister."

"Nor did I think myself so at the time," said Jane, laughing at the recollection of how she had denied this very fault to Mr. Mansfield on their first meeting. "But it is good that the wisdom of a little more maturity has shown me to have been so, for it was the contrast between those two remembered characters—old Mr. Mansfield and young Miss Austen—which gave me the idea for my new title."

"Well, tease me no longer, sister. What is this title?"

"I think," said Jane, "of calling the novel *Sense and Sensibility*."

**ALMOST AS SOON AS** she had finished *Sense and Sensibility*, Jane turned her thoughts to the other project she and Mr. Mansfield had discussed: a mock gothic novel that would poke fun at books such as *The Mysteries of Udolpho*. Her father, who detested the genre, took special delight in the story.

"What will Mrs. Radcliffe think?" he said, rubbing his hands together and smiling one evening as the party were settling in the sitting room to listen to Jane read from her story.

"Indeed, Father, I do not wish to cause offense to Mrs. Radcliffe or to any author. But of course if my stories remain forever within the confines of this rectory, I suppose I need not worry about causing offense to the great writers of the land."

"Your stories will one day burst the bounds of Steventon," said her father, "never you fear. And I should pay dearly to see the look on Mrs. Radcliffe's face when she reads this one. Now, I believe we had reached chapter six and you had promised us a conversation about reading between Susan and Isabella."

Jane settled in her chair and began to read the scene in which her heroine, whom she called Susan Moreland—though she was by no means certain that she should keep that name—was discussing the plot of Mrs. Radcliffe's novel *Udolpho* with her friend, the shallow and self-serving Isabella Thorpe.

> *"When you have finished* Udolpho,*" said Susan, "we will read* The Italian *together; and I have made out a list of ten or twelve more of the same kind for you."*
>
> *"And are they horrid?" said Isabella. "Are you sure they are all horrid?"*

*"Yes, quite sure; for a particular friend of mine, a Miss Andrews, a sweet girl, one of the sweetest creatures in the world, has read every one of them."*

"But you must name them!" said Mr. Austen, interrupting Jane's narrative. "Do not leave us hanging. What deliciously horrid books await Miss Thorpe? For myself, I should put *Castle of Wolfenbach* on her reading list."

"*Orphan of the Rhine*," chimed in Cassandra.

"Oh and you must include *Necromancer of the Black Forest*," said Mrs. Austen. "For I have never read a more horrid book."

"And *Midnight Bell*, and *Mysterious Warnings*," went on Mr. Austen.

"Very well," said Jane, holding up a hand. Interruptions from her readers were not unusual, but this one had been particularly enthusiastic. "I shall provide the particulars of Miss Thorpe's reading, but now may I proceed with the story?"

"You may," said her father, settling back into his chair with a smile. "And do let it be horrid."

Jane called the new story simply *Susan*. It was not that she disliked the title Mr. Mansfield had suggested; rather, she felt that her unfinished novel was not deserving of his title. As she worked through the autumn of 1798 crafting the adventures of her heroine and bringing her ever closer to that edifice where her fate would be decided, Jane wondered if she would be able to make of them a work that could live up to the title *Northanger Abbey*.

## *Hampshire, Present Day*

THE SUMMER HEAT was already bearing down even though it was only midmorning. Sophie and Victoria headed up the overgrown drive, happy for the shelter of the trees that provided shade. After about ten minutes of walking they rounded a bend and a vista opened before them. On a knoll about a quarter mile away they could glimpse a corner of what was certainly the main house. In the valley below was a small lake, with a copse of trees on one side and open fields on the other. Despite the warm fresh air, the park felt as neglected as the gatehouse. Several fallen trees lay untouched; the grass, without sheep to keep it in check, had grown tall and tangled; and even from this distance the lake looked green and choked with algae. No breeze stirred the leaves overhead, and the whole park was draped in silence.

Yet in spite of all this, Sophie felt she could see the park as, perhaps, Jane Austen had first seen it, as Eliza Bennet had first seen Pemberley—the sun sparkling off the blue water of the lake, the breeze whispering in the trees, the whole park pulsing with life and potential.

"I guess it was nicer in 1796," said Victoria.

"It must have been a beautiful estate," said Sophie with a sigh. "It's sad to see it so neglected."

"Who knows," said Victoria, forging ahead, "maybe one day it will be beautiful again."

Another few minutes brought them in full view of the house. It had once been grand, certainly—the epitome of the eighteenth-century country house. More like Rosings than Pemberley, Sophie thought—that is, it seemed more intimidating than romantic. But as they drew closer she realized this was due more to its obvious state of disrepair than to any arrogance in the architecture. Weeds grew in the gutters and several of the windows were boarded up. The rest were tightly shuttered. Several large pieces of stone had fallen from the facade. Two wings protruded from the center section of the house, and when they had walked around one of these they saw, a short distance down the hill, the chapel. It looked much older than the house itself, and stood in the shadow of a vast yew tree. A low stone wall surrounded the structure, and Sophie could just see the tops of a few gravestones peeking out of the tall grass.

Without speaking, she trekked off across the field toward the chapel, and in another minute she was pulling the grass away from one of the more imposing gravestones.

"It's hard to read," said Victoria over Sophie's shoulder.

"Nobody's cleaned it for a couple of hundred years," said Sophie, kneeling down and running her fingers along the inscription in the crumbling stone. "Edward Newcombe," she read. "Third Earl of Wintringham, 1750 to . . . I think it says 1811."

"And here's his wife," said Victoria, who was inspecting the adjacent stone.

"I doubt a visiting clergyman would get a stone this big or this close to the door," said Sophie. "Let's start at the edges." She took one side of the graveyard and Victoria the other and they began examining the smaller stones that lay near the wall of the churchyard. Sophie was kneeling in deep grass, trying to decipher the inscription on a stone in the most remote corner, when her ankle hit something hard and she stifled a cry of pain. She moved to one side and brushed the dirt and dead grass off of a fallen marker a little more than a foot wide and perhaps twice that long. There was no inscription on the side facing up, so she pried the stone out of the earth and began brushing the damp dirt from the other side. By the time she could read the letters carved on the stone, her hands were coated in dirt.

The stone read, simply, "R. M. 1796."

This was it. This was Richard Mansfield's gravestone and it told her nothing, pointed her nowhere. Sophie sat down in the grass and felt empty. She expected to be overcome with emotion, to finally cry those tears she had held inside since Uncle Bertram's death. But instead she felt nothing. Her world was a blank. The loss of her uncle, the loss of his books, the loss of the family library, and the loss of her literary idol weighed on her as one solid mass and seemed to press the breath out of her body. She might have sat there forever, she thought, but for the one bright thought that slipped into her mind like a shaft of light in the darkness. She had a sister, she thought, as she heard Victoria's voice. She still had Victoria.

"Hey Soph, don't you think we ought to look inside?"

Inside, thought Sophie. What if there was some further clue inside the chapel? It was a thread of hope—a thin, fragile thread, but she would follow it nonetheless. She hoisted herself up and walked to the west end of the chapel, where Victoria stood in front of a thick wooden door.

"Locked, I presume," said Sophie, seeing her glimmer of hope dim.

"There is a lock," said Victoria, "but it's a rusty lock." With one swift kick, she snapped the latch and the door flew open. "I knew those kickboxing classes would come in handy." The echo of the door bursting open died down and they stepped into musty gloom.

"It smells like death," said Sophie with a shiver.

"Come on," said Victoria. "Let's see what we can find."

The narrow windows admitted just enough light that they could read the memorials on the walls without the aid of the torch. On the north wall, wedged between elaborately carved memorials to various members of the Newcombe family, Sophie found a small marble plaque. She read it over several times in silence and then called softly to her sister. Victoria slipped an arm around Sophie's waist and with her sister at her side, Sophie read the words on the plaque aloud:

**In Loving Memory of**

# Richard Mansfield

**1716–1796**

**Rector of Croft-on-Tees, Yorkshire**

**Teacher, Writer, and Beloved Friend**

**Erected by his Students**

**R.N., S.N., and J.A.**

"What does it mean?" said Victoria, after they had stood in silence for a moment.

"Well," said Sophie, running her fingers across the text. "R.N. and S.N. must have been Newcombes. And J.A. has to be Jane Austen. It means she and Mansfield knew each other personally, not just through correspondence. And it means that she thought of him as a teacher and a friend, which is something. I mean, if she stole from him, would she have erected a memorial to him?"

"You're right, but it doesn't *prove* anything about *First Impressions*," said Victoria.

"No," said Sophie. "But I have a feeling that Jane Austen's relationship with Richard Mansfield was deeper and less . . . I don't know, less nefarious than what we've found so far makes it look."

"So what do we do now?"

"Give me a minute," said Sophie, squeezing her sister around the waist and then dropping her arm.

"Sure," said Victoria. She gave Sophie a light kiss on the cheek and walked out into the sunshine, leaving her sister alone in the ancient chapel.

Sophie suddenly felt the weight of her knowledge like a stone around her neck. No matter what Winston did, no matter what happened with Smedley, *First Impressions* and the evidence in Sophie's handbag would become public—and probably very soon. She knew she couldn't keep the secret much longer. Right now, this forgotten place was so apart from the outside world she could almost believe that when she stepped out of the chapel it would be 1796, and she would see Jane Austen and Richard Mansfield walking arm in arm along the shore of the lake. But when *First Impressions* became public, this place would be peaceful no more. People would flock from around the world to see the memorial to the man whose work spawned *Pride and Prejudice*. Or, thought Sophie, the true believers would flock to scorn the grave of the man who ruined Jane Austen's reputation. Sophie suddenly felt a great affinity for Richard Mansfield—after all, the two of them were in this together. If he ended up reviled by lovers of Austen, Sophie would be hated even more.

She reached out and ran her fingertips across the words on the memorial once more and whispered to Richard, "I'll do my best." As she touched the words RICHARD MANSFIELD she had a sudden inspiration. She took a moment to consider her idea and then walked briskly out of the chapel to where Victoria sat on the churchyard wall, gazing out toward the lake.

"I know what we need to do," said Sophie confidently. "We need to break into that house."

"OK, I'm all for action," said Victoria. "But just out of curiosity, why would we break into an abandoned manor house?"

"If there's one thing I know about estates," said Sophie, "it's that they keep records. Names of tenants, numbers of sheep, all that sort of thing. Some estate holders were obsessive about it."

When she had touched Richard Mansfield's name on the memorial, she had remembered a day when her father and uncle stood in her father's private study. Uncle Bertram had asked to see some of the estate records so he could show them to Sophie.

"Why would anyone want to know how many sheep were at Bayfield in 1920?" asked Sophie, as her uncle showed her the neatly penned entries in a musty ledger.

"Well, that's the thing about keeping records," said Uncle Bertram.

"You never know why someone might need them until someone does need them, and then you're glad you kept them."

"And what does the number of sheep have to do with Richard Mansfield?" said Victoria now.

"Nothing. But listen—Mansfield died here in 1796, the same time that Jane Austen was working on her original draft of *Pride and Prejudice*, the version she called *First Impressions*."

"Or possibly the version Mansfield called *First Impressions*."

"Possibly," said Sophie. "But Mansfield died right after he arrived here, according to the obituary. Hardly enough time for Jane to come to think of him as a teacher. So he might have been here before. Who knows what the estate records will tell us—dates of his visits, parties or balls that took place while he was here; there could even be letters from Mansfield to the earl. I don't know what we'll find, but we might find something." She could feel the excitement building inside her. She knew it was a long shot, that even if she could get into the house, even if the records survived, there would probably be nothing that would help her. But a slim chance was still a chance—one last chance to prove Jane's innocence. Then it wouldn't matter who presented *First Impressions* to the world—Sophie, Winston, or even that bastard Smedley. If Sophie could prove that it was Jane's original version and not Mansfield's story, Jane Austen's reputation would be saved.

"Do you really think there's anything left in there?" said Victoria, nodding toward the house. "It seems unlikely."

"Unlikely is not the same as impossible," said Sophie, repeating a favorite saying of her uncle's. He had liked to say this whenever Sophie had objected to some remarkable coincidence in, say, a Dickens novel as being unlikely. Never had his words held more meaning.

"All right, then," said Victoria, striding up the hill. "Let's break into the house."

## *Hampshire, 1800*

**FOR FOUR YEARS** after Mr. Mansfield's death, Jane had barely stopped writing. True, she found that she had more time to spare for her quill on some days than on others—visits to neighbors, journeys to see her brothers, and preparations for balls being a part of the rhythm of life. Nonetheless, in those years she had produced an entirely new version of what had begun as *Elinor and Marianne* and was now *Sense and Sensibility.* She had so enlarged and improved it from the original, not only shedding its epistolary form but also deepening many of the minor characters and extending the plot, that she did not even think of *Sense and Sensibility* as a new draft of *Elinor and Marianne.* It was, in her eyes, an entirely new book. She had also, in those four years, completed *Susan*, her satire on gothic novels.

During those years she had visited Mr. Mansfield's grave on the anniversary of his death—or as near to that day as her occasional absences from Steventon allowed. She had sat on the wall that enclosed the churchyard and read aloud a carefully chosen passage of her writing from the previous year. Since he was the one who had inspired her to continue, it seemed only right that she share her work with him in this way. But on a gray December day in 1800, she stood before his grave marker—which had dulled in color in four years—without any pages of manuscript in her hand. What she held was in her heart alone, and it was momentous intelligence indeed. It had been three days since she heard the news, and still she did not know how she felt. She had fainted away with shock when her mother had first told her. In the days since then she had wept with grief for what was passing away while, nearly simultaneously, feeling herself filled with excitement for what was ahead. On balance she believed herself to be devastated or at the very least disappointed, but she was not entirely sure.

"Well, Mr. Mansfield," she sighed. "First you have left Hampshire, and now I must do the same, though my destination is not quite so removed as yours. Father has decided that he is to retire to Bath, and we are to go with him. And not at some distant future date, but in May, not even six months hence. Oh, Mr. Mansfield, I am at a loss. Since the time that I was called from that place with the news of your final illness, I am afraid I have persisted with a very determined, though very silent disinclination for Bath. I find that the pace and noise of such a city leaves one with little time for that activity which you know is most dear to me as it connects me, so I feel, with yourself. I do not think Bath agrees with me, and now Bath is to be my home."

Jane waited in silence to hear in her recollection the voice of Mr. Mansfield offering her some sage advice, as he often did at these moments, but on the subject of Bath and of removal from the quiet lanes and open fields of Hampshire he was silent. She could only recall him saying to her, as they walked the lane toward Steventon one day, "How gently stimulating to the mind of the writer must be the peace of the countryside."

"Indeed, Mr. Mansfield," said Jane, "I find that nothing is more helpful in discovering the next step in a story than a long walk in the country. I am blessed to have the opportunity to take such solitary walks so frequently."

"I hope my presence does not quell your creativity, Miss Austen," said Mr. Mansfield. "For our walks are not solitary."

"Indeed not, Mr. Mansfield. I find your presence a constant stimulation. Just as the body needs both food and drink, my writing mind needs both solitude and companionship."

Solitude and quiet were likely to be infrequent friends in Bath, thought Jane. Her only consolation was that her eldest brother, James, was to take the curacy of Steventon, so she would still have cause to be a visitor in the neighborhood.

"I know this is not the last time I shall visit you in this way, Mr. Mansfield," said Jane. As the wind whipped her bonnet strings about her face, she laid a hand on the stone that marked Mr. Mansfield's grave and felt an emptiness in her heart. How, she wondered, could she survive such a place as Bath without even this meager communion with one who had inspired in her so much that she hoped was good?

**JANE'S FEARS ABOUT HER** productivity in Bath were not unfounded. In five years living in that city she started only one novel, but left off after only a few chapters. She was able to make some revisions to *Susan*—but only because the book was largely set in Bath and, in a failed attempt to change her own mind about that place, she took the opportunity to have her heroine adore everything about the city that Jane herself disliked. Following the death of her father in 1805, Jane, Cassandra, and their mother lived in Southampton for a time, and again Jane felt disconnected from the sources of her inspiration. By 1809 she had begun to despair of ever returning to that level of productivity she had known in the wake of her connection to Mr. Mansfield. But in that year, her brother Edward invited the Austen women to move into a cottage in the village of Chawton, on his estate. After nearly ten years away from the quiet of the countryside, Jane found herself back in Hampshire, living on an estate that could not help but remind her of Busbury Park. The flame of her writing could not be relit in an instant like that of a candle, but she felt as soon as they were settled in Chawton that the fire had been kindled and she had only to wait for the blaze to take hold. It was not long before she returned to her earlier novels, polishing *Sense and Sensibility* and *First Impressions* while waiting for new inspiration.

**EARLY IN 1811,** Jane paid a visit to her brother in Steventon. Against the advice of the household she ventured into the frigid winter weather for the long walk to Busbury Park.

"Well, Mr. Mansfield," said Jane, "I am back in Hampshire. Through my brother's generosity I am able to walk every day in a park which, though not so grand as this one, is a welcome relief from the streets of Bath and Southampton. And so I think perhaps it is time for a new story."

And though she knew that what she heard was the wind in the trees, and not some ghostly communication, that wind sounded very much like the whispered voice of an old friend saying, "It is time." The next day she returned to Chawton and began to write.

**"I AM ALMOST AFRAID** to ask about your work," said Cassandra one afternoon as the two sat by the fire. Jane had spent the morning writing, as she had done for most of the past month.

"In its early days," said Jane, "it may have been too precarious to withstand conversation. But now I find that the story has taken firmly hold of me, and soon I shall be able to share it with you."

"I am pleased to hear it," said Cassandra, "for surely, sister, I have not seen you so happy in many years as you have been these past few weeks."

"It is the happiness of one who, thinking that long ago a well had run dry, now finds oneself with a fount of cool fresh water."

"And have you chosen a title for this fount?" said Cassandra.

"I have, indeed," said Jane. "It is named in honor of the one who has so many times helped me to keep its waters flowing. I shall call it *Mansfield Park.*"

## *Hampshire, Present Day*

"HOW DO WE get in?" said Victoria as the two sisters stood staring up at the boarded windows of Busbury House.

"Somehow I don't think your kickboxing is going to do much good on *that* door," said Sophie. The front door stood at least ten feet high and felt as solid as a stone wall.

"Servants' entrance round the back?"

"It's worth a try," said Sophie.

Twenty minutes later they had made a complete circuit of the house without finding an unlocked door or an accessible window and stood back at the front, staring at the facade.

"Why do I think that just because there is no way into that house it doesn't mean you're going to give up?" said Victoria.

"Because you know me," said Sophie. "And you know how stubborn I am. If there is any way to stop the world thinking Jane Austen was a plagiarist, I'm going to find it."

"And since your friend Winston could be revealing *First Impressions* to the world at this very moment . . ."

"I'm going to find it now," said Sophie emphatically. "And he's *not* my friend."

"So we go around again," said Victoria.

This time they hugged the outside wall of the house and looked behind the overgrown shrubbery for any ingress they might have missed.

On the outside of the left wing, Sophie tripped and nearly fell, but Victoria caught her by the arm.

"What's this?" said Sophie, pulling dead shrubbery away from whatever had tripped her.

"Coal chute, maybe," said Victoria. "Looks like a pretty heavy cover."

"You don't really think it's too heavy for the Collingwood girls, do you?"

"I never said that," said Victoria, smiling.

They each did their best to slip their fingertips into the narrow gap around the edge of the wide metal disc. Alone, Sophie thought, she would never have been able to budge it an inch, but with Victoria's help she lifted one side enough that it slipped out of place and the two were able to slide it away, revealing a circle of blackness.

"Do you think we should tell someone we're going in there?" said Victoria, as the sisters stared into the narrow black hole. "In case—I don't know—in case we can't get back out?"

"First of all, *we're* not going in there," said Sophie. "*I* am. You're going to keep watch. But I take your point. We probably should tell someone."

"Not the police," said Victoria.

"No," said Sophie. "Announcing our own crimes to the authorities doesn't seem like the smartest move."

"Who do you trust?"

"Eric Hall," said Sophie, surprised at how quickly the answer leapt into her mind.

"I've barely got a signal on my phone," said Victoria.

"Me neither," said Sophie, pulling her phone from her handbag. "But it's worth a try."

"Eric," she texted. "Remember how you said to call if I need help? I'm not sure if I do or not, but I wonder if you could come to Busbury Park, Hampshire, to the main house. Some amazing J. Austen news to share. You might be right about Winston."

She showed the text to Victoria.

"A literary mystery, a damsel in distress, and his rival deposed. If that doesn't get him here then he's not much of a knight in shining armor," said Victoria. Sophie wasn't at all sure that Eric was the type to ride in on a metaphorical white steed; she only knew it felt right to reach out to him. She hit Send.

"Give me the torch," said Sophie. She flicked it on and shone it into the darkness. The coal chute extended below the house at a slight angle. She probably wouldn't get hurt, she decided. And if she did, so what; it was all in the cause of English literature. She sat on the ground and dangled her feet into the darkness.

"Be careful," said Victoria.

"You be careful," said Sophie. "I'm not convinced Smedley didn't follow us."

"Don't worry about me," said Victoria. "I can take care of myself. You go clear Jane's name." She leaned over and kissed Sophie on the cheek and Sophie shoved off, felt herself sliding down like Alice in the rabbit hole, and in a few seconds landed cleanly on her feet in total darkness. She did not think about how coated in coal dust she must be; she was just thankful to feel solid ground underfoot. She flicked on the torch and stepped forward.

It took her a few minutes to navigate her way out of the coal cellar, through the kitchens, and up the narrow flight of stairs that led to the main part of the house. In the servants' kitchen she found that the plumbing still worked. Though the brownish water that sputtered from the tap was ice cold, she did her best to wash the dirt and coal dust from her hands. Once abovestairs, in the high-ceilinged rooms that made up the public part of the house, she found that enough light seeped round the edges of the shutters for her to make her way without the use of the torch. The house was mostly empty, though here and there an old portrait still hung on a wall or a piece of furniture draped in cloth stood in the middle of a room. Even in this gloomy state, the house felt like a home to Sophie. The interior was certainly more like Pemberley than Rosings, and Sophie could imagine the happy sound of children's laughter echoing in the empty rooms. She could see those shutters thrown open to the bright summer sun, and the thought of the view across the valley and over the lake immediately suggested what Eliza had seen out the windows of Pemberley on her first visit.

"*Every disposition of the ground was good*," repeated Sophie aloud as she stood in what must once have been the dining room. "*And she looked on the whole scene—the river, the trees scattered on its banks, and the winding of the valley, as far as she could trace it—with delight.*"

Had Jane looked out the windows in front of which Sophie now stood and conceived the idea of Pemberley? Sophie longed to throw open the shutters and drink in the view, overgrown and untended though the park may be, but in spite of the inviting feel of the house, she reminded herself that she was a burglar. As long as she was committing a crime, she might as well get on with it.

She spent an hour searching every room on the two main floors of the house. Most were completely empty. One bedroom held nothing but a moldering pile of old magazines, another had a stack of copper pipes—as if someone had thought to update the plumbing, then given up before starting.

When her search yielded no study with shelves teeming with ledgers and no file cabinet full of bulging envelopes, she returned to what was, to her, the most melancholy room in the house—the library. She had walked through it quickly the first time. It reminded her too much of Uncle Bertram's empty shelves. A long room across the front of the house just to the east of the main entrance, it was adorned with beautiful woodwork—decorative enough to be special, but not so decorative as to detract from what was obviously the room's most beloved feature, the books. But the books were gone. The shelves held nothing but dust. In the case to the left of the fireplace lay a paperback copy of *Rebecca*, but that was all. Sophie pulled the book off the shelf and stared at the lurid cover.

So this was where it ended, she thought. Alone in a quiet, empty room. Soon enough, she imagined, this room would be filled with books again. The Richard Mansfield Library, she supposed they would call it. Some enterprising soul would buy up Busbury, rename it Pemberley, and wait for the tourists to pour in. For a moment, she thought she might like to work here. She could be the librarian. But then she thought of the looks on the faces of all those lovers of Jane Austen, parading around the site of their heroine's downfall. No, she preferred it like this—quiet and empty.

Just as she was replacing the paperback, her phone beeped and she saw that she had a text from Victoria. Only it wasn't from Victoria.

> I have your sister. If you want to see her alive come to the gatehouse with my book. Smedley.

But could Sophie come to the gatehouse—could she find a way out of the house? She had seen bolts on the tall front door that were high over her head. And she didn't have the book. Would he believe her if she told him that? Was this finally her opportunity to lure the rat bastard who killed her uncle into confessing his crime? That text would make a good piece of evidence. But would Victoria really be able to take care of herself? If she couldn't save Jane Austen, Sophie decided, maybe she could at least save Victoria. She texted back:

> George: I'm trapped in the main house. You get me out and I'll give you what I have.

She hoped her using his Christian name might shake Smedley a bit. She couldn't wait long before trying to find a way out herself; if she didn't hear back in ten minutes, she would see if she could wrench open one of the shutters and jump out a window. But she didn't have to wait that long. A minute or two after she hit Send she heard a crashing boom on the front door, as if someone was smashing it with an ax from the outside. Boom followed boom and Sophie tried to decide what to do. Should she confront Smedley as soon as he came in, or hide from him until she could assess how dangerous he was? She crouched behind the one piece of furniture in the room—a large sofa covered by a sheet. She could peer under the sofa and see the floor of the front hallway without being seen herself. Smedley would be tired by the time he got inside, she reflected, as the banging continued for five and then ten minutes. Finally the sound changed and light flooded into the house as the door crashed open.

Sophie saw a pair of men's boots stride across the hallway, but Victoria's hiking shoes, which she had put on before leaving the Land Rover, were not there. Smedley was alone, which meant Victoria was not in immediate danger. She listened as his boots pounded up the stairs and then heard the muffled sound of his voice calling out for her. Should she confront him now, or make her escape and find Victoria first? As his feet pounded overhead, she decided Victoria was the most important thing right now. She stood up and tiptoed across the library toward the front hallway.

Just as she was about to cross the threshold of the room, she heard Smedley's footsteps on the staircase. Without thinking, she pressed herself against the paneled wall and was surprised to feel it give slightly against her weight. Turning to look at the paneling as Smedley's steps came nearer, Sophie saw that carefully concealed in the woodwork was a door, ever so slightly ajar. She pressed against it, but it seemed to be blocked from the other side. She managed to shove it open just far enough to slip through. She quietly shut the door behind her and found herself in complete darkness just as Smedley's footsteps entered the library. The door was so thick she could barely hear his voice calling for her. No reason not to risk the torch, she thought. She switched on the light and gasped. She was in a tiny room, no more than a few feet square, its walls lined with simple shelves. A wooden stool stood in front of a small table, and next to that stood a wooden filing cabinet. What made her gasp, however, was that these shelves were not empty—they positively overflowed with ledgers, piles of papers, and file folders. Sophie had found the records of Busbury Park.

## *Hampshire, 1813*

**IF JANE HAD EXPECTED** the peace of Chawton to lead to success as an author, she was not disappointed. Not long after she began work on *Mansfield Park*, she received the news she had hoped for since her girlish scribbles had first taken the form of stories: Her work was to be published. *Sense and Sensibility* was accepted for publication by the firm of Thomas Egerton, and the day on which Jane first held those three crisp volumes in her hands had been a happy day indeed. The title page read: "*Sense and Sensibility* By a Lady."

She could just imagine Mr. Mansfield's reaction. "'By a Girl' would be more apt, for when Elinor and Marianne were first conceived you were little more than a child."

But *Sense and Sensibility* had come a long way from *Elinor and Marianne*, and much of that journey was thanks to the advice of Mr. Mansfield. With one book published, she turned her attention to the novel that was closest to her heart. It seemed to Jane that *First Impressions* lacked only a more original title—for that appellation had been given to two other books since she and Mr. Mansfield had first walked the paths of Busbury Park more than fifteen years ago.

"What was the novel you were reading on the day we first met?" Jane had said one summer day when an unexpected shower had prevented their walking in the park and they sat, instead, sipping tea in the gatehouse.

"Have I never told you?" said Mr. Mansfield. "It was the same novel you read in the garden that fateful night in Reading. It was *Cecilia.*"

"It was many years before I finally read the ending," said Jane. "But, in spite of the dreadful association the book holds for me, it remains one of my favorites. The stubbornness of an uncle who will pass his fortune to his niece only if she finds a husband who will continue the family name . . ."

"Meets the willfulness of a father who prefers to keep his family name rather than see his son happily married."

"A delectable conflict," said Jane, "and one I confess I wish had occurred to me."

"*The whole of this unfortunate business,*" said Mr. Mansfield, quoting from the novel, "*has been the result of pride and prejudice.*"

"*And,*" replied Jane, also in the words of Miss Burney, "*if to pride and prejudice you owe your miseries, so wonderfully is good and evil balanced, that to pride and prejudice you will also owe their termination.*"

"I am suddenly struck," began Mr. Mansfield, but he was interrupted by Jane.

"Is it possible that your mind leaps in the same direction as my own?"

"A title," said Mr. Mansfield.

"Exactly," said Jane. "A title. And all courtesy of Miss Fanny Burney."

At the time neither Jane nor Mr. Mansfield had suggested that the title be applied to *First Impressions*, but now it seemed to Jane to fit the work perfectly, especially as it connected the novel to that awful night in her childhood that had set her on the long road to its composition. And so, in late January 1813, Jane held another set of three volumes in her hand—volumes that then and for the rest of her life would hold greater meaning to her than any book she ever held. *Pride and Prejudice*, by the author of *Sense and Sensibility.* She felt a simultaneous rush of joy and melancholy when she turned to the first page and read the opening sentence. Jane was surprised to find that this simple combination of ink and paper brought a tear to her eye that dropped onto the page, leaving a small circular watermark. As soon as possible she arranged an excursion to Steventon, and early the morning after her arrival she walked across frozen ground to the chapel of Busbury Park.

"It is published, Mr. Mansfield," she said. "It is rather different from the last time you saw it, but nonetheless it is published at last. Only you will ever know what this book truly means to me. I only wish there were a way I could thank you for the part you have played in my own happiness even so many years after God took you to him." Jane looked down at the stone marker on Mr. Mansfield's grave. It was standing askew and the grass around it had grown thick with neglect. At the front of the churchyard, next to his wife, lay the earl whom Jane had known so briefly. His older son, Robert Newcombe, was no doubt the current Lord Wintringham, and she remembered that Mr. Mansfield's presence at Busbury Park had been a result of his having served as schoolmaster to Robert and his brother Samuel. Perhaps, she thought, there was something she *could* do to thank Mr. Mansfield.

Twenty minutes later, surprised at her own audacity, Jane found herself being ushered into the private study of the Earl of Wintringham.

"Miss Austen," said the earl. "How good to see you. We met at Mr. Mansfield's funeral, I believe."

"Indeed we did," said Jane, "though I am surprised you remember after all these years."

"I hope you will know that the invitation my father extended to you to walk in the park whenever you wish remains in effect."

"You are very kind, my lord, and I confess I have taken advantage of that hospitality, though on rare occasions, for many years. I sought you out today to make a proposal."

"And what form might this proposal take?"

"I believe that you may feel, as I do, that some of your success in life is due to the wise teaching and counsel of the Reverend Richard Mansfield."

"Indeed, Mr. Mansfield was as important in the formation of my character as was my own father," said the earl.

"It seems to me that a man who left such a positive imprint on the character of others deserves more than a grave marked with a small stone bearing only his initials. I wonder what you would think of placing a memorial to Mr. Mansfield *inside* the chapel."

"I confess, Miss Austen, I find that a capital idea, and I feel my brother would as well."

"If you are willing to undertake the task," said Jane, "I should like very much to contribute to the cost."

"I could not think of such a thing," said the earl.

"I beg you to allow it," said Jane. "It is only because of the encouragement and teaching of Mr. Mansfield that I am able to make such an offer, for his assistance and guidance in my youth has led to my having some success as a novelist. I should very much like to contribute five pounds to honor my old friend."

"I had no idea," said the earl, "that I was speaking with a literary figure. Certainly if the facts are as you present them, I cannot object to your generous contribution."

Two months later, Jane returned to Busbury Park at the invitation of the earl to attend a service of dedication for the new marble plaque on the wall of the chapel. She was touched to see that the earl and his brother had not only used the wording she had suggested, but had included her initials on the monument as well.

"That was most generous of you, my lord," said Jane after the service.

"My brother and I could not but include you among those paying tribute to Mr. Mansfield," said the earl. "For in addition to your contribution to the costs of the memorial, we remember that it was your idea that our dear friend should be so honored."

"I thank you, my lord," said Jane. "And now, if I may be so bold, I have a small gift for your library. It may pale by comparison to that splendid collection of literature, but I would be nonetheless honored if you chose to include it on your shelves." She handed him three slim volumes.

"*Pride and Prejudice*," he read on the spine. "Am I correct in assuming this is your work, Miss Austen?"

"You are, my lord. And it is a work in which both Mr. Mansfield and Busbury Park played an important role."

"Then I shall be pleased to place it on the shelves of the library, but only after I have had the pleasure of reading it."

"You do me honor, sir," said Jane.

The earl had sent a gig to Steventon to retrieve Jane from her brother's house for the service, but she preferred to walk home. She stopped outside the east gatehouse, still shuttered after all these years. She stood in front of the door for a few minutes, looking out toward the lake. The park still bore the bareness of winter, but to Jane, Busbury would be beautiful in any weather. She smiled and sighed as she laid a hand on the cold wooden door to the gatehouse and whispered, "Thank you."

Then she turned and left Busbury, never to return.

## *Hampshire, Present Day*

**AS LONG AS SMEDLEY** kept pounding round the house, Sophie reasoned, he could do Victoria no harm and Sophie could search the records for something that would exonerate Jane Austen. She knew that might not be long, but she thought she could buy a little extra time. She texted: "Stuck in servants' area," to Victoria's phone. If Smedley got the message he would have to search both the kitchens belowstairs and the servants' quarters on the top floor. She hit Send and a moment later the stomping and calling out stopped for a moment—long enough to read a text, Sophie hoped—before the footsteps moved off toward the back stairs. She had a few minutes, at least. She would have to work fast.

She began to scan labels on bundles of papers and on the spines of the ledgers. She knew a clue could be anywhere, but she only had time to look in the most likely spots, so she ignored labels such as "Busbury Farms," "Gardens," and "Tenants' Rents." On the third shelf she found a series of ledgers labeled "Guests." She pulled one down and opened it to see the heading "Guests, Busbury Park, 1801–1809." Too late, she thought, but the ledger to the left of that one covered the years 1789–1800.

She flipped the pages quickly until she found 1796. And there it was: "Richard Mansfield, arr. July 15, 1796 dep. Nov. 14, 1796 east gatehouse." He had been at Busbury during the very time that Jane Austen had begun writing her version of *First Impressions*. Sophie imagined the two of them, the eighty-year-old clergyman and the twenty-year-old future novelist, standing on the banks of the lake in Busbury Park and Richard Mansfield turning to Jane Austen and saying, "This would make a nice spot for a story. I could call it Pemberley."

Turning back to the register, Sophie found another entry a few lines below: "Richard Mansfield arr. Dec. 3, died Dec. 4, main house." He had arrived from Yorkshire having been taken ill and had been welcomed into the main house for his final hours rather than being sent to the—Sophie ran her finger back up the register—to the east gatehouse. What was the east gatehouse? Sophie pictured the way the morning sun had shone across the fields and realized that the east gatehouse must be the building she had broken into. Her exhausted mind suddenly experienced a moment of laser-like focus as she looked at those words in the ledger, "east gatehouse." She had seen those words before, and in the same hand. On the first shelf she had searched was a stack of bundles of documents, each tied together, like the packets at the Oxfordshire History Centre, with a decaying strip of once-white fabric. In the middle of this stack she found what she was looking for: a packet labeled "East Gatehouse."

The adrenaline surged through Sophie's veins as she untied the bundle. She heard footsteps on the main stairway as she rifled through the documents. Smedley had finished searching belowstairs and was on his way to the servants' quarters. She didn't have much more time. She tossed aside bills for repairs, inventories of furniture and paintings, and correspondence with other guests who had stayed in the east gatehouse. She was about to give up when, near the bottom of the pile, she found a browned slip of paper that read "R. Mansfield, d. Dec. 4, 1796." She took a deep breath, knowing the papers under this label probably represented her last chance to prove that Jane Austen alone had written *First Impressions.* She glanced at an undertaker's bill and a small printed memorial card, before unfolding a letter dated November 19, 1796.

**My Dear Lord Wintringham,**

**I write to thank you for your kind hospitality of the last few months. It has been a pleasure to see your sons, my former students, grown into such fine men, and to have the**

**honor of your own closer acquaintance. I do hope to return when I have completed the business which calls me back to Yorkshire, and am most grateful for your open invitation. You will know that I have grown quite fond of your neighbour Miss Jane Austen, and have even had the opportunity to pursue certain literary projects with her. In addition to my keen anticipation of continuing my intercourse with your family, I shall look forward to renewing my intimate association with a young woman of such promise.**

**Yours Humbly,**

**R. Mansfield**

Here at last was proof that Mansfield and Austen had not only been friends, but had "pursued" literary projects. But what projects? And how had they pursued them? Had Jane Austen given Richard Mansfield the idea for *First Impressions*? Had the two written the piece together? Or had he shown her the story and suggested it might be expanded into a novel? Sophie was beginning to think that the most innocent explanation of *First Impressions* being published in the second edition of Mansfield's book of allegories was that it had been a joint project between the old clergyman and his young friend. But even that would be hard to prove with the evidence she had in hand. Nonetheless, here, shortly before his death, Mansfield at least spoke of Jane Austen as one of whom he had grown fond. Perhaps people would look more kindly on Jane Austen knowing that she had borrowed from a friend, rather than plagiarized from a stranger. Then again, what could be worse, before one's "friend" was cold in his grave, than to steal his last literary work and eventually pass it off as one's own?

Sophie refolded the letter and put it into her handbag. The last item under the "Richard Mansfield" label was a receipt for a few books and other personal effects which had been sold at the time of his death—the proceeds being sent to his son, Tobias. Sophie was just about to retie the bundle when she realized that another item had adhered to the bottom of this receipt. She carefully peeled it away and saw that it was an unopened letter addressed simply: "Richard Mansfield, Busbury Park, Hampshire."

In her impatience, Sophie thought about dispensing with an archivist's care and simply ripping the letter open. But she remembered the voice of Uncle Bertram whenever they examined original materials in a library: "Remember, we are only guardians, protecting history for the next generation." She reached once again for her hair clip and carefully slid it under the flap of the folded letter. The centuries-old wafer adhesive gave way with little prodding, and Sophie unfolded the letter. As soon as she saw the date, she realized why the letter had never been opened. Richard Mansfield was already dead when this letter was sent.

***Leeds December 10, 1796***

**Dear Mr. Mansfield,**

**It was a pleasure to see you again and to receive the revised manuscript of *A Little Book of Allegorical Stories*. Having done the word count, I believe Miss Austen's "Cautionary Tale" will add about fifty pages, with a corresponding increase in expense. As you suggested, we will set the title page both with and without her name and send you both samples along with the galleys. I might add, with no disrespect to your own skills as an author, that Miss Austen's *First Impressions* is quite remarkable. I should not be surprised if you are correct about her one day outstripping Miss Burney.**

**Yours,**

**Gilbert Monkhouse**

## *Leeds, 1814*

**GILBERT MONKHOUSE HAD** purchased a copy of a new novel called *Mansfield Park,* in part because the title reminded him of an old friend for whom he had once printed a book. Richard Mansfield had not lived to see the second edition of his *Little Book of Allegorical Stories.* As Gilbert well knew, only a single proof copy had ever been printed, and that was safe in his own house. Theresa had read it to their daughter when Sarah was a child, but since then the book had sat untouched on the shelf. *Mansfield Park,* Gilbert read on the title page, was by "The Author of *Sense and Sensibility* and *Pride and Prejudice.*" Gilbert had read neither of these novels, but, finding that both he and Theresa enjoyed *Mansfield Park,* he ordered a copy of the latter from a bookshop in the high street.

He had not read beyond the second page when the tale recalled not only the final story in the unique copy of Mansfield's book but also his final visit with Mr. Mansfield himself almost twenty years earlier.

"As I was in Croft to find a new curate, I thought I would bring the manuscript to you rather than entrusting it to the post," said Mr. Mansfield as the two men sat in the small office of Gilbert's printing shop.

"This is more than just a revision, Mr. Mansfield," said Gilbert, weighing the pages in his hand. "Unless I am much mistaken your manuscript has grown quite substantially."

"That is mostly due to the addition of a new piece," said Mr. Mansfield, "the cautionary tale of the title."

"*First Impressions*," read Gilbert. "Your latest literary effort, I take it?"

"Not mine," said Mr. Mansfield. "Though the idea of a tale that would caution readers against the dangers of forming hasty opinions of their fellow men was mine, I cannot claim authorship of the story, which far exceeds in quality anything my humble pen might hope to produce. I coaxed and encouraged and even offered a critical eye, but the authorship of *First Impressions* must be claimed by a young lady—a dear friend named Jane Austen. I have undertaken to assist with the launch of her literary career by including her work alongside my own."

"And is this Miss Austen the next Fanny Burney, perhaps?" said Gilbert with a chuckle.

"Indeed, I believe she will exceed Miss Burney in every way."

"High praise indeed," said Gilbert, who had always admired the novels of Fanny Burney. "Well, I shall print your young friend's story and see if it earns me a place in literary history. How would you like her name to appear on the title page?"

"I confess, I have not given the matter any thought, nor have I consulted Miss Austen on the subject."

"It could be 'Miss Austen' or 'Jane Austen' or even 'by a lady.' There is certainly precedent for leaving her name off the title entirely."

"I shall consult with her when I return to Hampshire. In the meantime, perhaps you would set it both with and without her name so that I may let her choose."

"Of course," said Gilbert.

**BUT GILBERT HAD PRINTED** only one version of the title page before fire destroyed his shop—the one without Miss Austen's name. He had given no more thought to the name Jane Austen in the ensuing years but now he found himself in possession of what was certainly a novel by Miss Austen—an expansion of her story that he had set in type all those years ago. Here were the same characters and many more, fully realized in a way the limited confines of Mr. Mansfield's little book had not allowed. By the time he had read the novel and ordered *Sense and Sensibility* he had begun to believe that Miss Austen might very well outshine Fanny Burney. He was just thinking that perhaps he ought to add the words "by Jane Austen" in the margin next to the title of *First Impressions* in Mr. Mansfield's book when his thoughts were interrupted by the arrival of Joseph Collingwood, whose errand proved to be a request for the hand of Gilbert's sixteen-year-old daughter, Sarah, in marriage. Such a momentous conversation put all thoughts of Jane Austen and her literary legacy out of Gilbert's head, and so *Little Allegories and a Cautionary Tale* remained on his shelf, unmarred by marginalia.

## *Hampshire, Present Day*

**SOPHIE FORGOT ABOUT** the threat of Smedley for a moment as she read the words over again and tears welled up in her eyes: "Miss Austen's 'Cautionary Tale.'" Jane had written *First Impressions* and now Sophie could prove it. The book Winston now had was not evidence that Jane Austen was a plagiarist; it was the previously unknown original version of *Pride and Prejudice*. Suddenly the tension of the past few hours and days and weeks fell from her and she laughed and cried and collapsed with exhaustion onto the floor all at once. She could not tell where her tears left off and her laughter began; she could not separate grief for her uncle from joy at her discovery. All she knew was that here, at last, she felt the emotional release that she had not been able to find since that dreadful morning she learned of Bertram's death. Sophie did not know or care how long it took her to regain her composure, but her breathing gradually returned to normal. She pulled herself up from the floor and put the Mansfield documents into her handbag.

She now had a stolen book—the first edition of *Allegorical Stories* from St. John's College—and three letters: Jane's letter to Richard from the Oxfordshire History Centre, and letters from Mansfield to Lord Wintringham and from Gilbert Monkhouse to Mansfield from the Busbury Park records. She wondered what would have happened to all these items if she had not stolen them. The St. John's book and the Oxfordshire History Centre letter would have remained safe, but the Busbury Park files might well have been destroyed when the house was sold. So yes, Sophie thought, she was a thief, but possibly she was also a conservator. She doubted that any court would see it that way, but she hoped at least Uncle Bertram might have. She had stood up and brushed herself off when she was struck by a sudden and totally unexpected desire. More than anything else, she wanted to share this news with Eric and to hear his voice.

"Eric?" she said softly. "It's Sophie. Listen. How much do you know about the original version of *Pride and Prejudice*?"

"Sophie, is Winston—"

"Never mind about Winston. How much do you know about the original version of *Pride and Prejudice*?"

"I know that it was written between 1796 and 1797," said Eric. "I know that some people think it might have been epistolary, and I know that it was called *First Impressions*."

Sophie sighed. She had called the right person. She tried to think only of the literary bombshell she had to drop and not of the fact that her pulse had quickened as she had waited for him to answer, that her whole body had relaxed when she heard his voice, and that he certainly deserved a second chance to make his own first impression.

"What if I told you that I found it?"

"You found it?" said Eric. "What do you mean?"

"I found the original version of *Pride and Prejudice*. The version told in letters; the version called *First Impressions*."

"Are you serious?"

"Yes, I'm serious. I don't joke about Jane Austen," said Sophie. "You know that."

"Sophie, that's amazing. But isn't something like that . . . well, it must be worth an awful lot of money. I mean, are you sure it's safe? Are you sure *you're* safe?"

"Safe?" said Sophie. "Of course—" Sophie stopped speaking. She suddenly realized the house was silent. No footsteps. No voice calling out. Smedley had left.

"Get here," said Sophie into the phone. "Get here now. Come to the gatehouse on the east side of the estate."

She left the records room and dashed through the front door and down the stone steps. Smedley had said to come to the gatehouse, so that must be where he was holding Victoria. If he laid a finger on her, there would be no thought of coaxing him into a confession about Uncle Bertram. Sophie would kill him. She would kill him with her bare hands if she had to. Keeping to the grass next to the drive, where her footfalls would be quieter, she ran as fast as she could until she was only a few yards from the gatehouse. The east gatehouse, she thought. Had Jane Austen and Richard Mansfield sat before the fireplace in this little house and discussed the story that would grow into *Pride and Prejudice*? Someday soon, millions would flock to this unimposing structure to see the place where Pemberley had been born. She stood for a moment panting, considering whether she should go first to the Land Rover and find some sort of weapon, but before she could decide, a broad-shouldered figure emerged from the door of the gatehouse.

Sophie rushed across the few yards that separated them and slapped the man hard across the face, almost knocking him to the ground. The sting in her hand felt good.

"Fuck!" said the man. "Sophie, what the hell was that?" He turned back toward her and Sophie saw that it was Winston.

"You!" she spat. "You took Victoria? You're Smedley! You shit! Where's my sister?" She was raising her hand to slap him again but this time he caught her by the wrist.

"Jesus, Sophie, calm down. Victoria went to get the police. I didn't take her. I saved her, for fuck's sake. How do you think I got this?" Winston pointed to his face and Sophie saw that he had a huge bruise under one eye and blood trickling from what looked very much like a broken nose. "You slap hard but not that hard. That bastard Smedley, on the other hand, knows how to throw a punch." He let go of her wrist.

"You . . . you . . ." Sophie was not sure what to believe. "What happened?"

"When I went back to the Randolph and you were gone," said Winston, "I figured you'd come here. I got here about twenty minutes ago and saw the car and the open window of the gatehouse, so I climbed in and there was your sister tied up in a chair. I got the ropes undone just as Smedley came in the front door and I managed to get in a few good punches while your sister climbed out the window and drove away. Smedley ran off down the lane and then you showed up."

"So Victoria's OK?

"She's OK," said Winston. "How about you?"

"I'm really mad," said Sophie. "You stole my car! And what's worse, you stole my book. Where is my book?"

"God, you're in a mood," said Winston. "It's right inside. I told you I was just borrowing it."

Sophie strode past Winston into the gatehouse. There, on the table by the window, lay the Bayfield House copy of *Little Allegories*. She sat in the chair and picked up the book, turning to the last story. It was still there. With all that had happened, she half-expected the pages to be missing, or blank.

"Did you find anything in the house?" said Winston. Sophie hesitated before answering. Idiot or crook? she wondered. Winston had brought back her car and her book, but she wasn't sure she should trust him with the monumental intelligence of what she had found inside Busbury House.

As she ran her fingers across the opening sentences of "First Impressions" she closed her eyes and tried to imagine, in place of the gloom in which she now sat, a room lit by oil lamps with a fire dancing in the grate. A young woman and an old man sat in two chairs by the fire, warming themselves after a long walk through the grounds of Busbury Park. "I think in the story," said the woman, "I shall call him Mr. Darcy." "An excellent name," said the man. The scene was so real to Sophie that she almost expected to see the two before her if she opened her eyes. Their presence felt so strong that she did not understand what was happening when the muscular arms of Winston Godfrey pinned her from behind. Before she knew what was happening, her arms and chest were bound tightly to the chair with a thick cord.

## *Chawton, 1817*

"I **BEGIN TO DESPAIR** of recovery," said Jane as her brother Henry entered her bedchamber in Chawton. "And I have some instructions for you regarding my works."

"I wish you would not speak so," said Henry Austen. "Cassandra tells me you distress her with your talk."

"Nonetheless," said Jane, "I fear it is true. Else why would James be speaking of removing me to Winchester?"

"Only so that you might receive the best care for your recovery," said Henry.

It had been more than a year since Jane had first begun to feel ill. Now, in May 1817, she was confined to her bed and had not been able to write for the past two months. While her current project, *The Brothers*, remained unfinished, she wished to speak with her brother about two books that *were* complete, though unpublished. *Catherine* was the current title of what had begun life as *Susan*, the satire on gothic novels suggested by Mr. Mansfield. It had been Jane's intention to change the title to the one he had suggested only when she found a publisher, but the journey of the novel to publication had been rocky and was, as yet, incomplete. In 1803 the book had been sold to a London publisher who decided against its publication, but not until recently had Jane's brother Henry, who now served her as a sort of literary agent, been able to recover the rights to it. Her other finished work was *Persuasion*, which she had completed the previous year.

"It is kind of you to speak of recovery, brother," said Jane. "But I sent for you to discuss more practical matters. As you know, *Catherine* and *Persuasion* are of similar length—long enough to be novels, but shorter than those others which you have helped toward publication."

"So I have been told, though I have not read *Persuasion*."

"I have neglected you, dear brother, in not passing to you the manuscript, but I shall do so now. Cassandra will give it to you. I envision the two novels published together, perhaps in a set of four volumes."

"I can certainly begin to look for a publisher who may undertake such a commission."

"Do not begin your search yet, brother, for I believe my fame, though anonymous, may be enough that the publication may be more easily secured when you can present them as the *final* works of the author of *Pride and Prejudice*, to be published posthumously."

"Sister, I do wish you would not use that word."

"You are a man of God, brother, and I am one who loves him more than anything else in this world. I do not fear to make the journey to a further shore. Let us not deny the truth when the truth is a thing of such beauty."

"Scolded by my own sister to the last," said Henry, leaning to kiss her forehead. "I shall delay until the autumn my search for a publisher. By then God may have blessed us with your recovery, or he may have taken you to himself."

"Do your best to rejoice, whichever it may be," said Jane, smiling at her brother.

As she felt sleep beginning to overtake her, she realized she had heard those very words before, on the day when she and Mr. Mansfield had first discussed expanding her story of *First Impressions* into a novel.

"I do hope," said Mr. Mansfield, "that I shall live to see your work completed."

"Do not say such things, Mr. Mansfield," said Jane. "You are in good health and I do not think the work will take more than a year. No doubt by next autumn we will be sitting here reading of Eliza's encounter with Mr. Darcy at Pemberley."

"This time next year either I shall sit here reading with you, or I shall have been called home by the God I love," said Mr. Mansfield. "Do your best to rejoice, whichever it may be."

"There is one more thing, brother," said Jane as Henry turned to leave the room.

"Yes, sister?"

"*Catherine* is no more a title than *Susan* was. Let it be called *Northanger Abbey*."

## *Hampshire, Present Day*

"WINSTON, WHAT THE HELL are you doing?" said Sophie, turning to try to see him, but he came around the chair from the other direction and slapped her across the face so hard she saw nothing but black for an instant.

"That's for hitting me," he said in an angry voice. By the time Sophie had shaken off the shock of the slap, Winston had tied her feet to the chair and was standing in front of her, leveling a pistol at her head. "You and that sister of yours are a lot of damn trouble," he said. "That bitch kicked me in the face." In spite of her situation, Sophie felt a surge of glee. "I got her phone, though, and after what I did to your Land Rover, she won't be driving to fetch the police either. It'll take her a while to get anywhere on foot from here. You know, things would have been so much easier if you had just accepted that Mansfield wrote *First Impressions* and given the book to your boyfriend to publish. But you had to screw everything up by sticking your nose in where it didn't belong. Now what did you find in that damn house?" He snatched her bag off the floor where it had fallen and began rifling through the contents.

"You son of a bitch. You've been setting me up all along."

"It's amazing what you can accomplish with good looks and sexual technique," said Winston.

"Bastard," said Sophie.

"Ah, what have we here? A letter from Mansfield to Wintringham. Is this your little discovery?" He unfolded the letter and began to read as Sophie silently seethed. "'You will know that I have grown quite fond of your neighbour Miss Jane Austen, and have even had the opportunity to pursue certain literary projects with her. In addition to my keen anticipation of continuing my intercourse with your family, I shall look forward to renewing my intimate association with a young woman of such promise.'

"This doesn't prove a damn thing. 'The opportunity to pursue certain literary projects with her'?" Winston leaned down and whispered tauntingly in Sophie's ear. "It still sounds to me like Mansfield wrote *First Impressions*."

"That's not the only thing I found."

"Liar."

"There's a second letter. A letter from *my* ancestor Gilbert Monkhouse to *your* ancestor Richard Mansfield, sent after Mansfield died," said Sophie.

"And what does this alleged letter say?" asked Winston, running the cold barrel of the pistol along her neck.

She shivered, but recited from memory. "'I believe Miss Austen's "Cautionary Tale" will add about fifty pages.' Miss Austen's 'Cautionary Tale.'"

"And you expect me to believe that?"

"Believe it or not," said Sophie. "It's true. It's in my back pocket."

"So it really was Jane Austen all along," said Winston.

"It really was."

"Too bad no one will ever know."

"So what's your plan?" said Sophie. "Kill me in cold blood?"

"Not quite that simple," he said, reaching behind her and slipping the folded paper out of her pocket.

"You're doing all this just so you can pretend your ancestor wrote *First Impressions*?" said Sophie, who could feel tears welling up.

"Oh, Richard Mansfield's not *my* ancestor."

"But you said—"

"I said a lot of things, didn't I? No, I'm afraid it was Eric Hall who got drunk one night at Oxford and spilled the beans about his old family legend. American he may be, but *he's* the one descended from Mansfield."

"Eric?" said Sophie, trying to wrap her mind around this revelation. What did that mean? Was Eric trying to seduce her to get the book, too? Or had he been telling the truth when he warned her against Winston?

"So did he tell Smedley, too?" she asked.

"You're not as smart as I thought," said Winston. "George Smedley is my business partner. He helps me with . . . unsavory tasks. When you told me you didn't think you could find my book I decided you needed further motivation—hence the threatening phone calls and the irresistible mystery of two customers looking for the same book."

"So it really was Smedley who found the letter in the Oxfordshire History Centre?"

"I told him not to take anything; I just wanted to be sure you didn't keep secrets from me."

"And did he actually chase us through the street?"

"Well, I had to be your hero, didn't I? But no, George isn't much of a runner."

"And I suppose you had him kill my uncle, too," said Sophie.

"Sadly, no," said Winston. "He doesn't have the stomach for that sort of thing."

"Then who . . . ?"

"The problem with your uncle was that he left home at a different time every day. I was planning to break in and search through his books while he was gone, but when he opened the door just as I was breaking in . . . well, it was an awkward moment."

"Rot in hell," said Sophie.

"I don't think it's my afterlife you should be concerned about right now," said Winston.

"How did you even know to go there?" said Sophie, still trying to piece together the sequence of events that had ended with Uncle Bertram six feet under the rich earth of Oxfordshire and his shelves denuded.

"Ever since the night Eric told me his story, I've been patient," said Winston, leaning against the fireplace, seeming to enjoy prolonging his moment of triumph. "We were great pals at Oxford. He told me he never believed the story, but I was always on the lookout for books by Richard Mansfield just in case. Then I found the copy of *Allegorical Stories* at St. John's.

"The one inscribed to Austen," said Sophie.

"When I showed that to Eric, I think a part of him suspected it was all true. But he still didn't take it seriously. He went back to America and I figured I'd never see him again. I started collecting books printed by Gilbert Monkhouse, thinking one of them might have a clue to the riddle of *First Impressions*. Then a few weeks ago a friend sent me an article about Bayfield House from *Oxfordshire Life*. They had interviewed your uncle about the library, and he had said it was all started by a printer named Monkhouse. I knew Eric must have read the same article.

"I have to admit, he was more of an adversary than I thought. The French edition was a nice touch. But while he was following you round Oxfordshire, I got on with searching your uncle's flat. Didn't find anything, of course. Too bad old Uncle Bertram had to tumble down the steps for nothing."

Sophie ached to slap him again. To punch him, to bite him, to kill him, but he stood across the room and she couldn't move. She closed her eyes for a moment and willed rational thought to replace blind anger.

"You searched my room in Oxford, too, didn't you?" she said, suddenly remembering the transposition of two volumes on her shelf of Christmas books.

"I was afraid Eric had gotten there ahead of me," said Winston, "since you didn't have anything either."

They had both been using her, Sophie thought, but as soon as the thought was formed she wondered if she was being unfair to Eric. He had gone out of his way not to seduce her and God knows he had warned her against Winston. Eric had never actually lied to her—except about those wonderful volumes of Jane Austen in French. Unlike Winston, he hadn't killed her uncle or broken into her room. But had he been stalking her? Surely it wasn't a coincidence that they had met in Oxford. And then there was that kiss. Sophie could see so clearly now that everything with Winston had been a lie—every caress, every embrace—but maybe that kiss with Eric had been real. He may not have wanted it to be, but to Sophie it was the truest thing that had happened in the past few weeks, and even if he was a part of this whole web of deceit, it was hard for her to imagine that Eric didn't feel the same way.

"So what happens now?" she said quietly, almost certain that she knew the answer, almost certain that her first kiss with Eric would also be her last.

"Here's what's going to happen," said Winston. "In a few weeks I will announce to the world that I discovered, in my extensive collection of Gilbert Monkhouse imprints, the true first version of *Pride and Prejudice* written by Richard Mansfield and plagiarized by Jane Austen. It will be a simple matter to remove your uncle's ownership mark. I'll find a book at St. John's and a letter at the Oxfordshire History Centre that help prove the case. I will publish *First Impressions* and use the proceeds from its massive international sale to buy out the investors I'm assembling to help me purchase Busbury Park."

"You're going to buy—"

"Then I will generously sell the original book to the nation for permanent display for, say, a million pounds, renovate this estate, and . . . this is my favorite bit—rename it Mansfield Park. You've got to admit Jane Austen would appreciate that. The grounds and this gatehouse will become a major tourist destination and a few weekends a year I will open the doors to my lovely country home and let anyone with twenty-five pounds see what can be accomplished with one book."

"Why can't you do all that with a book written by Jane Austen?" said Sophie. "The Monkhouse letter proves she wrote *First Impressions*."

"That's a good story," said Winston, "but Jane Austen plagiarizes the most famous novel in English literature—that's a better story. And the better the story, the more people will pay."

"That's all you care about, isn't it?" said Sophie. "Money."

"Well," said Winston, waving the Monkhouse letter under her nose, "I'll need some funds to repair this place after the fire."

"What fire?" said Sophie, a cold sweat breaking out on her forehead.

"The fire that kills that girl who broke into the main house today. Oh, I'll see the flames and try to save her before I call the fire brigade, but I'm afraid I'll be too late." He drew a cigarette lighter out of his pocket and clicked it to life.

"Please," said Sophie. "Kill me if you have to, but don't burn that letter. Lock it up and let somebody find it after you're dead, I don't care, but just don't burn it." Winston moved the flame closer to the letter. "If you destroy that, no one will ever know the truth about *First Impressions*."

"I'm counting on that," said Winston.

Sophie watched as the flame licked the edges of the paper and then leapt into a brightness that illuminated the gloomy room. While the flame still burned bright through the haze of Sophie's tears, Winston held it to the bottom of the tattered draperies. At first nothing happened and the flame started to die away, but then it blazed to life and began climbing rapidly up the drapes. In less than a minute the room was filled with bright light and smoke was billowing through the air.

"Thanks for the help, Sophie," said Winston, stepping away from the fire, which had now begun to lick the ceiling. He leaned over and gave her a kiss on the cheek that stung the spot where he had slapped her. "Sorry it had to end like this." He swept *Little Allegories* off the table, grabbed Sophie's bag and its precious contents, dashed across the room, and disappeared out the door.

## *Winchester, 1817*

JANE KNEW THAT where she lay, in the bedchamber of a house just outside the precincts of Winchester Cathedral—a building she considered one of the most sublime works of man—was her deathbed. Cassandra had been her tender, watchful, indefatigable nurse since their arrival in Winchester nearly two months earlier. Jane felt blessed that she had retained her faculties, that her pain had been minimal, and that her two clergyman brothers had visited often—reminding her that her faith was not a mere consolation, but a cause for rejoicing. Yesterday she had received Communion and had been able to follow the service attentively, though she fell into a long sleep almost immediately afterward. Her dreams, of late, had been memories, and she almost didn't know when she slept and when she rested peacefully awake, recalling those moments of her life on this side of the divide most precious to her. Now, in such a state, she lived again that fateful afternoon with Mr. Mansfield that had set her on a journey to literary success.

"Now," said Mr. Mansfield, after Jane had poured them both a fresh cup of tea, "you have said that your sin—the sin that condemned Nurse to a life of misery—is that you allow first impressions to guide your opinions."

"In brief, it is true. But it is a sin of which I shall not only repent, but from which I shall turn away in the future."

"And that is well, for God shall both hear your repentance and see your reformation. But you have not yet heard all of what I propose as an act of atonement. In addition to helping me with my stories, I wish you to consider writing a moral tale of your own. A tale in which the first impressions of the heroine guide her falsely and which therefore warns against the very sins you have enumerated."

"I could envision such a tale with ease," said Jane, a sliver of excitement creeping into her voice. "Your description of Lady Mary and her gossip about her neighbors immediately suggests a departing point. But though the act of writing it may help me to avoid these sins in the future, how can it help others when the only ones who see my work are you and my family?"

"I would not argue that even that audience is beyond learning a lesson from your work," replied Mr. Mansfield, "but I confess I had a somewhat larger audience in mind. As I have told you, I intend to publish a second edition of my little book. What if I were to include your story in that collection? My readers do not number in the millions, but they may perhaps reach the thousands, to judge by the rapid sale of my modest effort."

"You do me unjust honor, sir. I come to you confessing a heinous sin, and you offer me the great reward of seeing my writing in print."

"Miss Austen, I have no doubt that your words will one day appear in print, regardless of whatever action I might take. If I could help you begin that journey, and at the same time find for you a way in which you might begin to heal the wound left by your accidental sin, I should consider that a service not just to you and to literature, but to God. So, do you accept my proposal?"

"I am both humbled and honored to do so, Mr. Mansfield."

"Excellent. With your assistance in the revision of my own stories, they may not yet be transformed into great literature, but perhaps they may rise a rung or two up the ladder of merit. And with the addition of an original story of your own, the book is certain to outshine the original edition. When the work is complete, I shall copy the whole for my printer, who is fond of my hand. Though I may lack your skills as an author, my script, I am told, is lovely."

"I shall relish the opportunity to work with you on your stories," said Jane.

"That is well. But your story must come first," said Mr. Mansfield. "That is the important thing."

"It seems a fitting tribute to Nurse," said Jane. "What would you think of calling it *First Impressions*?"

**"JANE? JANE, ARE YOU** awake?" She heard the voice of her sister as if it came from the banks of a wide river, across which Jane felt herself now to be drifting.

"Mansfield," whispered Jane.

"She speaks of her novels," said Cassandra to Henry, who was also in the room. "It is best to let her rest."

A few hours later, Jane woke to find her pillow supported by her dear sister. She had already begun to feel detached from the world, and she seemed to see the face of her sister and the room around them through a veil.

"Is there anything that you want?" said Cassandra.

Jane thought for a moment, and knew there was only one reply to this simple question.

"Nothing but death," she said, smiling.

Jane closed her eyes and felt herself again setting off across the river, this time with more intention of motion. And she saw waiting for her on the approaching bank the figures of Nurse and the only man outside her own family she had ever truly loved. This time she knew the words were unspoken, that no one on the earthly side of the divide would hear her voice again, but she smiled as the face of her friend came into view and she said quietly, "Mr. Mansfield."

## *Hampshire, Present Day*

**SOPHIE CLOSED HER** eyes as the smoke began to burn them. The heat washed over her in waves and the smoke tore at her throat whenever she took a breath. She tried to struggle against her bonds, but Winston had done his job well. Exhausted, she could feel herself slipping into unconsciousness when she heard voices. Richard and Jane, she thought, welcoming her. Perhaps she would walk the grounds of Pemberley with them when this was all over. She let her head fall against her chest, and began to smile as she saw an old man in black clerical garb and a young woman in a pale blue dress with an Empire waistline walking on the shores of a deep blue lake. "I think," said the woman, "I shall call it *First Impressions*." "Sophie," said the man, turning to her. "Sophie, stay with me!"

Her bonds fell free and she slumped forward in the chair into someone's arms. How had he done it? How had eighty-year-old Richard Mansfield come from beyond the grave to catch her, to hoist her out of the chair, to run with her from the gatehouse into the cool evening air? A scream rent the air and tore Sophie back to the present. She lay on the ground coughing out the horrid smoke and looking into the face of Eric Hall.

"My knee!" came a voice from nearby, and Sophie turned to see Winston Godfrey, also on the ground, Victoria standing over him with a tire iron. "The bitch took out my knee," he said.

"Oh, take it like a man," said Victoria, leaning over to retrieve Sophie's bag and *Little Allegories* from where Winston had dropped them. "I would've done a lot worse if Sophie hadn't come out of there alive."

In another minute Sophie was sitting up, Eric holding her as she sucked the clean cool air into her lungs. Behind them, flames leapt through the upper windows of the gatehouse.

"You still didn't save your precious Jane Austen," gasped Winston, propping himself up on one elbow. "The only thing that proved she wrote *First Impressions* went up in that fire."

"That would be true if you weren't incredibly stupid," said Sophie. "But lucky for me you burned an invoice for two thousand tulip bulbs. The Monkhouse letter is still in my bag." Winston sank back to the ground with a groan and Sophie started to laugh.

"The police and firemen will be here any minute," said Eric. "We need to get you to the hospital, and I suppose that vermin, too," he added, nodding toward Winston.

Sophie felt more clearheaded now, and as lovely as Eric's arms felt, she pulled away from him as she sat up further. "So is what Winston said true?" she asked. "Are you Richard Mansfield's descendent? And have you been stalking me?"

"Well, the first part is true," said Eric. "But I wouldn't exactly say I've been stalking you. I really was staying in Oxford and shooting my mouth off at the Bear every night when I saw that article about Bayfield House. I knew the way Winston preyed on women and I was afraid he'd come after you looking for that book, so when I found out you worked at Christ Church, I thought maybe I should check up on you."

"To protect me from this scum," said Sophie, nodding toward Winston, "or to get access to the Bayfield library?"

"I honestly didn't believe the book existed; I just didn't want Winston to hurt you. And then everything changed."

"Because you found out the book was real after all."

"No. Because I fell in love with you. I thought you knew that."

"Well, how could I know it if you never told me?" said Sophie, smiling.

"I'm telling you now, aren't I?" said Eric, pulling her back into his arms.

"And you're not just saying that to get hold of *First Impressions*?"

"You can do whatever you like with the book," he said. "I'm only interested in you." Sophie believed it now. She relaxed into the support of Eric's embrace and let his love wash over her for a moment until she heard sirens in the distance.

"What am I going to do about the books, and the letters?" she said, looking into his eyes.

"The stolen pieces you'll return," said Eric. "But from what your sister says, *First Impressions* belongs to you."

"I stole that, too," said Sophie, "from Bayfield House."

"You did no such thing," said Victoria, who, Sophie now saw, was holding the book. "This book has Uncle Bertram's ownership signature in it. And you know he wanted you to have his books."

But Victoria's voice sounded faint to Sophie, who had not dropped her eyes from Eric's gaze—a gaze that reiterated the words he had spoken a minute earlier. He loved her.

"Sorry I didn't get here sooner," he whispered. "I guess I wasn't very good at protecting you."

"Well, kiss me," said Sophie, "and let's see if you're any good at that."

# *Epilogue*

Dear Gusty,

Would you believe it, Eric was seriously considering changing the name of Busbury Park to Pemberley, but I convinced him that the only thing Winston Godfrey was ever right about was that this place should be called Mansfield Park. It seems the only way to honor both Jane Austen and Richard Mansfield. And so you couldn't have picked a better wedding present than my Uncle Bertram's first edition of *Mansfield Park*. It was far too generous, but I am nonetheless grateful to you not just for tracking it down for us, but for the way you have presented my case to so many of the booksellers who ended up with my uncle's books. Many of those books are now in the library here—though I know it will take the rest of our years to fill all those shelves. Father kindly bought back for me the copy of Newton's *Principia* which I returned to the dealer from whom I had purloined it. I now have almost half of my uncle's beloved Christmas books.

*First Impressions* has reached its twenty-third printing and is translated into forty-five languages, with more coming every day. It has kept our agent and publishers busy, and I like to think that Jane Austen would be happy to know that her little story has brought Busbury Park back to life.

We are having a little service of "Thanksgiving for the Life of Richard Mansfield" at the chapel next week on his birthday, and I do hope you will be able to come down. I still walk to his grave every Sunday, no matter the weather, and whisper him a thanks for all he has done for me—not just in helping Jane Austen to become a writer, but in establishing the line that gave me my wonderful husband. I don't think I ever understood just how happy Eliza was with Mr. Darcy, but living here with Eric, now I know. He is calling me for a walk down by the lake even now, but I know he joins me in sending thanks for the perfect gift.

Yours Most Affectionately,

Sophie

# *Author's Note*

**THE CHARACTERS OF** Jane and Cassandra Austen, their parents, brothers, and their niece Anna are all based on historical figures. The basic facts of Jane Austen's life—her family relationships, where she lived, and when she wrote and revised her novels—are essentially as presented in the novel. Jane and her sister did spend a year in Oxford and Southampton under the tutelage of Mrs. Ann Crawley and attended the Reading Ladies' Boarding School from 1785 to 1786. Jane did travel to Kent in September 1796. Little Anna Austen, at the age of four and a half, "was a very intelligent, quick-witted child, and, hearing the original draft of *Pride and Prejudice* read aloud by its youthful writer to her sister, she caught up the names of the characters and repeated them so much downstairs that she had to be checked; for the composition of the story was still a secret kept from the knowledge of the elders." I am grateful to *Jane Austen: Her Life and Letters, a Family Record*, by William Austen-Leigh and Richard Arthur Austen-Leigh, for this information.

The original version of *Sense and Sensibility*, titled *Elinor and Marianne*, was an epistolary novel, and some have suggested that *First Impressions* (which later became *Pride and Prejudice*) may have been so as well. The letters in my fictional version of *First Impressions* rely heavily on Jane Austen's language from *Pride and Prejudice*. The letter Jane writes to Mr. Mansfield, but never sends, from Bath includes an account of a ball very similar to one in *Northanger Abbey*. The text of the letter from George Austen to Thomas Cadell is from the original.

Busbury Park and Richard Mansfield are completely fictional. The summaries and excerpts from his work *A Little Book of Allegorical Stories* are taken from an anonymous book of 1797: *The Selector: Being a New and Chaste Collection of Visions, Tales, and Allegories, Calculated for the Amusement and Instruction of the Rising Generation*. All the titles of Mansfield's allegories are taken from this work, except for "General Depravity of Mankind," which is a chapter title in Mary Martha Sherwood's didactic children's book, *The Fairchild Family* (published between 1818 and 1847).

There was, in fact, a printer in Leeds named Griffith Wright who published the *Leeds Intelligencer*, and his son Thomas did take over the business in 1784. The text of the article about penalties for using fireworks is taken from the *Leeds Intelligencer*, November 7, 1796. The character of Gilbert Monkhouse is entirely fictional.

# *Acknowledgments*

**I AM GRATEFUL TO** have grown up in a home where books were valued both as texts and as physical objects, and for that I especially thank my father, Bob Lovett, who not only collected books but also taught literature. His passion for the eighteenth century and for Jane Austen led me into the world that much of this novel inhabits.

Humble thanks to Janice Lovett, whose wisdom has contributed to *First Impressions* as it has to so much of my writing; David Gernert and Anna Worrall, who saw the potential in a rough manuscript and gave me direction; and Lindsey Schwoeri for her expert editorial guidance. To the incomparable Kathryn Court I must express thanks for so much more than brilliant editing—the energy to write this novel is due in large part to her support and encouragement.

Thanks also to Stephanie Lovett for assistance with Latin, to Victoria Huxley for a lovely tour round Jane Austen's Adlestrop, to the Wake Forest University library and Megan Mulder for allowing me to handle (and even read) their first edition of *Pride and Prejudice*, to Mark and Catherine Richards for so much hospitality in their book-filled Maida Vale flat, and to Chris and Delphie Stockwell for helping me understand English gardens and so much else about life in Oxfordshire.

In addition to William Austen-Leigh and Richard Arthur Austen-Leigh's *Jane Austen: Her Life and Letters*, I am particularly indebted to the anonymous work *The History of Printing*, published in London by the Society for Promoting Christian Knowledge in 1855.

To all those at the Gernert Company and Penguin Books who have brought my work to the world—especially Will Roberts, Rebecca Gardner, Rebecca Lang, Annie Harris, and Scott Cohen—I am eternally grateful.

Finally, thanks must go to my family, in particular to the aforementioned Janice, whose patience, love, and support make being a writer possible, and to Jordan and Lucy—my children not only inspire me; they also read my novels.

Charlie Lovett's first book,

***The Bookman's Tale,***

is available from Penguin Books.

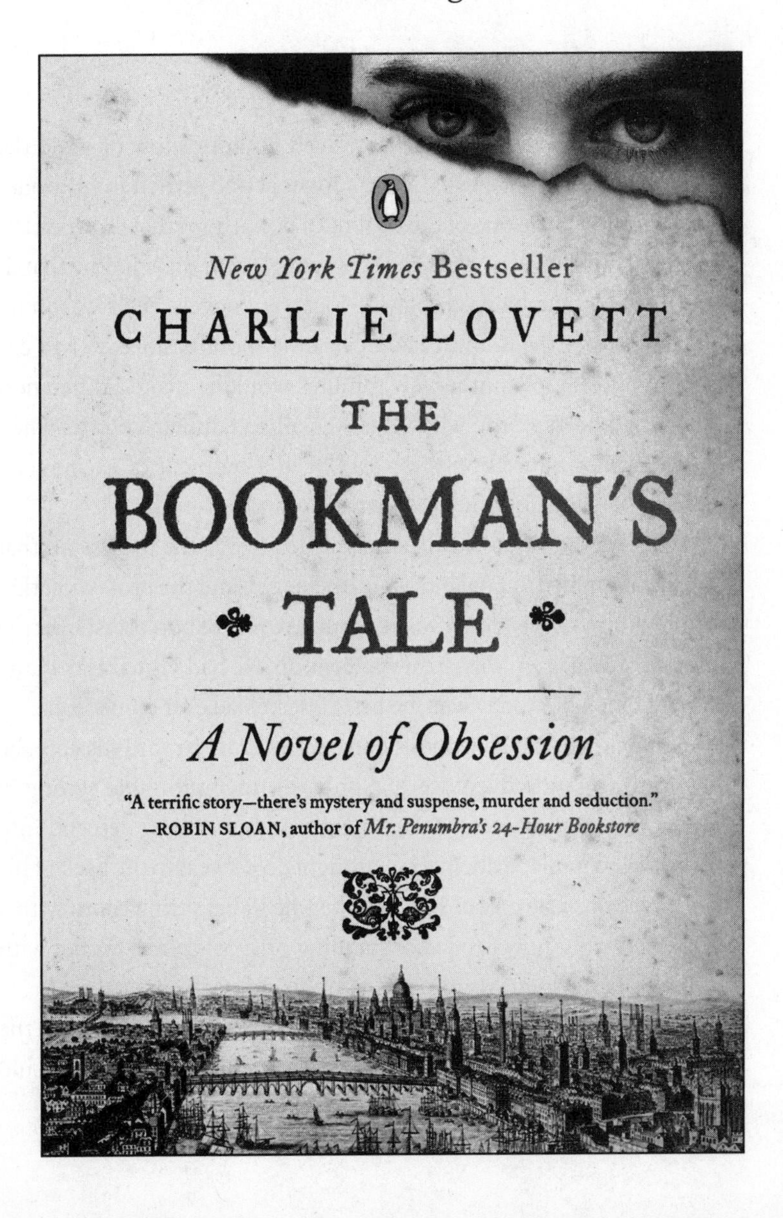

*Hay-on-Wye, Wales, Wednesday, February 15, 1995*

Wales could be cold in February. Even without snow or wind the damp winter air permeated Peter's topcoat and settled in his bones as he stood outside one of the dozens of bookshops that crowded the narrow streets of Hay. Despite the warm glow in the window that illuminated a tantalizing display of Victorian novels, Peter was in no hurry to open the door. It had been nine months since he had entered a bookshop; another few minutes wouldn't make a difference. There had been a time when this was all so familiar, so safe; when stepping into a rare bookshop had been a moment of excitement, meeting a fellow book lover a part of a grand adventure.

Peter Byerly was, after all, a bookseller. It was the profession that had brought him to England again and again, and the profession that brought him to Hay-on-Wye, the famous town of books just over the border in Wales, on this dreary afternoon. He had visited Hay many times before, but today was the first time he had ever come alone.

Now, as the cold ache in his extremities crept toward his core, he saw not a grand adventure but only an uncomfortable setting, a stranger, and the potential for shyness and unease to descend into anxiety and panic. Anticipation brought cold sweat to the back of his neck. Why had he come? He could be safe in his sitting room with a cup of tea right now instead of standing on a cold street corner with a sense of dread settling into the pit of his stomach.

Before he could change his mind, he forced himself to grasp the door handle and in another second he was stepping into what should have been welcoming warmth.

"Afternoon," said a crisp voice through a haze of pipe smoke that hovered over a wide desk. Peter mumbled a few syllables, then slipped through an open doorway into the back room, where books lined every wall. He closed his eyes for a moment, imagining the cocoon of books shielding him from all danger, inhaling deeply that familiar scent of cloth and leather and dust and words. His rushing pulse began to slow, and when he opened his eyes he scanned the shelves for something familiar—a title, an author, a well-remembered dust jacket design—anything that might ground him in the world of the known.

Just above eye level, he spotted a binding of beautiful blue leather that reminded him of the calf he had used to bind another book—could it have been nearly ten years ago? He pulled the book from the shelf, reveling in the smooth, luxurious feel of the leather. Taking a closer look at the gold stamping on the spine, Peter smiled. He knew this book. If not an old friend, it was certainly an acquaintance, and the prospect of spending a few minutes between its covers calmed his nerves.

*An Inquiry into the Authenticity of Certain Miscellaneous Papers,* by Edmond Malone, was a monument of analysis that unmasked one of the great forgers of all time, William Henry Ireland. Ireland had forged documents and letters purporting to be written by William Shakespeare, and even the "original manuscripts" of *Hamlet* and *King Lear.* Peter turned past the marbled endpapers to the title page: it was a copy of the first edition of 1796. He loved the feel of heavy eighteenth-century paper between his fingers, the texture of the indentations made on the page by the letterpress. He flipped a few pages and read:

> It has been said that every individual of this country, whose mind has been at all cultivated, feels a pride in being able to boast of our own great dramatick poet, Shakespeare, as his countryman: and propor-

tionate to our respect and veneration for that extraordinary man ought to be our care of his fame, and of those valuable writings he left us.

Peter smiled as he recalled reading "those valuable writings" from an actual copy of the First Folio, that weighty 1623 volume of Shakespeare's works in which many of his plays were printed for the first time. He was calm now—all sense of dread and panic banished by the simple act of losing himself in an old book. Remembering how that First Folio, given the opportunity, always fell open to the third act of *Hamlet,* he spread the covers of the Malone and let the pages fall where they would. The book opened to page 289, revealing a piece of paper about four inches square. The brown foxing on the pages between which the paper had been pressed told Peter it had been there for at least a century. Out of habit more than curiosity he turned the paper over.

The sharp pain that stabbed his chest almost made him drop the book onto the dusty floor. He thought he had outrun that pain, that he could escape it with distance and distraction, but even in the corner of a bookshop in Hay-on-Wye it had found him. Knees suddenly weak, he slumped against a bookcase and watched, as if in a dream, as the paper fluttered to the floor. The face was still there; he closed his eyes, willing the face and all that went with it to retreat, willing his pulse to slow once more and his hands to stop shaking. He took a deep breath and opened his eyes. She lay there calmly, serenely, looking up at him, waiting. It was his wife. It was Amanda.

But Amanda was dead—buried nine months ago in the red earth of North Carolina, an ocean away. A heartbeat away. And this painting, so much older than Amanda or her mother or her grandmother, could not possibly portray her. But it did.

Peter leaned over to retrieve the paper from the floor and examine it more closely. It was an expert watercolor, almost imperceptibly signed with the initials "B.B." He looked again at the book from which it had fallen, hoping for a clue to the watercolor's origin. On the front endpaper was a penciled interlocking "EH," the monogram of some long-forgotten owner. The description printed on a card inside the cover made no mention of a watercolor, only the price: £400. He had seen copies cataloged for half that. Copies that didn't hide a century-old painting of his dead wife.

On the shelf in front of him was a shabby copy of Dickens's unfinished final novel, *The Mystery of Edwin Drood*. The original cloth binding was worn at the corners and spine, the hinges were broken, and a few pages were loose, but nothing was missing. He could easily restore it to be worth two or three times the asking price.

Glancing around, he found himself still alone in the room. His hand trembling, Peter slipped the watercolor into *Edwin Drood*. He could not leave Amanda here, so far from home. He reshelved the Malone and tucked *Drood* under his arm. Twenty minutes later he had purchased a stack of books, including the Dickens, and was walking toward the car park on the outskirts of town, two heavy bags hanging at his sides.

The drive from the Welsh border to Peter's cottage in the Oxfordshire village of Kingham took just over two hours. Peter's cottage was down a narrow lane from the village green and, like the rest of the village, built of golden Cotswold limestone. It was in the middle of a row of terraced cottages, but in five months of residence, Peter had yet to meet either of the neighbors with whom he shared the thick stone walls.

By seven, he had a fire in the grate, a cup of tea in his hand, and the watercolor propped up on the coffee table. Despite Dr. Strayer's advice, he had boxed all his pictures of Amanda and left them in the attic of the house in Ridgefield. So how could she be here, in what suddenly seemed like *her* cottage? She had, after all, picked out the William Morris fabric on the sofa and curtains. She had overseen the renovation of the kitchen and the addition of the conservatory. She had spent weekends in Portobello Road buying the Pilkington vases that stood on every windowsill and the Burne-Jones prints that hung in the upstairs hall. She had gone to country auctions to buy the furniture and had found the carpenter who installed the floor-to-ceiling bookshelves in the sitting room. The shelves had been her gift to Peter, the outward and visible sign of her passion for his passion; but everything else in the cottage was pure Amanda. She had never spent a night here, but that Peter could have lived here for five months and actually come to think of it as his cottage seemed silly now that she stood on the coffee table staring at him.

The painting showed a woman seated in front of a mirror, combing a long tress of dark hair. Her shoulders were bare, and her hair just covered her breasts. The dark hair and the pale skin were Amanda's as were the straight shoulders, and even the insistent way that she gripped the brush, but the most remarkable similarity was in the countenance that stared out from the mirror—teasing and challenging at once. The resemblance was uncanny—the narrow face, the high, pale forehead; and above all the deep green eyes that could laugh and demand to be taken seriously simultaneously. Amanda could do that. Of course the face couldn't be hers. She had been born in 1966; the watercolor was definitely Victorian. Still, Peter sat staring into Amanda's eyes, wondering where she had come from and wishing she had never left.

He lost himself in those eyes, and in the past, for a few minutes, then roused himself, stood up, and began pacing the room. Here was a mystery that demanded a solution. During his years as an antiquarian bookseller, Peter had solved his share of bibliographical puzzles, but he had done so with the same emotional detachment with which he solved crosswords. This was different. The mystery of the watercolor's origins felt deeply personal and Peter could already feel curiosity and grief melding into obsession. He had to know where this painting came from—how a hundred-year-old portrait of his wife, who had been born only twenty-nine years ago, had come to be tucked into an eighteenth-century book on Shakespeare forgeries.

The problem was how to begin. Peter had never worked with paintings before. It took him another hour of staring and pacing to remember what was in the bookcase in the spare room upstairs. He had not set foot in that room since he moved to Kingham. It had been intended as Amanda's sanctum sanctorum, and though she would never spend afternoons sitting there in the armchair reading her books, it still seemed an inviolable space. Now he opened the door slowly and looked into the stale silence. In the distance he heard the church bell toll nine and he waited until the last chime had died in the wet winter air before turning on the light.

In the bookcase by the window were sixty-five nearly identical volumes—Peter's wedding gift to Amanda. Because it had been a Royal Academy exhibition catalog that brought them together, and because Amanda so loved her Victorian paintings, Peter had resolved to give her a copy of the catalog for every year of Victoria's reign—an illustrated journey through seven decades of English art. It had taken him a year to track down all the volumes, but it had taken Amanda almost that long to plan the wedding. Now the books stood patiently on the shelves of the room she would never use.

Peter stood in the doorway for several minutes wrestling with the eerie sense of Amanda's presence. It wasn't just that this was Amanda's room furnished with her books and her favorite chair and the lamp she'd picked out from the antique shop in Stow-on-the-Wold. Peter was used to living with Amanda's taste. This was different. This was a feeling that Amanda might return at any moment—not the evanescent Amanda who sometimes spoke to him, but the real flesh-and-blood Amanda. It was a feeling Peter longed to embrace, but which he knew he must fight. He felt the same nausea and dizziness he had felt when they first met, and he had to lean against the doorway to steady himself.

"It's okay," said Amanda. "You can go in." She stood at the end of the hall and Peter looked up just in time to see her fade away. Her words gave him the courage he needed, though, and he entered the room, crossed to the bookshelf, pulled out the volume labeled "1837," and sat gingerly on the edge of the chair. *These are just books; these are just things; this is just a room; and that was just my imagination,* he told himself. And although he didn't really believe it, he opened the book and began looking at paintings.

Before Peter had left for England, Dr. Strayer had given him a typed list of things he needed to do in order to move on with life. The second item was: "Establish Regular Eating and Sleeping Habits." He had been making progress on this—going to bed by eleven, sometimes falling asleep as early as one, and sleeping until about ten. It wasn't ideal, but it had become regular.

Peter had opened the first Royal Academy volume at nine o'clock P.M. He closed the last one at seven o'clock the next evening. He had not eaten or slept. Now he sat, bleary-eyed and exhausted, amid piles of books on Amanda's floor. He had looked at thousands of paintings, read thousands of captions. He had not seen Amanda's face; he had not seen the initials B.B. or discovered any artist with those initials.

It wasn't until he was standing in the doorway looking back at the books he had left heaped on the floor that he realized that Amanda's presence, which he had felt so strongly when he entered the room, was gone. After twenty-two sleep-deprived hours he honestly felt that this was nothing more than a room. He listened for Amanda's voice telling him not to leave her books on the floor, but he heard nothing. He turned out the light, left the door open, and staggered downstairs.

---

For the first two months, Peter had left the cottage only to buy food at the local shop. He had ventured into nearby Chipping Norton on a couple of errands before Christmas, but had avoided the bookshop, where he might be recognized by the proprietor. The excursion to Hay had been the beginning of his attempt to address the fourth item on Dr. Strayer's list: "Re-establish Your Career," and he had to admit it wasn't a wholly unpleasant experience to discover that the world of books still existed, that he could escape what Dr. Strayer called his "secret lair."

"What do you mean by that?" Peter had asked.

"You've spent most of your life in hiding," said Dr. Strayer. "Your secret lair is the only place you feel truly safe. When you were a child it was your room where you'd hide so you didn't have to interact with your parents. In college it was the rare-books room; once you married Amanda, it was your basement book room. You bury yourself in these places, Peter. You avoid life there."

"I left my lair plenty with Amanda," Peter retorted.

"Yes, *with* Amanda. She was your trusty sidekick, the person who made the world safe for you. Be honest, Peter, the only places you ever really went without her were bookstores and libraries—and there you didn't need Amanda to run interference because you could interpose the books between yourself and any meaningful human contact."

And so he had started the process of emerging from his secret lair in Kingham with an excursion to bookstores. And just as Dr. Strayer had predicted, he had done everything he could to avoid any conversation.

Still, wouldn't Dr. Strayer be pleased that Peter had taken some small step toward restarting his career? He hadn't looked at his own books—the bibliographical reference library he had built over the past several years—since he lost Amanda. Even when he had boxed them up to be shipped to England, they had been only rectangular solids to be fit into empty boxes—boxes now stacked in the stone shed in the garden.

He thought he might have one or two books on Victorian illustrators so he turned on the lights in the tiny back garden, shoved open the door of the shed, and began carrying the boxes into the sitting room. Two hours later, he had opened them all and emptied the contents haphazardly onto the floor-to-ceiling shelves. On the coffee table he left two books: *A Treasury of the Great Children's Illustrators* and Percy Muir's landmark study *Victorian Illustrated Books*. Not sure he could bear another dead end without at least some sleep, Peter left the books where they were, picked up the watercolor, and went upstairs to bed. He slept soundly for the next twelve hours, dreaming of those Royal Academy catalogs and the building where he first encountered them.

*Ridgefield, North Carolina, 1983*

When it opened in 1957, the Robert Ridgefield Library had been the tallest building in Ridgefield—a nine-story neoclassical behemoth of granite and glass, columns and cornices, with an incongruous cupola perched uncomfortably on top.

The Ridgefields had come to North Carolina from Scotland just after the revolution and had spent the next two centuries going from success to success. A moderately wealthy nineteenth-century merchant family, they had become impressively wealthy in tobacco, then excessively wealthy in textiles, and now obscenely wealthy in banking. Along the way, they had turned a backwater two-year Bible college into the nationally recognized Ridgefield University.

The library had been built atop Ridgefield's highest point—a hill on the edge of campus previously favored by students for late-night trysts. From the upper floors one could view the countryside around Ridgefield for miles—a patchwork of corn and tobacco, clouds of dust rising from the horizon as pickup trucks sped down gravel roads. In the Georgia granite above the library's main entrance were carved the words, "Let those who enter here seek not only knowledge but wisdom."

The moment Peter walked into the library for the first time, passing from the blazing sun of a North Carolina August into the cool dimness of its narrow corridors, its miles of shelving, its million and a half books, he felt at home. He was eighteen and had lived his life on that very farmland that was visible from the top of the library—a world in which he had always felt awkwardly out of place. His family had run a general store in a small town eight miles from Ridgefield, until his father's neglect of the business sent it into bankruptcy. After that his parents seemed more interested in drinking and fighting than in spending time with their son. He had often gazed at the strange white building on the horizon and dreamed of a different life, a life free from the encumbrances of family and the daily interactions at school with people who understood him no better than he understood them. He dreamed of a life protected from everything outside of himself, but protected by what he could not imagine.

He had tried various ways of insulating himself over the years. As a youngster he spent most of his free time in his room with his stamp collection, meticulously mounting stamps and trying not to think of the wider world that those little rectangles of paper represented. During high school, he had taken to sequestering himself in the basement with a pair of headphones and a stack of classical records. But however carefully he mounted the stamps, however loudly he played the music, he could never quite escape. A part of him always knew that the world still existed outside his door and that, ultimately, he could not avoid it.

Peter had won a scholarship to Ridgefield, and freshman orientation had been a harrowing experience, focused on "getting to know" people. Peter did not want to know people. What he wanted was to find that world-within-the-world where he could be himself by himself. Following his tour guide through the foyer of the library into the stacks, he suspected he may have found that place. Lagging behind the tour and slipping into the rows of stacks that disappeared into darkness, Peter discovered exactly what would protect him: books.

It took him only a few weeks to secure a work-study position in the library. It was nirvana. Peter spent four hours a day reshelving books. Technically, he was part of the Circulation department, but he worked alone, wheeling his cart down the narrow aisles between towers of books, easily avoiding contact with anyone who might be browsing.

Even on those occasions when he had to push his cart through the main reading room, with its wide oak tables and banks of card catalog drawers, Peter remained invisible to his fellow students. The cart would glide almost silently across the smooth marble floor and heads would remain bent over books, his passing no more remarkable than a change in the light streaming in from the high clerestory windows as a cloud moved across the sun.

On a dark and rainy October day in his sophomore year—he would later tell her the exact date, October 14—Peter Byerly wheeled his cart into the reading room and first laid eyes on the woman he would marry. She was sitting alone at a table, poring over a biography of William Morris. She sat ramrod straight, with her book propped on the table in front of her, her posture almost daring the work to get the better of her, while all around her students slumped with the weight of impending midterms. She wore, in place of the unofficial uniform of jeans and a T-shirt, an impeccably tailored black suit, with pleated trousers and a crisp white blouse. Not a strand of her shoulder-length black hair was out of place.

She was slim, though not as slim as most college girls aspired to be. She was tall, though not as tall as those girls whose height inspired envy among their peers. Both her figure and her stature were enhanced by the one quality completely lacking in most coeds but which she possessed in abundance—poise.

He did not at first see that she was beautiful—though it would not take him long to notice. What he saw was that she was different, that she seemed, like himself, to inhabit a world on the margins of Ridgefield University. She did not fit in, and this intrigued him, made him want to shout, *Comrade!*

Peter slid quietly into a chair at the edge of the room and pulled a book from his cart. For the next thirty minutes, he pretended to read, while watching her. Except to turn a page, which she did frequently, she did not move. At six o'clock she closed the book, put it on a pile of others, picked up the books and her red leather purse, and headed toward the exit. Peter followed. When she returned several of the books at the circulation desk, he swept them off the counter as soon as they had been processed.

Ten minutes later he was sequestered in the stacks perusing her books. In addition to the William Morris biography there was a book on the Pre-Raphaelite painter Holman Hunt, a volume of Edward Burne-Jones prints, and two volumes of the catalog of the annual exhibit at London's Royal Academy of Arts—1852 and 1853. He glanced through the volumes of artwork and the Holman Hunt biography before reshelving them. The Morris biography he slipped into his bag without checking it out. He wasn't sure what made him do it; for some reason he felt a need to illicitly possess a book she had read. He returned it to its shelf a week later, afraid that if she was as complex and multifaceted as Morris, she was way out of his league.

Over the next month he watched her for at least half an hour every afternoon. Her schedule was precise—she arrived at the library every day at two, spent fifteen minutes in the stacks, and read at the same spot in the reading room until six. She never varied her posture; she always wore smart clothes; she took notes with a fine pen in a black journal.

She read voraciously—biographies of Victorian artists along with poetry of the period and a smattering of history. She worked her way through the Royal Academy catalogs at the rate of one every two or three days. It was three weeks after he first saw her that he noticed, while shelving the volume for 1863, that the front cover of the 1865 volume was completely detached. He couldn't abide the idea that she should find it in such condition, so he carefully removed the book and its detached cover from the shelf and trekked up six flights of stairs to a sturdy wooden door marked CONSERVATION.

The brightly lit room into which Peter stepped looked as he imagined an autopsy room might—but, instead of human cadavers, books lay on the counters in various states of disassembly next to neat lines of knives and piles of various kinds of paper. On a shelf to his left were a dozen or so beautifully restored books, some in leather bindings with gold decoration. The room was not a morgue, thought Peter, so much as an intensive care unit, from which all patients would one day be discharged, if not fully cured, at least substantially improved. A man in a white lab coat leaned over a strange sort of vise that held a disbound book. He was spreading something that looked like cold oatmeal on the exposed spine.

"Can I help you?" he asked, standing up. The man looked at Peter through round gold-rimmed glasses. He looked to be about thirty and had blond, almost white, perfectly straight and groomed hair hanging to his shoulders and an equally pale beard sticking several inches straight out from his face. He smiled through his beard and Peter's first thought was that he looked like a Muppet. Peter couldn't help but smile back.

"I have a book that needs repair," said Peter.

"It has to be referred by library personnel," said the man, his smile fading and his tone of voice indicating that Peter was not the first person to come barging into the Conservation department uninvited.

"I am library personnel," said Peter. "I work in circulation."

"Put it over there," said the man with a sigh, nodding to a high pile of damaged books on a table near the door and turning his attention back to his work.

"When do you think it will be done?" asked Peter.

"We're running about six months right now, assuming nothing major comes down from Special Collections."

"Six months," said Peter. "But I have . . . I mean, we have a client . . . That is, a student who needs this book in a couple of days. It just needs the cover attached." Peter held up the book in one hand and its wayward front cover in the other. The man in the lab coat turned back toward him and considered both the book and Peter for a moment. His face softened and his smile returned.

"I'll tell you what," he said. "I'll put it in the girlfriend pile." He took the book and cover from Peter.

"The girlfriend pile?"

"Usually when a guy comes in here in a rush to get something repaired it's because his girlfriend needs it. What can I say, I'm a sucker for love and chivalry and all that. How about I have it for you Monday afternoon?"

"Monday would be great," said Peter, and he backed slowly out of the room, watching the young man return to his oatmeal paste.

Back in the stacks Peter could not get the Conservation department out of his mind. Suddenly he was seeing damaged books everywhere he looked: a frayed spine here, a torn endpaper there. He had thought of books before only as his shield, but now they seemed to be taking on lives of their own, not so much as works of literature or history or poetry, but as objects, collections of paper and thread and cloth and glue and leather and ink.

When he returned to the Conservation department on Monday afternoon, the book was waiting for him on the counter near the door. Peter inspected the front cover, the spine, and the front endpapers. "I can't even tell it was ever detached," he said.

"What can I say, I do good work," said the man in the lab coat.

"I don't suppose you ever let students work in here," said Peter.

"We sometimes have a student intern," said the man, "but they usually come from Special Collections."

"Special Collections?"

"Yeah, you know, the top floor. The Devereaux Room."

"What's the Devereaux Room?"

"You've never been to Special Collections?"

"No," said Peter.

"You're a book lover, right?"

"Absolutely," said Peter, who had never thought of himself as a book lover before this moment.

"Well, if you love books, you're going to adore the Devereaux Room," said the man. "Listen, I think there's a work-study position available up there right now. I could put in a good word for you with Francis."

"Francis?"

"Francis Leland, the head of Special Collections. I'll tell him we've got a budding bibliophile on our hands and maybe he'll take you on."

"That would be great," said Peter, wondering what exactly one did in Special Collections.

"I'm Hank, by the way," said the man, holding out a hand. "Hank Christiansen."

"Peter Byerly," said Peter, returning Hank's firm handshake. "Thanks for the . . . the recommendation."

"Sure thing," said Hank.

Peter turned to go, but stopped in the doorway. "And thanks for this," he said, holding up the repaired volume of Royal Academy pictures.

"I hope she likes it," said Hank.

Peter returned the book to its place in the stacks. The next day, she checked it out.

# ALSO AVAILABLE

## THE LOST BOOK OF THE GRAIL

Set in an English cathedral city, *The Lost Book of the Grail* tells the story of bibliophile Arthur Prescott as he works to uncover a long-lost secret about Barchester Cathedral's past. But when the cathedral itself is threatened, Arthur's search takes on grave importance, leading him to discoveries about the Holy Grail and about himself that he never expected.

## THE FURTHER ADVENTURES OF EBENEZER SCROOGE

**A Christmas Carol Continued**

Twenty years after his famous conversion to kindness, Ebenezer Scrooge still roams London spreading Christmas cheer, much to everyone's annoyance. But when Scrooge decides to help his former partner, Jacob Marley, he will need all the help he can get, including from the three ghosts who visited him many years ago.

## THE BOOKMAN'S TALE

**A Novel of Obsession**

After the death of his beloved wife, Amanda, Peter Byerly relocates to the English countryside, hoping to outrun his grief. But upon leafing through an old book, he discovers a Victorian watercolor of a woman who bears an uncanny resemblance to her. Peter follows a trail of clues back across the centuries to find the truth about the woman's real identity.

Ready to find your next great read? Let us help. Visit prh.com/nextread